THOSE
FATAL
FLOWERS

THOSE FATAL FLOWERS

A NOVEL

SHANNON IVES

DELL
NEW YORK

A Dell Trade Paperback Original

Copyright © 2025 Shannon Ives
Book club guide copyright © 2025 by Penguin Random House LLC

Published in the United States by Dell,
an imprint of Random House, a division of
Penguin Random House LLC, New York.

DELL and the D colophon are registered trademarks
of Penguin Random House LLC.
RANDOM HOUSE BOOK CLUB and colophon are trademarks
of Penguin Random House LLC.

LIBRARY OF CONGRESS CATALOGING-IN-PUBLICATION DATA
Names: Ives, Shannon, author.
Title: Those fatal flowers : a novel / Shannon Ives.
Description: New York : Dell, 2025.
Identifiers: LCCN 2024010718 (print) | LCCN 2024010719 (ebook) |
ISBN 9780593725306 (trade paperback ; acid-free paper) |
ISBN 9780593725313 (ebook)
Subjects: LCSH: Proserpina (Roman deity)—Fiction. | LCGFT:
Mythological fiction. | Lesbian fiction. | Novels.
Classification: LCC PS3609.V53 T48 2025 (print) |
LCC PS3609.V53 (ebook) | DDC 813/.6—dc23/eng/20240329
LC record available at https://lccn.loc.gov/2024010718
LC ebook record available at https://lccn.loc.gov/2024010719

Printed in the United States of America on acid-free paper

randomhousebooks.com

1st Printing

Book design by Jo Anne Metsch

To Ruby—

*You give me the courage to reach
for my most impossible dreams.
This book only exists because of you.
My love for you overflows all oceans.*

What reason
Was there to give Achelous' daughters feathers
And claws, but let them keep the faces of girls?
Was it because they were with her when she gathered
Those fatal flowers? They were her dear companions,
The Sirens, skilled in singing, and they sought her
Through all the lands in vain, and came to the ocean
And prayed that they might seek her there, be given
Wings for their quest, and hover over the waters,
And the gods were kind, and gave them golden plumage,
But let them keep the lovely singing voices,
So dear to the ears of men, the human features,
The human voice, the dower of song forever.

OVID, *Metamorphoses*

AUTHOR'S NOTE ON CONTENT

At its core, *Those Fatal Flowers* is a book that explores the effects of loss and guilt on the psyche, but it's also a book about structural violence. In the following pages, there are depictions of sexual assault (both in the abstract and on the page), homophobia, racism, sexism, pregnancy loss, ritual sacrifice, cannibalism, and colonial violence. As such, there are certain passages that are quite graphic in nature.

THOSE
FATAL
FLOWERS

PROLOGUE

The night before Ceres's palace becomes a tomb, its halls are filled with music. The warm melody is plucked from lyre strings and blown through silvery flutes, and it meanders through marbled corridors, all empty save for one young girl. Thelia runs, clutching her sandals in one hand and a letter in the other, her bare feet padding silently against the polished floors.

When the music finds Thelia's ears, a song rises instinctively in her throat to meet it. But tonight, Thelia forces herself to swallow it down. Luck, she believes, has been on her side, and she doesn't risk drawing attention to herself. Not even with a hum. Amid the din of the visiting pantheon currently reveling in her throne room, Ceres has yet to notice that her daughter, Proserpina, is missing from the crowd. For now, the elder goddess is too busy assessing suitors for the younger's hand, a fact that would have normally soured Thelia's mood for days. But in this moment, the celebration provides the perfect distraction.

When her sisters' glittering voices rise to accompany the

instruments, Thelia flies out into the warm summer night with Proserpina's letter pressed to her heart.

Please meet me. It's been harder and harder to leave notes like this, with Ceres actively preparing Proserpina for marriage. Their affection, which Ceres first ignored and then merely tolerated, has now caught the goddess's full attention.

"A needless distraction," Ceres called their love. "One that will hurt."

Servants were ordered to scour both their quarters for messages; Thelia's sisters were commanded to always accompany them. Ceres stopped short of forced separation only because Proserpina would never allow it. This note, placed so perfectly on Thelia's pillow, should have been an impossibility. Her sisters chattering excitedly ahead of her on their way to the party, not noticing as she slipped away, another. Miracles, Thelia believes, and in a way she's right. What she doesn't understand is that carefully orchestrated plans across centuries are clicking into place, teeth into gears that propel her forward into the woods she and Proserpina are fated to be in.

What she doesn't understand is why.

The note didn't say where to find Proserpina; it didn't have to. The location for their trysts has been the same for weeks— the small clandestine pool tucked away in Sicilia's forests, as far away from Ceres's disapproving eyes as they dare venture.

It's at that pool, through parted willow branches, that Thelia finds her goddess.

Her raven curls, her skin painted silver by moonlight. And all around, fireflies blinking in and out of existence, as if Proserpina's pulled the twinkling stars down from the heavens to share with her. Thelia marvels at the sight. She isn't the only one to fall to her knees in awe before Proserpina, but Thelia's devotion isn't bound to temples. As Proserpina's handmaiden, Thelia worships her each time she slides a comb through Proserpina's midnight hair. Her hands fastening the silk panels of Proserpina's tunic in place are prayers. And when they find time to steal away alone, Proserpina's lips are ecstasy.

But though their bodies are an exciting new frontier of exploration, her feelings are more than simple lust. In the coming weeks and years, Thelia will try to puzzle out when, exactly, she realized she was in love with Proserpina, but it's an impossible question to answer. They've grown up together, ever since Thelia's mother, a Muse, came with her children to serve in Ceres's court. And there have been as many moments when Proserpina dazzled her as there are stars in the sky.

Watching her now, Thelia revels in that honeyed ache that comes only from loving someone. But then the memory of her eldest sister's warning sucks away its sweetness.

"She's not yours to love." Raidne's voice rings in her ears.

How many times have both her sisters cautioned that this could end only in heartbreak? For even sweet Pisinoe, always drunk on infatuation for someone new, never defends their young love.

Resolve tightens Thelia's fists at her sides. If their time together is as fleeting as everyone cautions, then she doesn't want to waste tonight worrying. But how, exactly, to recapture the magic?

A single lily blooming at the base of an oak tree gives her an idea: a crown of flowers for her goddess. And so before Proserpina notices her, Thelia slips back into the shadows of the trees, guided by the promise of Proserpina's smile when she presents her with the gift.

The forest's music is different from the palace's, but no less beautiful. It's cicadas chirping and animals rustling underfoot, and here, Thelia joins without fear. It feels good to sing like this, to hear her voice harmonize with the night's. To lose herself in song and to fantasies of Proserpina's embrace.

She doesn't notice the cicadas fall silent, the animals still.

The next gear locking into place.

All at once he's on her, his cold claws squeezing her neck, his hot breath on her face. Terror unleashes the warnings she ignored to be here, desperate whispers from her mother, her sisters, the other nymphs, about what happens to those who find themselves alone in the path of a ravenous god.

All those women of the past, split apart for pleasure.

But this god doesn't want her. As he crushes the scream inside her throat, it's Proserpina he demands. Her vision darkens with his tightening grip. His voice grows distant. It isn't until he releases her that she feels her raised finger, revealing Proserpina's location. But before she can call out to stop him, to try to take back her treachery, he's gone—a wolf on a yearling's trail.

Every instinct in her body screams at her to run home. He might kill her if she intervenes, but as Proserpina's handmaid, she's duty bound to protect her. Though it's not her role that drives her to her princess's aid—it's love.

A horrible, jagged scream cuts through the air. It snaps her from her stupor. He's already found his prize. She nearly chokes on the realization, but for a moment, she dares to hope: Would he really be foolish enough to lay a hand on the Goddess of the Harvest's daughter?

"Be careful," Pisinoe cautioned whenever they slipped from the palace. "The gods show respect in Ceres's hall, but there's no telling what they'll do outside of it."

She takes off through the underbrush. Sharp stones cut at her feet and twisted roots turn the hem of her tunic into ribbons, but there's no time to waste. The path back to the pool is short, and no more screams rise to join the first, no pleas for mercy. Perhaps there's still time. When she spots a large stone at the base of a birch, she picks it up and weighs it between her quaking hands. The rock is heavy enough to crack a skull. It won't kill him, no, he's too powerful, but hopefully it will buy them enough time to escape. What will the punishment be for striking a god? Whatever the penalty, protecting Proserpina is worth it.

But the pool, bathed in pale silver light, is empty. The only occupant of the water is Luna's rippling reflection. How can such an awful moment be so beautiful?

"Proserpina?" There's no answer.

The sloshing water laps at something on the bank: Proserpina's belt. Thelia's stomach churns. She moves to retrieve the clue and spots a scorched patch of soil at the edge of the pond. In its center, encircled by burnt reeds, is a hideous black split in the earth. Steam rises from the healing crack with a hiss. Her throat tightens: It's large enough to swallow a person, a princess, or even a god.

She falls to her knees at the rift, fingers clawing desperately through the hot soil.

"No, no, no," she begs. "Please, no." The tears break free and blur her surroundings. It's too late; the hole is already closed, and the portal is gone. Dis slipped back to the Underworld, and he took Proserpina with him.

All those warnings. They didn't listen; *she* didn't listen. And look what happened because of her foolishness.

Then she thinks it, the thought that will haunt her for millennia to come, long after the dust of this event settles. At first, it will demand all her attention, playing on an endless loop, haunting all her waking moments, scaring away sleep at night. Only after months, years, will it finally slip from the forefront to settle in place as a constant background, muddled into regret and sorrow, where it will remain for centuries. And then, when she no longer expects it because it hasn't visited her for years, it will find her again. She'll carry it with her until the day she dies, this great, unanswerable question.

What have I done?

1

ⵕⵕⵕⵕ

NOW

When my eyes crack open, the world is veiled in shadow. It's a darkness I remember, the same shade as the pit that swallowed Proserpina, and it's just as cold. After all these years, did the Underworld finally claim me? I brush my lips with trembling fingers and find no coin for passage placed between my teeth. But the relief that swells in my chest at this fact is crushed by the memory of climbing into my small boat.

If I'm dead, I died alone.

Shapes slowly emerge against that inky blackness: a billowing white fabric, so much like Proserpina's gowns, with hundreds of tiny lights blinking into existence behind it. My mouth falls open in awe as I remember the sight of her in that pool surrounded by fireflies. But I taste salt on my tongue, and the illusion is shattered. It's not my long-lost love descending to greet me at the Underworld's gates. It's a sail swelling with a fresh gust of wind, and behind it, a blanket of stars. There are some familiar faces in the constellations, although they twinkle down without offering any hope.

So I'm still alive.

Nothing delights the gods more than a cruel twist of destiny, so the Fates must have been gleeful as they wove and apportioned my life's thread. A tragedy written across centuries, full of more despair than a single human life can hold. And now Morta's shears finally tease along its fibers. The old goddess is surely salivating as her sisters press beside her, their shared eye wide with anticipation as they wait for my final, most humiliating moment to reveal itself. That will be when the blades clamp down, when the stars go dark.

The moon emerges from behind a veil of clouds, as if Luna's decided to revel in my plight. She's already over halfway full again. When I left, she was a sliver in the sky, barely more than a dark void in the heavens, but I've been in this boat long enough to watch her swell into a perfect circle and then fall back into shadow once more. One precious full moon lost to the sea, and my second only a little over a week away.

A cold breeze blows across my cracked skin as I slide onto the floor for another trying night. Coins clink as I settle atop them, and the sharp edge of an ornate ruby ring presses into my back. I push it aside with a frustrated sigh. How many more mornings do I have left? The stars of Cetus, fellow monster, scintillate in sync with the waves that slosh against the boat's edges. But the gods won't honor my death by hanging my image in the heavens like they did hers. I'll turn to carrion, and this tiny skiff will be my grave—the punishment that I alone deserve.

A dry sob escapes me, splitting open my bottom lip on its way out, but I'm too dehydrated for any tears to join it. I should have known it would end this way. When has fate ever been on my side, truly?

Ceres will be thrilled.

My mouth falls open to the sky for one last plea. The words dig their claws into my throat, fearful of the pain that speaking them into existence will bring, but I force them out anyway.

"Let me save them."

The voice that fills the air is one I don't recognize: It's scratchy and weak, a far cry from the sonorous one capable of driving men into the sea. The wind carries it away as if it never existed at all. Overhead, Luna retreats behind another gauzy cloud. I must be too pitiful to look upon.

Damn them all.

My tongue tastes copper, and I raise a weak hand to wipe away the blood that oozes from the crack in my lip. But my fingers falter before I can. Instead, I roll onto my side and press my mouth against one of the planks. When I raise my head, a gory kiss looks back at me from the wood.

Take it. May this small offering seal my prayer.

I owe my sisters this, and I beg all who will listen for help: the waves, the stars, Proserpina.

The boat shudders around me. A monster must have heard my cries, drawn to the surface by the promise of an easy meal. An awful scratching fills the air, so much like claws on wood, and my shaking hands grab hold of the gunwale in a poor attempt to steady myself. Immediately, my knuckles turn white.

What waits for me below the water's surface? Perhaps Scylla, human from the waist up like I was, but with a monstrous bottom half too maddening to behold in its entirety—the giant serpentine tail used for dragging ships into her vast sea cave, the snarling mouths of rabid hounds that encircle her waist. Or maybe I've found myself on the lip of Charybdis's infinite maw just as she's poised to turn this section of sea into a whirlpool that will swallow me down into her rows upon rows of glittering, concentric teeth. Will my final resting place be among the cemetery of ships she holds in her belly? It takes the last of my strength to muster my courage to peer into the depths below.

But there are no gleaming scales, no eyes of an angry leviathan looking back at me—there are only stones. I've washed ashore.

"Thank you," I whisper as my eyes sweep over the rocky beach before me. Luna reappears, her silvery light glinting off the white sea-foam that collects where the waves meet land. A tangled mess of trees sit just beyond the beach. Their empty branches sway in the chilly late autumn air.

A shaky laugh escapes from the back of my throat. It hurts, but I don't care. I did it. I survived. Despite the cold wind that swirls all around me, an unfamiliar warmth gathers in my belly. Is this what being blessed feels like? I wouldn't know— I'm not used to my prayers being answered.

When a light flickers in the trees ahead, I can't help but smile. A man stumbles out onto the beach, lifting his torch in my direction. He's far enough away that his face is buried in shadow, but when his body straightens, I know he's caught sight of me. I don't move until he's standing over me, his confusion painted orange by the torchlight. He wears simple linen clothes, though they're soiled, and his smell, a mixture of stale sweat and even staler alcohol, burns my nostrils. He slurs something down at me, but his words are undecipherable. Instinct brings my fingers to the small pendant around my neck, nestled above my heart. Only then do the consonants that fall from the man's lips warp into a shape I recognize.

Does this small miracle belong to Jaquob's saint?

"Wh-who are you?"

My mouth splits open instinctively to let my song pour out, but my throat is too raw to make music. The sound that escapes instead is ghastly—it's wind blowing over dead leaves, it's the beating of locust wings. The man hears death in it and runs back into the woods without another word. If he returns, he won't be alone.

Good. I need more than one.

The stars above don't have time to move across the vault of the heavens before I hear them, a whole mob, and I lie back down and close my eyes. My lips fall open just so, as if asking for a kiss. Even without magic, men are easily manipulated.

"S-see! I t-told ya!" the familiar voice rattles. I picture him pointing at me with a victorious smile splashed across his reddened face. "But she was . . . she was awake!"

A different man guffaws. "Are you mad, John? I'll concede that there's indeed a woman here, but look at her! She's dead. You let the alcohol get the best of you. Again."

"I didn't, Thomas. I swear it," John says, but even I hear the hesitation that now laces his voice.

"See all the treasure?" Rocks crunch beneath Thomas's feet as he draws closer. "This is a funerary ship."

Gods, I can feel him standing over me, feel his eyes examining the sight before him. Somehow, my parched mouth grows even drier.

"A funerary ship?"

"Of course. The Vikings used to send their dead to sea with all sorts of riches. Perhaps the Croatoans do as well."

The boat creaks as Thomas grabs hold of its edges to lower himself beside me. He scrapes together a handful of coins and gems and lets them slip through his fingers slowly, reveling in the *clinks* and *tings* they make as they fall into place among the other treasures in my hoard. Then he touches me.

His caress is light at first, but it still burns through my

gown. Cold fingers flatten into a heavy palm that takes its time crawling up my midsection. Suddenly, I'm that young girl again, and it's the first time sailors arrived on our shores, all those unknown hands grabbing for me—except now I have no way to protect myself from him. From them.

How much of me would he feel entitled to explore if there wasn't a crowd behind him?

His palm finally settles atop my heart and finds what he wasn't expecting—a beating organ; his shock is revealed by the slightest hitch in his breath.

"She's . . . she's alive!" His voice is now clipped, controlled. "Quick! This woman is alive!"

Murmurs erupt through the crowd, and a few seconds later, a gentler hand lifts my right wrist to find the artery at its base.

"We must get her inside."

Though her speech is hurried, it still sounds like music, like the lyres that graced the halls of Ceres's palace. The glittering sound is both a balm and a blade—I never considered that women might be caught in my plans.

"Hurry!" she says, and the lyres play louder. How would our lives have been different if I'd followed their notes instead of sneaking from the palace that fateful night? If I'd joined my sisters in the throne room to sing songs so beautiful they made the gods weep? Would our voices have been even half as lovely as this woman's? I don't think so. It sends stars exploding across the blackness behind my eyes, and when they fall, the shadows in their wake are heavier than they were before. It's all so strange, confusing, but I can't make sense of what's happening to me, can't open my eyes, can't breathe—

Then the music is gone, too, and all is dark and quiet.

᠍᠍

I can save them.

She speaks, drawing my consciousness forward again. It's my stolen princess, Proserpina, rousing me with the voice I've been so desperate to hear.

"Are you awake?" This voice is different. The lyres have returned—the woman from the beach. A fire crackles gently behind her music. I'm warm. Cramped and sore, yes, but no longer cold.

I don't know, I say, or I think I say, but all I hear is a groan that emerges in place of words. *Am I? You tell me.*

"Who are you?"

I don't have an answer for her. Someone—no, something—scarred by loss, a monstrous shell that once held a girl. But that's not exactly true, is it? It's not the loss that wears on me. It's that face, those hands. And, above all else, it's my traitorous finger revealing her location to him.

We were children. I was scared. I didn't mean to—

Mean to. Mean to. Mean to. A bitter laugh racks my chest. How little intention matters when the consequences are so great. No, it's not the loss that destroyed me. It's the guilt. I'd hoped that the years, the centuries, would wear down its edges into something softer, a stone at the bottom of the riverbed. But instead that ever-present weight in the pit of my stomach grew teeth and talons of its own.

It's mutated into rage.

My eyelids are heavy, and the voice has fallen quiet. Did I imagine her? My hands reach out into that still darkness, desperate to find anything to anchor me to this place, this realm. They find nothing, and a broken cry shatters the silence. The sound is pitiful, an animal toiling in its final, terrible moments. The rush of skirts accompanied by a gentle *shhh, shhh, shhh* . . . makes me realize I was the one who made it.

There's a warm hand on my forehead, followed by a murmur of approval, and then the blessed cool of water against my lips.

"Slowly, slowly," the voice cautions. "Drinking too quickly will make you sick."

The water is delicious enough that it could belong to the dream world, and its effect on my raw throat is nothing short of miraculous. But I can't focus on that little wonder—not with this woman so close I can smell her. Roses doing their best, but failing, to mask the salty sweetness of sweat. The heady scent is intoxicating.

I can save them, but I need more blood.

"Proserpina?" I whimper softly, my newfound sense of calm already shattered by the desperate need to hear her voice again. But Proserpina speaks when she pleases, not when I want her to. Again, she falls silent.

"What was that?" the unfamiliar woman asks, but a knock at a door draws her from my side. She's swallowed away in a flurry of whispers, leaving only her scent in her wake. Without her to anchor it, the essence slowly dissipates, and then there's nothing left but my own rank odor to offend my nostrils. It's particularly upsetting after hers, but also oddly comforting, for it offers at least one concrete answer: The Fates still haven't cut my thread.

I open my eyes, and again, the world takes its time coming into focus. I'm alone in a small room. The walls are made of wood, and a fire flickers in the hearth directly before me. Its gentle snaps and pops obscure the creaks from the bed that accompany my shifting. The warm glow it casts signals that it's still night.

Footsteps and muffled voices filter up from below. Slowly, I ease myself down onto the floor, my muscles screaming. Tears have collected in my eyes by the time I place my ear to the wood, along the seam where two boards meet, and wait. Breath rattles through my lips, shallow inhales and exhales that I keep as quiet as possible. There are two people speaking, I think, but their words are garbled together. At first, trying to untangle them is as futile as trying to separate commingling vapors, but then, slowly, they each begin to take their own form.

"She must be royalty—" It's a male voice. Thomas's.

"But from where? The francs could hint to trading with the French, but there are no reports of a civilization here . . ." a female voice murmurs. This one is new, distant, and calculating. It holds no music.

"A place of great wealth, apparently. To send her to sea with all that treasure . . ."

"A place like Spain, perhaps?"

Thomas laughs. "You think she's a spy?"

"I *think*"—the woman's voice climbs an octave on the word—"it's quite an incredible coincidence a mysterious woman has arrived on our shores with such a hoard, along the very route their treasure galleons travel."

"So what would you have me do?"

"She belongs in the pillory until we know exactly who she is."

"Have you been drinking seawater? Our purpose here is to find this land's riches—to find that exact gold! And you want me to lock up the best lead England has ever had?"

"Thomas, please. Think! Bringing a strange—possibly dangerous!—woman into our home . . ."

"Master Sutton inspected her. She's starving, in desperate need of water. What kind of spy is that?"

"And you've upset your betrothed."

"Putting her in the pillory would have upset Cora more! She knows it made the most sense to bring her here."

"Is that why she kept vigil until Will finally came to collect her? Don't be foolish. She didn't want you alone with her. The amount of treasure stays the same no matter where this woman sleeps." Her voice drops a register. "I don't need another mess to clean up."

"Now, hold on—"

"I've said all I have to say on this subject," she snaps, killing his reply mid-sentence. "It's late. We're both tired. We'll determine the best course of action tomorrow."

"Yes, Mother."

The house creaks as they cross it and ascend to my floor. I hold my breath as their footsteps pad past my door, but thankfully, no one stops before it. Only now, under the weight of their suspicions, do I notice how my palms are slick with sweat.

I don't know if I am safe. I've already lost a moon. It's not only men who live here, wherever here is, but women as well.

In the hurry for my departure, I never considered what living with them would be like. How dangerous it could be.

I don't try to stand until I'm certain everyone in the household is asleep. It hurts more than lying down did, but I still manage to pull myself to my feet and tiptoe to the door. Its wooden latch is rough in my hands, and I lift it slowly to peer into the hallway.

The bedroom opens to a small landing. To my right, a narrow set of stairs leads down to the floor below. The hallway continues to my left, a dark place with no windows. The only light, the moon's, filters through a tiny window straight ahead of me. Underneath it sits a small wooden table with two matching chairs on either side. Dust hangs suspended in the air like slow-falling snow, visible only because the exact angle of Luna's beams has exposed it.

I take one more look down the depressing corridor. Two doors line the opposing wall. Beside each door is a sconce, but the candles are no longer lit. Thin trails of smoke rise up from their wicks, weaving transparent ribbons in the air. Someone blew them out before retiring.

I hear my heart beating in my ears, and my first instinct is to soar down the stairs, to flee from this home. Instead, I take a deep breath and retreat into my room. Disappearing into the night would be dangerous, and I must keep calm. Raidne and Pisinoe are depending on me.

But from where?

Despite everything, the woman's question brings a smile to my lips, for how could I ever possibly begin to answer it? I'd love nothing more than to describe Sirenum Scopuli to her. To explain that my prison was an archipelago formed by three islands: the main landmass, Scopuli, and two smaller isles. One we call Castle because of its three stone spires that look like turrets against the setting sun, and the other Rotunda simply because it's round. I'd tell her that Scopuli looks like a porpoise from the air, and that its sweet half-moon body creates the archipelago's eastern boundary, with Castle and Rotunda completing it to the west. It's inside this net that ships break upon our reef, the lucky sailors smashed to their deaths against the cliffside of the porpoise's belly, the unlucky ones washing ashore alive onto the beach located, quite fittingly, inside its mouth.

But her son will learn all about that soon enough.

I crawl back into the bed. It doesn't take long for Proserpina's voice to find me one final time.

My dear Thelia. I can save you all, but I need more blood.

What would it feel like to be the girl who balked at such a

request? The question leaves a bitter taste in my mouth. That girl died for the first time on her hands and knees, clawing at scorched earth that swallowed the one she loved, and she's died a thousand deaths since then. She was weak; there's no place for her here. Not with one full moon already lost and the next only a week away.

Six turns of the moon, Proserpina had said, and now I'm down to five. That's all I have before her magic wears off, before my sisters and I will be officially sentenced to death.

When I speak, there's no hesitation. "Then you shall have it."

2

NOW

Despite my exhaustion, sleep doesn't come easily. I toss and turn in the strange bed, surprised to find no relief in its soft linens. I'm untethered without the sound of the waves lapping at Scopuli's shore, without the ocean sloshing against the edges of my boat. Wherever I am, it's far enough inland to hide these comforts from me. The house is still and silent.

Streaks of light eventually filter into the room from a window behind my bed. The air that slips between its shutters is cold, and I draw my blanket around my shoulders as I peer through them. A line of thatched-roofed cottages sit in view, and behind them, a timber wall so high that it's impossible to discern what the world holds on the other side of it. The architecture is dark and angular compared to the marbled palace of my youth, with exteriors stripped of any embellishments; these homes are purely functional. They look nothing like the warm mud-brick dwellings of mortals past. Are they a mirror of what lives inside their builders' hearts?

People are already meandering past. Men with curious

metal devices slung over their shoulders and conical hats on top of their heads, a woman with a basket of mushrooms resting on her hip. Many wear shades of brown and black, as muted as the dying earth beneath their feet. All slow their gait before this home, eyes lingering on the windows, no doubt trying to glimpse the strange woman who arrived the previous night. I pull back from the aperture before I'm spotted, sinking down into the mattress.

A light knock at my door catches me by surprise, and I lift my head in time to watch an unfamiliar woman slip inside. The sight of her takes my breath away. When was the last time I saw a woman? Alive, that is. My throat closes at the memory, and I shove those waterlogged corpses as far out of mind as possible. It must have been Ceres, perched on her golden throne, the same color as late autumn wheat. She'd been so furious that her anger formed its own entity, a dark shadow that twisted up the wall behind her. After all these years, I can still see it, *feel* it, as the shade shifted from beast to beast—first a wolf, then a bear, then some unknowable monster of teeth and claws, but always a predator bearing down on us.

At the time, I didn't understand how rage could be so potent. Now I do.

This woman is nothing like Ceres. Her garb is plain, made of a simple gray linen, and wisps of blond hair escape from beneath a strange little white hat to delicately frame her thin face. Her eyes are a deep brown, and a dusting of freckles adorns her cheeks. She's young but worn past her years. There are deep purple bags under her eyes, dark as bruises, and her limbs are bordering on too thin. To call her beautiful would be a stretch to most, but not to me—after all these years, she is a miracle. A tray of food is balanced on her left hip, and she kicks the door gently closed behind her. When she finds me sitting upright, she gasps with surprise. Is this the mystery woman who watched over me last night?

An unfamiliar voice dashes my hopes.

"Mistress! I didn't expect to find you awake!" She shuffles over to set the tray delicately down on a small end table beside the bed and offers me a biscuit. "My name's Margery Harvie. I'm the Bailies' maid. Mistress Bailie told me all about you. How they found you on the beach last night with so much treasure . . ."

I look at the biscuit blankly, too stunned by her presence to move. Is it safe to eat? Attitudes toward wanderers varied among mortals the last time I interacted with them. Some treated travelers with respect, opening their homes and their pantries to those who could be sages, mystics, or even gods. Other groups ravaged and murdered those unfortunate enough to cross their path. What type of people do I find myself with now? The offering of food suggests the former, but humans have never been above poisoning. My stomach, unafraid of injury, gurgles loudly at the sight of food.

The maid's expression crumples. "I know it's hardly a worthy meal, but it's all we have. Provisions are already low, and with winter so close . . ."

I still can't bring myself to take it from her. What would become of Raidne and Pisinoe if I died now? And over something so foolish.

Realization washes over her features. She smiles softly, placing a warm hand on top of mine. The feeling of her palm, calloused by work, on my skin makes my heart leap into my throat. "It's safe, mistress. Here, I'll show you. They're more palatable if you soak them in the soup."

To the audible protest of my stomach, she cracks the biscuit in half, sending crumbs raining down into the steaming broth below. The liquid is a pale yellow and woefully empty, a mockery of Raidne's soups during times of plenty, colorful creations packed with herbs, mushrooms, and meat. Saliva pools beneath my tongue at the memory.

Only after Margery's swallowed her piece do I wolf down mine. The broth is tasteless, but at least it's warm.

"What's your name, mistress?"

It feels as if a piece of the hardtack is stuck in my throat, but the sensation's caused by nerves. The importance of this moment isn't lost on me. This is where my test truly begins. Up until now, my journey was passive. I climbed into the boat, and the boat brought me here. I was discovered on the shore and carried to this home. And now, finally, an actual person sits before me, asking me who I am and what I want. I try to gulp down the blockage as my hand finds the golden relic around my neck. The delicate oval pendant fits easily in my palm, though the sapphire in its center bites into my skin as anxiety tightens my grip around it. Will it translate my words for Margery's ears like it does hers to mine?

Proserpina, please, let this work.

She's the only god I know is listening.

"Thelxiope," I say softly. Margery tilts her head to the side, considering the unfamiliar syllables. "But people call me Thelia."

I don't know what makes me offer the nickname to her— the same one spoken by Proserpina all those eons ago. Maybe it's desperation to finally, after centuries, hear it again on the lips of someone new, spoken softly like a prayer. I crumple my brows in my best impression of confusion. "Where am I?"

"Oh, Mistress Thelia, forgive me! I—" The poor maid stumbles over her words, but I don't mind—she understood me. She said my name. My skin tingles at the sound of it, remembering how it felt to have it whispered into my palms, against my neck, upon my lips.

Thelia.

"—You're in Virginia Territory. In the City of Raleigh."

My eyes glance toward the window. The town outside is a far cry from a city. Calling it an outpost would be too generous.

Margery reads the criticism on my face. "We've only been here a year and a half. This was previously just a small military colony, but—" Her mouth snaps closed suddenly. "But Mistress Bailie can explain all that later, once you're feeling better."

"Mistress Bailie?"

"The lady of the house. Her son, Thomas, brought you here to recover. They found you last night on the beach."

"The beach?" I lace my voice with confusion; it's not dissimilar from weaving promises into a song, though the effect is markedly less impressive.

Margery abruptly abandons her place at my side and motions toward the fireplace, where a large basin of water waits. "Let's get you cleaned up. Come, can you stand?"

I nod and swing my legs over the side of the bed. Despite rising slowly, I stumble after my first few steps. This, unfortunately, isn't an act. My body is still weak from my time at sea.

Margery rushes to my side and catches me in her arms. "Careful, mistress!"

She supports my weight to bring me to the basin and then, without a word, works to unfasten the dragonfly fibulae that clasp my gown closed at my shoulders. Seeing them makes me think of Pisinoe, the softness of her face as she fixed them in place the morning before I left.

My gown slides easily from my shoulders. The act feels symbolic, like I'm shedding my old self to be reborn once again, but there's no joy in this.

Now I stand truly naked before her, save for the relic around my neck. The room is chilly, and my anatomy reflects it. Margery makes no indication that she notices and guides me into the tub, where warm water waits to envelop me. I savor its embrace as she wipes away the weeks of sweat and sea salt from my skin.

"Thank you," I murmur softly, my speech languid. Despite everything, her touch is soothing.

"No need to thank me, Mistress Thelia. It's my job."

"Then I thank you for your kindness instead."

A strange expression flickers in her eyes, and her delicate mouth parts ever so slightly before it falls closed again. I raise an eyebrow expectantly, but she stands quickly, hands brushing out her skirts. "I have new clothes for you. Mistress Bailie asked that you be dressed in something more . . . decent."

My eyes wander to the stola still in the middle of the floor. I wouldn't have called this style immodest before, but I can't help but feel underdressed compared to Margery. She wears several layers, as if her skin is a thing that must be hidden at all costs.

She holds up a plain blue dress. I've never seen a piece of clothing look so depressing, and its true horrors aren't revealed until I'm out of the bath and Margery slips it over my head and laces up its back.

I inhale sharply, surprised by the sudden constriction. I've made a mistake. This woman is trying to suffocate me, to kill me. I whirl around to meet her, my fingers like claws, my teeth bared—

"Mistress Thelia, please stand still," Margery scolds gently before I'm upon her, and there's something in her tone that softens me, but it's too late. I already have her by the shoulders. Even in this form, I'm stronger than she is. I could crush her frail bones in my palms if I wished to, and she knows it. Her eyes become large, frightened disks. The fear is genuine. I've seen enough of it to know.

"I'm sorry, I . . ." I release her, holding up my hands in apology. I what? Thought she intended to strangle me? It sounds absurd now that the gravity of my mistake is looking me in the face. ". . . I didn't know it would be so tight."

The maid's expression is strained, but she forces a nod. "No, I apologize. I should've warned you . . ." A silent, agonizing moment passes. "May I continue?"

My hands fall to my sides in defeat as she finishes her handiwork. The fabric is heavy and itchy against my skin, but somehow, the final product isn't as uncomfortable as I feared it would be. I can still breathe.

"I really am sorry."

"It's all right," she replies, though her voice suggests she isn't so sure. "Traveling all alone, it . . . it must have been frightening."

She reaches to brush a stray lock of hair behind my left ear. The act is so gentle that I bite my lip to keep from tearing up. It's something Pisinoe would do. Pisinoe, who, in my place, would never have lunged at an unsuspecting woman.

But I shouldn't be too hard on myself. Raidne would have torn her apart.

"You're quite a beauty." Her eyes are somewhere far away, like she's watching a bruised sunset sinking into the sea, and her voice contains the smallest touch of sorrow. Ah, how little has changed—drawing the attention of men is still a dangerous game to play.

A gruff voice barks an order from down below. The floor muffles the exact contents of the call but can't mask its irritation.

The maid bristles, then moves to collect the empty tray

from my bedside. "That'll be Master Thomas wanting his breakfast. I'll let Mistress Bailie know you're ready."

"Can I come with you?" I ask, but Margery has already retreated into the hallway, and my answer is the *thunk* of my door falling shut. She's already gone, drawn by Thomas's yell with more speed than men are drawn into the waves by our song.

Our song. Without the wings, without the feathers, without the magic, can I still claim it as my own? The gods gave us those forms to find Proserpina, and when we failed, they did not take them back. The dark magic that wove itself into our voices came later with Ceres's curse. But our song, our beautiful song, has always belonged to us. Raidne, Pisinoe, Thelxiope: the fallen handmaidens to the Goddess of Spring, banished to Scopuli's shores with the voices of Muses and the bodies of monsters.

Sirenum Scopuli. That's what the sailors in the early days called our island home: the cliffs of the sirens. *Scopuli* for the literal cliffs, but also as a metaphor for something to overcome. Few did, save for those who were clever enough to stuff their ears with wax.

The first time I saw that wild piece of land, my hands were bound, and my mouth was gagged. But I left Scopuli free from restraints, blessed by a different goddess than the one who cursed me, and imbued with different magic—a human body in place of the monstrous one. That will last only five more turns of the moon.

Which means I must hurry.

🝮🝮🝮

Margery's final words implied that Mistress Bailie would be my next visitor, but I don't need anyone's permission to leave this room. Margery didn't lock me in. The wooden door creaks in protest, but I ignore it. In the pale light of morning, details emerge that darkness concealed last night: that the sconces that hold the candles are gold, that there's a plush scarlet rug that pads the floor.

I extend my leg across the threshold to let my toes caress the rug's fibers. They're soft and warm beneath my bare foot, enticing me forward. Thomas's voice floats up through the floorboards. Holding my breath, I take my first step down the stairs to the main floor. The weight of the unfamiliar gown catches me by surprise and I nearly lose my footing, but miraculously, I find my balance. I release my captured breath and continue, emerging into a large kitchen. Margery's domain.

She's folded over an iron pot, stirring furiously. Herbs hang from wooden beams that line the ceiling above as they do on Scopuli, although there are admittedly fewer varieties here. In fact, the entire kitchen is surprisingly bare. There are no baskets overflowing with dandelion greens, no salted meat spread across the table in the room's center, no bins of root vegetables overflowing in its corners. Margery gingerly ladles some broth into a clean bowl, then exits the kitchen through a door on my right, too distracted by her current task to notice my presence on the landing. Directly ahead, on the opposite side of the wooden table that anchors the room, is a door flanked by two windows. My heart trips over a beat—it's the only thing separating me from the rest of this strange world, and it beckons.

I rush across the kitchen and push open a window's shutters to peer into the streets from a different angle. Here, the people who pass don't linger; this entrance is for servants, and they don't expect to spot me in its windows.

A cloaked woman floats past, glancing in my direction for a split second to reveal a flash of pale skin, lips the color of wine, and curls as black as midnight. My chest constricts, and an overwhelming array of emotions threaten to swallow me: longing, mostly, and deep regret, but also a tantalizing thrill.

Proserpina?

How her eyes would sparkle as I chased her through her mother's hedge mazes. It was one of her favorite games, running through the labyrinth, her hair a sea of black billowing in her wake, always just out of reach. I'll never forget how mischief slithered between the green and gold flecks in her irises when I caught her, or how warm her body felt pressed against mine. I was never happier than when I was wrapped in her arms, in the safety of the world we built for ourselves. More than anything, I miss those moments after our passion's blaze. When she'd hold me to her chest and stroke my hair, when we were equals. To know another person's heart, and to have them know yours, is a gift not many are given. I never believed I'd be foolish enough to think I'd find that again, but . . .

Proserpina's visited me in dreams, and I've heard her voice on the cusp of them. Is it possible she's discovered a way to somehow be here? That this village is only a new maze to pursue her through?

My hand flies to the door's latch, but a cold voice addresses me before I can dash into the streets after her.

"Going somewhere?"

Its owner materializes on the stairwell, still cast in shadow, but there's no denying that it's the same woman I heard through the floorboards last night. When she descends into the kitchen, the first feature that emerges from the darkness is her pale yellow braid, the color of early spring daffodils. Gray strands entwine themselves with the blond, but despite her age, she carries herself with the air of a queen. Her eyes are an icy blue, and I recognize that cutting stare. It's one I've made countless times over the years: She's assessing if I'm a threat, if she can handle me. Her lips curl up in a cold smile; so, she believes she can. "It's good to see you're awake. My name is—"

"Mistress Bailie," I respond coolly.

She bristles at my interruption, which wasn't entirely intentional. I'm so used to finishing Raidne's and Pisinoe's thoughts or having them finish mine. But this woman isn't kin, and she interprets the interjection as insolence. Shit. I don't need to make an enemy of her. Not yet, anyway. I lower my eyes to the floor and force myself away from the door, but each step into the kitchen, away from *her,* drives a sword through my heart.

"Forgive me, I'm not myself." My aching legs sway beneath me, and the truth of my words softens her accusatory stare into irritation. Thankfully, she decides that my rudeness isn't worth berating me over. Not when she doesn't know who I am, or why I'm here. My boat filled with centuries of wealth has bought me a little safety, if for no other reason than she's desperate to know where it came from.

She sweeps into the kitchen. "It's good to see you looking decent. You arrived dressed like a nymph from some sort of tragedy. That, or a harlot."

My lips curl into a forced smile at her intended slight, which is a curious choice given the relatively opulent home I find myself in now. Of course, it doesn't compare to Ceres's palace from my childhood, but Mistress Bailie stands before me in a maroon silken gown, her slender neck dripping with pearls. This woman is wealthy enough to employ servants, and compared to the townsfolk I saw through the windows this morning, it's clear that the Bailies are richer than most. Unless women are allowed to make their own wealth in this land, she sold her body in some way for this life. *Or it was sold for her,* I caution myself. But Mistress Bailie struts around the kitchen with the confidence of a woman who's only ever dominated; her hypocrisy is stunning.

Before I can reply, Margery bursts back into the kitchen, an empty bowl in hand. "Mistress Bailie, good morning! Thomas is requesting your— Ah! Mistress Thelia, is there something I can do for you?"

"No, no, Margery. I was simply stretching my legs." Already, I regret burdening her with my presence. Her brows pinch together with alarm. She's unsure of who she should address first: her employer or the mysterious newcomer.

"That will be Lady Thelia, Margery."

I recognize this voice from last night, too. Low and penetrating, it makes my skin crawl at the memory of his hands on my body. Thomas.

He darkens the same doorway that Margery just spilled in through, no more than a menacing shadow before Margery's hearth illuminates him. He has his mother's severe cheekbones, and her fierce pale blue eyes, though their effect is different. Her gaze studies and catalogs; his devours.

"Lady?" Mistress Bailie repeats, a thin yellow brow cocked. I didn't register the different title until now, but from the way her face contorts to try to hide her displeasure, I glean that *lady* falls above *mistress*. Who's the slattern now?

Raidne's letter, the one we spent an entire day composing, is clutched tightly in Thomas's hands. My sisters sang its contents into the parchment, hoping to imbue some trace of their voices' magic into the ink, to charm whoever found me into understanding our words. We didn't know if it would work, but Thomas's hungry expression reveals that it did. Mistress Bailie snatches it from him the moment he offers it.

I can barely breathe as her eyes dart across our tale, but the letter is only one piece of the deception. Men adore

weak things, after all—either to save or to crush. Which will
Thomas choose?

"What's that?" I allow myself to draw closer to Mistress
Bailie, peeking over the paper's edge, as if I don't have every
single line of its ink memorized. "Was that with me . . . ?"

"You don't know?" Thomas's question is loud with surprise.

My teeth find my lower lip and tug it between them in a
display of embarrassment. His hungry stare follows them,
then lingers on my mouth. How predictable.

"Lady Thelia's having some trouble remembering what
happened to her," Margery says.

"Was there anything else with me?"

The question brings Thomas's eyes back to mine, and he
laughs, delighted by it. "Come, I'll show you. Perhaps it will
jog your memory."

"Thomas—" Mistress Bailie starts, but her son hasn't taken
last night's conversation to heart. He's already lost in the dazzling relief of my smile, and when he extends his hand to me,
I accept it, trying to ignore how badly my heart aches.

Leave this place, my heart begs, as the image of that cloaked
woman comes to mind. *Go find her.*

But I can't. To abandon the Bailies' home in this moment
would be to fail my sisters. Thomas's grip tightens around my
hand.

Mistress Bailie follows on our heels as her son leads me
from the cottage's kitchen into a large main room where a
polished wooden table gleams before another brick fireplace.
It holds a cataloged fraction of my trove, all glittering with
the fire's reflection.

"We found you last night," he says. "You washed ashore in
a little boat filled with treasure—"

"Filled?" I ask, unable to help myself. The riches before us are impressive, surely, but they wouldn't fill much of any-thing.

"The rest is locked away upstairs. For safekeeping."

I nod, as if this doesn't essentially amount to theft.

"I'll admit, I thought you were dead. That this was all part of an elaborate funerary ritual . . ."

My feet carry me to the table's edge, and I let my fingers trace over the familiar items—the golden openwork bracelet with its elaborate lattices and shiny pearls, the beaded emer-ald necklace, the pile of gold coins of all different origins.

". . . but little did I realize that this was all—"

"A dowry," I finish for him, realization dripping from my voice as I pluck a silver ring from the hoard. "My dowry. I remember now."

The lie spills easily from my lips, though I suppose it should. I had all of early autumn to practice.

"Princess Thelia." Mistress Bailie finally speaks, lowering the letter to her side. "Who left a place called Scopuli in search of a husband."

The corner of her mouth twitches into a fanciful grin, and she drops into a deep curtsy. She's no better than the women who clung to Ceres's side, fanning her with palm leaves and feeding her grapes in thinly veiled attempts to garner her favor. In fairness, Ceres was generous in those early days, so their efforts were typically rewarded. A correctly timed glass of wine guaranteed a bountiful harvest; a perfectly recited poem, a pregnancy. Back then, she'd even smile when she saw Proserpina take my hand in hers. True smiles, as warm as summer soil. Those golden days seem impossible now. After Proserpina bled, Ceres's kindness evaporated. Where I was once a treasured confidant, a childhood crush, I became a liability to her plans for Proserpina's future. But what Ceres never understood was that Proserpina didn't need me to whisper poison into her ears about her mother's preferred matches; Proserpina hated them all on her own.

To fall out of favor with Ceres was to fall out of favor with the women who served her—women I'd known for years, friends to my mother and my aunts, who suddenly refused to meet my eyes. As if I were blight on crops that would spread to them on contact. They made me sick then, and Mistress Bailie makes me sick now.

Her bowed head hides her face, though the way her knuckles turn white as she grips her skirts betrays that she's not as deferential as she'd like me to believe. "Forgive me, my lady, I had no idea."

"We must celebrate the arrival of such a distinguished guest! Mother, fetch Margery and tell her the news—tonight, we'll throw a feast in Lady Thelia's honor!"

The only evidence of Mistress Bailie's irritation at his order is a smile that's slightly too wide. "Excellent idea, Thomas. Why don't you go share the exciting news with the Council?"

"The Council?" I ask.

"The six of us who govern this colony."

"I'm coming with you. I want to explain—"

Thomas holds up a hand to silence me, then extends it to Mistress Bailie for the letter. "No need, Lady Thelia. Everything we need to know is right here."

"But—"

"There will be plenty of time for business. Relax today, and ready yourself for a celebration tonight."

I don't have time to protest before Thomas is gone.

"A princess!" Mistress Bailie's voice slices through the air. "I can hardly believe our luck."

"I understand this must be strange," I offer, this time my tone a little kinder. I allow a shred of vulnerability to coat my words, trusting that she'll latch on to it as something she can manipulate. Antagonizing her, while tempting, would be a mistake. If I push her too far, too quickly, she'll gladly lock me away. "It's been an extraordinary couple of weeks for me as well."

"I can only imagine," she responds measuredly. "Given what you've been through, you should return to your room and rest. Tonight will be a big night."

I look behind me to the kitchen, to the door that offered such a tantalizing promise: the flash of pomegranate lips, the spark of green eyes. "I'd really love to see more of the city—"

"Absolutely not, my lady. After the journey you've had, you must gather your strength." The words alone are friendly enough, but I hear the secret meaning layered beneath them: *You won't cause me any trouble. Do you understand?*

Back in the safety of my quarters, I pull a chair to the window. If I can only search for her through this small aperture, then so be it; I'll do it.

The slightest movement above its frame catches my attention. A tiny spider weaves a web in the corner of the ceiling. Her movements are delicate, as if it's yarn she spins and not a net. She looks like her sisters on Scopuli, and in this strange new place, her familiarity is reassuring. I smile. I've always admired the gracile beauty of their spindle legs, the plump roundness of their bodies. I've always admired their cunning.

I've seen humans recoil from spiders, disturbed by their craft. They've tricked themselves into believing there's no honor in how these arachnids feed themselves, building traps and lying in wait, but they never bother to analyze their own actions through the same lens. After all, they eat animals bred too docile to ever imagine death at their hands. Where's the honor in that?

I admire the spider's ingenuity, and perhaps envy it a little. As a predator myself, I feel like its method is divine, as if whatever lands in its web was destined to end there. Then again, we must have seemed divine—no, profane—to those we lured to shore, with the voices of angels and the bodies of monsters.

The divine, the profane. They're two sides of the same coin.

᠎ 🜲

The marble hall of Ceres's throne room is barren, save for the boughs of dead poppy stalks that still adorn its walls. Their petals, once red as blood, collect in decaying piles along the hall's edges. No new blooms have grown these past few weeks to replace them, and Ceres refuses to take them down. The flowers' shriveled corpses serve as a reminder of what was lost.

What I lost.

I swallow hard, risking a glance to Pisinoe beside me. I've never seen the hall like this, so devoid of life, so solemn. This place that has always been a joyous one, where music constantly plays, and ambrosia always pours. But without Proserpina, it's a tomb.

The Lady of Grain perches on her golden throne, and my sisters and I drop to our knees before her, folding our wings to our backs and pressing our foreheads to the cool marble floor in submission. My face flushes hot with shame.

"Well?" Her voice reverberates through the hall's columns. It's laced with anger, yes, but also the smallest dash of hope— that's what brings the tears to my eyes.

"We couldn't find her," Raidne begins.

"We scoured the earth; we spanned the sea . . ." Pisinoe continues.

It's up to me to deliver the final blow. "But she's . . . she's gone."

We moan in turn, telling the entire tale together, one picking up when another fails. Our voices are a song, its tone silvery, tiny bells caressed by a gentle breeze. We pour our heartbreak into it, but, though it may win us some sympathy among Ceres's court, it does nothing to soften the lady's anger.

"You three had one task, and that was to protect her. And when you failed, I gave you a chance to redeem yourselves by finding her." Rage brings her to her feet, and my eyes fall closed as I steel myself for what's to come. She's already cursed the land—entire fields of crops lost to blight, both men and livestock murdered in fits of rage. How quickly the giver of life can take it all away.

"And now you grovel before me having failed again."

"We went to Lake Avernus, my lady, but the door to the Underworld wouldn't open for us—" Raidne begins, but Ceres cuts her off with a cruel laugh.

"How is it that mortals are constantly wandering into Dis's realm, but you three can't find your way in? Not that it matters now. That vile god tricked my sweet child into eating from his garden. Six pomegranate seeds, and now not even Jove can bring her back to me."

My hands press back into the marble floor to steady me as the world begins to spin.

She ate the food of the dead?

Finding her will be impossible now. A whimper escapes from my lips before I can stop it, and the lady's focus is on me once more.

"You foolish girl!" Ceres shrieks down at me, and I drop my gaze as terror digs its claws into my heart.

"My lady, I'm sorry . . . !"

"How many times did I warn Proserpina that your"—she sputters, as if she cannot bear to name our relationship—

"your childish *infatuation* would hurt her? But she wouldn't listen!"

Infatuation. The gross simplification of what Proserpina and I shared brings fresh tears to my eyes. Was it merely infatuation all those times she whispered poetry into my ears to soothe me when I was afraid? Merely infatuation that let us learn the languages of each other's thoughts in the curves of the other's shoulders? The various cadences of the other's breath? Until that night, we were a single soul split across two bodies. And now, without her, I am only half of the person I once was. I rise to my monstrous feet, talons scraping against the marble floor. "My lady, I *love* her."

"And look what that love got her. Imprisonment in a world of death and darkness. How is that fair?" she spits.

"It's not."

A flicker of surprise ripples across the ravaged goddess's features, and for one glorious moment, I believe that maybe, just maybe, Ceres's fury might soften.

Except, of course, it was Proserpina who could conjure that rare miracle of quelling her mother's fits. Without her, Ceres's surprise transforms into a violent rictus grin. "So let's make it fair, then."

"My lady, please, Thelxiope didn't mean to offend . . ." Pisinoe rises to her feet as well, hands clasped in capitulation, but Ceres raises a palm, and Pisinoe's plea dies in her throat.

"I banish you three to your own prison. Like Proserpina's, it will be filled with death and unspeakable darkness. And when I decide I've lost pleasure in watching you suffer for what you've cost me, you'll shrivel away slowly, across eons, until there's nothing left of you but dust."

"M-my lady . . . !" Suddenly, I feel every piece of this large, lumbering body, awash in the horror that Ceres means to leave us in them. Means for us to die as monsters.

"And if some mortal hero brings me your heads before then, I'll hang his image in the stars." Ceres sits back on her throne, her muscles relaxing as her anger dissipates. Our sentence has brought her peace, which means there will be no reversing it. "Now remove them from my sight."

Hands with the strength of manacles clamp around my wrists and drag me across the floor.

"No, my lady, please!" Pisinoe pleads.

And Raidne, still prostrating on her knees before the goddess, begs, "Please, my lady, forgive us!"

But Ceres only laughs.

≈≈≈

The weight of a hand on my shoulder jolts me awake, and I nearly topple from the wooden chair I'd dragged to the window's edge.

Margery jumps back. "I'm sorry, my lady! I didn't mean to frighten you!"

I shake my head to banish the dream and turn my attention to the window, where the wooden shutters remain pushed open. Where I waited desperately for another glimpse of her. Where my traitorous body defied me once more and succumbed to its exhaustion.

Margery steps between me and the view and draws the shutters closed. "It's time to dress . . . I let you sleep as long as I could, but we don't want to be late. Everyone will be waiting."

This time, she ushers me into multiple layers of garments, naming each component, but my tired mind can't hold on to them. It's the emerald gown that sits atop the rest that steals my attention—its fabric buttery beneath my fingertips: silk, no doubt. As soon as my arms are inside the sleeves, Margery laces it closed. A clever way to ensure I'll never escape without her help. She collects my hair in a braid and pins it at the base of my neck, then steps back to admire her handiwork.

Even I can't deny the final result is breathtaking.

"You look beautiful, Lady Thelia."

"Are we finished, then?" I ask, hoping desperately that the answer is yes. These clothes are far more complicated than the garments of my youth, and by the time we're done, the sun has disappeared from the sky, leaving a deep orange stain in its wake. It's the same hue as the lily I found this summer, and its memory brings a sad smile to my face. If everyone is going to be there tonight, will she? My stomach is suddenly full of wings, and without a task assigned to them, my hands brush out my skirts.

"Almost," Margery assures me, interrupting my reverie. Inspiration flashes across her eyes, and she arranges my fibulae into my hair. My fingers reach back to brush each dragonfly delicately, thankful for the one piece of familiarity in this entirely foreign, though not wholly uncomfortable, style of dress. Finally, I'm decent.

"Mistress Bailie and Sir Thomas have already left. Let's join them," Margery says.

I leave the house for the first time since I was carried into it. The pointed roofs of the surrounding cottages cast sinister shadows that spill onto one another's walls and into the streets. Can buildings be vicious? These stand at attention, sentinels keen to defend their builders. My stomach twists at the thought. Somewhere in the distance, a blackbird caws, heralding winter's arrival. I shiver in the gloaming, cheeks flushing with nerves, and look over my shoulder at the Bailie home once more. It's like all the other cottages here, but the Bailies' is the only structure that stands two stories tall. Something about the way it towers over all the others is almost perverse, and my gait draws me closer to Margery.

"That's the meetinghouse." The maid points to a large building at the end of the street, and I am thankful for the distraction. "It's where we hold services, but also where we celebrate."

It's painted white and has two rows of tiny square windows adorning its facade. Between them sits a large wooden door. Light spills forth onto the street, and a cacophony of voices follows it, like thunder trailing in the wake of lightning. My trembling hands remember that the last time I appeared before a hall of people, it ended in my banishment, but my fluttering heart tells me tonight is different. This crowd is boisterous, composed of booming laughter and the clinking of glasses, and even—my heart swells to hear it—the notes of music. But my mood is quickly dampened by the article pinned to the door:

LAWS DIVINE, MORAL, AND MARTIAL
OF THE CITY OF RALEIGH

1. *No man may speak impiously or maliciously against the holy and blessed Trinity or against the known Articles of Christian faith, upon pain of death.*
2. *No man shall use any traitorous words against her Majesty's Person or royal authority, upon pain of death.*
3. *No man shall commit the horrible and detestable sins of Sodomy, upon pain of death . . .*

"Are you ready?"

Margery's voice interrupts me before I can read the rest, though the first three are enough for my palms to grow slick with sweat. But despite the fear that tightens my throat, my dream is still fresh in my mind—my sisters' faces as we were torn from the only home we had ever known. How no one, not even our parents, spoke in our defense. Even then, I'd already promised myself a thousand times over that if I ever had the chance to right what happened, to see her again, I'd take it without hesitating. I nod.

Margery pushes the door open, and light and music spill forth to greet us. My eyes flutter as they try to accept the sudden brightness. For the faintest moment, when the room's details remain obscured by white, I almost see the willowy nymphs and muscled demigods of Ceres's palace in their forms. But then, of course, my vision adjusts, and the ghosts of my past are gone.

In their place, three men pluck at oblong stringed instruments in the center of the room. Another blows on a conical one made of some sort of metal. I don't recognize these variations of lutes and pipes, but the melody is surprisingly pleasant. The room is so enchanted by its notes that no one notices Margery beckon me forward. I cross inside and scan the scene before me. Nearly one hundred people fill the hall, and to my surprise and relief, most of the faces belong to men. I hadn't expected the ratio to be so striking, but there are only twenty or so women and perhaps ten children scattered throughout a sea of beards, heavy brows, and thick jaws. My heart races at the sight of them all—there are more than enough here to save my sisters, and for the first time since arriving, I allow myself to find comfort in fate. For once, it finally seems to be on my side, though it's hard to relax in this form. Longing for my old body floods me, a twist so bitter it sours my stomach. To miss that monstrous frame, that prison of feathers and talons . . . but it was powerful. It kept me safe. If these men decided to, they could tear me apart.

My eyes scan the crowd for her.

Please, Proserpina. Don't let them tear me apart.

The door crashes into place behind me, drawing the room's

attention. The man with the metal instrument lowers it from his lips, while the other three remove their fingers from their strings. More than two hundred eyes find me, all wide as they take in the mysterious princess who washed onto their shore.

The attention is petrifying, but Thomas's voice cuts through the tension.

"Welcome to our guest of honor!" he booms from a large table at the back of the room. It spreads out horizontally with seats for twelve, perhaps for the Council members and their partners. Thomas rests in the center, the place of a king, and stands to raise a glass in my direction. Six smaller, notably less striking tables sit perpendicular between us.

A large, unsettling smile is plastered across Thomas's face. A wave of nausea hits, but with the help of my binding gown, I manage to keep the contents of my stomach in their rightful place. Mistress Bailie sits to his left, and I'm struck by another similarity they share—the same obvious lust for power. They wear it so brazenly, on their lips and in their gleaming eyes, and with so much conviction. What fools. Haven't they learned that the gods love nothing more than to knock pompous men from their thrones? If these two haven't drawn their attention yet, they will soon. A ripple of satisfaction cascades down my spine as understanding dawns—but of course, they already have. Why else would she bring me here?

I look away from the pair, and my attention falls to the woman on Thomas's right. I didn't see her until now, a fact that is instantly unimaginable. I'm looking at a ghost. It takes all my courage to meet her stare, to not lower my gaze in deference, or shame, or both. I've dreamed of this moment since the day I lost her, and yet here she is, and I'm unable to move. She watches me intently, her eyes so green that I am certain the first spring must have erupted from them centuries ago.

The rest of the room, all its noise and its people, falls away as if we've broken free from this realm and slipped into one entirely our own. My breath catches in my throat, and my legs tremble beneath the large circumference of my skirt. The only sound is the pounding of my heart.

A single loose curl, the color of raven wings, the color of shadow, falls free from the rest of the hair pinned behind her neck. It spills over the gentle slope of her shoulder onto a crimson gown. Her lips have been painted the same smoldering shade of carmine, and the contrast against her porcelain skin is breathtaking. I haven't seen anything so lovely in thousands of years, but is it truly her? Or is this a trick being played on me by the gods?

I make myself a promise: If she's merely an illusion meant to harm me, I won't give them the satisfaction. It seems impossible, but only now do I realize how the years watered down my memory of Proserpina's beauty, waves slowly erasing footprints in the sand until they're lost to time forever. Except now time has given them back. To see her again like this in full relief, flesh and blood, as a woman, no longer a girl bathed in moonlight—my throat tightens, and tears threaten to spill over my cheeks. I blink them back furiously. No, if this is a trick, I'll be grateful for the chance to stand in her radiance once more, to remember what it feels like to be a flower in the light of her sun.

I search her face for signs of recognition, but her expression is unreadable. She makes no move to look away, and those blood-red lips part briefly before snapping closed again. There's a distance between us, but of course there is—we've lived a thousand lives since we last saw each other, and though it will hurt, I want to hear about every one of hers. My mouth falls open to speak, to call to her, to beg her forgiveness, and to confess my devotion, still, after all this time—

3

𝖘𝖘𝖘𝖘

BEFORE

Our first decades banished on Scopuli are gorged with elaborate designs for liberation. Raidne is the first to attempt to escape. Other lands are visible from our cliffs, and she's certain she has the strength to reach one. The sky is an infinite and blazing blue, so deep it's hard to discern on the horizon where the heavens end and the sea begins. Pisinoe and I sit atop Castle's middle turret and watch her fly west. She rises and falls on the currents of wind, a dancer, farther and farther away, closer and closer to salvation. I reach for Pisinoe's hand to give it a squeeze, confident in our imminent victory.

We're foolish to think we can best the gods so easily, but we're still young, each equivalent to less than eighteen mortal years. We hold the arrogance of youth to prove it.

Pisinoe stands, unfurling her wings to follow Raidne's lead. She's no more than a dark speck on the horizon, but then she shoots upward as her body slams into a wall of wind. Our necks crane as she ascends toward the zenith until we need to fall onto our backs to keep her in sight. When she's nearly overhead, she drops like a boulder straight into the choppy ocean below.

We launch toward the spot where Raidne hit, but the water churns like Charybdis, vicious and punishing. I'm certain Raidne is dead, lost to us forever.

We spend the remaining daylight hours gliding around the island, low above the water, buzzard-like, searching for any sign of her. We don't return to the beach until the sun sinks beneath the sea and twilight envelops us in a half-hearted embrace.

What were you thinking? the island seems to ask with each murmur of waves, but we don't have an answer. We're silent and heartbroken.

Our own self-importance clouds our judgment: We never consider that a quick death could be a kindness. Raidne washes ashore under the rising moon, choking on the water in her lungs and badly beaten, but alive. And so we try again.

And again.

And again.

The day, the time, or the season—none of the innumerable variables we tweak changes the outcome. Whichever direction we venture, there's always a point where the wind blows us right back to Scopuli and discards us fiercely into the ocean. So we try sailing away, hopeful that we might glide across the surface of the water unnoticed. But as soon as our rafts leave our little archipelago, a wave either crashes us into the reefs or swallows the vessel entirely. All our attempts end the same way: with us struggling beneath the surface, tortured for hours as the water steals our breath, as the current pummels our bodies. Only when we're certain that we'll die do the waves release us.

We're too distraught by our confinement to accept our prison's feral beauty—how Scopuli is a land of extremes, with her unscalable cliffs and towering trees, bathed in soft-spoken sunrises and violent, bruised sunsets. Instead, we spend our time in the sky, frantically circling, and along the beach, desperately hoping for a sign from the gods. But neither the heavens nor the depths hold the path to our salvation, and as the decades roll into centuries, our designs for freedom dissolve into sea-foam.

All the while, I speak to Proserpina. Not in prayer, nor in hope of forgiveness, but as a companion in imprisonment. I whisper my treason into Scopuli's soil and water it with my tears. Whenever the checkered adder that resides in the birch grove crosses my path, I beg it to carry her messages below.

I hope that you're safe.

Please stay strong.

I miss you.

I miss you.

I miss you.

I don't expect an answer, but when we wake one morning to discover Scopuli ablaze with lilies, I know she's heard me. Lilies were Proserpina's favorite flower. When we were children, we'd lie beneath them in the fields surrounding the palace. They were so regal, both the flowers and my princess, silhouetted against the sky. It was the perfect backdrop for sharing feverishly whispered secrets and girlhood imaginations. Later, when we were older, we stole our first kiss beneath their shadows, their elegant stalks arching over us like graceful protectors. Proserpina's lips were as soft as petals each time she found mine, and I'll never forget the feeling of our fingers curling into each other's, the black waves of her hair engulfing the light strawberry of mine.

Lilies were planted around the palace grounds in her wake, but they died in the earth as if her radiance was what they had thrived on; without it, they rotted in the fields. I understood their refusal to take root in a world without Proserpina.

Raidne and Pisinoe marvel at the curiosity, how all the other plants bow down to the lilies, ceding their own claims to sunlight. But when I tell them who's responsible, they only smile sadly. My sisters know what she meant to me; though skepticism is written into each of their faces, they love me too much to take away this last little piece of her.

But regardless of their origin, that's how we learn: The ships appear when the lilies bloom.

The first time a ship materializes on the horizon, the sailors aren't drawn by our song. We haven't discovered its magic yet. No, it's curiosity, for a new land perhaps, that lures them close. We are desperate for a chance to escape, so when they sail inside our curse's bounds, we fly to meet them. We're still young and naïve, so we lead them through the rocky waters to our beach. They happily disembark to share our food and drink our wine, entranced by our forms. They regale us with tales of their travels. Some flirt. We don't realize that they see us as beasts to slay, their own Gorgon heads to claim, until night falls. When we're drunk and unsuspecting, they overpower us.

There are too many of them, on us all at once. What silent call alerted them to begin their attack in unison? How did they know to switch from jovial to vicious? Did some god whisper the truth of us into their ears? They bind our hands and feet and drag us into a sea cave, its chambers too shallow to allow our wings to spread. And then they discuss what to do with us.

Not about our lives—no one disagrees that we must die. After years at war, though, they're curious if the slit between our legs would feel the same as a human woman's. If taking us offends the gods. *Taking*, they say, as if they speak simply of plucking fruit from its vine.

"No," one argues. Our form already speaks to divine punishment. No creatures so hideous could exist unless they were guilty of an atrocious crime. He isn't wrong. "Any further degradation would only please the gods more."

He isn't wrong about this, either.

In the blackness of the cave, Raidne's stare hardens as she steels herself for what's coming. If only we were Gorgons, able to freeze our attackers in stone. But Medusa wasn't born with such incredible power; she was cursed with it, just as we are.

No, our stare does not hold our salvation. Our mouths do.

Sing.

The sound of that voice—*her* voice—makes every part of me thrum, like I'm a lyre and she's just run her delicate fingers across my strings.

It's Proserpina.

My back straightens, and I search for my sisters' faces in the darkling cave, expecting to find their eyes alight with the same joy that now sparks in mine. But Pisinoe's body is slumped forward, her face hidden beneath a curtain of blond curls. And though Raidne's stare is locked on the cave's mouth, it holds nothing but fear. I remember those sad smiles on their lips this morning, and my epiphany disintegrates into ash.

What if that voice is nothing more than a hallucination produced by a terrified mind? But Proserpina doesn't abandon me as I abandoned her.

Sing, Thelia, she urges once more, and I swear that I feel the warmth of my name whispered against the back of my neck. It undoes my resolve, and my mouth falls open, letting the same notes that once comforted us as children fill the cave until they eventually spill onto the beach.

Pisinoe and Raidne join, and before long, the song takes on a shape of its own, a plea for release with the knowledge one won't be coming. Except, inexplicably, the sailors listen. With clouded eyes and slackened jaws, they untie our bonds, then fall back on swaying legs. We scurry from the cave and take to the sky, circling overhead. The melody still tumbles from our lips. Our voices have always held power, to coax out smiles or tears, but these men aren't temporarily entranced in the face of art. No, this song contains something new: the promise of their futures, courtesy of either Ceres's curse or Scopuli itself. We don't know which, but they're bewitched by it. The sailors reach for us again, this time in exultation, but it's too late. All our truths are laid bare, and there's no taking them back. The terror passes, leaving fury in its wake.

They make us into monsters.

Are all human men like this? Vessels for profound violence that simmers just barely beneath the surface, ready to overflow when they believe no one watches? In the safety of Ceres's palace, there was little need to think of them at all. But now, staring into those clouded, stupefied gazes, we're presented with our own tantalizing promise: bloody, painful vengeance.

Together, as one, we take it. Pisinoe, with her keen attention to detail, becomes the eyes. Raidne, the quickest, is our hands. And me? My rage has only one outlet.

I am the mouth.

〜〜〜

We stop wearing clothes; we let our hair go wild. Scopuli's game, once abundant, begins to dwindle. Her deer become ghosts that haunt the twilight, dissolving into the night before we can hunt them; her fish, slippery shadows beneath the waves. Even her beach plums and hickories yield less and less fruit.

And so we purposefully lure a ship to shore, hypnotizing

the sailors with our song, and we gift the worthy ones to Ceres in feral, offensive displays. Her curse is what locks the chains around our wrists, and her growing apathy is what keeps the animals from our traps and withers our fruit on its vines. It's her we must appease.

We follow the old rites, the ones we've seen priests and priestesses perform countless times before, though their gifts were bulls, sheep, and pigs. But our offense was great, and so too must be our offerings.

We purify ourselves in the sea. We lead our victims to our altar. We pour libations over their heads. The first sailors know the rules of sacrifice: They've seen the same trick pulled on livestock to make them bow their heads, to make them consent. But observing is different from experiencing, and each man drops his gaze to keep the wine from trickling into his eyes, and in doing so, agrees to his fate. We slit their throats, and Raidne reads their entrails for signs of forgiveness. Then we burn them on a pyre, and the smoke delivers our gifts to Ceres.

Our hatred for Dis, for those first sailors, transfers onto each man who wrecks here. We make them suffer. We bleed them slowly, paint our bodies with the gore, and revel in the pain our power brings. Their bodies belong to Ceres, but their suffering is ours alone.

Compassion never squirms its way into our hearts, but even if it did, we wouldn't stop. We can't. Ceres promised our lives would be defined by death and darkness, and in the smoldering light of that first pyre, we watch as our time collected here melts from our skin. She cursed us with unending life, but not eternal youth, and yet . . .

Their souls make us ageless.

4

𝗅𝗅𝗅𝗅𝗅

NOW

"Loyal subjects of the Crown, allow me to introduce Lady Thelia!" Thomas bellows, his voice an axe to the moment that held only us. Proserpina's double cuts her attention to him, shifting uncomfortably in her chair. My mouth turns sour. If she really was Proserpina, surely she would've acknowledged me by now. Unless—

She despises you, that ancient fear chides. *How could she not?*

I force myself to stand tall, to stay still, refusing to succumb to the very real desire to fall to my knees and beg for forgiveness.

It's not her. It's not her. It's not her. Is the realization a blow or an answer to a prayer? It's a bit of both, though it still feels like being pummeled by Scopuli's waves.

The room is disturbingly silent. Perhaps my ruse is easily detected, and they've already determined I'm not who I say. I turn to Margery for guidance just in time to watch her step away from me. Mistress Bailie rises from her chair, a sickeningly sweet grin painted across her lips. It takes all my strength to keep from collapsing beneath the weight of her stare—does she mean to introduce me or decry me?

The older woman fans out her arms in a display of presentation. I think of the sweet-eyed cattle that humans paraded through the village streets during my childhood, straight to the center of the town, where they met their fates as gifts to the gods. Is this what it feels like to be an offering? I've never been on the receiving end of a sacrificial blade, and I don't doubt that, given the opportunity, Mistress Bailie would happily drag one across my throat.

"When our fair queen granted us our charter, she entrusted us to explore these remote and dangerous lands with the intention of establishing the first permanent colony in the Americas. We've secured our outpost here, on Roanoke, but our queen also wished for us to seek out and meet other peoples," Mistress Bailie says, projecting her voice to fill the large space. "Tonight, we do our queen proud. Lady Thelia comes to us from a land called Scopuli. Her people, as you may have suspected, are noble and wealthy. We're proud to have her as our guest, and we look forward to forging a fruitful alliance between our countries."

The townspeople turn to one another with excited chatter. I use the cacophony to ground myself. The next few minutes will be important. I must appear strong, not meek, or else my ruse will never work. Raising my chin higher, I push forward to the center of the room to face Thomas and the woman who must be his betrothed. His love, though she looks so much like mine.

"I thank you all for your kindness," I say. "I was at sea for several weeks, afraid the waves would claim me, unsure of what to expect if they didn't. I'm so grateful I washed upon your shores."

"And what, exactly, brings you here?" Thomas asks for the

crowd's benefit, though after his meeting with the Council, everyone likely already knows.

"Scopuli has run out of eligible suitors, so I've been sent to find a worthy man for my hand in marriage. The treasure you saw is only a fraction of my dowry, but I hope it's enough to convince you of the seriousness of my offer."

Another burst of prattling fills the room, and Thomas offers me another toast. "To the mysterious and beautiful Princess Thelia! May she find her king among our ranks!"

"Hear, hear!" Everyone raises their glasses in unison. I bow my head in thanks, trying not to lose myself in my racing thoughts. The details of my story swirl around the one thing that dominates my attention: the woman before me, the very likeness of my stolen love.

"Come, Lady Thelia. Sit and enjoy the meal!" Thomas motions toward the seat beside him where Proserpina's twin is currently positioned. "Cora, do you mind?"

Cora's spine straightens, and those red lips press into a cold, thin line. But she acquiesces and slides into the empty seat to her right. In the halo of her radiance, I can't help but feel silly by comparison. But all eyes are on me, not her. The vast fortune they believe me to have helps me compete with her natural beauty.

I step onto the platform with the other high-ranking members of the village and take my seat beside Thomas. My hands press into my stomach, and I keep my eyes trained on the empty plate on the table before me. I fear if I look at her, I won't be able to look away. Or worse, she'll vanish.

And then, there it is: the same elusive smell that intoxicated me last night. So it was she who guarded my side. The realization is enough to pique my curiosity, to encourage me to speak, but before I can, Thomas is once again talking.

"Rose, fetch these ladies something to drink!" he says to a wisp of a girl, then turns to me. "Wine or ale, Lady Thelia?"

"Wine, please." I respond slowly, trying to hide my irritation at his intrusion. Men, always inserting themselves where they're not wanted. He snaps his fingers, and the girl pours me a large glass of the scarlet liquid before moving to fill Cora's cup as well. It doesn't go unnoticed by either of us that Thomas didn't ask her preference. She swirls her goblet aggressively before taking a long pull from it. A knot grows in my abdomen, and I follow her lead with my own large gulp. The alcohol warms my throat, but it does little to calm my nerves.

The excitement dies down enough that everyone begins to eat. A spark of jealousy kindles in my stomach as I watch them. There's Margery, bouncing a baby on her knee. Another woman scolds her own children, but she does so with a smile on her lips. These people have families; they have lives. Things that I was forbidden from having a long time ago.

But maybe that's not true anymore.

The thought dampens the glint of rage, and with my resentment tempered, relief floods in. I'm no longer the center of attention.

"If you're looking for a worthy suitor, the most likely candidate is already betrothed," a man says from behind Mistress Bailie. He moves to stand behind Thomas. "I'm Master Will Waters. His oldest friend." He claps his hands onto Thomas's shoulders to emphasize his point, laughing as he does so, before nodding to Cora. "And Cora's older brother."

As I observe them in the candlelit glow of the hall, I'm surprised to see how much the two siblings look alike. He's a large man, no doubt, but his features are soft and gracile— almost feminine. The same dark curls frame his face, which is markedly softer than the hard lines and sharp angles of

Thomas's. However, where Cora is reserved and calculating, Will is exuberant. It would be hard to remain cold toward him if thoughts of my past didn't immediately sour me against him. The last time I let my defenses down around a man, I allowed evil to go unpunished. I won't make that mistake again.

Will's intrusion is far from subtle. Thomas and Cora have an arrangement, and Will senses Thomas's curiosity toward me. Nervous thoughts begin to swirl, but the sight of Thomas's eyes darkening at the mention of his betrothal keeps me anchored to the conversation. He wears the same expression as a child who realizes he won't be allowed to play with a new toy.

I lift my chin away from Will in the best display of dominance this body allows. When the lie spills from my lips, it does so easily. "A competition will be held to win my hand. It's tradition."

"A competition?" Thomas responds with glittering eyes. A flicker of something flashes across Will's face, but it ripples away too quickly for me to catch exactly what it is— indignation at Thomas's disrespect toward his sister? Irritation at the allure I hold for him?

Jealousy?

"What type of competition?" Will draws his gaze back to me.

"A display of strength," I respond. "Becoming the heir to Scopuli's throne is an honor not fit for the weak."

"When will it be held?"

"As soon as—" I start at the same time Thomas asks loudly, "What's the hurry?"

Will drops his hands from his shoulders. Only now do I realize he'd been touching Thomas this whole time, as if he were reluctant to let go.

"Let the woman rest and regain her strength before we send her on her way with a new husband-to-be in tow," Thomas adds.

"Of course, I didn't mean to be rude. I hope you can understand that a man is simply eager to try his luck for such a reward."

I feel the color rising in my cheeks, and I turn to look at Cora. She's nearly finished her meal, while my plate remains untouched. I take another sip of wine and reach for a stale roll from a basket in the center of the table, but the gesture is for show. I'm not hungry.

Despite an apparent shortage of food, there's no shortage of alcohol. Rose, the girl who poured my wine, finds herself rather busy, refilling goblets all around the room. The din grows as people start talking louder and moving heavier, banging the tables with their fists, clinking glasses. I scour the room, counting the women as best I can. When I can't make it past ten without realizing I've double-counted someone or losing my place, I determine that the alcohol hit me harder than I intended.

Proserpina and I used to sneak sips of Bacchus's wine when Ceres hosted feasts. We'd hide beneath the elaborately set dinner tables and wait patiently until the adults were ripe with drink and my sisters lost interest in keeping an eye on us. Only then would we snatch their goblets from above and return them once they were drained. One or two glasses was enough to send us scampering from the banquet hall, giggling as we dashed through the emptied corridors of the palace. If anyone ever knew what we were up to, no one stopped us. Only Ceres had the authority to scold her, and the Mother of the Fields was still jovial back then. The memory is a warm one, and without thinking, I reach for Cora's hand beneath the table.

Cora's face snaps to mine as she pulls her hand away. The look of shock I wear betrays my situation, and although she's irritated at first, her expression softens. When she stands, she motions for me to join her. Whether her intention is to rescue me or simply to draw me away from the crowd, I don't care—I'd follow this woman anywhere.

"Lady Thelia, you must be exhausted. Would you like me to walk you home?"

This is the most she's spoken all evening. At first, the sound of her voice sends my expectations soaring, but although it's just as lovely as last night, Proserpina isn't in it.

"Yes, thank you," I reply softly, trying to hide my disappointment. I'm suddenly desperate to escape the room's hundreds of appraising eyes. Thomas studies us both, as if calculating how this could play in his favor. If he discovers an answer, his expression doesn't reveal it.

"Of course. Good night, Lady Thelia, Mistress Waters," he says.

We exit into the chilly night air. I wrap my arms around my frame as a shiver traces down my spine. The wine has made my mind foggy, but there's a sense of security under the cover of Nox's cloak; out here, I allow a few tears to fall as I watch the outline of the woman I love walk ahead of me. The woman I lost.

Cora is quiet for a few steps, but we don't make it far before she whirls around to face me, those green eyes flaring.

"Master Thomas seems rather fond of you," she says. The subtext is clear. She's warning me.

I raise my hands in submission. "I have no interest in your betrothed, Mistress Waters." Not in the way she's implying, anyway—what I have in store for him is far, far worse, but what good would saying such a thing do for either of us?

Her smoldering gaze lingers on mine for the span of a

breath, then she turns on her heel without another word. We walk back to the Bailie house in silence. When the shadows of the cottage finally catch me, I open my mouth to thank her. But she's already several paces down the street, and soon, darkness engulfs her completely.

I stare after her, mouth agape and eyes wide, watching the last place her form is visible before it's overtaken by shadow. After a time, I step into the warmth of the foyer, but the image remains with me deep into the night, long after the Bailies have returned, when the house is as silent as a crypt.

I can barely stand it: Proserpina and Cora, both swallowed by darkness. When it took Proserpina, it was over so quickly. One moment she was there, the next she was gone, devoured by a stygian mouth that carried her straight to the Under-world. I always believed nothing could be worse than the shock of her sudden disappearance, but now I wonder if I was wrong. For it's Cora's dissipating shape that haunts me tonight—the shade slowly eating away at her, piece by piece, until nothing is left but black.

5

BEFORE

On Scopuli, years feel like days. The chill of morning is spring, and summer is the glow of the afternoon sun. Autumn arrives at twilight with winter in tow once more under the blanket of night. And when the passage of time starts to take its toll, when our food stores grow slim, we scan the horizon for sails, and we sing. We sing for Proserpina, we sing for ourselves, for all who've felt unwanted hands encircling their wrists, their throats—we sing those dark souls into the sea. And when a sailor loses his battle against the waves, or is torn to ribbons by coral, or chokes on his own blood after meeting our blade, we feel it: The ache in our limbs dissipates; our skin grows firmer, brighter. Our youth is restored once more, but their deaths alone don't sate the growing hunger in our bellies.

Their meat does.

It's during these centuries that I learn Scopuli's location isn't fixed in the physical world. Overhead, the positions of the stars change. When our exile began, it was in Mare Nostrum, the Tyrrhenian Sea, but ships from all over the world have crashed here since those early days. Survivors insist they were sailing on the Sea of Sanji, the Caspian Sea, the Black Sea, the Sea of Antilles, the East Sea, the North Sea, the South Sea. I don't know why Scopuli appears to certain ships and not to others. Perhaps it depends on who's aboard and whether the gods believe they must be punished.

Life here is monastic, lonely. But it's also safe. Or at least it was, until the ships stopped coming.

Without the ears of men to hear our song, without their deaths to roll back time, and their meat to feed us, we begin to die. Our feathers turn white, as does our hair. Our skin wrinkles, breasts sag. Teeth loosen, talons crack. Pisinoe tries to hide her aging form beneath the treasure that washes ashore, her arms and neck draped in emeralds, sapphires, rubies, and other gems with unknown names. Raidne finds this habit irksome, but she's always been more ready to torment herself, preferring to live an ascetic existence, still hoping to atone.

When it seems like we can't get any older, we shrink. We once stood more than six feet tall. Now we hover closer to four.

"How small will we get?" Pisinoe asks one day. She's recalling the story of the Cumaean Sibyl, a great oracle who asked the gods for immortality but didn't specify her wish to remain forever young. The gods revel in punishing mortals for lack of clarity, so when the Sibyl spurned Helios's advances, he granted her wish. As the years passed, she grew so small that she fit inside a bottle, and then she continued to shrink until she was no more than dust.

Did she reach a point at which she died, when her frame became too diminutive to support any life? Or is she still shrinking, a creature so infinitesimal and alone that she prays for a death that will never come?

I think about the ceiling of our cottage—how I once could brush it with my fingertips. But I haven't been able to reach it for years now, and each day, the distance grows larger.

"We won't find out," Raidne insists. "More ships will come."

It's not that she believes our supply of sailors is unending; she clings to the hope that even after eons, Ceres's anger still burns hot enough to find pleasure in our suffering. Time has given us droughts before, she's quick to point out. "Remember that first harsh winter?"

How could we forget? The unusually bitter season came after a year without ships, and its freezing temperatures sent the rest of Scopuli's already scarce animal populations into hiding. How quickly we deteriorated without those willing ears and without any source of food.

But then Proserpina came to me in a dream. *I won't let you starve,* she said, and the next morning, a single lily had pushed through the snow. An hour later, a ship graced our horizon. As we sorted through the survivors fit for sacrificing, I realized what Proserpina meant. Mortals offer only an animal's organs and blood to the gods; the meat they keep for themselves. Raidne and Pisinoe would never agree to hold anything back from Ceres, but what of the sailors too old and too battered to offer her?

I told myself if my sisters reacted poorly to the idea, I'd lie and say I was simply speculating out loud and had no intention of eating human flesh. But more shocking than my suggestion was how quickly Raidne and Pisinoe agreed to it. The allure of a meal simmering over the hearth after several frigid months without one was simply too enticing to dismiss.

Besides, do our sisters Scylla and Charybdis refuse the men they ensnare? Like us, they were women once, before heinous acts of magic turned them into something unspeakable. Scylla by Minos, as he gleefully dragged her behind his ship bound for Crete. The gods supported his cruelty because instead of simply dying, she was transformed into a creature that could survive it. And Charybdis by Jove himself for helping her father, Neptune, in a petty sibling feud. We were all made into monsters, and what do monsters do?

They feed.

🔄

Nearly a decade passes without sightings of lilies or ships. In more fruitful times, the passing of ten years feels like the passing of days, but without the ships and the men they bring, we wither away, and withering is painful.

The first year without them is the hardest. Their numbers have dwindled for years, but Raidne insists if we continue to sacrifice the survivors, continue to send their spirits upward on the ritual fire's smoke, Ceres will finally forgive us. In the early days, our prayers were for mercy, to regain our divine forms, to be free of the prison of rocks and cliffs. Now we simply pray for the return of eager ears, for an end to our slow and painful rot. But nine more years pass, and my messages whispered into the earth go unanswered.

I watch my skin turn pallid, see the strawberry kiss drain from my hair, feel my breasts shrivel. No one speaks it out loud, but we all fear we've entered the final stage of Ceres's curse, and now there's nothing left to do but wither away. Until we're only dust and shadow, too, companions for the Sibyl. Sometimes I consider throwing myself from the cliffs to cut my suffering short, but the thought never lasts long. It's not death itself I fear, nor the fact I'll be prohibited from entering Elysium. It's that even after all these years, I'm still not ready to face her—my darling, dreadful Proserpina, the queen of the world of darkness.

ธธธ

Watching my sisters slowly decay is the cruelest part of Ceres's curse. If we were human, these gnarled bodies would never last longer than a few years. But here, we'll endure for centuries. It's the sight of Raidne's grimace as she limps slowly to her bookshelf that brings me to my own aching feet. She's clutching another tooth in her palm. It's the fourth she's lost, and she means to add it to her jewelry box where she stores the others.

My heart sinks. How is it that Raidne, the most pragmatic of us, still clings to hope? If a miracle brings us another ship, she plans to nestle those fallen teeth back into the gaps in her gums where the curse's magic will help them take root again.

"I'll gather some mullein leaves," I say. Brewed in a tea, they'll soothe some of her pain. The only thing that can ease it completely is the snap of Morta's shears.

It's a bright late summer morning, though a light blanket of fog still envelops Scopuli's meadow. This time of year, it's filled with goldenrod, meadowsweet, and, of course, mullein. Bumblebees flit through the haze from bloom to bloom, and the field vibrates with their communal hum. If we were younger, I'd close my eyes and let the soothing frequency wash over me, but today, there's no peace to be found in quiet moments. There's only Raidne's pain.

Mullein's familiar clusters of browning yellow flowers crest above the tall grasses, but before I can push through to collect the large, soft leaves, an unfamiliar sound rises behind me to join the bees' song. It's a delicate, silvery tinkling, and it halts me in place as my ears rush to place it. Pisinoe?

I look to the sky for her. She jingles as she moves, courtesy of the countless jewels she adorns herself with. But this noise is more delicate than the clinking of gold against silver. No shapes materialize through the fog, and there's no whir of wings to indicate her arrival; there's only the buzzing of bees and the soft cascade of bells.

A shiver prickles along my spine. During our first weeks on Scopuli, Raidne took jewelry from the ships that wrecked here and hung it in Scopuli's highest branches. She was mimicking the behavior of mortals who understood that the gods could communicate with them through the wind. They hung chimes and bowls in the trees surrounding their settlements, and their oracles deciphered the cryptic messages delivered through the various *tings* and *bongs* created when wind filtered between the artifacts. Raidne spent hours in the woods, her body nestled in vacant deer beds, her head craned toward the sky as she prayed for a response. Wind swished through the leaves, but the baubles remained untouched and silent, and the message was clear: There would be no answers for us.

Like a lover scorned, she stopped dressing the trees centuries ago, but I still catch Pisinoe with a string of bells or an old flute heading into the woods on occasion. These attempts at divination have also gone unanswered. Until now, it seems, when someone finally speaks.

Could this be a trick of the light reflecting off the haze, some sort of strange recall of memory? It sounds just like the tintinnabula, the tiny assemblages of bells that hung in the palatial gardens when we were children. When we lived with her. I look to the treetops, but no golden sheen or metallic reflection catches my eye, no logical source for the tones.

My throat tightens as my mind races for an explanation.

But my heart, its thuds growing louder against my ribs, already knows it. Each beat is the mysterious, shimmering song's refrain: *It's her. It's her. It's her.*

When I finally turn around to face the path home, I see it. My ancient body can't absorb the shock, and in the time it takes to blink, I fall hard onto my knees with a sickening *crunch*. But if there's pain, I don't feel it. I can't—there's no room for anything other than wonder.

A lily blooms in the crook of a maple root. Its bright orange petals are a beacon, stealing my attention from the other members of the forest's undergrowth. It towers over the narrow, fine-toothed blueberry leaves that mingle with the simpler, serrated margins of the sweet-pepper bushes. The honeysuckle vines with their trumpeted blossoms don't crowd the noble flower; instead, they snake up the opposite side of the maple, forgoing their claim to sunlight. The lily, with its deep amber hue, even outshines the bunchberries, which punctuate the rest of the underbrush like crimson staccatos in a larger symphony. They accentuate the foliage around them, but the lily doesn't need their help to highlight its beauty. The lily is a solo.

I don't breathe, afraid that any disturbance to the air will shatter the image before me, but this electric unknowing is too raw to perpetuate for long. The hair on my arms stands at attention; my feathers quiver with anticipation. After I've done my best to memorize the curve of each petal, the arc of each stamen, I finally teeter from the edge of being terrified to lose it and tumble forward into needing to know if it's real. Inhaling deeply, I force myself to look away from the flower. My eyes find a wren on one of the maple's limbs, and I listen to a few moments of its song, giving my mind time to exorcise the fantasy, if it is one. When my focus returns to the spot at the base of the maple, relief floods my veins. The flower is still there. Sunlight filters through the gold-kissed leaves above, and the lily stretches its petals to lap up the light.

The first lily in a decade. In all my years trapped here, I've never seen one so deep an orange, as if blood courses through its stem and soaks into its petals, like ink on papyrus. The beauty of its symmetry, its six petals radiating from its darkened center, where stamens erupt like little tongues, brings a knot of emotions to my throat, and when it escapes, the sound is neither a gasp nor a cry: It's a noise that has no name.

"A ship's coming." I crawl to the bloom and whisper into the lily's center, an act that feels shockingly intimate.

Shielded by the maple, we're safe from wind, and still the lily leans forward to answer. Gratitude, sorrow, or some mixture of the two emotions wells in my chest, and I let its petals graze my lips. They're as soft as Proserpina's kisses were, and I close my eyes to take in their sweet scent. The bells, this flower. They're messages.

The thought is interrupted by something crisp and wet hitting my right cheek. I look up to discover darkling clouds swirling furiously overhead, and more raindrops follow the first. I blink back the tiny pearls of water as others land on the bridge of my nose, my lips, as they cling to my eyelashes. A storm is coming. If the clouds didn't announce the approaching tempest, the scent in the air does. Suddenly, it's sweet and electric all at once; it's kinetic. I know this island's weather patterns like I know my own moods. We are both mercurial, this land and me. I lean close to the lily once more and inhale deeply, trying to crystallize its scent in my memory. It's time to return home.

Raidne and Pisinoe need to know what's coming.

ᛋᛚᛋᛚᛋ

The rain falls heavier now, thousands of cold droplets kissing everything in their trajectory, from the leaves on the trees all around me to my exposed flesh, forming goosebumps on contact. The beads roll over me, descending dramatically into puddles at my feet. Lightning streaks across the sky in a brilliant flash that illuminates the forest all at once before it's over. Thunder's low rumble follows.

The dirt path beneath my feet winds gently upward, and when I emerge from the cloak of trees, our little hut is visible on its perch on the cliffs. It's a tiny dwelling, no more than a single room, a crumpled hat that sits atop the highest, rockiest point of the island. We built it ourselves with large gray stones, following the hurried instructions given to us by some nameless survivor years ago. He thought the architecture lesson would sway us to spare him. It didn't.

A muted light from within the structure flickers through the two windows that flank the front door, which creaks open to receive me. Pisinoe sticks her ashen head out from behind it, beckoning me forward. Her bracelets jingle on her wrist, but their sound is carried off by the quickening wind. Gusts shoot rain against my body like hundreds of little daggers. As if to underscore Pisinoe's insistence, another lightning bolt tears across the sky, and the thunder that follows this time is no mere rumble. It sounds as if the heavens above are shattering.

I take off toward the door. Tiny rivers are forming, creating small waterfalls that descend off the cliffs into the sea below. Pisinoe steps aside to let me enter. I'm soaking wet. Small puddles collect on the dirt-packed floor, and I know what's coming. I hear Raidne before I see her.

"Wash your feet." She leans over the ancient iron pot hanging above the hearth and hasn't yet looked at me, but instinct tells her that I'm making a mess anyway. She raises one arm and points a sharp finger at the large basin filled with water near the door. Her other hand keeps stirring the contents of the pot with a large wooden spoon, and the warm scent of basil mingling with thyme fills the cottage. The knowledge that Raidne's stews will soon contain meat again makes my stomach rumble. "And dry yourself."

Our home is humble despite our having accumulated the wealth of kings. Shadows cast from the fire flicker across the walls. A variety of drying herbs hang from old wooden beams that crisscross overhead. We don't have much in the way of furniture, save for a large, creaky table in the middle of the room and the pallets along the left wall where we sleep. It would feel rather roomy if it were not for all the piles of books strewn about. Raidne can't bear to leave them in the caves with the rest of our hoard.

I take a seat on a small stool inside the entryway, which we keep there for this very purpose, and stick my right foot in the basin to wash the mud from my talons. These feet used to disgust me, the three hooked nails in the front and the fourth behind, their only purpose to cut into flesh. However, the revulsion quickly faded. It was hard to remain disgusted by such strength. They've served me well.

The sound of Pisinoe's gasp draws Raidne's attention from the stew and mine from my washing.

"Thelia! What happened to your knees?"

Twin bruises have bloomed where I hit the ground, already a sickly purple and green. Only now do I stop to wonder how bad the damage is, though it doesn't matter. In a few hours, it will all be erased. I put the washcloth in my lap and lean forward. "I found a lily."

Pisinoe inhales sharply and looks to Raidne, who freezes before the cauldron, spoon still in hand. Her expression is blank, but I know from the way her body tenses that she's running the same calculations I did: Was it simply a trick of the light? Of my aging, failing mind?

"It was beautiful, Raidne, so deep an orange it was nearly red. I can't explain it, but it's different from the others somehow."

Though age has softened Raidne's features, her gray eyes are as exacting as ever. They study me: the arc of my brows, the curve of my shoulders. The answer she seeks is in the culmination of my details. What she finds makes her grip tighten around the spoon's handle. Before I can ask her if she believes me, she hobbles to the window that faces the sea and forces two of the wooden slats in the shutters apart to peer between them. I hold my breath as she stands there, suspended. The only indication that she hasn't turned to stone is the sound of her own labored breaths as she directs that severe stare onto the waves. But then those breaths hitch in her throat, breaking her stupor: Something has caught her attention, and she unlatches the wooden panels to get a better look.

"What are you doing?" Pisinoe shrieks, throwing herself toward Raidne. Outside, the wind roars. "You're going to let the storm in!"

"Help me open these!" Raidne snaps back, and Pisinoe abides. When they finally muscle the shutters open, the wind whips inside and nearly knocks them from their feet. It tears through the cottage, sending the cockled pages of Raidne's books flying open as if looking for a specific passage.

The sound is all-consuming. Pisinoe yells something to Raidne that I can't make out as Raidne points to the swirling ocean. I squeeze myself between them to take in the sight. A wall of stygian clouds has formed in the space where the water meets the sky, and a gale shrieks to warn us that the most dangerous part of the storm has yet to come. The unfathomable blackness is broken at first by only lightning strikes, but then I see it. For the second time today, my heart stops in my chest.

A light bobs furiously up and down on the waves. It's so faint that I can barely make it out, a will-o'-the-wisp dancing on the storm's swells. No one says a word, and we watch it rise and fall with the churning sea, leaning our bodies into one another's until another flash of lightning confirms what we already know in our hearts: There's a ship on the horizon.

6

NOW

I rise before dawn to catch Margery as she arrives. She's surprised to find me perched in the kitchen and grows more perplexed when I beg her to take me to Cora. I can't bear to be trapped in this cottage all day, I tell her, and is Cora not the closest woman to both my age and rank in the village? Who better to spend my time with? Margery looks unsure, but she can't concoct a reason to say no to me. I'm a guest in the Bailie home, not a prisoner, and although we both know Mistress Bailie won't be pleased, my rank prevents Margery from denying me. I regret taking advantage of her in this way, but memory and fantasy made sleep nearly impossible last night. Seeing the familiarity of Proserpina in Cora is the only way I can think to calm my racing mind.

"She'll likely be at the market. Come on, then." Margery hands me a cloak from a peg beside the door, and we take to the streets. Our breath creates small clouds of mist, barely visible in the gray light of morning that spills over the horizon as the city wakes. Men stumble out of cottages with weapons slung over their shoulders, with fishing nets in hand, with axes in tight grips. The clanging of hammers rises around

us—on metal from the blacksmith's shop, on wood as car-
penters erect more buildings, and on the palisades as others
strengthen the city's fortifications. I'm thankful for the noise.
It hides how loudly my heart beats.

Margery is quiet as she leads me along a row of angled
houses, and only then does it hit me that she won't be the one
to break our silence first: Her rank forbids it.

"How long have you been working for the Bailies?"

She shoots me a look out of the corner of her eye. "Since
last September. After Dyonis—my husband—passed."

"Oh, Margery, I'm so sorry."

"Hard to believe we sailed all the way here only for him to
catch a late summer fever. He was a good man, but he was
the one who believed in this place. On my worst days, I wish
he'd died before the governor returned to England for supplies. Maybe then Jeremie and I could've gone back with
him."

"Jeremie?"

Her entire face lights up. "My son."

I recall the child she cradled in her arms the night before,
and my stomach turns. "Are they good to you? The Bailies?"

"Good enough. Mistress Bailie can be a little exacting, but
without them, I'd likely have to remarry. At least this way I
have a choice."

"Between?"

"Claiming my late husband's promised acreage as my own,
once we've found a more permanent location to settle, or
returning home with the next supply run. Ah, there she is."
The street opens before us, though *market* is a generous
word for the handful of stalls that line either side of the
road. Cora stands before a woman selling bars of soap. Beside her, a boy oversees a display of tallow candles. There's
a butcher offering unimpressive cuts of meat, a warrener

selling skinned rabbits. Another woman hawks a handful of stunted bluefish—far too small for this time of year.

"Master Warner will be back shortly with some crabs!" she hollers, but her promise doesn't draw any potential customers to her display.

It's a far cry from the forums I remember—street after street of vendors selling food, spices, colored silks, perfumes, and jewels from all across the known world. Though each seller's wares here differ, one thing among them remains constant—their tables have far less goods than they should.

"Not up to your standards, Lady Thelia?" Cora walks toward us now, and my cheeks burn at her observation—was my distaste so plainly written on my face, or is she just unusually good at reading it?

"I thought you could show Lady Thelia around the city this morning." Margery ignores her slight, and I could hug her for pretending the idea was her own.

"Is Agnes busy?"

Margery's lips curl into a knowing smile, one I'd yet to see. "I think you and I both know that Mistress Bailie would prefer Lady Thelia stay inside."

"We have that in common." Cora's green eyes are cold as they bore into mine. It's hard to reconcile this version of her with the tender hands that brought water to my lips, that wiped sweat from my brow. It's as if she offered me a gift only to snatch it away, and I'm overcome with the urge to make her feel as unmoored as I do.

"Master Thomas will be waking shortly," I say, refusing to break our eye contact. "Perhaps he'd like to give me a tour instead."

Cora huffs, folding her arms across her chest. "All right, all right!"

"Great!" Margery says. "Then I'll head back—your betrothed will be wanting his breakfast. Have fun, you two!"

Before I can say goodbye, Margery's already turned to be on her way.

"Shall we?"

"I don't know," I admit, turning back to Cora. "If my presence is truly such a nuisance, then maybe I'll just go back with Margery."

She has the decency to thaw, though just slightly. "It's just that I have chores to do. The Bailies are one of the few families here wealthy enough to employ help."

"Then let me help you," I say too quickly, too eagerly.

"I wouldn't want you to dirty your royal hands, Lady Thelia."

Shit. Another mistake. Even Proserpina, despite our closeness, never offered to help me with my duties all those years ago. It simply wasn't, and isn't, the way of things. And now Cora has discovered a loose thread at the edge of my tale. How can I be certain she won't unravel the entire thing?

"Please, just call me Thelia."

Now she does soften: Her arms unfurl, her jaw unclenches, and a hint of warmth sparks in those verdant eyes. "All right, then. Thelia. Come with me."

She says my name slowly, and I savor each syllable as it drips from her lips.

⌗⌗⌗

Cora leads us west out of the market, through rows of cottages that grow smaller the farther we get from the city's center. Ahead of us, the wall draws closer, composed of hundreds of vertical logs. She scoops a stick off the ground in one graceful motion and then waves me to her side.

"Come, I'll draw you a map."

I relish the opportunity to draw close to her again, to smell the delicate kiss of rose water on her skin. But my excitement withers into dread as Cora drags the stick through the dirt, as her coastline begins to curve in on itself—another island. This one's oblong, with the land bending gently to the west. Its western shore has a small cove, and another, sharper inlet of water cuts in from the sea on the south.

"The colony is here." Cora draws a circle in the middle of the northern edge. Then she takes a step away and draws another line farther west. ". . . And this is the mainland."

Then she marks an "X" at the top of the sharp inlet of water. "This whole area is a swamp, though I haven't seen it myself."

"Why not?"

"Because it's dangerous. There are few good reasons to leave the fort, let alone wander that far away from it."

I frown. This island is roughly the same size as Scopuli, and Cora is suggesting that most of it is off-limits.

Next, she draws a quick outline of the actual village. It's composed of three concentric rings, all orbiting the meeting-house. The Bailie home is directly north of the meetinghouse in the first ring. Cora's home is in the second ring, to the northeast. The village is encased in a fourth, final circle—the wall before us, intended to keep the city's occupants safe. There's a gate in each cardinal direction, and each is guarded by a sentry posted on a ladder.

"What are they watching for?" My eyes snap to the man who sits atop his perch.

"Natives," she concedes, "and for ships at sea."

"How many people live here?"

"One hundred and twelve now. Though far fewer will likely survive the winter."

A somber mood settles over Cora, but I bite my lip to keep

from shrieking with joy: More than one hundred people call this place home. The number makes saliva pool under my tongue. If I can convince even a fraction to return with me . . .

"Come, let us walk around the wall."

We continue west, weaving our way among tiny thatched houses and curious stares. The guard on duty eyes Cora from his post as we approach. I recognize him immediately; he's the one who found me first. At least today his clothes aren't soiled.

"He's a drunk," she whispers before we enter his range of hearing.

"Good day, Mistress Waters and . . . oh!" In the light of day, I can see that his eyes are a dark brown, and that they're leery.

"This is Master Chapman," Cora says.

"It's good to meet you," I offer, and his face crumples as he tries to parse whether our initial encounter truly was a hallucination brought on by too much alcohol. His expression doesn't betray where he lands.

"I'm showing Lady Thelia the city. Can we look across the sound? It would only be for a few minutes."

"If you're quick about it."

He doesn't speak again until both feet are on the ground, and then he locks his eyes on his leather boots, missing how Cora rolls hers before she proceeds up the ladder.

"Why such fortifications?" I ask as I climb after her. From above, it becomes clear how many men are tasked with the city's defense—many, like John, posted as sentries, but even more fortifying the wall with larger pieces of timber. What type of people do I now break bread with?

Cora watches the horizon, scanning the distant shoreline as if she's looking for answers there. When she speaks, her voice is so hushed that it nearly gets lost on the wind that whips past us, chilling her words midair. "Because of what Grenville's men did."

"Grenville's men?"

She turns away from the view, leaning her back against the wooden palisades, and for a moment, she doesn't speak. Guilt is a powerful silencer, and it's etched all over her face, impossible to ignore. My stomach sinks. Out of all the ships I've seen carrying soldiers—for isn't that what these people are?—how many of them fought for just causes? They're preparing themselves for revenge owed for a past atrocity, which means I've found myself in a bed of snakes. Every time I speak to someone, the City of Raleigh grows more dangerous. A curious quiet hangs between us, refusing to drift to the ground below, demanding to be acknowledged.

"There was a group here before us." Her voice is a bit louder now, but the tone is detached, as if she's sharing an old story she's heard countless times. "They were led by a man named Sir Richard Grenville. He sent a party to Aquascogoc, a Secotan village on the mainland, to broker trade deals. During the negotiations, someone discovered that a silver cup was missing. Stolen by one of the Secotans, they assumed, and Grenville and his men were quick to retaliate." Cora pauses, teeth digging into her lower lip. "Men's egos are so fragile. Can you imagine? Razing an entire village to the ground over a silver cup? Aquascogoc smoldered for days . . . The wall was built immediately after. It needed to be, to protect the colony from the savagery that was owed to us."

I think of the centuries of men deposited onto our beaches, their helmets and shields scattered among their broken bodies, their spears and bows still bobbing in the surf. So many on their way to and from wars, to and from committing atrocities of their own. In their final moments, did they see their death as clearly as Cora sees this—as a violent debt finally being repaid? Will the rest of the City of Raleigh's inhabitants? I imagine Thomas's smug and confident smile; there's my answer. But his arrogance will be his downfall. When I cut his throat, the tear of my blade across his skin will break our song's enchantment. He'll die choking on his own blood with the knowledge that no god saved him. But what of Cora, and her role in it all?

"It's time to come down now, Mistress Waters!" John hollers up at us. Cora waves a hand to indicate she heard him, then begins down the ladder without another word. When I reach the ground again, my hands are shaking. Cora's already a few houses away, eager to put distance between me and her confession. I have to run to catch up to her, the late autumn air whipping my face.

A chill dances down my back in spite of the midmorning sun that shines brightly overhead. In the palisades' smothering shadow, the fort loses any remaining pretense of safety. Suddenly, it's hard to breathe.

"Can we leave?" I ask. I hate how weak my voice sounds. How desperate.

"And go where? I told you, there isn't much to see out there."

My hand finds my heart racing, and I close my eyes and force myself to slow down. There, behind my eyelids, I see Scopuli's shores and hear its waves; I know exactly where I want to be.

"Show me where I was found."

᚛᚜᚛᚜

We exit the settlement through the northern gate, escaping into a sparse forest. The trees here are different from the ones on Scopuli. They're not as tall, similar to the ones on

Rotunda, though they're covered in moss. It hangs from their limbs like a strange and beautiful fabric. I lift my hand to graze my fingers against it, bringing a handful of the plant to my nose to take in its deep, earthy scent. Already, I feel my body relaxing. Seeing such unique flora brightens my mood considerably, and I don't try to hide the smile of relief that spreads across my face. Cora watches me, her lips pressed into a tight little ball. She doesn't know what to make of me.

Fair enough. I don't, either. I've only ever known myself in the context of someone else. As Proserpina's handmaiden. As Raidne and Pisinoe's sister.

As one of a trio of monsters, tasked with luring these men back to Scopuli.

I release the moss so we can continue along. I almost ask her if Roanoke is home to its own shy dryads, though even if it is, she'd never know. Only Proserpina could coax them out from the variegated shapes in their trees' bark, and even still, not for very long. Some loud sound or unexpected movement in the underbrush always inevitably sent them lunging back for the safety of their oak or elm. They had good reason to be skittish. Their beauty brought them unwanted attention.

"Why did you come back here?" I ask after her, trying to shake off the heavy silence that's settled over us once more. "After what you did."

Cora's head snaps to face me. "What I did?"

"Your people, I mean."

She straightens, and her hands turn to fists at her sides. The reaction surprises me, and a bitter laugh escapes from my throat.

"Oh, come now. That was a confession you just gave me, wasn't it? Or do you condone leveling entire villages to the ground over supposed theft? Even if the cup was stolen, that wouldn't be an excuse."

I expect her to hurl another insult my way, but instead, her gaze falls to the ground. Shame paints her cheeks red.

"We didn't intend to stay here," she admits. "Our plan was simply to collect the last of Grenville's men on our way north to build"—something stops her mid-thought—"elsewhere."

"Elsewhere," I repeat flatly, remembering Agnes's accusations from my first night, and how Margery's lips snapped shut the following morning after revealing the city was previously a military outpost.

"When we stopped in Dominica after crossing the Atlantic, we received news that being at sea was no longer safe. So instead of a temporary stop, this became our final destination. But the fort was abandoned. Grenville's men were gone."

"Why you, specifically? Why come here at all?"

She scoffs. "My father and Will couldn't resist the promise of five hundred acres, and I couldn't stay in England alone."

I smile sadly. Cora talks as if she had no other choice, but that's nothing more than a comforting lie. Choices always exist. Even I had one, when I raised my finger and betrayed the one I loved.

"And why stay?"

"We're waiting for Governor White and the relief ship. The ship we have isn't large enough to bring everyone back across the Atlantic, though even if it was, we don't have enough supplies to survive the journey. Seeds seem to die in the soil around here."

Another sign the gods are punishing the colony.

The sound of waves interrupts us, and the trees finally part to expose the sea. A thin strip of rocky beach is all that separates the tangled woods from the ocean, but there, stranded high on the smooth stones, is my little skiff. Beyond it, anchored offshore, is the colony's ship. Too small to carry the entire city to Scopuli, but plenty large for what I need.

"John was the one who found you."

"The guard from this morning?" I ask for the sake of maintaining my cover.

She nods. "He came tearing through the village in the middle of the night screaming for Thomas. His poor wife, Alis, she was so embarrassed. We all thought he'd imagined you, but here you are . . . though he reported that you were bewitched."

I turn away from the boat, from the sea, to look to Cora. A gentle breeze blows wisps of her dark hair across her face, and she reaches to tuck them behind her ear. In the full light of midmorning, I can see the light dusting of freckles that adorns her nose, and I think of the mole on Proserpina's left shoulder. Would I find its twin on Cora's?

"Bewitched?" I repeat, a bemused smile overtaking my lips. "Do you believe him?"

Her eyes bore into mine as if they can find the answer there. "You were unconscious when we found you. He was drunk and imagining things."

"The night will play tricks on a drunkard's mind."

She nods as her eyes wander to the blue-green waves that lap at the shoreline, but her thoughts are etched in the way her brow furrows: *What if . . . ?*

I'm a woman, and I'm alone, two facts that immediately make me suspicious.

The distant expression her profile wears should be a reminder to tread carefully, but instead, my instinct is to do anything, say anything, to bring her attention back to me. "I prefer that to Mistress Bailie's theory. She thinks I'm a Spanish spy."

Her face snaps back to mine as she sucks in a sharp breath. Gods, those green eyes are bulging. I can't help myself— a grin cracks across my lips.

"Evidently a poor one," she says slowly, a mirrored smile slowly emerging. "Given that you'd tell me so."

We both dissolve into laughter.

"It's wise of her to be wary," Cora adds once we've finally regained our composure. "The Spanish are unbelievably cruel."

"And the English aren't?"

"I didn't used to think so," she admits. "Now I'm not so sure. What does it feel like, to find yourself among us?"

"Like a dream, mostly."

"I know that feeling well. Sometimes in the mornings before I open my eyes and remember I'm here, I'm certain that I can feel my old bed. It's so real that I hear my old town waking up around me."

Her words spark an idea, and I take her hand and drag her toward the sea.

"What are you doing?"

I'd answer, but we're already at the water's edge, and I'm collecting salt water in my hands. Before she has a chance to process what I'm about to do, I hurl the water at her, hitting her playfully in her midsection. The ocean is cold, and she shrieks at its touch.

"Looks like you're awake after all!" I grin as she stares incredulously at the stain that blooms across her bodice. Her mouth hangs open, and when she raises her head to meet my gaze, her eyes are filled with fire.

Oh, gods, I've made a grave mistake—but then she's reaching into the water to splash me back. A laugh erupts from my chest, and I turn to dodge her attack. She doesn't relent, and I'm left with a soaking wet shoulder.

The heavy garments dull some of the water's bite, but not much. I must look surprised, because Cora laughs as well.

"And I suppose you're not actually dreaming!" She cackles with delight, and I'm stunned by the sound of it—the pure, uninhibited joy. When did I last hear a laugh like that? I scour through memories of Proserpina's for one that could rival Cora's, but Proserpina was a princess always destined to be a queen. A goddess. The only times I saw her composure truly melt away were when we found ourselves circling each other, enchanted by the promise of being tangled together . . .

"Are you all right?" Cora asks. "You look a little red."

Gods, what am I doing, allowing myself to get distracted like this?

"I'm such a fool! You're still recovering, and I dragged you all the way out here!" She reaches a hand toward my face, likely to check for a fever, but before she can, I've already flinched away, out of her reach.

"It's fine." My words come out too quickly, and if my cheeks were flushed before, they're burning now. "I'm all right, Cora, really—and I was the one who asked you to take me here."

Her hand still hangs there in the air, my first error, but it's the way her lips part just so that gives away my second—I've called her by her first name. It came out so quickly, so naturally, that I never would have realized. "I mean Mistress Wat—"

"You can call me Cora." Her words are kind, but she snaps her hand back to her side. And is it a trick of the light, or are her cheeks turning scarlet as well? Gods, why did I recoil from her?

Because she's not what you're here for.

Is that Proserpina's voice or my own? Guilt pools in my stomach, thick as oil. Of course she's not, I know that, so why am I wondering what it would feel like to have those fingers cup my face?

"Cora," I repeat, my tongue exploring the shape of her name against my will. It would feel so good there if I could just relish it, if I wasn't me. But Cora doesn't let me wallow. She retreats from the water back toward the tree line without another word. All I can do is collect the soaking bottoms of my skirts and rush after her. "Wait! Where are you going?"

"We've been gone too long. I'm going to be late."

"Late? For what?"

"Bible study with the other women. You should join us."

My heart swells at the invitation. When I reach the trees myself, I sneak a glance toward the ocean one last time, trying to commit its sights, scents, and sounds to memory—the swirling blue waves capped with white foam, the sharpness of salt on the wind, the mewing of gulls. These are all friends, my threads to home.

Go, they urge as the forest swallows Cora ahead. And although it pains me, my best choice is to listen.

᠍᠍᠍᠍᠍᠍

Emme Merrimoth's home, this week's Bible study location, is in the outermost ring in the southeast corner of the city. At a single story—and, from the looks of it, a single room—it's markedly smaller than the Bailies'.

"I live next door," Margery says, pointing to an equally humble dwelling beside Emme's. I force a smile, my thoughts on Cora and her change of mood.

Before I can offer Margery a half-hearted reply, an infant comes toddling out of Emme's doorway into the street. Cora steps aside to let him pass, and his face is swallowed by a smile as Margery drops to his level and extends her arms to catch him. A third woman watches from the doorway, laughing as she struggles to retain her grip on another squirming child in her own arms.

"Sorry, Margery! He was too excited to see you!"

Margery scoops the boy up and spins him around before placing a wet kiss on his forehead. Not much more than a year old, he's too young for the act to embarrass him; instead, the sloppy sound makes him giggle, and he buries his face in her chest. I tense at the sight of him. Jeremie's sweet now, of course, but what will he grow into? Cubs always mature into bears, lions, wolves—never sheep; their anatomy doesn't allow it.

Dis was a child once. Look what he became.

Margery turns to me, coaxing the boy to look in my direction. "Lady Thelia, this is Jeremie."

There's no one else he could be. He looks identical to his mother, down to their sickly constitutions.

"Hello, sweet one." I force the words out as convincingly as I can, though the singsong inflection my voice takes on sounds like talons scraping across rock. Thankfully, the child is as foolish as the adult men around him. Jeremie beams at me. Behind the smiling moon of his face, Cora slips inside the house, abandoning me with the mothers.

"And this is Elizabeth and her son, Ambrose," Margery says, nodding her head to the woman in the doorway. Shit, another boy.

"Nice to meet you," Elizabeth says with a smile.

A new round face appears from behind Elizabeth's shoulder. Even as she stands in Elizabeth's shadow, warmth radiates from her slender frame. Although she doesn't look as thin as Margery, here's another woman with hardly any meat on her bones. Her skin is sun-kissed, dappled with freckles, and her frizzy red hair is stuffed unceremoniously beneath a coif. Wild crimson tendrils break free, giving her the appearance of someone touched with a hint of madness. But she must be, if this is Emme—from what Margery shared on the walk here, she was one of seven single women who decided to make this colony her home. She gasps when she sees me, a sun-speckled hand rising to cover her mouth. "Oh—my lady!"

"Please forgive my intrusion," I offer, unsure of what exactly to say.

"It's my pleasure!" Her voice rises an octave, hinting that it's not.

"If it's not too much trouble. Cora invited me, but I don't have to—"

"Don't be silly!" Margery interjects. "You're more than welcome here!"

Emme shoots a dark look back into the room, no doubt cursing Cora for bringing me along without asking, but when she looks back to us, the warm smile has returned. "Come on, then. Get inside before you both catch a chill."

The doorway swallows Emme and Elizabeth, and Margery follows their lead. I stand there for a moment, listening to the soft tinkling of laughter spill into the street. It's easy to pretend that I'm back home, standing outside my own humble dwelling. Inside, Raidne prepares dinner while Pisinoe reads poetry aloud. I can almost hear her perfect meter: *As for me, the sacred wall with its votive tablet declares that I have hung up my dripping garments to the god who rules over the sea.*

The laughter quiets when I step inside. As I suspected, Emme's house is a single room, not unlike mine on Scopuli, save for one noticeable difference—believing their stay on Roanoke would be short, the cottage's builders apparently deemed a chimney an unnecessary luxury for the likes of a poor single woman. The entire space is thick with smoke from the fireplace that dominates the back wall. But even the haze isn't enough to hide me from seven new pairs of curious eyes.

"Ladies, we have a special guest today," Emme says, fanning her arms out to present the group to me. "Please introduce yourselves."

A woman seated at a small wooden table speaks first. Another baby is in her arms, sleeping peacefully, nestled in her mother's embrace. An emotion I can't quite identify claws at my heart.

"I am Elyoner," she says, "and this is my daughter, Virginia."

The rest of the ladies follow her lead. There's Wenefrid, the group's oldest member, with wiry graying hair, and a second Elizabeth whom everyone calls Liz. A woman named Margaret rivals Wenefrid in old age, and the two could easily be confused if Margaret weren't missing one of her front teeth, though this doesn't stop her from smiling widely. And then there are Rose, the same girl who poured wine at the welcome feast, and Jane, both as young as I was when Scopuli became my prison. A mousy, timid woman introduces herself last as Alis. The name catches my attention.

"Alis Chapman? Is your husband the one who found me?"

The woman's face turns a deep scarlet. "Yes, my lady."

I take off a pair of gold earrings and place them in her palms. "It's not much, but please thank him for me. I would have frozen if he hadn't gotten aid."

The act makes Alis blush harder. "Oh, my lady, I couldn't—"

I close her fingers around the jewelry. The other women watch with their eyes wide.

"Accept the gift, Alis, please," Cora urges. "John did a good thing, and God wants you to be rewarded for it."

Alis fiddles with the earrings but eventually slips them into her pocket. "Thank you, Lady Thelia."

"Well, then," Margaret says, the words whistling through the gap in her teeth. "Shall we?"

Emme points to a large leather-bound tome on a small table beside her bed. Cora clears her throat as Wenefrid hands it to her.

"Slow down, Cora. You're forgetting the most important part." A devious grin lights up Emme's face. The others start laughing, and Cora smirks.

"Go on, then."

Emme pulls a large crock from a shelf beside the hearth, pausing only to wiggle her fingers gleefully before dividing its contents into mugs for us all.

As Emme prepares the libations, my attention returns to the book in Cora's lap. This must be the Bible that she mentioned earlier. Cora's fingers graze the cover gingerly before she teases it open to the first page. The paper is delicate, like a butterfly's wings.

Cora catches me watching her, and our eyes lock. Her stare is intense, searching, and it strikes me that she's trying to discern if I recognize the book. I smile, hoping to encourage her that I do. The way she handles it shows how important it is to her, and the fact that these readings occur weekly suggests that she's not alone in revering it. She smiles faintly in return. It's a far cry from her spontaneous laughter on the beach, but it's an improvement. As Emme passes around the wine, Cora clears her throat once more.

"Let's start at the beginning. It's been a long time since we read about the creation."

"I love Genesis," Rose says on a sigh, resting her head in her palm as her focus settles onto Cora.

"Reader's choice," says Margaret with a shrug, and all the other ladies laugh. Ah, yes. Cora is the only one who knows how to read.

"In the beginning God created the heaven and the earth. And the earth was without form and void, and darkness was upon the deep, and the Spirit of God moved upon the waters . . ."

It's always strange listening to mortals recount their origins—which details they get right, and which they get wrong, though even I don't know the whole truth. No one does. The memory of the gods isn't infallible, as old as they are, and many are happy to embellish the details of their histories to willing ears. Still, though, I crack a smile, ready to lose myself in the familiar.

"Then God said, Let there be light: And there was light. And God saw the light that it was good, and God separated the light from the darkness. And God called the Light, Day, and the darkness he called Night. So the evening and the morning were the first day."

My smile fades. There's no familiarity to be found here after all. Only a single god? How could that be, when I've played in the woods with dryads? When our fathers, though lesser, were gods in their own right?

I served ambrosia to the Goddess of the Harvest. I kissed the lips of the Goddess of Spring, and I lost her to the God of the Dead.

Cora's brows knead together in concentration, and a flush crawls up her neck. She's enraptured by what she's reading; she believes it, every last lie, and so do the rest of the women in the room.

When her god creates man from dust and breathes a living soul into his body, I resist asking how he obtained the ability to grant life in the first place. Did he steal it from a goddess lost to time? Why choose to make a man first, when a woman could have birthed her own children of flesh and blood?

Because he, too, is a man.

So where are the goddesses?

Cora finishes the part about how the primordial couple is banished from their home in Eden and looks up to face the rest of us. This is the story that Rose loves? It makes my stomach roil.

"I'd forgotten that God creates beasts and birds for Adam as companions before he creates Eve," I say. It takes all my strength to keep my features from twisting into a sneer. To be no more than an afterthought—why believe such a story?

Emme barks with laughter. "It seems a bit silly now, doesn't it?"

"I just like the part about the serpent tricking Eve," Rose says, a bit defensively.

"But he didn't trick her." I can't help myself.

"He convinced her to eat the fruit!"

"He told her she wouldn't die if she ate it. And she didn't, did she?" I don't bother asking why this god would put such a tree in Eden in the first place; just like mine, he enjoys setting humanity up to fail. An apple and a pomegranate. Two women damned for their taste in fruit.

"The serpent is Satan, Lady Thelia!" Elyoner's face darkens, and she draws Virginia closer to her chest as if I've invited evil into the room by defending a snake.

"I—I know," I begin, unsure of how to recover. I don't know what else that giant book contains and can only speak confidently about what we just heard. "I'm just saying that he didn't actually lie."

"But he deceived her."

"Did he?"

"Do you think Eve would have eaten that fruit if she knew what it would cost her? What it would cost us?"

Virginia nuzzles at Elyoner's chest, looking for a breast,

and I soften. She's still young; the memory of childbirth must be fresh. "I'm not sure. But even Eden might grow to feel like a prison after an eternity of it."

"I think we all know how quickly Eden can spoil," Cora muses sadly as she turns to Elyoner. "After all, didn't your father describe the New World as Eden on earth? Isn't that why we're all here?"

Elyoner's cheeks turn scarlet, and she pulls Virginia closer. "He believed that, Cora; otherwise he would've insisted I return with him on the supply run."

My eyes grow wide. "Your father is Governor White? And he left you behind?"

"Virginia was only nine days old when the fleet returned. My husband thought it safer to stay."

"I know your father believed it, and that your husband did, too," Cora says softly. "But if the choice was yours, would you have stayed here?"

Perhaps it's a trick of the light on the haze or a result of the smoke itself, but Elyoner's eyes are suddenly glassy. "Of course not. We knew it was dangerous here that first day we disembarked."

"Some places more than others," Emme murmurs, her eyes wandering to me. Her stare, previously so warm, is now sharp with warning. Cora bristles at the comment.

"What are you implying, Emme?"

"Only that Lady Thelia should be careful in the Bailie house."

Cora's eyes turn into slits. "Say what you mean plainly."

"Ladies, please!" Wenefrid interjects. Emme's lips fall open in protest, but Wenefrid holds a hand in the air to silence her. The woman's age must carry weight, because Emme's mouth snaps closed, though her silence isn't enough to quell Cora.

"I won't sit here and listen to you slander my future family." She stands abruptly, her movements frenzied, save for when she turns to delicately place Emme's Bible on her empty chair. I push forward in my own, ready to follow her, but Margery places a hand on my knee. No one else tries to stop her, and before I can untangle what just transpired, Cora has already bolted from the home. The door slams loudly behind her.

Emme shakes her head, huffing with frustration.

"You shouldn't have been so blunt," Margaret chides her. "What would you have her do? The engagement is already set."

"Would you prefer I say nothing? She's about to marry a monster. Lady Thelia is *living* there!"

"What are you talking about?" My palms grow slick with sweat.

"He was a little rough with me one evening," Margery whispers, looking to the floor. "Master Bailie walked in before anything happened, Lord protect his soul, and he scolded Thomas properly . . ."

"Margery . . ."

"It was right after Dyonis died. I think he was trying to make me feel better, but—" Her voice cracks, and she shakes her head as if pushing away a bad memory. "It's why they employed me. Master Bailie offered me a position to make it right. After he passed, Mistress Bailie agreed to continue the arrangement—"

"—because she likes the status it brings her—" Emme interjects.

"—and nothing has happened since."

"But do you feel safe there?" I ask.

"Mistress Bailie is always present."

"And what if she wasn't?"

Margery buries her face in the top of Jeremie's blond curls, and the room falls silent.

"Someone should make sure Cora is all right," I say softly.

Elyoner bobs her head with approval, though perhaps she's only eager to see me leave, too. Emme shrugs, and the other ladies give various levels of agreement in their nods and their stares.

"You shouldn't go alone," Margery says, rising to her feet as well. "I'll walk with you."

ᒥᒥᒥᒥ

Outside Emme's cottage, Cora's nowhere to be seen. Our conversation gave her plenty of time to put a healthy distance between us. Margery heads north, with Jeremie on her hip. The little boy watches me from over her shoulder; I do my best to ignore it.

I replay the conversation as we duck through the streets, pulling my cloak over my face to keep away unwanted attention. From their own lips, these women think Thomas is dangerous. Poor Cora. The sex between her legs has saddled her with an impossible choice: Either accept the proposal of a violent man for the comfort of food and shelter, or reject it and risk starving, or worse. Neither outcome has the potential for a truly happy future.

The thought darkens my mood, until another counteracts it: Cora's fate isn't as set in stone as it seems. When these men return with me to Scopuli, Thomas will either drown beneath the waves or I'll slit his throat in the ritual cave. Whatever the method, he'll be dead, leaving Cora free to pursue another destiny. That is, of course, if she wants one.

"Here we are." Margery stops before another cottage that looks indistinguishable from the two beside it. "The Bailies' home is a street over that way."

"Is that where you're going now?"

"I'll take Jeremie to Elizabeth's first, but yes. The Bailies will be expecting their dinner soon."

"Thank you. For everything today."

Margery smiles before looking to the doorway. "I can't promise she'll be happy to see you."

"I have a feeling she won't be," I say with a laugh. Margery returns it with a smile.

I knock lightly on the Waterses' front door, but it's not Cora who answers. It's Will. A grin overtakes his face when he finds me.

"Lady Thelia! What brings you to my doorstep?"

"I came to see Cora. Is she here?"

"She's out back feeding the chickens, but I'm not sure now is a good time."

"I know she's upset. I wanted to check on her."

"Ah, yes. The women often pester her with their gossip, but she never tells me what they actually say. Any chance you'll spill the secret?" He leans against the doorframe and folds his arms across his chest. There's something effeminate about him, though he conceals it beneath his bravado and exaggerated smile, as if the gentler nature is something he learned to hide long ago. What a loss. That buried softness is the only reason I feel safe standing outside with him alone.

"Cora's secrets are her own, and I won't be the one to betray them. May I see her?"

He tosses his head toward the side of the house. "Just go around. You'll find her."

"Thank you, Master Waters."

"Anything for you, my lady."

There's something beneath his words . . . a light flirtation, perhaps, but it feels forced, like it's an impression of what he believes he should say. We exchange goodbyes, but I look back to him as he closes the door, and the pinched expression he wears when he thinks I'm not looking makes me wonder if he's as confused by the performance as I am.

Cora's hunched over a small plot of soil behind the house, just as Will said she'd be. A sack is positioned on her left hip, and she reaches into it to sprinkle seed onto the dirt below. Several chickens scuttle around her feet, pecking at the feed eagerly. There's a part of me that wishes to melt into the shadows and drink all of her in, but the sound of her sniffling draws me out of their dark, safe embrace.

She lifts her head toward the sound of my footsteps and quickly moves to brush her cheeks with her free hand, but it's too late—she knows I've caught her in a moment of weakness, and the eyes that moments ago held such sorrow now blaze with rage.

"What are you doing here?" Her voice is clipped, though she begrudgingly adds, "My lady."

"I came to see if you were all right." My skin flushes hot under her scorn.

She snorts. "Why you?"

Compassion withers inside me into indignation. "Maybe I'm the only one who hasn't grown tired of your hostility."

Her eyes widen, but she's alone in being shocked by the words that leave my mouth. I would never have spoken to Proserpina like this; despite being her dearest friend, her lover, I was also her handmaiden. A servant. But I'm not Cora's lesser—here, I'm the one with the higher rank. The one with power. I don't have to hold myself back.

"You shouldn't be so cold to them. They're only trying to protect you. You know that, right?"

Her fury dissipates into an expression I can't quite decipher. Only when her teeth find her bottom lip do I notice that it's trembling.

"Yes," she admits. "I know they worry for me. But what would they have me do?"

I take a step closer. "Do you want to be Master Bailie's wife?"

"I don't owe you an answer to that."

Gods, she's frustrating. My blood rushes through my ears, and I can't tell if I want to slap her or—

No.

"You can speak plainly to me," I say.

"Can I, truly?" A bitter laugh escapes from her throat. "I've seen the way Thomas looks at you. And now you ask me to spill my secrets? How do I know you won't use them against me?"

Her accusation stings, not far off the mark, and I shoot back coldly before I can stop myself. "You think I'm your biggest threat? After what I just heard, isn't it Thomas who earns that title?"

Cora falls silent at my retaliation, and my lips threaten to curl into a victorious smile, but a fresh glistening in her eyes melts the satisfaction from my features.

"My father's dying," she says, tears spilling over her cheeks. "If we're not wed before he passes, there'll be no one left to make a suitable match for me."

"Couldn't Will help?" Her attitude be damned, the sight of those tears draws me to her side, and without thinking, I take her hands in mine.

"There's a thin veil of order here that grows weaker with each Council member's passing. There isn't much Will could do against a pack of ravenous men. Yes, Thomas has a cruel streak, but he's respected for it. And as Mistress Bailie, I'll never want for anything. Food will always be on the table, and money will always be in our coffers. Of course I worry about what our life together will be like . . . But Alis's husband beats her, and she has no money to show for it. Charles Florrie made certain that Emme would never find a decent match. The pool of gentlehearted men is smaller than the number of single women. That's why I need him. Why I need the Bailies. And I might lose everything to you."

She looks down at our hands, but she doesn't pull away from me. I slide in closer, so near to her that I can feel her breath against my fingers as I reach to wipe the tears from her cheeks. Her skin is like silk, and the desire to feel more of it takes root in the pit of my stomach.

"Cora," I begin, my voice dropping to a gentle whisper. "I didn't cross the sea to steal another woman's betrothed." The words fall from my lips so easily that even I believe them for a moment—until I remember what I actually plan for Thomas. Suddenly, the words taste like dirt in my mouth.

"We're trapped on an island a world away from anyone who owes us kindness, so I ask again, what would the others have me do?"

Let me take them, I want to say, but of course I can't. Instead, I envelop her in an embrace, bracing for the moment she pushes me away.

But Cora doesn't. Instead, she leans her frame into mine, nestling her head into the base of my neck. The scent of roses rises from her hair, and I'm suddenly aware of every part of my body—the places that connect with hers sing with anticipation, while the parts that don't cry out for their turn. Everywhere aches for more. Her breath on the bare flesh of my neck is a small miracle. How is it that she fits so perfectly in my arms?

"It seems a woman's fate is the same no matter where you're from," I whisper into her raven hair as a wave of homesickness crashes over me. I viewed those shores as walls to a prison for centuries, but is it possible that we had our own little Eden on those rocky cliffs, safe from the ravages of men? After what I've seen of the outside world these few days, will I even want to leave Scopuli again if I'm able to break Ceres's curse? "I wish you no harm. I swear it."

It's a truth hidden inside a larger lie, but I hope it brings her comfort nonetheless.

When she lifts her head to look at me, I find that those vibrant green eyes believe me.

"Can I ask you something?" Her voice is barely a whisper.

I want to say, *Anything,* but I know how that word will sound leaving my lips—like a plea. I settle for a nod.

"You looked . . . upset while I was reading. Like you'd never heard Genesis before, and every part of it offended you."

I can feel crimson rising to my cheeks. I was so certain that I'd hid it well; was she the only one who noticed, or did the others catch sight of my deceit, too?

My pause lasts too long, and Cora sighs, finding her answer in the void between us. "So, what—you're a heathen, then?"

"A heathen?"

"You don't believe in God."

I think of the laws pinned to the meetinghouse's door. "Of course I do."

She looks unsure, but she doesn't pull away from me. "Try harder to look like you know what's happening at church tomorrow."

I smile grimly, suddenly uncomfortable beneath her scrutiny. Less than a day with me, and Cora's already discovered one of my secrets. What else will she find if she looks close enough?

"Cora!" Will's voice shatters us apart as his face appears in a back window, an axe through flowers. "Oh—you're still here, Lady Thelia."

"She was just leaving," Cora calls out to him before turning back to me. Did I imagine it, or was her voice a little rushed? "It's nearly dinner . . ."

"I understand." And I do, though it doesn't make leaving any easier.

Later that evening, after Margery helps me undress, I slide a chair in front of my bedroom door before crawling into bed. If I've learned anything today, it's that this city, this house, isn't safe.

7

BEFORE

Raidne and Pisinoe stand in stunned silence. They can't accept the ship is real until another lightning flash confirms it, but I saw the lily, its ethereal glow—I need no more convincing. The third time light streaks across the darkness, instinct takes control. My wings twitch, my talons sink into the dirt floor, anticipating muscle between them. We strip ourselves bare. Anything extra will weigh us down, a dangerous proposition in the fury of the squall. Pisinoe has the hardest time of it, bedecked in all those jewels. She tears them from her body with a ferocity that appears only in these moments, when our humanity recedes and the raptor emerges.

Men to hear our song. To follow its promises into the waves.

Tonight, we survive.

Raidne is first out the door, then Pisinoe, then me. We run in a line toward the cliffs. When Raidne reaches the edge, she jumps from the precipice without hesitation. Pisinoe and I follow with equal confidence. With our black wings folded against our backs, we dive down toward the rocky shore below until, suddenly, our feathered limbs snap open to catch a plume of air. Into the heavens we ascend. Here, among the clouds, we're weightless.

Thunder crashes and rain pelts our forms, but any discomfort is obscured by our excitement, by our hunger. I lick the ocean's salt from my lips. When we're close enough that those aboard can hear us, I begin our song. Thelxiope, for pleasing voice.

The notes are high and drawn out, head tones that fall from my mouth and travel to the sailors' ears. Raidne and Pisinoe join. The melody is seductive, but it's also haunting. We pour our souls into it, and we carry so much sorrow.

The sadness of losing Proserpina. The shame of being banished. The power of our new bodies. The isolation. The beauty of our voices. The obscenity of our forms. The thrill of bringing men to heel. The hope for a different life. These sentiments rush toward the ship, but they're not what the men aboard hear.

As it slips between thunderclaps and the howling winds, our chorus spins magic.

"Come, stop your ship so you may hear us."

The men scatter across the deck as we approach. This ship, with only two masts, isn't the largest that we've seen, but it has plenty of ears to meet our needs.

"We know all that happens on this bountiful earth . . ."

A few sailors who have yet to hear our notes on the wind are trying desperately to keep the vessel afloat. They work the ropes and sails to steer it through the squall as best they can, but large waves send seawater crashing over the deck and make simply standing a struggle. But once our song, and its promise, reaches them, their frantic efforts cease. Ropes fall from slackened hands; open-mouthed faces peek out from the portholes. All are rendered still. Lightning teases our forms, but the cover of night obscures our haggard, aging bodies, the danger of our talons. To them, we're winged women dancing among the thunderheads—a sight to marvel at, not to inspire dread. Surely nothing dangerous could sing so beautifully.

I land on the deck first, followed by Pisinoe. Raidne remains in the air, uninterested in taunting them. Now they're close enough to see our ghastly bodies, but the sailors aren't frightened—our song has given them glimpses of the futures they crave most, and a glimpse is never enough. The man closest to me clutches his chest, devotion pooling in his dark eyes, as if he's gazing upon Venus herself. When I take a step closer, he falls to his knees, his clasped hands raised to me in desperation. He's not dead yet, but already, I feel myself standing taller.

Tell me, his expression begs. I reach to stroke his bearded cheek. As soon as my fingers connect with his skin, his hands rush to his chest. Then he crashes to the ground. This wouldn't be the first time a sailor's died overwhelmed by his own anticipation. But this man twists his body closer to me even as his heart begins to fail. I take a step back, and then another, and all the while, he claws desperately to close the gap I create between us. My wings spread wide, and I take to the air, hovering just over the ship's edge. The wooden deck tears at his fingers as he pulls himself along, leaving scarlet stains in his wake. Good. What bloody trails of mine would he create if given the chance?

"Come," Pisinoe sings, and another, larger sailor steps on the fallen man's hands with a sickening *crack* as he rushes for her. But the sailor on the ground doesn't scream—he still drags his broken body forward, his mouth open in awe. I can't understand the words he says, but the meaning is clear from the desperation in his tone: *Tell me my fate.*

I have to swallow the violent smile that threatens to consume my features as I open my arms to him.

"Come, and I'll tell you everything."

The deck tries to stall him, wooden planks cutting ribbons into his clothes and marring his skin with abrasions. Pain must bloom with each shove forward, but the sailor doesn't stop. Finally, he reaches the ship's edge and extends a single bloodied hand as he muscles himself over it, broken fingers outstretched to me as he falls. But he doesn't hit the waves first: His body shatters on a cluster of rocks, and then I'm soaring. Ecstasy washes over me as he's swallowed by the brine. It's thousands of seedlings unfurling in the spring from dormant ground; it's being kissed by a warm summer rain. And then, for the first time in years, I take a slow, deep breath without my chest rattling. My hands form fists.

I sing even louder. And so do my sisters.

We guide the ship toward the rocks that lie in wait submerged beneath the waves between Scopuli and Castle. Like jaws cracking open bones, they do their job splitting the hull. The ship roars, and more men dive into the frothing water below. We circle overhead until the vessel is no more than shattered planks of wood, never once wavering in our melody. Some men sink beneath the surface. Others cling to floating detritus. A few attempt to swim to shore. But the waves, enraged by the storm, are too big, too powerful. They pull the men below one by one and flood their lungs with seawater, and with every single death, we grow stronger. The years dissolve from our bodies as if it's the rain that washes them away.

There won't be any survivors. Not having sacrifices is a disappointment, but only those who survive the churning sea make appropriate gifts for Ceres.

When the depths claim the last set of listening ears, we fly

back to the cliffs. Tomorrow, our beach will be littered with
corpses.

᠑᠑᠑᠑

Pisinoe erupts in a triumphant laugh as soon as her feet
touch the ground, and I follow her lead. Even Raidne joins,
and we find one another's hands and dance and howl in the
storm, reveling in our victory. Only when the rain begins to
soften do we finally return to the cottage, and I marvel at the
long-forgotten vitality that now courses through my veins. Inside, I stretch my arms overhead to find that my fingertips
once again brush the wooden beams that span the ceiling.
Raidne's stew still simmers on the hearth, and she rushes
forward to stir it as Pisinoe follows in pursuit of the hand
mirror she keeps on the mantel. It's a scene I've lived an
uncountable number of times before, but tonight, it blurs
behind a veil of tears. I never thought I'd see this again—my
two beautiful sisters, young once more, painted in the warm
orange glow of a crackling fire.

While I wait for my turn with the looking glass, I run my
hands over my body, relishing the feel of my own transformation beneath my palms: Taut skin where it previously sagged,
free from wrinkles once more. Wiry hair made soft, and brit-
tle talons sharpened back into blades.

"Who's next?" Pisinoe asks eventually, but Raidne is too
busy nestling her lost teeth back into place. I take a deep
breath and accept the ancient mirror, lifting it slowly to find
myself inside it.

A young woman stares back at me, so beautiful that I
barely recognize her. The ghost of a smile graces her oval
face, and I reach first to brush her lips, then my own. They're
soft and pink again, two petals parted. My fingers slip inside

my mouth and gently wiggle each tooth. The bones don't budge. The firelight highlights the dusting of freckles across my reflection's nose and makes her blue eyes sparkle. A strange feeling washes over me as I behold myself—I'm no longer a crone, but I'm still older than I was when we were banished. We were children then, me just shy of sixteen, Raidne and Pisinoe only eighteen and seventeen, respectively. Would Proserpina recognize this woman? Would I recognize her?

"It's your turn, Raidne."

She turns to face me with a full, glittering smile, and a small gasp escapes her throat as she surveys herself. I force my melancholy away and enjoy the sight of her instead. Though I've come to appreciate the beauty in all youth, I was always the plainest of us three.

Raidne is the most beautiful, her lips a deep plum, her eyes the same color as the sky on a stormy day—a capricious and seductive gray that simultaneously draws you in while warning you to stay away. Her moody stare is supported by cheekbones that must've been chiseled by the gods, and when she smiles as she does now, it's enough to make even the most sullen soul's heart stop.

"Look at us!" Pisinoe screams, jumping to her feet in a giddy fit. "Look at us!"

"Bless the sailors," Raidne says, her voice full of reverence. "Bless their willing ears."

After we've eaten our fill of stew, Raidne kisses the tops of our heads.

"Let's try to get some rest," she whispers into our hair. "Tomorrow will be a full day."

I collapse onto my pallet, and Pisinoe follows, cuddling in close. Raidne joins. Even she can't resist the joy of the moment. Within minutes, Pisinoe snores softly beside me, and Raidne's breath is so shallow that I barely hear it at all. But sleep doesn't offer me its release.

I think of the men aboard the ship. How long did it take those who clung to its scraps to realize that their destiny was to drown? Did that broken sailor who flung himself from the edge understand what his fate was as he rushed toward the ocean's surface, or was he still enraptured as his lungs filled with brine?

I hope that in their final moments, our song brings them no solace. I hope that they suffer.

We could never make Dis suffer, but we can punish the sailors in his stead.

We can lure them into the rocks with our song. We can eat the ones who wash ashore, ripping their flesh apart with our talons, tearing into their skin with our teeth. We can cut into their stomachs and inspect their bowels for signs, then slice their throats in a prayer to Ceres for forgiveness.

These images accompany me to the cusp of sleep, and my last coherent thought is how strange it is that such violence makes me smile. But I force it, and its implications, away and let sleep claim me and my monstrous musings. Tomorrow, I won't remember them anyway.

A tangible excitement draws us out of our slumber before the sun breaks over the horizon. I wander to the window, and when I push open the shutters, the only creaking comes from their hinges. My joints are blessedly quiet once more.

A cool breeze greets me, a reminder that summer is at its end. The storm has passed, leaving behind a world glossed in a sheen of raindrops. It's beautiful, but the damp will quicken the decomposition process. If we're going to salvage anything, we must hurry.

Raidne gravitates to the wooden shelf beside the hearth where the tools are kept. She lifts the blades to the light one by one, letting their razor-sharp edges scintillate for us: hooked knives to skin and gut, sleeker blades to separate meat from bone, saws to dismember. Pisinoe prepares a pot of water over a fire.

"I wish we could've drawn them in on gentle seas," she says, monitoring it for a boil. When bubbles burst across the water's surface, Raidne hands each knife to Pisinoe, who gingerly deposits them into the pot. It's important to make sure the blades are clean before we begin our work. "I want to sing for an audience during the warm afternoon sun . . . It's been so long."

We all prefer hunting to scavenging.

The knives roll in the boiling water for several minutes before Pisinoe extracts them from the pot with a hook for this purpose. Raidne has already spread a rag across the table to catch them until the metal is cool enough to the touch. Then we reach for our favorites. My gutting knife has a round wooden handle that has long since been stained a deep purple. My boning knife is the thinnest of the three, and my saw is the shortest. I tuck them into a satchel around my waist before turning to my sisters. We're ready. Raidne leads the way over the edge of the cliff as she did last night, but this time we glide down to the beach where carnage awaits.

The ship is now thousands of fractured pieces scattered across the sand. The spaces between them are littered with its contents—everything from clothes, food, and tools to bodies.

There are dozens. All dead, all in various conditions. Some

are so pulverized, their bowels torn open by coral and the meat already poisoned, that processing them isn't an option.

Our first step is to sort them: which we can salvage, and which must burn instead.

The piles have barely grown (six too bloodied, too broken; two we can butcher) when Pisinoe shrieks from behind one of the ship's masts. The sound slashes through the air with the same ease as a knife through skin.

"Pisinoe?" Raidne screams, worried she's been hurt. Did a sailor survive, only to ambush her? No, that can't be possible; they would still be enchanted by our song . . .

"Come quickly!"

Her voice draws us both to her side. Raidne immediately begins scouring her arms for signs of injury, but Pisinoe stands in stupefied silence. I find what caused her outburst and grab Raidne's shoulder roughly, redirecting her attention with a trembling finger.

There, lying in the sand, is the body of a woman. For a moment, I can't make sense of what I'm seeing. In all our years here, a female body has never washed ashore. It's always been men: men going to war, men buying and selling goods, men on an odyssey. The sight drops me to my knees beside her.

She's wearing a woven tunic, its shoulders adorned with an intricate pattern of red, yellow, and black, made from what I first mistake as some kind of thick thread. But recognition slowly reveals that the motifs aren't made with thread at all— they're individually dyed porcupine quills. How many hours did it take, to stitch each one in its perfect place? The artistry takes my breath away, but then tears rise to my eyes. Something so beautiful should never have ended up here, like this. The same design lines the bottoms of her leggings, which are made from an animal hide. A deer's, I think, though it's been centuries since Scopuli's allowed me to see one up close. A beaded necklace made from seashells still hangs from her neck—somehow, it survived the rocks and the waves.

The woman's body is relatively intact, which I'm thankful for, relieved that she was not ripped open like some of the others. But this is the smallest mercy. What was she doing on the ship? I delicately tuck a few locks of long obsidian hair behind her ears and brush the sand from her tanned face. A sense of uneasiness washes over me with the feeling she wasn't aboard the ship of her own volition. The contents of my stomach swell into my throat.

"Look." Pisinoe gingerly lifts the woman's hand to inspect it. A raw red ring encircles each of her wrists. "She was bound."

Tears pool in our eyes, and we sit in the anguish that men have wreaked upon her.

"Take her from the beach," Raidne whispers. "She deserves her own pyre."

Pisinoe and I nod. The discovery shakes us, bringing back uncomfortable memories. We were never mortal, but such horrors aren't reserved for the mortal realm. How many gentle dryads bore the unwanted burden of a god's attention? Proserpina's sacred lineage didn't stop Dis. Pisinoe kneels beside me and scoops her arms beneath the woman's frame and lifts her as if she's made of air. Such is the strength of our chimeric bodies. Pisinoe unfurls her great black wings and ascends from the beach.

The day reveals six more women. We bring each to the grassy area at the forest's edge atop the cliffs so that we can bury them properly. The men's corpses don't receive the same treatment. By midmorning, we finish sorting them. Fifty-four dead total, including the females.

Only eleven sailors are in good enough condition to

butcher, and we start work on those first. We use the jagged
rocks of the cliff face as anchors to hoist the bodies into the
air, hanging them by their feet. Then we cut the clothes from
the carcasses, slit their throats, and drain their blood. The
fluid spurts onto the sand, staining the ground a brilliant red.
Their fingers graze back and forth across the grains as we
work, coloring the fleshy tips crimson.

Once the blood is entirely drained from a body, the next
step is to gut it.

I carefully slide my blade into the soft skin of my first sail-
or's lower abdomen, right below where a patch of thick, curly
black hair begins. Starting in the wrong spot risks puncturing
his stomach and spoiling the meat, but I've had plenty of
practice. The blade scores easily down his midline to the
base of his neck, but the rib cage is more difficult to overcome. The man's lifeless eyes bulge down at the ground as if
in protest; if he were alive, he'd gag on his bloated tongue. It
was a gruesome sight in the beginning, but the effect hasn't
fazed me in centuries—the whole process is now more familiar than dressing a deer.

I split him open, and a hot wave hits me in the face. Good.
Releasing this heat will slow the decomposition process as
well. Sawing through the ribs takes a bit of effort, even with
my strength returned. Their bodies are designed to protect
their organs, even in death, and they don't offer their insides
willingly. I must work for them.

But with the ribs removed, the rest is straightforward. I
scoop out the stomach, the lungs, the heart, the intestines,
all the viscera that made him, until the cavity is empty.

All that's left is to skin and quarter him. Everything
unusable—the threadbare clothes, extra flesh, fat, and
bowels—is tossed onto the pile to be burned. Once we're
finished with all the bodies, we'll set the heap ablaze. We

save this step for last, though. Everything that preceded is a necessity to cheat death; but this little violation, this final jab, is for us. Let them rot. The goal is to be profane.

Back at the hovel, our table becomes a preparation space. We cut the meat into long strips, then rub them generously with salt before stacking them inside a large crock, adding more salt between each layer. The mineral will preserve the meat for several weeks, and we'll stretch it as long as we're able. It's a shame it's early autumn and not winter. Freezing the salted meat makes it last nearly forever—in this way, we have something in common.

ςςς

We work until the sun reaches its midday zenith, managing to process six carcasses. The remaining join their mangled brothers on our pyre.

We need the rest of the afternoon for what's next. Raidne and I make our way to the bluff where we've laid the women. Pisinoe joins us with a bucket of water and washcloths in hand. We take care to clean them—wiping the salt from their skin, removing the sand from beneath their nails. Raidne brushes their hair, and I help Pisinoe stitch closed the tears in their clothing. Then we dress their necks and wrists with more jewels, but we leave their original ornaments in place— delicate earrings carved from animal bones, white and purple bracelets made with beads cut from clam shells. So much has already been stolen from them by the men on the beach, by the sea, and even by us. We won't take anything else.

Once they're ready, I delicately insert a gold coin between each set of teeth. Then we dig graves and fill them with dried wood. Raidne adds handfuls of elderberries and persimmons to each, and Pisinoe inters casks of wine. After we've laid each woman onto her own pyre, I place bouquets of asters and goldenrods in their hands. Then we set them ablaze. Their fires burn until the sun hangs low in the sky, and when only embers remain, we return the displaced earth and mark each site with a stone.

Back in our cottage, I light incense to lift away today's death from our home, then Raidne prepares us a large roast with some of the fresh meat. Pisinoe pours mugs of blackberry wine, and finally, a sense of relief breaks through the exhaustion of the day. We did it. We survived.

"Want to explore the wreckage tonight?" Pisinoe asks as she picks the last bit of meat from a bone, and although I can barely move, the idea is too enticing to ignore. Our larder might be full, but there's still hunting to be done: This time, it's for treasure.

As with our preferences for knives, we've developed unique salvaging techniques over the years. Raidne is drawn to the paper items first: waterlogged books and letters written in tongues we can no longer decipher, large maps with bleeding ink. In the coming days, she'll meticulously separate the soaked parchment pieces as best she can and hang them to dry before the fireplace, as if our home were purposefully decorated with paper garlands. At night, firelight filters through the parchment, casting strange and beautiful shadows onto the walls where they dance for us.

Pisinoe heads straight toward chests, barrels, and bags, her hawkish eyes scouring for jewelry and other valuable personal effects. She adds each new locket, golden cross, and hair ornament to her hoard as she uncovers them, admiring her image in each reflective surface she finds. This time, it's an elaborately carved silver hand mirror. She loses herself in the swoops and curls of its filigree, unbothered by the large crack in the glass that leaves her image shattered. She's content to revel in the drama of it all, pretending to be the bejeweled goddess she never had the chance to become.

A salty, metallic tang hangs like a cloud over the entire scene. Whether the tinny odor is from the scattered iron nails, chains, and other metal objects from the ship or from the sailors' blood, I can't say. Most of the crimson sand is gone already, the violence committed here softened into pale pink by Scopuli's lapping waves.

I prefer to take stock of each wreck in its entirety before I begin to sift through its subtleties. I move south along the shoreline, dodging the tattered wooden remnants of the ship's bones. The wreckage gradually thins until eventually, there are hardly any artifacts at all. From here, my sisters are no more than two dots bobbing gleefully in the glow of the rising moon, treasure hunters dancing among the carnage. They're immune to its horrors as they revel in the comfort of their first full bellies in years and in the knowledge that they won't go hungry for months. The violence of the day does nothing to stifle the excitement that's returned to our frames; if anything, it fuels it.

As I consider where to begin, the hair on the back of my neck rises to attention. The sensation stops my feet in the cool sand. My sisters' laughter, so loud just moments ago, is now muffled. I feel my face pinch with confusion, but then I realize: It's because of the air. It's somehow heavier, and there's a whisper of a scent mingling with the salt and brine that I can't quite place. When I do, the breath leaves my lungs. It's sweet, spring soil with the kiss of flowers. The way Proserpina smelled.

I know this feeling: the flutter of anticipation in my stomach, the tingling on my skin. It's the same way I felt that time, all those years ago, when I heard—

Look.

The sound of Proserpina's voice crashes into my back with the force of a wave. I'm no match for it, and I stumble forward into the sand. I barely manage to keep myself from falling completely, but the second I find my balance, I whirl around, heart in my throat, half expecting to see her . . .

But there's only the empty shoreline.

"Proserpina?" I whisper, but my question is lost on the breeze. I force myself to stand a little taller, and when I speak again, my voice is more assured. "Look where?"

The only answer is the sound of my pounding heart. I stomp around the sand, kicking over pieces of wood, trying to find whatever it is that she wants me to see. It's just as a curse forms on my lips that I catch sight of an object sitting on the brink of the tide. The waves lap at its edges, as if they're trying to beckon it back into the depths. What's it doing so far away from the rest of the ruin? Every part of my body sings with anticipation.

There. I don't know if it's she who speaks the word or me.

I approach cautiously, though with night setting in, my eyes can't identify the mass until I'm nearly on top of it.

It's a man's corpse.

The sound of blood rushing through my ears overtakes the sound of the waves. His back is to me, his body coiled into a ball and face half buried in the surf. I press a talon to his shoulder and drag him onto his back. He's handsome, his face colonized by a bushy red beard peppered with gray. His nose is crooked, but a splash of freckles makes the imperfection somehow charming. Significantly chapped lips are barely parted, as if he died hoping for drinkable water that never came. There's a dark, bloodstained wound behind his left ear that still seeps. I observe his stillness. He looks relatively whole—another piece of meat to burn. My mouth falls open to call for Raidne and Pisinoe.

Don't.

"Why not?"

A hoarse, desperate cough from the corpse is my answer, and I clamp a hand across my lips to ensure I don't accidentally disobey Proserpina's command.

This man is alive.

As if to underscore my revelation, he hacks up seawater all over himself. It splashes at my feet, and I recoil.

No one else lived. They drowned in the current or were shredded by coral before the sea deposited them on the beach. How did he survive the gauntlet? How does he continue to draw breath now?

He groans and reaches a weak, quaking hand toward me, but I step away before he can make contact. His clothes are in tatters, and his body is covered with gashes. Some look severe. He'll be lucky if he doesn't already have an infection.

I look north to my sisters' whirling silhouettes. *A sacrifice!* I should scream. *I found a sacrifice!* Instead, my voice lodges itself in the back of my throat and doesn't budge.

"What do you want me to do with him?" I whisper, desperate for an answer. The longer the silence grows, the more dread pools in my stomach.

My body moves of its own accord, driven by the desire—no, the *need*—to hear her voice again. It's as if I'm watching from above as a chimera of raptor and woman drags the battered man into one of Scopuli's sea caves. Not the ritual cave, but a smaller grotto embedded in the cliffside. As soon as we're tucked away inside the tiny alcove, my mind has a chance to catch up with my actions.

What am I doing? I should be signaling to Pisinoe and Raidne; we must offer him to Ceres—

As soon as her name materializes, I taste venom in the back of my throat. Ceres isn't listening. How many centuries have we already wasted performing sacrifices in her name, only to be met with hateful silence in return? The lily, the ship—this man, whoever he is, was sent by Proserpina. He's important; whether a gift, a message, or a warning, I don't know yet, but I'll keep him alive long enough to find out. Until her purpose reveals itself, he's mine.

His breath is shallow and labored, rattling his chest as he exhales, but a sense of urgency tugs me away. If I'm gone much longer, Pisinoe and Raidne will trace my steps in the sand and discover my secret.

"I don't know if you can hear me, sailor, but if you value your life, don't stray from this spot. You're safe here, and I'll come back for you in the morning."

He stirs but doesn't wake. I leave him there, slumped against a boulder.

As I head back up the beach, I try to shake the nerves from my trembling hands.

My darling Proserpina, what will you have me do?

8

𐌆𐌆𐌆𐌆

NOW

A deep red stain appears on my nightgown between my legs, and when I stand, I discover its gory twin on my mattress. I don't have time to wonder at the horror of it before my insides contract so forcefully that I fall to my knees, fingers grabbing hold of the sheets to keep myself from spilling onto the floor completely. A raw metallic scent confirms what I already know.

This is blood.

With the understanding formed into a coherent thought, it's harder to breathe. Am I dying? I groan as a terrified hand wanders between my legs to find a slick, warm wetness. My fingers return a deep maroon, the dark hue indicating that the blood is old. I've been bleeding, and for a while.

A current of panic surges through my limbs. I need help. I stumble to my feet and reach for the bedroom door, pushing aside the chair that blocks it. When I finally fling it open, Margery already stands at the threshold. She nearly drops the tray of gruel she's prepared me, her eyes flooding with concern when she reads my expression.

"Lady Thelia! What's happened? Are you all right?" She

pushes past me into the room to deposit my breakfast and notices the sanguine spot on the mattress's center. It looks like the bed's been gutted. I haven't moved, still frozen in place with my soiled hand in the air, unable to find the right words to express my terror.

She chuckles knowingly, her right hand moving to rest upon her heart. "Oh, my lady! It's only Eve's curse! You frightened me!" I watch wordlessly as she opens a chest at the far side of the room to retrieve a new mattress shell. "I'll fetch you a rag."

Eve's curse? I don't understand the phrase's meaning, though I remember Eve from yesterday's Bible study. But Cora never referred to Eve and Adam's exile as a curse—was there more to the story? Was banishment from Eden not punishment enough? No, of course not. Expulsion is hardly a creative penalty to a god. Better to dress it up with feathers and talons, or in this case, blood.

Margery strips the soiled sheets from my bed, and her calm allows another, less alarming thought to surface: Am I flowering? I hadn't yet before my transformation, and after, there was no reason for it. Hybrids can't bear children, and although Pisinoe and Raidne bled before our mutation, they lost their menses when they gained their wings. My jaw drops, and I turn from Margery to try to hide my disbelief. She takes this as a display of modesty and laughs.

"No need to be embarrassed, Lady Thelia. It's quite natural."

But not for me, I want to scream. Instead, I stumble to the tray and take a large gulp of cider. The fermented drink slides down my throat, and for the first time since I woke, my heart finally begins to slow.

Does this mean I can conceive?

My chest tightens. When we were young, Proserpina and

I often dreamed of being mothers. We would carry dolls lovingly in our arms, swaddling and cradling them, cooing gentle songs into their unhearing ears. A visiting oracle predicted that she would bear two children. When I asked how many I'd have, the old woman only smiled sadly. At the time, I didn't think much of it, but once we were banished to Scopuli, I realized she didn't want to be the one to tell me what my future held.

After that, I ceased to dream of children.

"Of course," I stammer through trembling lips, forcing away the thought. "It just caught me by surprise. It's early."

Margery nods knowingly as she picks up the sullied linens. "I'll be right back with a rag, my lady." Her eyes find the red between my legs. "And perhaps a bath for good measure. Though we'll have to be quick about it. We don't want to be late."

"For what?" I ask, but Margery, consumed by the task at hand, is already gone.

᭝᭝᭝

Everyone files into the meeting hall. The jovial atmosphere that filled the space earlier this week is gone, replaced with an air of severity. The tables have been pushed to the walls, and their benches are aligned in several rows before the elevated platform at the back of the hall. People crisscross one another to slide into specific spots as if they've been assigned. Thomas and Mistress Bailie head to the first row, where she claims her place at the end of the pew. I follow, leaving an empty space between Thomas and me. He moves to fill the gap, but before he can, Cora slides into it. My skin flushes at the sight of her, but she's not here for me. Thomas resigns himself to his current spot, but he still folds his arms across his chest in a display of irritation. Mistress Bailie watches the scene play out, but her face is like carved stone—it's completely unreadable, betraying no emotions. I almost envy her ability to hide her thoughts beneath such a placid exterior; I seem incapable of it.

"That's Master Sampson," Cora whispers, nodding toward the older man who arranges himself behind the pulpit. His sharp eyes cut to her, and he clears his throat dramatically. The *hrgn-hrgn-hrgn* snaps Cora's attention back to the front of the room as a flush crawls up her neck. I look over my shoulder and find everyone else's attention is locked on him as well.

He leads the villagers through a morning prayer, and then more than one hundred voices speak "Amen" in unison. It's an unsettling sound that makes me rock forward in my seat, but Cora reaches for my leg to steady me. Her hand is hot on my thigh. Its warmth permeates all the suffocating layers of clothing and sears into my flesh. It makes my breath quicken, my heart pound.

Why does this friendly gesture cause a ball of anticipation to form in my root? The last time someone's touch made me feel like this was with Proserpina. I can almost see the delicate outline of her jaw that I once kissed, the gentle curve of her shoulder where I rested my head. I bite my lip, my gaze wandering to Cora's hand. Her fingers are so slender and elegant, with trimmed and clean nails like bows atop a present. My mind wanders to things I suspect Master Sampson considers blasphemous.

What would the tips of those fingers feel like brushing against my lips? What would they taste like?

I have to hold myself tightly to keep from trembling at the thought, and then her hand is gone, back in her own lap. The place where it rested burns cold in its absence, as if it was never whole without her touch. I am left wanting in a way I can't begin to put into words.

The service passes by in a blur of ritual and sacrament that means little to me, except for the part where a giggling child is called to sit in a chair before the entire congregation as a form of punishment.

I know how it feels, to be a girl punished before a crowd. As soon as Master Sampson snaps his Bible shut, she's the first to dart from the meetinghouse. My heart aches for her, but at least she was allowed to leave on her own two feet. She wasn't dragged away, strong hands clamping down like shackles on her wrists.

"The Chapmans are always causing trouble," Mistress Bailie remarks self-righteously. "If it's not John making a drunken scene, it's one of their brood interrupting services. Despicable."

Outside, the little girl has found comfort in Alis's arms. Alis looks exhausted, but still she rocks her daughter gently, a dejected but loving expression settled across her face. I can't help but watch them like that, mother and daughter finding comfort in each other. I'm so transfixed that I don't notice Will appear beside us.

"I miss having you sit with me," he says to Cora, his breath forming a small cloud in the cold air as he speaks. "Church is certainly less entertaining without you."

"You know I have to sit with my betrothed now," Cora says, exasperation filling her voice. Even after our talk last night, I wonder if she truly must sit with Thomas or if she insisted on it because of me.

As if summoned by my thoughts, Thomas breaks into our huddle, sliding an arm around Cora's waist. She beams at his touch, and resentment stirs inside my stomach. Even if her exuberance is only a show to endear herself to him, it still makes me feel things I didn't expect: possessiveness, jealousy. A darkness flickers across Will's face as well, but he quickly masks it beneath a smile.

I'm reminded of the same reaction he had at my welcome feast. I thought his displeasure was directed at me, but what ill will could he hold against his sister? Unless . . .

"Care to join us for a walk, Lady Thelia?" Wenefrid's voice materializes from behind me, and I turn to find the older woman with Emme in tow. Thomas snorts, and Emme's expression darkens. Wenefrid acts as though she didn't hear it, but the slight twitch of her hand at her side reveals that she did.

"Mistress Powell, don't be sil—" Agnes begins, no doubt intending to chide her about how such an activity is below my rank. But the thought of returning home with them, with Cora as she watches Thomas with that glowing expression, makes my stomach twist.

"I'd love nothing more," I interrupt, and though Cora opens her mouth in surprise, I link an arm into Emme's. "Shall we?"

Wenefrid leads us both to the eastern gate. "Fun little secret for you, my lady." The older woman's eyes twinkle as she tilts her head up toward the empty post on the palisade. "The guards usually take their time returning to their posts after services."

"Where are we going?"

"Into the woods," Emme answers. "Wenefrid's teaching me how to make bayberry candles."

Wenefrid clicks her tongue, her features growing dark as she peers into the future that winter threatens. "The way we're burning through livestock, there soon won't be any tallow left."

"Maybe if Sybil Browne would lift her curse from the traps . . ."

How strange memory is, that a name's enough to transport you to a different time and place. I'm suddenly curled up at Raidne's feet, flanked by Pisinoe and Proserpina. Raidne's perched on an old rocking chair in Proserpina's palatial room, a large book spread across her legs. It contains the story of Aeneas, and his desire to find his father in the Underworld. In order to reach him, he needed guidance from the Cumaean Sibyl, the only person capable of straddling the lines between the living and the dead.

Trojan, Anchises's son, the descent of Avernus is easy.

All night long, all day, the dark door of Dis stands open . . .

But that's where the story was wrong. We stalked the shores of Lake Avernus for months looking for Proserpina, watching as entire flocks of birds fell dead from the sky into its waters, but Dis's dark gates never opened for us.

Wenefrid turns on Emme with an admirable fierceness for such an old frame; it takes the younger woman by surprise, but not me. I'm well aware of how far anger can carry an aging body. "Be careful how you speak about other women, Emme. With Sybil cast out, they'll soon need a new person to pin all our misfortune on."

Emme swallows hard, scarlet rising to her cheeks. "You're right, Winny. I'm sorry."

"Who's Sybil?"

"She's a skilled healer," Wenefrid says. "One this pitiful city desperately needs. Her expansive knowledge of medicinal plants is why she was recruited to come here in the first place."

"So where is she?"

Emme sighs. "A few days after we first landed, a scouting party reported that they'd seen natives circling the fort. The men on watch fired shots into the trees but found no bodies. But Mistress Bailie noticed Sybil slipping out of the fort at odd hours and had her followed. She'd found an injured Croatoan man and was nursing him back to health."

My brows furrow. Did I hear her wrong? "They punished her for helping someone in need?"

"Our laws forbid us from bartering with the natives without explicit approval from the Council. Mistress Bailie said the supplies Sybil used to treat him were equivalent to theft from the colony, and that by healing him, she'd traded those goods without permission. It's absurd, of course. Everyone knew Mistress Bailie and Sybil didn't get along. But both theft and bartering are offenses punishable by death. Agnes convinced the Council it was a mercy to simply exile her from the city."

"That way, if someone is truly sick, they can still beg Sybil for help." Wenefrid's features are pinched with disgust, and she waves a hand in the air to brush the conversation away.

A large, dense shrub appears before us, and we follow Wenefrid's lead to separate its tiny blue fruits from its serrated leaves until our skirts are filled with them. The process is tedious but far from over. Next, we return to her cottage and boil the berries to coax their waxy finish from the flesh beneath. The concoction is then strained through a cheesecloth to separate the fruit from the liquid. As it cools, a light olive-green wax floats to the top, where it hardens, finally ready for collection. It smells of pine and winter.

"We were friends," Wenefrid admits as she dips a wick into the remelted wax. "But I still let them chase her out into the woods."

"Sybil?" I ask softly.

She nods. "Some days, I wish I'd left with her. Now it's been so long, and I never tried to visit . . . I was too afraid to find her when she needed me, and I'm still too afraid to go to her now."

The admission stokes the embers of my own guilt. Although the novelty of being here allows me to temporarily forget, regret has been my most intimate companion over the course of my long life.

"If no one would punish you for it, would you go to her?"

"Of course," she answers sadly. "But how could such a thing be possible?"

A knock on the door interrupts us. Emme opens it and a weathered Elizabeth draws inside, Ambrose crying in her arms.

"Sorry to bother you," Elizabeth says, her voice cracking.

"You're no bother, child. What's the trouble?"

"It's my goat again." Ambrose squirms, and Elizabeth shifts him to her other hip. "I can't get any milk from her . . ."

The child in her arms sobs harder, and Elizabeth coos into the top of his head. When she looks back to Wenefrid, I notice that dark circles ring the young mother's eyes. "Can you try? You're always able to coax something out of her, and he's starving."

"Come, I'll show you my technique," Wenefrid says, pushing herself to her feet. "Lady Thelia, can you take him?"

I balk, hands rising to my chest. "Oh, I don't think that's—"

But Elizabeth is already handing Ambrose to me. The moment she releases him, the boy unleashes an ear-piercing scream.

Emme moves to follow them.

"Wait—" I start, but Wenefrid turns to me with a warm smile.

"We'll only be a minute. Just bounce him gently."

Before I can speak another word of protest, the three women are gone.

I didn't think it possible for the boy to cry louder, but he loses his grip on reality the second his mother vanishes from sight. I pull him closer to my chest and do my best impression of Elizabeth's coos, bouncing him gently in my arms. His hair is soft beneath my fingertips, little copper curls that catch the muted light that filters in through the slats in the window shutters.

There's only one way I know to soothe him. I sing—a quieter melody than I'm used to, almost a whisper, that promises to tell him his future glories if he can quiet himself long enough to hear them. I don't expect much without the curse's magic, but Ambrose reminds me that my voice is beautiful without it. The little boy's wails dwindle into hitching sobs, which eventually soften into the occasional whimper. When he rests his head against my shoulder, I know I've won. Exhausted by the tantrum, he lets his thumb find its way into his mouth. It takes only minutes before the child is asleep.

I keep swaying and humming, and my eyes fall closed as well. A strange sensation settles over me—an expansive feeling in my chest that's hard to put words to, and so I don't try. Instead, I marvel at the little body so warm against mine, so breakable. At what age does evil sink its teeth into a boy? Because the sleeping child in my arms seems shockingly innocent.

"Oh!" Elizabeth makes a surprised sound, and my eyes snap open to find her and Wenefrid smiling in the doorway. When she speaks again, her voice is much softer. "I've been trying to calm him for the past hour but haven't been able to."

To my dismay, my arms are reluctant to return him. Why do I suddenly feel so exposed? "He must have just tired himself out."

Elizabeth's blue eyes twinkle as she pulls Ambrose in close. "You're good with him."

"I should be heading back to the Bailies'." I brush out my skirts, suddenly eager to put time and distance between myself and this moment.

"I'll walk with you," Elizabeth says, and after bidding Wenefrid goodbye, we both return to the streets.

᠍᠍᠍᠍

Mistress Bailie is seated at the head of the table with Thomas to her left. A large roasted bird that's already been carved rests before them, and their plates are piled with its meat.

"There you are, my lady," Thomas says, motioning to the empty setting to his mother's right. "Please, won't you join us?"

I've barely had time to settle into my chair before Agnes clears her throat.

"Perhaps this isn't my place," she begins, "but those women are far below your rank. Surely you know that?"

She's testing me and my story, and, of course, she's right. Proserpina would never have run off to spend the entire day with commoners. I slide my hands, my fingers stained blue by the bayberries, beneath the table and away from her prying eyes.

"You're right," I offer, and when Agnes smirks triumphantly, I add, "it's not your place."

Her expression sours into a scowl.

Thomas rushes to change the subject. "Now that you've settled in, tell us more about the challenge for your hand, my lady."

I think of my wings, my talons, my old form to give me the strength to keep from melting beneath the heat of their combined attention. Thomas tears into a bite of meat as he waits for my answer; juice from the roasted bird leaks from the corners of his mouth.

"On Scopuli, it's tradition to hold a wrestling match for a woman's hand," I say, bringing a finger to my chin to mirror where the juice runs. "The men fight until only the strongest remains."

Thomas grabs the napkin from his lap and wipes his face, then turns to his mother with a grin. "That sounds like exactly the kind of competition I'd excel at."

"If you weren't already happily betrothed," Mistress Bailie adds, a pale eyebrow raised, though I can't tell if her admonition is genuine or simply an act for me. The glint leaches from Thomas's eyes, leaving behind an empty smile that's somehow worse to behold. The sight of it makes my stomach churn.

"Of course," Thomas answers coolly, then turns to me again. "When will it be?"

I reach for the glass of wine before me, swirling its contents. That moment of softness with Ambrose, the appearance of my menses—gods, even the jealousy toward Cora's affections for Thomas. They're all just distractions, pulling my focus away from my one true purpose.

I can save you, she'd said. *But I need more blood.* And to give that to her, I need men to follow me to Scopuli.

"In four days' time. On the next full moon."

Perhaps its light will bless the endeavor.

"And what happens after you've found your husband?" Agnes asks, stumbling, just barely, over the word *husband*. It's the obvious next question, but that tiny slip of her tongue gives her away—despite what she read in my letter, Agnes is still suspicious of me and my motives. But can I really fault her for that, given her son is what's at stake?

"I want to return home with him before winter truly sets in. Though he shouldn't be the only one who joins me—I've heard talk of the city's rations. People say there's not enough food to keep everyone alive through the season."

Thomas's eyes widen with consideration, but Agnes shoots him a cutting look. "We can't blindly send the entire colony to a place we've never been, my lady. And even if we wanted to, the only ship large enough to carry us all returned to England two summers ago. The pinnace that you've seen offshore only holds about twenty people."

Twenty is hardly one hundred, but it's still enough.

"So send a scouting party to accompany us," I offer. "If Scopuli passes their assessment, formal plans to move the colony can be made after they return, if winter demands it."

Agnes strokes her chin, her cold eyes finding Thomas's.

"We'll need to discuss the idea with the other Council members," he says slowly. "But I don't see a reason why we shouldn't explore it."

"After the competition is held, how quickly can we leave?" I ask, my stomach twisting as I prepare myself to flirt. "And would you join us? I'd love to show you my home."

Especially the hidden sea cave, whose sand will swallow your blood below.

Thomas smirks, and immediately, the biscuit I barely managed to eat threatens to come back up. If Cora heard this, she'd hate me.

So what? You're not here for her.

Was that my voice, or Proserpina's?

"Within the week, I imagine. And I'd never decline an invitation to stand at your side."

I force a soft smile, suddenly exhausted.

"Are you tired, my lady?" Agnes asks. I fear I've given myself away once more, but Mistress Bailie's attention is locked on Thomas. She wants me gone from this room as much as I want to be.

"Yes, actually. Would you mind if I retired for the evening?"

"Not at all, Lady Thelia. Go rest." Agnes waves a hand to dismiss me and then slides her chair closer to Thomas's. Immediately, the two descend into whispers, so lost in their plotting that they barely notice my retreat.

9

⌐⌐⌐⌐

BEFORE

For the second day in a row, I wake without pain. But today there's no joy in this fact, because its absence is tempered by guilt. It conjures the sailor's image from the shadows, and now that he's here, all I can do is hide my nerves in a task and pray that Raidne and Pisinoe don't notice them. I pull myself from my blankets and add some wood to the dying embers in the hearth, then move to prepare tea.

Pisinoe raises her head from her pillow with a smile. "Should we start cleaning the wreckage today?"

The procedure is always the same: collect the scraps of wood and burn them, along with anything else we don't want, and move the valuables into a sea cave for safekeeping. The work is hard but enjoyable, but that's beside the point—if we didn't comb through each wreck, the shore would be so littered with debris that there would be no beach at all. We'd be buried by the ruin.

I hand them each a mug of tea, and we sit before the fireplace, sipping slowly.

"Let's only worry about the bodies today," Raidne says.

"Once their stink is gone, I want to savor sifting through our treasure."

"I might head to the beach early," I say slowly, bracing myself for the coming backlash.

"You don't want to go to the lake first?" Raidne's voice is laced with concern. After the last hundred or so times our youth was restored, Pisinoe and I snuck away to the clandestine pool in the center of Scopuli's forest to admire ourselves in the water's glassy reflection and to anoint ourselves with it. Although a relatively new habit given our age, it's already become somewhat of a tradition. Pisinoe's face crumples so quickly that Raidne doesn't have time to press me further before she displays a rare moment of kindness. "I'll go with you, Pisinoe."

Pisinoe tries to muster a smile, but we both know Raidne's mood will last only so long. "Why the rush to go to the beach?"

Only some semblance of the truth will keep their curiosity at bay; they'll be able to smell an outright lie. "She's trying to tell me something."

Pisinoe raises an eyebrow and turns to Raidne, whose back has straightened. Even after all these years, they aren't sure what to believe about the lilies or my insistence that they're messages from Proserpina.

"I can't shake the feeling maybe there's something she wants me to find. It sounds silly, I know, but I just . . . I want to look."

What if, out there in the surf, there lies a clue to the man's purpose?

"Of course," Pisinoe murmurs, and she slides in to wrap her arms around me. It's only inside her embrace that I realize I'm shaking. "We'll join you later, after sunrise."

"Thank you." My voice quivers under the weight of both my appreciation for their understanding and the guilt of withholding the entire truth from them. The room falls silent as I collect a bladder of water and a pouch full of meat and nuts they assume are intended for me. I'm about to push my way outside when Raidne speaks.

"Thelxiope, wait—" she says, and I turn to meet her gaze. "If you don't find anything . . . try not to read too much into it, all right? If Proserpina could reach you, I know that she would."

Would she? The words sting for a reason Raidne doesn't understand, but I force a nod to acknowledge that I heard her, then disappear into the early morning darkness.

The moon's position in the sky tells me that I have two hours before dawn.

ᕯᕯᕯ

Nerves scratch at my stomach lining as I tumble over the cliff's edge to descend to the beach. For now I ignore the battered pieces of wood and other detritus strewn about the sand. The tide is low, and the waves gently lap at the ever-shifting edge between the land and the sea. My path is hidden in the shadow of the escarpment, but I still feel exposed as I scramble down the strip of beach untouched by the waves. I'm a lone dot on a wide stretch of shore, an easy target for the what ifs.

What if Raidne and Pisinoe catch me? What if the man's gone? What if he's dead?

What if he's dangerous?

All men are dangerous.

What if Proserpina never speaks?

I force my focus to the vertical cliff face to my left, an unscalable wall of gray granite. The grotto where I left the sailor appears, its maw a dare. The opening is evident only by its darkness, a somehow blacker void against the rest of the cliff's shadows. I curse myself for forgetting a candle, and a metallic tang rises in the back of my throat—the taste, I realize with surprise, is fear. When was the last time I was afraid on Scopuli? I can't recall. It's been so long since I didn't know exactly what my future held.

My right foot takes a reluctant step forward and my left follows suit. *Right, left, right:* The words guide me until I'm standing at the cave's threshold, on the precipice between outside and in. Here, my feet lose their motivation. I waver, allowing shapes the time to slowly emerge from the unimaginable blackness: Small stalactites just a tad brighter than the nothingness behind them hang from the ceiling, and boulders are scattered along the ground. Pools of water, trapped here from the last high tide, circle the stones' varying circumferences.

The rock where I left the man comes into focus. I crane my neck to try to find his broken frame, but it's no use. I need to fully enter the cave to know for sure.

Right, left, right. As I peer around the stone, my mouth goes dry. He's gone.

"Damnit." I take a few more steps into the cliff's cavity.

A swift force hits me bluntly in the back of the head, and I fall forward, my face barely missing the cave's wall. Before I can call out in surprise, a large weight presses into my spine, cramping my wings, pushing me farther into the dirt. A rough hand grabs my hair at my crown, and something cool and metallic slides against my throat. It's a blade. The irony isn't lost on me.

This can't be what she wants, can it?

A deep voice growls in my ear, but he speaks no words. The knife presses harder against my flesh, but it doesn't yet slice.

I nearly laugh with relief, despite my current position. I

was afraid that I'd lost him, but he was lying in wait the entire time, as much a predator as I. His attack caught me by surprise, but he's woefully mistaken if he thinks he can keep me pinned here. I'm far too strong for him.

"Clever." The sound of a woman's voice coming from the winged creature beneath him must shock the sailor, because he lightens the pressure on the blade. "But how are you not enchanted?"

"What are you?" He ignores my question. Although his voice is cold, there's a sliver of curiosity lurking beneath the ice.

"What, exactly, I can't say, but I'm the one who saved you. You washed ashore yesterday. I hid you here to keep you safe."

"Why should I believe you?"

"If you don't let me help you, you'll die. Even if you do, you might die still." Raidne's favorite sentiment rings in my ears: Why offer these men hope if there is none to be found here?

The man lowers his weapon, but he doesn't release me.

"Where's the rest of my crew?" he barks. His voice is rough, as if the sound is passing through sand before it finally crosses over his lips.

"They all drowned, except for you."

A garbled cry escapes from the back of his throat. It cracks mid-release and hangs in the air between us. The sound, revealing his dehydration, makes me wince.

"That must be difficult to hear, but you're in danger here. Let me bring you somewhere safer, and then I'll get you something to drink."

The promise of water breaks him. He relents and climbs off me, but he doesn't offer to help me stand. If I were making a list of offenses, this would be his second: first the attack, followed by a serious lack of manners. My jaw clenches. He's not making a good case for me to save him.

Gods, what am I doing?

I pull myself to my feet, brushing the dirt from my body. When I look at him, he's staring, a mixture of horror and awe.

Under his scrutiny, I'm desperate for my aging body. Maybe then he wouldn't be gawking so openly, though it's not the human parts of me that he's having trouble reconciling. It's the feathered legs, the talons of a hawk, and the incredible wings that adorn my back.

I can almost hear his thoughts, for he wears them so readily in his stunned expression: *Is she the same as a human woman, between her legs?*

It's a look I've seen before.

My wings spread instinctively, but they don't fit within the narrow width of the cave. At their full span, they're twice his height. Still, he stumbles backward, recognizing this display for what it is: A sign of dominance. A warning. "Are you ready?"

I give him a moment to process my question. In conjunction with my appearance, it takes him longer than I prefer, but he eventually concedes with a nod.

"Good. Come," I say as I brush past him. He can barely stand; he must have used most of his remaining strength to tackle me to the ground. But I don't help him. He shuffles along behind me, cursing under his breath. Outside, the beach spreads before us, and beyond it, a thin stretch of sea holds the faces of Rotunda and Castle illuminated red in the fiery blaze of dawn.

"See that island across the way? The one lower to the horizon without the crown of rocks?"

Another bob of the head for yes.

"I have to carry you there."

I don't give him time to react; he should be thankful for

the warning. Without a word, I spread my wings wide and take to the air. We don't have much time before the rest of the dawn comes spilling over the border between sea and sky, before Raidne and Pisinoe return to the wreck.

My talons slice into the linen shirt near his shoulders, and I'm careful not to slip my razor-sharp claws into his flesh. My sudden closeness elicits a terrified gasp. I relish it.

His shirt tears as I lift him from the ground. The flimsy brown fabric can't support his weight, and his body sinks inside of it, like a turtle retreating into its shell. When we're well off the ground, I release him just long enough to encircle my talons around his arms instead of through them. My claws itch to tear into his skin, but I force myself to maintain a loose grip. Any more wounds will kill him, and I can't risk his death until I know what he's for.

He makes a variety of sounds as we fly: deep groans, rapid bursts of cursing and *oh-oh-ohs,* and even soft whimpers as he tries to make sense of what's happening. Thankfully, the trip isn't long. I set him down gently onto Rotunda's eastern beach a few minutes later. The small isle is entirely shrouded in trees, which makes it the ideal spot for hiding him. This sandy haven is the only island in our little archipelago that doesn't feature staggering, unscalable cliff faces. Our little home is visible from here, a silhouette perched upon Scopuli's highest crest with the blazing sun rising behind it.

"We have to get to the other side of the island. It's not far, and I can carry you if you'd prefer, but you must be quiet—"

"No!" the man shouts up at me, shielding his body with raised hands. "I can walk!"

I can't help myself—the sight of him like that, with his eyes wide, his arms arranged in a defensive posture, brings a laugh to my lips, and I disregard my own demand for silence as I touch my toes to the sand and begin toward the tree line. To my surprise, he follows without arguing. The trees on Rotunda aren't as high as Scopuli's. They barely cover the tops of our heads, and we duck to avoid the low-hanging limbs. Katydids blare the final moments of their nocturnal song all around us, but the sailor doesn't notice.

"Here we are," I announce as we emerge into a clearing. It sits on Rotunda's westernmost edge. The sea is visible again through the tangled tree trunks, and the sound of the waves mingles with the bugs' softening chorus. There's a small lean-to overlooking the beach, as well as an old singed firepit encircled with stones.

Very early in our exile, we discovered that a different sailor had washed ashore here. He must have instinctively known to hide from the watchful eye of Scopuli, but a poorly timed afternoon fire gave away his secret.

We, in turn, gave him to Ceres.

I take the water bladder from my hip and hand it to the man, fulfilling my earlier promise, but he gulps the liquid down with such a ferocity that most of it doesn't make it into his mouth at all. It spills over the sides of his parched lips and rolls down his face.

"Slowly, slowly. You'll make yourself sick if you drink too fast."

He heeds my warning and lowers the vessel from his face, wiping water from his mouth with the back of a salt-stained arm. His eyes lock onto mine. "Who are you?"

"My name is Thelxiope." I pause, watching his face crumble at the unfamiliar chain of sounds.

"Thelxiope," he repeats, stumbling over its music. "What are you?"

"Unlucky, just like you." The truth is that I don't know what I am, exactly, besides cursed. I'd never heard of creatures like us before our transformation, and poring over books the sailors brought with them while they were still written in tongues we could read offered very few clues.

Once, several hundred years ago, Raidne found a broken shard of pottery in the surf after a large fleet of soldiers crashed upon our cliffs. The clay was black, and the fragment depicted the image of an ochre bird with a woman's head. Her eyes were closed and her lips parted, as if either waiting for a kiss or lost mid-song. It was the only clue we ever found, but the sea claimed the rest of the vase, and there were no accompanying words to describe what the image was.

We must have been known. Our sin was too great, our punishment too unique to go unsung. People revel in tales with tragic setups and doomed protagonists, and our story has both. The fact that our history ended with a metamorphosis would only make it more popular, more enduring.

"That's not what I meant," he objects. "I have never seen a being—"

"If there's a name for what I am, I don't know it," I confess, cutting his sentence short.

He falls quiet for a moment before responding with another question. "What did you mean by *enchanted*? Back in the cave?"

"What do you remember from last night?"

"I was on the lower gun deck during a bitch of a storm . . . I heard a bunch of commotion above, but before I could make it back up, something hit me." He touches the side of his head above his ear, the same wound that was oozing last night. The bleeding seems to have stopped, but he still snaps his hand away. "Maybe a lantern? Everything was getting tossed around as the waves battered us. But whatever it was, it knocked me unconscious. I woke up in the cave."

So that explains his coherence. He was unconscious before our song could reach him.

The sun has risen above the horizon, although it still sits low in the sky. I grow uncomfortable under the man's watchful eye, which still waits for an answer. Instead, I offer the small satchel of nuts and meat to him, anxious to draw his attention from my form. "Hungry?"

He takes it from me roughly, then lifts softened eyes to meet mine in apology. I scowl back; I don't want it. "I need to go, but I'll be back later with more water and food. If you value your life, don't stray too far from here. And never light a fire during daylight hours unless I'm with you."

"What happens next?" he asks, a fresh glimmer of fear beneath his words.

"I don't know," I admit. I can't be sure when, or if, his purpose will be revealed to me. *Please, Proserpina, tell me what to do.* "But first we'll need to clean those wounds."

"My name is Jaquob, by the way!" he calls out to me once my back is turned. There's something in his tone that catches me by surprise—playfulness.

Jaquob. What in the name of the gods am I supposed to do with you?

Raidne and Pisinoe, still glistening from their swim, find me on Scopuli's beach. Pisinoe's eyes are large and expecting, desperate to hear if I discovered the message I claimed to be searching for. When I shake my head, her lips turn downward in a sympathetic frown. Raidne doesn't say a word. Instead, she heads straight for the pile of bodies. All that's left to do is burn them.

We get to work constructing a wooden platform of slow-burning oak logs, interweaving twigs of birch between them.

The birch will catch the entire structure ablaze quickly, while the oak will smolder until only ash remains. When the structure is nearly as tall as us, and stuffed with kindling, we place the corpses, stacking them like logs until they tower over us.

Pisinoe places additional branches and birch bark between the tangles of limbs and lolling heads, and finally, we're ready. By now the bodies are putrid. Good. The outsides of these men reflect their fetid insides, and their sweet rot lures clouds of flies to the beach. The insects crawl over the corpses' milky dead eyes, looking for entry. Pisinoe frowns; she feels bad that they, too, will fall victim to the flames. For a moment, I think she'll try to shoo them away, but instead she nods to Raidne, who strikes two rocks together over the formation.

Chtt, chtt, chtt, the stones chirp before emitting a single spark that sets the entire heap ablaze.

The flames erupt along the kindling and consume the clothes. Eventually, when the conflagration is hot enough, they find the skin and the meat. Darkling smoke billows up toward the heavens, and although Pisinoe says a prayer under her breath, there's no formal dedication. These bodies are too soiled and too broken to gift in offering. Instead, they burn for no one.

When all that remains is bone, we return to the wreckage. We find personal artifacts—pouches of gold and silver, letters, and the occasional locket—along with a large quantity of animal pelts. Raidne is thrilled to discover a wooden trunk filled with maps, but Pisinoe's left disappointed when she finds nothing grander than last night's mirror. A treasure ship this is not. By now the sun is low in the sky, and my stomach rumbles. Jaquob must be starving, but he'll have to wait.

Only when I'm certain that Pisinoe and Raidne have been claimed by sleep do I cross the small stretch of sea, but not before retrieving two casks of alcohol we discovered in the wreckage. I'll need them to clean Jaquob's wounds. Even still, I keep low to the water as I fly, like a seabird searching for food to bring to its children back on the shore.

I used to wonder what it would be like to be those birds, but I no longer torment myself with such thoughts.

Jaquob sits on one of the large gray stones that encircle the firepit, wearing a dark expression. He's built a small pyramid of wood, but he hasn't set it aflame.

"You told me not to light it without you." A pause. "From the looks of it, you had your own fire this afternoon."

"We had to clear the bodies," I say.

His jaw tightens. For a moment, I worry he might lash out, but instead he turns back to his log pile to start a fire. "Honestly, I wasn't sure if you were coming back."

"Well, here I am." My tone is harsher than I intend it. "Come on, then. Let's see how bad it is."

He nods and peels his tattered shirt from his frame. The sight of what lies beneath it makes my lips press together in a thin line. His body is littered with bruises and cuts, and there's a large gash on his left flank. He wrapped some fabric around it to stop the bleeding, but the blood that stains the bandage is an angry purple tinged with green. What comes next will be unpleasant.

I kneel before him, and my nose shrivels instinctively; I smell the wound before I see it. The sweet, rancid scent, so much like his compatriots', climbs into my nostrils and settles there. I do my best to ignore it, distracting myself with peeling the makeshift dressing from his side. Combined with the smell, what I find beneath it makes me gag.

"That bad?" he asks sheepishly.

A piece of coral scooped out a chunk of his side the size of my fist. It left a deep laceration, with yellow tissue pockets scattered throughout the crimson. The flesh surrounding the wound is red and hot. My stomach sinks. It's likely infected. I press gently on its right edge, and Jaquob hisses out air, recoiling. A creamy pus emerges in my finger's wake.

I retrieve a clean rag from my bag and douse it with the alcohol.

"This is going to hurt." I hand him the bottle. He takes a large swig of the liquor before turning his gaze away. I do my best to clean the wound before wrapping it in a fresh bandage, but only the Fates know if it'll be enough.

I continue sewing the tinier cuts closed, and he continues gulping down alcohol.

"All right, that's it for the top half," I say after some time. "Let me see your legs."

The liquor and the pain have made him delirious, and he chuckles a bit before standing to unbutton his pants. "As you wish."

They're so badly torn that they nearly fall from his frame. He retakes his seat next to me. I suddenly feel flushed. This is the first man that I have seen both naked and alive.

Don't look down, don't look down, don't look down.

I chant the words to myself, hoping the incantation will ensure my focus. It doesn't. I can't help but glance at the limp member between his thighs. I'm curious despite myself.

He catches me looking and snorts. "What, like what you see?"

My stomach turns. What rests between his legs looks just as grotesque as it does on the corpses I've gutted. I was certain there'd be some difference in its presentation on a living man, but this revelation only leaves me more baffled. How can such an ugly organ be the root of man's oafish pride? What about it causes them to strut about so proudly?

"Don't be foolish."

I reset my attention to scour his legs for more injuries. Thankfully, his bottom half is mostly unscathed. It's the wound on his side that remains the most serious.

That wound might kill him.

"You look like a woman," he says, hiccupping. "A beautiful one, at least from the waist up."

As if to underscore his point, his eyes linger on my breasts. I forgot to be ashamed of my nakedness before, but now I flush beneath his scrutiny.

"But you're not a woman, are you? Not a human, anyway. Can you even—"

"You're right," I snap back, eager to change the subject. "I had the form of a human once, but that was a long time ago." I stand up again, putting a few paces between us. "I'll bring you a fresh set of clothes tomorrow."

"I didn't mean to embarrass you," he says. "Truly, I'm thankful for your help."

"You asked me what I am. What about you? What were you doing on that ship?"

"I'm a trapper returning to France. We were only at sea for a few days when the wind blew us off course, and then that fucking storm hit . . . I've been sailing since I was fourteen and crossed the Atlantic three times. Never in my life have I seen a storm like that. It was like Hell opened above us and let loose its fury."

Most of what he says means nothing to me. I don't know the names of cities, seas, or countries anymore. But the part about the storm piques my attention. I think about offering my sympathies, but they would be a lie. I sway on my feet, already weary of the worry he's brought me.

"Are you leaving already? I've been alone all day, and apparently my whole crew is dead, and I'll soon be joining them. Spare a few minutes of your company for a dying man?"

"What would we talk about?" I ask, surprised to find myself considering his request. But there's a reckless part of me that's desperate to discover what it is about this man that caused the Goddess of the Dead to intervene on his behalf.

"Anything. Tell me about yourself. How long have you been here?"

"Eons."

"Were you born here?" The question makes me bristle, and I turn away from him.

"Fine, fine! No more questions!" he pleads, desperate to win back my favor.

"We're not friends, Jaquob. Don't make the mistake of believing that we are."

His mouth snaps closed.

"There are others on this island, like me, and if I'm gone too long . . . well, they might come looking. And they won't spare you like I have."

He bites his lip, his dark eyes wandering back to the flames.

"Of course, Thelxiope. Thank you again."

I don't answer as I walk along the shore away from him. Only when I'm around the bend, out of sight, do I unfurl my wings. He's decided not to fear me for now, but I don't want to remind him that I look more eagle than woman with my wings spread to their full length. If he saw me in the skies, I'd lose the fragile trust we have built—instinct would take hold, and he would recoil, the way a mouse naturally avoids a cat, or a fish flees from the gaping jaws of a shark. Until I know what Proserpina wants with him, I need him to trust me.

I take to the heavens.

Every time that I fly, song builds in my stomach instinctively. It takes all my self-control to keep the notes buried deep in my body, away from my lips. The air tonight is still, and if I let it, my aria would carry across the distance to Jaquob's ears. It would drive him mad, straight into the sea to try to find me. He would drown, like all the others, and then I'd never discover his use.

When my feet finally touch the ground again on Scopuli's western cliffs, a stifled hum bursts from the back of my throat. It's a small concession to my instincts, but until I know Jaquob's purpose, it will have to be enough.

10

NOW

With the challenge date officially set, the men watch me more closely. I catch them sharpening their knives, carrying larger loads, and practicing their shots, training for a test without knowing exactly what it is—everyone except for Thomas. If he prepares, he's smart enough to do it privately—or, more likely, Agnes demanded it. But the knowledge of what's to come paints his features with a new shade of arrogance, and Cora senses the change in him like a hound on the scent of a boar. When she glimpses Thomas emerging from the locked room where they've stored my treasure, she cuts her suggested Bible study short and calls him to us. Thomas barely looks at her as he shares the news that the Council has agreed to send a scouting party to Scopuli with me and my betrothed. His hungry gray eyes swallow me alone. When he excuses himself, Cora rushes after him, and though it makes me ill, I don't try to stop her. Instead, I make myself scarce.

Elizabeth, Emme, and Wenefrid open their homes to me. I do my best to blend in, especially after my misstep at the first Bible study. But despite the notable differences in our ranks, they quickly grow accustomed to my presence. With their blessing, the others follow. Even Elyoner, who I was certain despised me after my defense of the serpent.

"Is there truly enough food for all of us on Scopuli?" she asks, her eyes wandering to little Virginia in her arms.

"More than enough," I say, hiding my heartbreak behind a warm smile. The scouting party will never return here, and Elyoner and Virginia will never reap Scopuli's bounty.

Relief softens her usually harsh features. "God is good to have brought you to us, Lady Thelia."

It's not her god who brought me here, but she's right that they need help.

Young Rose, while showing me her needlework, clicks her tongue disapprovingly when Emme saunters past the Bailies' front window with a sailor named William Berde.

"After what happened with Charles Florrie, she really should be more careful," Rose whispers, so softly I wonder if she intended for me to hear it at all. "Master Berde won't marry her, either."

"Do you wish to marry?" I venture carefully, and when Rose looks to me, it's as if she's aged several decades. Deep purple bags collect beneath her bright blue eyes, and her usually plump lips are pressed into a thin straight line.

"My lady, I am already married. To Master Sampson."

The air leaves my lungs as I remember the old man from Sunday's church service. I try to catch my features as they fall, to keep my expression neutral, but Rose has seen the crack. "He's just so much older than you, I didn't realize . . ."

She smiles sadly. "It's the way of things."

These interactions reveal the truth of this place: Wenefrid, Elizabeth, and Cora aren't the only women who feel restless, trapped. I begin to wonder . . . Could they become my allies?

On the night before the challenge, the near-full moon

shines brightly over Roanoke. Despite Cora's warning of dangers, I easily slip through the city's eastern gate, courtesy of a passed-out Master Chapman, and make my way to the beach once more. Luna bathes the sea in the same luminous light as she does on Scopuli, but here, it makes everything appear harsher, more exposed. Is this how the world looks through Raidne's eyes?

Notes rise into my throat at the thought of her, of Pisinoe. Instead of swallowing them down, I spill them onto the waves, losing myself in the thought of the white-capped crests carrying them all the way to Scopuli. A message for my sisters, just like those messages I whispered into the earth for Proserpina.

I will save us. I promise.

"Your voice is beautiful."

The words shatter my cocoon of sea and song, and I whirl around to face the tangled mess of trees behind me. Cora emerges from them, a lantern raised in one hand.

"You frightened me!" I scold, and though I'm grateful to see her, my hands still tremble. "What are you doing here?"

"I could ask the same of you," she murmurs, drawing in close. "I come here sometimes. To think."

"I thought it was dangerous?"

"It is, so I usually have the beach to myself. What were you singing? I couldn't understand the words."

I shrug, looking back to the waves. "I don't know, really. It just poured out of me."

"It sounded sad."

My eyes flick back to find Cora's emerald stare locked on me. She holds her bottom lip between her teeth, and now I know for certain that my song's magic is gone. Cora doesn't look like a woman enraptured; she looks like she's seen a ghost.

"It was about my sisters," I offer. "I miss them terribly."

"Then it's a good thing you'll see them soon. Do you know when exactly you'll be leaving us?"

My chest tightens—of course she wants me to go. How can I blame her for that, after what she's shared about her future? The one that my presence threatens. "In a few days. Once the ship is loaded with supplies."

"I think Will might try for your hand."

I force myself to keep my expression blank. I hope she's wrong, and I don't want Cora to see that truth written across my face. Regardless of how I feel for him, Cora clearly loves him. How could I keep him from returning with me to Scopuli if he were to be my husband?

"Would you like it if he did?" she asks.

"Your brother is a kind man. I'd be lucky if he won."

"Is that all?"

"What do you mean?"

"I catch you watching him sometimes," she says softly. Her expression is unreadable.

"He looks like someone I loved once." I leave out the second part of that thought—that so does she, and even though they both share features with Proserpina, it's Cora's I search for in Will.

Her desire to ask me more is written in the crease of her brow, but instead she says, "If I was a good person, I'd want him to win for you. But I'm terrified by the idea of him leaving me behind. Of being alone here."

"It wouldn't be forever." Speaking the lie feels like pushing glass through my throat. "You'd join us as soon as the scouting party returned. And until then, you'll still have your friends. And Thomas."

"Will I?"

"What do you mean?"

"He's planning something, Thelia. Please don't make a fool of me and pretend you haven't noticed. Has he told you if he means to compete?"

My hand reaches instinctively for hers, just like it did that first night, but this time, Cora doesn't pull away. How easily our fingers lace together. It makes me want to tell her that I've been falling asleep to the imagined sound of her voice, that I hold the image of her smiling like a treasured secret pressed to my heart. That being near her feels like being with Proserpina again, and that in my weakest moments, I wonder if kissing her feels the same, too. If it feels better.

But I say none of those things. Instead of a confession, what falls from my lips is another lie. "Cora, of course not."

Those spring-ripened eyes search mine for what feels like hours before she eventually nods. Only then does her focus fall to our hands, still clasped.

"Do you believe in fate?" I whisper, and when Cora nods, I squeeze her hand in mine. "You're going to be all right. Fate is on your side."

"How can you possibly know that?" she asks, but for the first time tonight, the ghost of a smile crosses her lips.

I return it with a playful shrug as my attention wanders up to the moon. A sense of calm washes over me as I stand on this foreign shore on the eve of my next victory, fingers still intertwined with Cora's.

How do I know? Because this time, the Fates are finally on mine.

※※※

When the meetinghouse's bell strikes ten, the City of Raleigh will gather to compete for my hand. I still have a few hours to prepare. There's a chill in my bedroom this morning despite the fire that burns, and Margery fills the bath basin with bucket after bucket of water. The steam swirls into the air, inviting me in, and finally, it's ready for me.

Margery disappears to prepare Thomas's breakfast. My eyes flutter closed, and I try to relax into the quiet warmth while I still can. A few moments pass, and the bedroom door creaks back open.

"That was fast," I say, and the only response is a pregnant silence followed by the door clicking back into its place. My eyes flash open, but the room's empty. The hair on the back of my neck prickles with alarm.

"Good morning, Master Thomas." Margery's voice travels from the stairs. Despite the hot water, my body turns to ice. How long would he have gawked if I'd kept quiet? What would I have done if he tried to come inside? I draw my knees to my chest, instinctively trying to make this weak body smaller. The best way for human women to protect themselves is to hide. To shrink into the background, to not draw attention. My sisters would think me mad if they could see me now, curled in on myself and terrified, desperate for the protection of talons and wings.

A gentle knock startles me. But it's Cora who slips inside this time.

"Cora." My voice betrays my surprise. After how much time we spent together on the beach last night, I didn't expect to see her until today's festivities.

"I thought you might need help preparing," she says, her fingers smoothing over her skirts. Is she nervous? "Thomas can be prissy before big events . . . I expect Margery will be busy doting on him."

I nod softly, giving her the space to say more, to ask if he's given any clues to his plans in the short span of hours we've been apart. But Cora doesn't use the opening, and today, we'll discover if the extra attention she's been lavishing on him has worked. My eyes fall away from hers back to the steaming water; I don't want her to read in my gaze what I suspect will happen.

"Let's get you dressed." She holds open a towel for me, and I become acutely aware of my heartbeat, of every single bead of water that rolls down my skin, as I push myself to my feet and will her to look at me. My body aches for her to see me completely bared before her, to take me in, but Cora drops her gaze to the ground and clears her throat. I let her enfold me in the towel's warmth.

We follow the same ritual I did that first morning, except now it's Cora's hands guiding me into the various layers this world requires of its women. Throughout it all, I wish the process were occurring in reverse. My eyes fall closed as she pulls a chemise over my head and straightens it across my shoulders. Although there's a thin layer of fabric between us, her fingers still burn hot against my skin. I want to turn around and take her into my arms, to kiss their calloused tips. Instead, I remain firmly planted in place with a hand on my stomach to steady myself. Her breath kisses the back of my neck as she tightens the laces of today's gown, making my toes curl beneath my skirts. What would it feel like for her to whisper my name there, against my skin?

"It's a beautiful gown," she murmurs, running the warm peach silk through her fingers. "Agnes may be difficult, but she does have good taste." The bodice is embellished with flowers, stitched in blues and pinks, their leaves unfurling across my abdomen. Unlike the other dresses I've worn here, the sleeves on this gown are fitted, save for the areas immediately over my shoulders, which puff out into two little circles. The skirt underneath is full and accented with gold. Cora motions for me to twirl before her. I laugh, suddenly nervous, but concede. Why is it that fully dressed, I blush beneath her stare? It doesn't matter—in this moment, there's nothing I wouldn't do to make her grin, and she does.

It's a dress made for spring, not for the dreadful beginning of winter, which is probably why Agnes deigned to part with it for this occasion. But the fact that its color is out of season doesn't bring Cora any comfort—as she watches me, her features take on a strange, resigned expression, and I know suddenly that Agnes has never bothered to shower Cora with such a lavish gift.

I take her hand in mine, desperate to pull her back to me. "How should I wear my hair?"

Cora mulls over my question as she picks up a comb. "Hmm. Down."

"Really?" I ask, raising an eyebrow. I've yet to see a woman here wear her hair freely.

"You look like our Virgin Queen, with your strawberry hair. It'll excite the men, and besides, it's so beautiful—it would be a shame to hide it. Now come, let me brush it."

Color rises to my cheeks at the compliment, but Cora's thankfully too focused on teasing the tangles from my locks to notice.

Once she's finished, she pulls a tiny pot of red dye from her apron pocket and touches her finger to the concoction. I start to ask her what it is, but then she brings her painted fingertip to my lips to apply the ruby mixture. Energy courses down my spine; my spirit catches in my throat. I don't breathe, afraid even the tiniest shift in the air between us will send her running. But it doesn't. She's close enough that I can smell the roses on her skin. My mind races, incapable of forming a single coherent thought—there's only the marvel of her touch and the overwhelming desire to take that slender finger into my mouth. She steps back to admire her handiwork before I lose myself entirely.

"Well?"

Cora sighs contentedly. "You look perfect."

Before I can bask in her compliment, Margery comes rushing back into the room, flustered.

"Lady Thelia, I'm so sorry. Sir Thomas required my help— Oh! Cora!" Then her eyes fall to me. Her mouth drops.

"Wow." The single word is all she can manage. I blush harder.

"Stop, you two! You're making me nervous!" How strange it is, to almost forget that I'm not who, or what, they believe me to be.

"One of those men is about to become very, very lucky . . ." Margery sighs, and Cora nods in agreement.

"Well, then," Cora says. "Let's go find your future king."

᠌᠌᠌᠌᠌᠌

There is a bite to the morning air, a sharpness that claws down my throat, as if I'm breathing in the salt crystals that form in Scopuli's rocky tide pools during the hot summer months. Their memory coaxes a smile to my lips. Those afternoons spent collecting the briny granules felt so tedious, and though I noted the swaying starfish, so like their twinkling sisters in the heavens, and the colorful crabs scuttling about, I didn't appreciate them. Only now, when the kiss of Scopuli's summer sun feels farther away than it ever has, do I fully understand what I've left behind. A light dusting of snow has settled over the City of Raleigh, and stray flakes still fall slowly from above. They catch on my dress as I make my way to the town square. Margery accompanies me, and I catch her stealing glances in my direction. Her movements are stiff, and although this could be a result of the cold, I have a feeling that it has more to do with her nerves. I force my gaze back ahead, afraid that her anxiety might spread to me, like ink in water, if I watch her for too long. Today, I can't risk being rattled.

Today, I must be strong.

The square is empty when we arrive, and Margery hands me the broom that she carries. The wood is coarse between my palms until I find the worn-in places where she typically holds it, the spots where her work has smoothed its rough exterior into something almost soft. Beads of perspiration collect on the back of my neck. I'm supposed to be preparing for a familiar ritual, and I do my best to appear assertive and proud, though only Margery can say how successful I am. With a deep breath, I flip the broom around so that its bristles face the sky. The broom's tip cuts into the shallow drifts of snow like a blade, and I use it to carve a large circle into the ground. The ring is spacious enough that ten men can stand inside it, packed together shoulder to shoulder.

"Thomas aims to compete," Margery says once I've finished, likely so that I couldn't feign distraction.

"Do you know for certain?" I ask, knowing full well it's a foolish question. Thomas Bailie would never let the chance to be a king fall into someone else's hands.

She scoffs. "He didn't tell me so, but do you really believe he means to sit this out?"

"No," I concede, gritting my teeth.

"Tell him not to. Tell him that you're not interested in him."

Now it's my turn to laugh. "Do you really think he cares if I'm interested or not?"

Margery snaps her mouth closed into a tight, disappointed line. "Cora can't lose him."

Resentment blooms in my stomach at the mention of their union, at the suggestion that its success has anything to do

with me. Shouldn't she know better than most the impossibility of trying to control Thomas's urges?

"I thought he was dangerous," I snap, my tone close to a
hiss.

"Lady Thelia . . ." Margery's blue eyes are wide, worry crin-
kling her brows so close together that I think they might kiss.
"You know what this marriage means for her."

Of course I do. I hear Cora's words ringing in my ears—
I'll never want for anything—and I am suddenly grateful for
the light, tasteless breakfast. Anything rich would be coming
back up.

Never want for anything. Not even for me? I've caught her
stealing glances when she thinks I'm not looking, her bright
eyes filled with a curiosity that extinguishes the second she
knows she's been discovered. But it's foolish to hope that
those looks contain the same desire that's taking root in
me—I have no proof that they do, and even if they did, just
like Proserpina, Cora belongs to another.

For now.

"Then hopefully he abstains for both our sakes," I say
coldly.

Margery doesn't look convinced, but before she can continue the conversation, other townspeople begin to filter into
the square to meet us. The nausea threatens again, and my
right hand moves to rest atop my stomach in a vain attempt
to calm it. It's no use. My breath quickens, but I force my
hand to my side. This chance, this moment, it's what I've
been begging the gods to grant me for centuries. I must be
brave enough to take it.

Instinctively, my eyes close and a song fills my throat, the
same melody that Raidne and Pisinoe sang to me as I left. I
didn't know then what I do now—that the song wasn't only a

goodbye; it was also a gift. The melody grounds me; it reminds me who I am, and when its notes fill my chest, I feel as powerful as I ever have—as if I could snap open the wings I've lost and take to the sky, as if I could raze this entire village to the ground. I'm singing out loud now, but I don't care. Let them believe it part of the ritual. Only when the song ends does a smile crawl upon my painted lips as a satisfied sigh escapes them, as if this is a day I've always known would come and not one that I spent centuries begging for but never believed I'd see.

When I reopen my eyes, the square is full. The crowd watches me with expectant, though not enchanted, stares. As anticipated, the entire village has appeared to watch, though different camps have already emerged: the women and children to my left; a group of about sixty men, who I assume plan to participate, in the center; and a group of older and married men off to the right. Everyone is quiet, but restive, eager for the festivities to start.

And who am I to keep them waiting? I clear my throat.

"The test is straightforward," I say. "Here behind me, I've drawn a circle into the earth. Those who are interested in my hand may wrestle for it. The rules are simple. You may not strike each other, you may not gouge each other's eyes, you may not bite each other, and you may not grab each other's"— I hesitate, looking for the primmest descriptor—"delicate areas. If you leave the confines of the circle, you lose. Two of you will fight at a time. The first person to make the other fall three times is the winner. The winner remains in the circle to compete in the next round. Any questions?"

The men nod their heads, confirming their understanding.

"Who wishes to go first?"

A young boy approaches the circle, and the crowd erupts into cheers. The excitement is so palpable that even I'm buoyed by it. A wisp of blond facial hair adorns his chin, more of a shadow than an actual beard. He's hardly old enough to consider taking a bride, let alone fighting for one.

Is this the age that evil starts to blossom inside a boy's heart?

"What's your name?" I ask sweetly.

"Lewes," he mutters, his face flushed bright red. I grin as I motion for him to enter the circle. His bashfulness would be endearing if I didn't know the violence that his boyish frame will someday be capable of.

"And who challenges Master Lewes?"

An older man named Marke steps forward to join the boy inside the circle. Despite the gray that tinges his hair, he's not frail, and Lewes's fair eyebrows raise to touch his hairline. Marke's skin is weathered and tanned in a way that I would recognize anywhere—this man has spent his life at sea. He's a sailor. My toes squirm in my shoes instinctively, but today, they're only toes, not talons.

Marke assumes a wide stance to plant himself firmly on the ground, and that first action tells me that he'll win.

"Begin!" I command, and almost instantly, Marke has one arm around the boy's throat, pulling his thin frame up off the frozen earth. Lewes kicks his legs wildly, to no avail. Within moments, Marke has thrown him down into the snow with a surprising amount of power.

"One," I count, and even though he still needs to be tossed twice more, Lewes has had enough. The young boy scurries out of the circle, forfeiting his claim as the crowd bursts into laughter. I force a small smile to mirror the townspeople's emotions, but there's no pleasure for me in Lewes's defeat. If anything, may this flirtation with violence sate him for a lifetime.

Marke, on the other hand, is visibly desperate for more.

He clenches and unclenches his fists, skirting the edges of the ring with a victorious smile that cuts across his face like a hideous gash. His bravado makes my own lust for gore take root in the pit of my stomach, and my lips curl back; it's time for someone else to crush him since it can't be me who has that honor. At least not today. "Sir Marke wins the round. Who will challenge him?"

Hugh Taylor, one of Thomas's men, steps forward. Unlike Lewes, Hugh is prepared to take on the older man. As soon as I give the signal to begin, Hugh kicks the back of Marke's knees to force him into a kneeling position. Everyone, including me, lets out a gasp, though I suspect only mine contains pleasure. One. When Marke stands again, Hugh shoves him with such force that the older man stumbles back into the dirt. Two. This seems to galvanize him, because Marke throws himself in Hugh's direction, but Hugh deftly jumps to Marke's left and sticks out his leg. Marke stumbles over it back onto the ground for his third and final fall.

I don't need to ask who's next. Mauris Allen, another of Thomas's inner circle, enters the ring to face and defeat Hugh. Then he beats Cuthbert White, but he is too exhausted to keep his streak going, so Charles Florrie quickly outpaces him. Emme's expression darkens as she watches Charles, and it dawns on me that most of the women here have secret histories with these men I'll never be privy to. It's hard to see Emme's round face with none of its usual warmth, and though Charles loses his next match, the pain he feels right now doesn't absolve him of the debt he's accrued by hurting Emme.

I'll make him pay. I swear it.

Emme's eyes flick to mine. Her stare is cold and distant, just like the sea that brought me here. Does she somehow sense the vow I've just made? The sound of bodies colliding draws her attention back to the ring, and I exhale my relief slowly through gritted teeth.

One by one they fight, throwing each other's frames into the ground, crushing each other into the dirt. The snow inside the circle melts under the heat of their bodies, and the number of participating men begins to dwindle.

After several matches, Griffen Jones stands triumphantly after forcing Brian Wyles from the circle. No one moves to challenge him, and I've stepped forward to declare Griffen the winner when I catch sight of Cora from across the ring. Her eyes have grown wild, and Emme, who's moved to stand beside her, meets my gaze with an equally alarmed expression. And then I see why.

Thomas has entered the circle. A series of hushed whispers tear through the spectators. Only Agnes looks calm, having known this moment was coming. Her close confidant, Jane Mannering, whispers something into her ear, but Agnes holds up a hand to silence her.

"What are you waiting for?" Thomas goads. "Start the match."

I look again to Cora, but her eyes are no longer on Thomas—they're on me, and they're pleading. I have no reason to object, no reason to stop this, but still, I find that my words waver on my tongue. Thomas clears his throat expectantly.

I can save you all, but I need more blood.

I'm sorry, Cora.

I close my eyes and say it. "Begin."

When I open them again, something in Cora's expression has broken, and I'm swallowed by the fear that allowing this was a grave mistake. Griffen is far larger than Thomas, and for a moment, I dare to hope that Griffen will trounce him. But to my horror, he bows to Thomas instead.

"I'm not worthy of the prize of your hand," he says, but it's hardly a reason. That was true before he entered the ring, and it didn't stop him from crossing into its boundary.

"You forfeit?" My voice betrays my surprise. Griffen answers by excusing himself into the crowd.

Thomas smirks and folds his arms across his chest, looking back over the faces of the eligible men. No one moves. My heartbeat rings in my ears, and despite the cold air, I feel suddenly flushed.

"Who challenges Sir Thomas?" I ask, and still no one comes forward.

"Well, then," Thomas says, turning to face me with a wicked smirk. "It looks like I'm the winner—"

"I'll challenge him," Will shouts, pushing himself from the throng to step into the circle. Somehow, this only makes things worse.

Rage flashes across Thomas's face, but he manages to bury the emotion beneath a collected exterior. "Are you sure, Will?"

If the question is meant to force Will into submission, it has the opposite effect. Something in his expression hardens, and he nods.

"You may—" I start, but before I can finish speaking, the two men are at each other's throats.

The only sounds that fill the otherwise silent square are the *thuds* of their bodies colliding. Thomas is bigger than Will, more muscular, but he's also slower. Will dodges most of Thomas's blows, and for a glittering moment, I'm hopeful that this won't end badly. But Will's ability to elude him only makes Thomas more aggressive, and he somehow manages to grab Will by his sable locks. As soon as he does, he yanks Will's head back. Bile rises into my throat—he'll snap his oldest friend's neck for my hand. Cora must fear the same, for she lets out a pitiful wail, and the sound breaks Thomas's attention away long enough for Will to throw his entire weight backward onto him. The force sends them both into the dirt.

"One. For both of you. Now separate," I command, though my voice delivers it as a plea.

They obey, but only long enough to get back onto their feet, and then they're at it again. This time, Thomas grabs hold of Will's arm and, with surprising strength, lifts him to throw him over his shoulder. Will drops like a stone onto his back.

"Two-one."

When Will rises to his feet, there's a determination in his eyes that makes me sick. What if it's not enough? But having the lead makes Thomas cocky, and he charges to try to repeat the same move for the final toss. Except this time, Will sees him coming and expertly steps aside to copy Hugh's tactic, leaving his foot in Thomas's path. It's too late for Thomas to stop himself—he trips over Will's ankle and falls to the ground.

"Two-two."

Now Thomas is furious, but despite my wishes, he doesn't charge again. The two circle each other, their chests heaving. The vapor from their combined breaths cocoons them in a haze. They orbit each other like that for what feels like hours, but then Thomas cracks. He throws a fist at Will's face that connects squarely with Will's left eye, and then he sends his other fist into Will's jaw. The blow splits open Will's lip, and a trail of blood flies through the air.

"Stop!" I shriek. "You're not allowed to strike each other!"

But my words have little effect. Will's doubled over, one hand holding his face, the other propping himself up against his knee. Thomas uses the time to sidle behind him, and with one swift movement, he wraps a muscular arm around Will's neck and begins to squeeze. For a few painful moments the only sound is Will's gasps for air; his face turns a sickening shade of red.

"Enough!" I say. "That's enough!"

But no one moves to stop them. Even Cora seems resigned, for she's turned away to bury her head in Emme's shoulder.

And then Will's body goes limp. The blood rushes to my head, but I see what Thomas doesn't: Will's feigning his defeat, and Thomas, convinced of his victory, loosens his grip. The exact moment he does, Will grabs hold of Thomas's arm, his left hand atop Thomas's elbow and his right on Thomas's wrist, and then he throws his weight to the left. It opens enough space between their two bodies for Will to strike the top of Thomas's right thigh with his right fist.

Thomas is shocked by the sudden hit and looks down to see the cause. As he does so, Will swiftly raises his right arm back up and connects his elbow with Thomas's jaw with a sickening *crack*. The blow is enough to force Thomas to release him, and when he does, Will whirls around and gives him one final, forceful shove into the ground. Thomas lands on his back with a loud *thump*.

It's time to end this now, before any other surprises occur.

"That's three!" I scream. "Will is the winner!"

The crowd, equally unsettled, remains quiet.

Thomas's face flickers as he processes the unlikely turn of events, but Will spins around and extends him a hand. Thomas takes it and rises to his feet, and Will claps his shoulder. The two lock eyes, and neither one speaks until Thomas erupts into an exaggerated smile. It chills me, but it has the opposite effect on most of the crowd. Lulled into a sense of security, they go wild with applause. Except for the women. Though smiles grace their lips, their eyes are all haunted.

"Congratulations on a good fight, Will!" Thomas says. Will looks unsure but ultimately nods, apparently deciding to believe him. Then Thomas releases Will's hand and turns to the crowd, sweeping his arms open as if to invite the entire square into an embrace. "Shall we celebrate?"

᠄᠄᠄

I try to reach for Cora, but I lose her in a sea of people swelling to the meetinghouse. I'm handed a goblet of ale the second I cross the threshold. Someone is already playing a stringed instrument, its music upbeat and lively. If this were any other day, I'd be tempted to ask its player to show it to me, but my eyes are already scanning the room for familiar faces. Elizabeth, Elyoner, and Rose flock to me, followed by Margery, who looks as shaken as I feel.

"Where's Cora?" My voice betrays my concern. Rose lowers her eyes, and Elyoner excuses herself. They all know how furious she must be, and it's clear as day in the way they worry at their lips and fingernails that, on some level, they find me responsible. Indignation at the injustice of their blame paints my cheeks red, but it burns as brilliantly and as quickly as a falling star. This is my fault, after all. Without my curse, without me, none of this would have happened.

"There." Margery tilts her head to the back corner of the room. "But give her some space for now."

I follow the motion of her nod. Cora's back is to me, but her posture is rigid. Thomas, with his exaggerated smile, is visible from over her shoulder as he offers all sorts of explanations to placate her. I wish I could see her face, I *need* to see her face, to know if she believes his words. But how can she? He's just exposed the undeniable fact that her feelings matter very little to him, and he's done it before the entire colony.

Besides the cloud over the two of them, the mood is jovial.

A few couples begin to dance, and even Agnes giggles over her glass of ale, though it's hard to believe her upbeat attitude is anything more than an elaborate farce. It's more likely that she's already divining some scheme or another, but there's no need for that. I'll allow Thomas to join us on our trip back to Scopuli, along with any other willing men. But what of Cora and the other women I've come to know?

I sip my own drink and scan the crowd. I don't know who I'm looking for until I find Will's face, but when I do, a wave of relief, of gratitude, floods over me. It feels strange, to be this happy to see a man all right. But his intervention is the only reason I haven't lost Cora entirely, a fact that endears him to me more than I care to admit. If Thomas had won, she would rightfully despise me. But he didn't, thanks to Will. Will smiles when he finds me staring, and he slides through the crowd to meet me, taking my hand into his.

"Want to dance?" he asks, a single green eye glittering. The other is purple and swollen shut, and the skin across his neck is still raw from Thomas's choke hold. His clothes are torn and covered in filth from being thrown to the ground. Will is an attractive man, but currently, he looks pitiful.

"Absolutely not!" I reach to touch just below his bruised socket. He winces and jerks his head away from my fingers. "Let's find something cold to put on this . . ."

"I've had worse, Lady Thelia. It's all right. The best remedy is a dance." I open my mouth to protest, but he's already pulling me toward the dance floor.

"No, Will!" I say, moving quickly to keep the sloshing ale in the goblet away from my expensive dress. "I don't know the steps!"

"You, my queen, don't need to," he says, and the next thing I know, we're spinning around the circle, my drink spraying as we go. The room becomes a blur of color, with Will's smile the only thing in focus.

In the cacophony of the celebration, and with the kiss of alcohol on everyone's breath, it's almost easy to forget that he hasn't won my hand in marriage or the treasure of an ancient kingdom, but rather a horrific death by my hand.

Does he deserve to be a sacrifice for our freedom? I think about how he watches Thomas with a desire he'll never be able to name aloud, and against my better judgment, my heart softens for him.

But what about the story Cora told me about the indiscriminate slaughter of the people on the mainland? Will still chose to sail across the sea knowing what his predecessors did. And since arriving, not a single person has tried to right the violence their forebears wrought. Instead, they happily erect walls and point their weapons in the faces of those whose villages they razed, whose families they murdered.

"I need some air," I say, pulling myself from Will's arms. He releases me without question.

"Of course, Lady Thelia, but try not to linger—it's unusually cold this year, and though the ale will warm your bones, don't be deceived by it."

I nod, touched by his thoughtfulness, and slip from the group to head outside to the meetinghouse's southern edge. There are no people out here; my only company is the orange glow from the windows and the sounds of laughter and music that waft through the air. Will is right about the temperature. I hold myself tight to keep warm.

The sun is low in the sky, and pointed roofs pierce the twilight. In the eastern sky, my second dazzling full moon crests the horizon, painted orange by the last light of day. A shiver snakes up my spine, but the chill isn't the cause. It's the anticipation of what's to come: In the next few days, I'll bring Will and as many men as the Council will allow to Scopuli. With any luck, we'll break the curse well before the third full moon graces the sky. But then what? I could return here for the women and children, but would they want my help after the incredible cost they unknowingly paid for it? Would Cora?

Movement in the shadows pulls me from my thoughts. It's Thomas, emerging from the darkness. The mask of happiness he wore before the crowd is gone. In its place is something sinister. He staggers as he approaches, and the scent of alcohol hits me before he's within arm's reach. Whatever he's drinking is stronger than the ale being served inside.

"You were mine," he growls, reaching out for me. I take a step back to dodge his touch. "And then that bastard—"

"Beat you," I finish for him. "We weren't destined to be, Master Thomas."

"Bullshit," he sneers. "No one else here deserves you. They're all peasants, the dregs of society forced to come here because they had no other options back in England. My father was one of the men chosen to lead this sorry lot with me as his successor, and I *will* make it profitable."

"Funny," I say, a smile creeping onto my lips, "I heard your father decided you weren't fit to lead."

He pins me against the meetinghouse so hard that the wooden wall scratches my back through my chemise, bodice, overdress, and cloak. My heart beats wildly in my chest; I haven't felt this particular fear—the sense of dread that comes with knowing that you are weak, that you are the prey—since that night those first sailors bound our wrists and plotted our demise. The type of fear known only to us deemed lesser, when the powerful decide to take what they want from us by force.

And this time, I have no song to save me. I'm as helpless as Proserpina was that fateful night, all those years ago. Terror courses through my veins as Thomas presses his body harder into mine. I speak so much of justice, but what about the justice owed to me? Was my curse truly penance enough for Proserpina's fate, or was all of this—the human form, the ability to leave Scopuli, the loss of my magic—meant only to bring me here, to this exact moment, so that Thomas can take me as forcefully, as brutally, as Dis took her? I close my eyes, desperate to recoil from his hot, sour breath, but there's nowhere to escape to, though even I can't deny that this is exactly what I deserve.

"Enough, Thomas," a sharp female voice scolds, and Thomas releases me like a retriever drops a duck at its master's feet. My eyes snap open, shocked at the sudden cold that replaces Thomas's closeness. Agnes stands behind him, arms folded across her chest and a dark look plastered across her features. For the briefest moment, I think that she'll scold him for his vile behavior, but it isn't disgust that paints her delicate features. It's irritation. His boorishness offends her, not his actions, as if he merely trampled her favorite flowers. "Leave us."

Thomas growls like an animal, but he listens to her, trudging from the meetinghouse's glow into the shadows and out of sight. My heart still beats like a caged bird, and I watch the spot where the darkness swallows him, but the rebuked man does not return.

"My son can be impetuous when he drinks," she explains, as if this is a valid explanation for restraining a woman against her will. I look up at her incredulously, but she continues before I can retaliate. "Pay him no mind."

"Thelia?" Will rounds the corner and finds us both standing there. "Ah, Mistress Bailie, good evening!"

"Good evening, Will," she nearly sings, her voice now sweet. The quickness with which she can shift between personalities is something to behold. "I was just saying good night to Lady Thelia."

"Retiring so early?"

"Someday you'll be as old as me. Then you'll understand." She winks at him before taking a few steps back from us both. "Enjoy the rest of your evening, you two! What a handsome match you make."

If Will hears the venom that coats her words, his face doesn't betray it. In fact, he smiles after her affectionately, as if he were watching his own mother retreat. Only once she's gone does Will notice my expression and ask, "Is everything all right?"

"Thomas," I say, and Will's eyes darken.

"I knew he'd be upset," he admits. "But I needed to do something. For Cora." Shame swells in my gut—of course. Will had no intention of competing for my hand until his sister's future demanded it.

"Be careful, Will," I warn. "He was furious. I worry what he might do."

"Thomas is my oldest friend," he says. As he speaks of him, his eyes soften, despite everything he knows. "He's petulant and spoiled, certainly, but he just needs to drink this off. He'll take a few days to lick his wounds, but then he'll be all right. We settled our differences in the ring. That's where they'll stay."

I chew on my bottom lip, unsure of what exactly to say next.

"I hope you're right."

It's all that I can muster because I know that he's not.

Overhead, the moon glitters as brilliantly as a diamond. The sight should bring elation, but as Will and I stand bathed in her ethereal light, I can't shake the feeling that I'm on the brink of losing everything.

᛬᛬᛬

Will's prediction about Thomas proves true enough. The day following the challenge, I barely see him at all. I wake early to join him for the Council meeting, but instead I find a flustered Margery in the kitchen.

"Where's Master Thomas?"

"Gone already." Her face is pinched with worry.

"What's wrong?"

"Have you looked outside yet?"

I shake my head, and Margery tilts her chin toward the back door. "Go see."

Light spills inside, so bright that it blinds me. In this moment of weakness, the air, now far colder than last night's, rushes forward and snaps my skin between its teeth. The combined effect is disorienting, and several breaths pass before shapes begin to form in the wall of white that my vision's become—the City of Raleigh is covered in snow, its harsh edges softened beneath a glittering white blanket. Smoke curls from the top of each cottage's chimney, and the scent of burning pine hangs heavy in the air. All the while, large, wet flakes continue to fall from the heavens.

And it's quiet. This is the first time I've seen the streets completely empty. Margery's footprints entering the kitchen and Thomas's footprints leaving it, both already half filled once more with fresh powder, are the only indication that anyone's managed to rouse themselves from bed. It's as if the entire colony collectively decided that today is a day for rest. Its beauty erases Margery's worry from my mind until the frigid air forces me to close the door to the sparkling world.

"We have no record of it getting this cold, of it ever snow-ing like this here." Margery's voice is grave as she adds more wood to a pile of coals in the hearth.

"It's going to be all right, Margery." I draw closer to her, holding my hands before the budding flames to warm them. "I'm going to meet with the Council today to plan our departure—"

Her tone takes on a sympathetic lilt that can only be pity. "Oh, my lady, they won't let you join a Council meeting."

"What do you mean? I'm the only one who knows where Scopuli is. How can they plan to sail there without me?"

"They won't be planning to sail anywhere. Not with the weather like this. It's too dangerous to be at sea when it's this cold."

A soft ringing begins in my ears, and I shake my head to try to expel it. "No, that's not right—Master Thomas said that we'd leave within the week."

Margery smiles sadly. "Was that before or after he lost to Master Waters?"

I turn away from the hearth, unable to bear the truth of her words. It makes the ringing in my ears grow even louder, and my hands find the back of a chair to steady myself. "I need to speak to them, to Thomas, right away. Do you know where he went?"

"No, my lady, but he's never gone long." An iron pot clangs behind me as she hangs it over the fire, and then two warm hands find my shoulders. "Come, sit with me and wait for him."

But morning creeps along, and Thomas doesn't return. Even Agnes remains scarce, and the idea of them both colluding somewhere makes me want to crawl out of my skin.

"Why don't you go rest?" Margery asks after a time, her nerves shot after a full morning of balancing my worry with her own. Being alone is the last thing I want, but I owe her some peace, so I retreat to my room and suffer time's sluggishness alone.

The sound of his footsteps finally graces the stairwell sometime well into the afternoon. They pause before my door, and my ears strain, expecting to hear the *creak* of hinges. But the sound never comes, and so I throw open the door for him.

"Master Thomas, there you are!" I say, doing my best to strain my lingering irritation from my tone. "I've been wanting to speak with you."

A coy smile crawls over his lips as he closes the gap between us, his hands moving to brace himself on my doorframe. "Is that so? What about, my lady?"

I force my feet to remain planted where they are, even when he leans his body in closer to mine. "Did you speak with the Council today? When can we return to Scopuli?"

Thomas's smile falls into the impression of a pout, and he reaches to take a lock of my hair between his fingers. "Why would I rush to send you into another man's marriage bed?"

I balk, stunned by his brazenness. "You said we'd leave within the week."

"Even if I wanted us to leave now, the weather isn't on your side, my lady."

"What are you saying?" I hate how my voice climbs an octave without my permission. "That we're stuck here until spring? Thomas, your own people will starve—"

I should have known that a plea to his humanity would have no effect; his stores are fuller than the other villagers'. He'll survive the winter regardless, and the smug smile that still graces his lips confirms it.

"Don't fret, my lady. This weather is unusual. It'll warm up soon enough."

"But even if it does, I'll still be promised to Will—"

His fingers curl into a fist around my hair, and instinct drives me away from him. Thankfully, Thomas releases me without a fight, but the relief is short-lived as his smile contorts into a hideous, knowing grin. I'm frozen by the sight of it, by the knowledge that we're both remembering last night and how it felt for him to press me against the meetinghouse. He uses the opportunity to devour me with those cold blue eyes. But the slightest shift of his body forward is enough to shatter the spell, and my hands fly to the lip of the door, ready to slam it closed.

Thomas laughs and raises his palms in submission as he falls back, turning to continue to his own room. I watch him for several breaths, closing the door only once I'm certain he won't come charging for me.

But distance doesn't stop him from landing one last sickening blow. His voice floats down the hall, slipping into my quarters just before my door clicks into place.

"I guess we'll have to wait and see what happens, won't we?"

11

BEFORE

I wait for times when Pisinoe and Raidne are occupied and slip away to Jaquob's hut. His strength isn't returning, and despite my insistence, he refuses to eat the meat that I bring him, feigning fullness. A trapper by trade, he has a deep familiarity with landscapes and the food they're capable of producing. He suspects the meat for what it is, but he never questions its origins. After a time, I stop bringing it.

His wound festers for the first few days, the open gash irritated by the midday heat. Thick yellow pus drenches his bandage. Flies begin to linger on his camp's periphery, hovering in the heavy air like sentinels, their one-toned drone nature's death knell. I try to prepare myself for the likelihood that he won't survive, but the thought is painful—if he dies now, my deceit will have been for nothing. Proserpina hasn't revealed his purpose, and her silence burrows beneath my skin like a tick on a deer; I can't shake the unease it brings, leaving me no choice but to bear it.

And yet, to my surprise, Jaquob lives. After his first week, the wound stops leaking. It begins to close after the second.

The flies end their vigil, and Jaquob's energy slowly returns. He starts to laugh; he starts to leer.

My bare breasts distract him, so I take to wearing clothes around him. It's been centuries now since those first sailors' ropes burned my wrists, but in Jaquob's presence, the memory is never far. It lingers in the shadows that pool beneath the beach plums and speckled alders, begging me not to let my guard down. But Jaquob never threatens me, and slowly, that kindness softens my edges.

"Was your mother a fae?" he wonders aloud one afternoon. He's finally stopped asking me what I am, accepting that I'll never give him a satisfactory answer. Now he offers suggestions of his own. His angels didn't fit, nor did the Valkyries. The afterlife I guide deserving men toward isn't a glorious one.

We're curled up inside his tent made of sticks and pelts, lounging on a pile of furs. Very little space separates our frames, a distance that seems to grow smaller and smaller as the days pass. To my surprise, I find that I enjoy his company.

Would I have enjoyed other men's company, too? The question lingers uncomfortably, a more palatable version than the one I'm too scared to ask: *Was killing them wrong?*

The air is heavy today, and heat collects inside the tent. Summer, Proserpina's favorite season, is officially over. Still, Scopuli's meadows are heavy with flowers: purple asters and coneflowers, though no new lilies emerge to join the bloom that brought Jaquob's ship. It's been nearly three weeks now, and its elegant stalk now bends beneath the weight of its blossom; its vibrant orange petals curl at the edges. Each day that passes brings it closer to returning to the earth, and still, Proserpina is silent.

"A fae?" I respond slowly, reluctant to leave my reverie.

Even the newness of Jaquob isn't enough to lure me away from the thought of her.

"A fairy. Like Melusine."

I've learned during our short time together that he loves to tell stories; though we both have chimeric bodies and an affinity for water, I have little else in common with his half-serpent woman.

"I don't know if there are any fae in New France, but there are definitely spirits."

"Tell me about some." I lean into his words, desperate for more. Spirits, humans call them, when they're so often more—lesser gods and their children. Could there be others like us close by, separated by only a thin boundary of magic?

He props himself up on an elbow to face me.

"There's one that's said to arrive with the winter. They're emaciated creatures with pallid skin, as large as giants. They eat human flesh."

My gaze locks on the crude ceiling above, where I trace the cracked lines in the dried leather, hopeful that my silence doesn't betray the dread that pulls my muscles taut.

"Each human they consume makes them grow larger, so their stomachs are never full. They roam the northern forests, always hungry, always in pursuit of meat."

I've punished so many men, and it's never been enough to sate the fury I carry in the pit of my stomach. My mood darkens. "It sounds like they're cursed."

Like me.

I turn my head away from him, trying to hide the tears that mist my eyes at the recognition of myself in his tale: a bewitched immortal, doomed to feed on the flesh of men.

"Tell me another story," I add, knowing the task will keep him from scrutinizing the dark cloud that's swallowed me. Jaquob has no problem complying.

"Have I told you about this pendant I carry around my neck? Supposedly, it's a relic of Saint Jerome. His remains were originally interred in Bethlehem, and although the Church won't admit it, when they transferred his body to Rome, he didn't make it there in his entirety."

I don't understand most of what he says, but my ears do know one word: *Rome*. A smile tugs at the corner of my lips—so the city Anchises prophesized still stands.

Jaquob is too busy pulling a golden chain from beneath his shirt to catch the flicker of recognition in my eyes. Once it's free, he lifts its pendant so the sapphire in its center catches the light. My fingers brush against it, as softly as a whisper.

"It opens here." He turns the pendant onto its side to reveal a small seam between two golden plates, and the clasp that keeps them closed. It's a locket. "There's a piece of his robes inside."

"What's a saint?" I ask, turning to face him again. Surprise sweeps across his features, widening his eyes, parting his lips. But he doesn't laugh at my ignorance, nor does he linger on it.

"A saint," he begins, "is a person who is holy, who has a closer likeness to God than the rest of us."

"Are they gods, too, or just their children?"

This question elicits another smile, and he reaches to trace his fingers along my cheek as if he's not sure exactly what he's dealing with, as if he needs to prove to himself that I'm real. They're a shock against my skin, and I recoil instinctively. Outside the tent, the memory of being bound vibrates in the shadows, warning against the warmth that rises in my chest.

He smiles sadly, but he doesn't press me. "Where I'm from, we believe there's only one God, and he only had one son. Saints are mortal men."

Now it's my turn to look shocked. "Only one child? Why? Did his son castrate him?"

Jaquob erupts with laughter. The sound's infectious, and soon we're both howling.

"When I was young, there were many gods *and* goddesses. But that was a long time ago. What made Saint Jerome more godlike than other men?"

"He was blessed with an ear for languages. He translated our holy text from Hebrew into Latin."

"And why do you wear a scrap of his clothing around your throat?"

"Because saints are sacred. I figure it can't hurt to keep a conduit to God close. Think of all the miracles it might be performing without me realizing it."

I shrug, conceding his point, and a pregnant silence settles in the space between us. He slides in closer to me, and my pulse thumps loudly in my ears.

"What happened to you, Thelxiope?" His voice is a whisper, so quiet I have to strain to hear it. His hand reaches for my face again, and when I try to look away, his fingers gently guide my gaze back to his. I feel the color rising to my cheeks beneath his stare.

"Being here, like this, is a punishment." I don't have the energy to explain everything to him; I don't owe him access to my most painful memories.

"Your gods are cruel."

"*All* gods are cruel," I counter, and he has nothing to say in response.

Instead, he leans his head closer and presses his lips against mine. I've never been kissed by a man, only by Proserpina, and though he's gentle, it still feels treacherous. Outside the tent, insects churr in the afternoon haze and my memory screams.

My hands find his chest, and I push him away as a storm of emotions clash for control: the terror, yes, of him managing to physically hurt me, but also desire—why shouldn't I let myself enjoy this? Is that why Proserpina sent him? And, oh, gods, now the guilt. "I already told you—I'm not your friend, Jaquob."

"Don't be cruel, Thelxiope." His eyes are pleading, and he reaches for my hand, but his baiting has the opposite effect. As soon as the word *cruel* passes over his lips, I'm struck by the image of the dead women who washed ashore with his ship. Suspicion unfurls inside my gut, but I don't voice it yet.

"Being cruel would be allowing you to believe you're safe here."

The sparkle of longing vanishes from his eyes, replaced by a flash of annoyance. "You never let me forget."

His words hang in the air before settling into silence, and I draw my feathered knees into my chest.

"Can I ask you something?"

"Anything." His desperation to route the conversation back to flirtation is palpable in how he lifts his chin to me. He wants me to offer myself. Men, even the ones who are pleasant to be around, are obnoxiously predictable.

"The day your ship washed up on the beach, we found seven women."

In the moment of a blink, his lips press into a cold, straight line, but then they twist down with confusion. "That doesn't sound like a question."

"Who were they?"

He turns his attention to the tent's entrance. A gentle breeze blows through the glade behind us, rustling the autumn-soaked leaves. "I didn't know there were any women aboard."

"How could you not have known?" I ask incredulously, but then I remember the marks around their wrists. Is it possible that their presence was hidden from him? "Don't lie to me. Please."

He takes my hand in his and brings it to his lips, then meets my gaze once more. "I don't know anything about them, I swear it. It's unlucky to have women aboard, so perhaps their presence explains how we ended up here."

A lump rises in my throat, and I cough gently to clear it.

No, dear Jaquob. You and your men were fated to land here, women aboard or not. But why?

Am I simply supposed to save him? Because I didn't save her the night she was taken, and after she ate those pomegranate seeds, no one could?

I've never been able to fully accept she was tricked into doing so. As her closest friend, her other half, I tell myself it's because she was too clever for that. But isn't believing so the darkest kind of wish fulfillment? If she chose, then her fate isn't entirely my fault.

Except what reason could she possibly have had to commit herself to that place? To Dis? Heat blisters beneath my skin, and my palms grow slick. This is usually where my line of questioning comes to an abrupt halt, a book slammed closed to avoid learning its ending.

Did she do it because she decided to love him? Is that what all of this is? Her way of showing me that it's safe for me to love someone, too?

I won't love again, I *can't* love again, not without her explicit blessing.

"What happens next?" I blurt out, and he looks puzzled. But of course he is—it's not really a question for him. "What's your plan? You can't stay here."

He watches me measuredly, taken aback by my outburst.

"I suppose I'll need to build a boat," he posits. "But that's no small task. It'll take a few weeks."

My body vibrates with the suggestion. Three weeks. It's been three weeks with no word from her, so I will force her hand. Either she can tell me what he's for or he can return to the sea. I'll no longer sit idly by and wait for the gods to dole out their favors, and for one single time in the entirety of our pitiful existence here, I won't grovel in blood for her mother's mercy.

"I understand," I say, and I do. "Is there a way I can help?"

"I could find a lot of what I'll need if you let me search Scopuli's beach—"

"No." I'm surprised by the power behind my voice, the finality. "It's not possible, and I forbid you to ask me again."

"But you said—"

"Draw me the pieces you need, and I'll find them for you, but you can't go anywhere near Scopuli."

"I'm growing restless here," he admits.

"This will give you something to do, and then you'll be off," I say, marveling at how quickly relief unspools the tension in my muscles. This isn't a perfect plan, but it's something. For the first time since stumbling across his broken body, I feel a semblance of control.

"Well, then. It sounds like I'm building a boat."

⌕⌕⌕

Cursed spirits and drowned maidens visit me in dreams. I'm soaring over Scopuli headfirst into an approaching storm. The clouds are rolling in too quickly, too fast for any natural squall. Lightning forks across the sky in a thousand different directions, its force sending me spiraling downward. All around me, thunder tears open the heavens.

I fall to the beach where the dead women from the wreck stand vigil. They face Rotunda, pointing decaying fingers at the island across the strait. Their eyes have rotted away, but they watch me still with wide, empty sockets. Bloated tongues fill their open mouths, which try to wail, but the only sound that escapes is the gurgle of the water that choked them as it spills out of their throats. Their sorrow, their rage, it's so heavy, and it's directed not only at Jaquob, but at me—I want to beg for forgiveness for my part in their fates, want to ask them how I can fix it, but before I can, their swaying bodies fade, replaced by a field of lilies.

Proserpina lies in its center, and a gaunt creature crouches over her middle. Its skin is gray and too small for its frame, stretched so tightly across its body that all the bones beneath are visible. It's a monster of vertebrae and ribs and scapulae, all angles and edges. A set of horns—or are they branches?—adorn its misshapen head and stretch to the sky like a crown. When it raises its hideous face to look at me, my feet fall back in alarm. I know the black eyes that bore into mine. Although he's little more than a skull, I'd recognize him anywhere.

Dis.

Blood drips from his razored teeth, and his lips curl into a twisted smile. He's been feeding from her, eating the contents of her gut cavity. A swarm of black flies erupts from the wound and encircles his head in a dark, pulsating halo. Their buzzing fills my ears. I turn to run as Dis unleashes a victorious, hateful laugh.

"Thelia!" Proserpina screams for me, her voice broken by my betrayal. And although there's nothing I want more than to save her, I don't look back.

12

NOW

Dread's grip on the settlement is temporarily relieved at the end of the month by Yule. The holiday draws us to the meetinghouse, now adorned with laurel and holly leaves, to celebrate two nights after the solstice. Their green and red flashes are a welcome sight—they're the only color that winter hasn't buried beneath an unrelenting cloak of white. Candle flames dance in every window, and the air inside the meetinghouse is heavy with cinnamon, cloves, and wine. Alcohol warms my frost-kissed cheeks, and when I spy the rosy complexions on Margery, Wenefrid, and Rose, I find I'm not alone.

All around, the townspeople swirl in their finest clothes. There's Agnes, her tinkly, forced laugh emanating from across the room as she speaks with Master Sampson. Rose stands by his side, doing her best impression of a captivated wife, but the way her fingers strum along the side of her mug reveals her boredom. When her friend Jane rushes past, dodging the obvious advances from Master James Lacie, Rose politely excuses herself from her husband's side and inserts herself between the two, allowing Jane time to escape. The simple act of kindness makes me smile.

Thomas bursts through the large wooden doors with a piece of a tree trunk in his arms, its roots dangling near his feet. The colonists erupt into applause as he carries the log to the center of the room, where he makes a show of sitting on top of it. Everyone gathers around him, but I hang back, apprehension slowing my limbs as the comfort I felt moments ago dissipates like dew in the late morning sun.

My mind wanders to my sisters. Imagining them before a roaring fire inside our little hut as Scopuli's fierce winter winds roar outside makes my chest ache with longing.

Thomas clears his throat, returning my focus to the scene at hand. Cora, dressed in emerald as his winter queen, hands him a mug of ale. Watching her with Thomas is worse than it was watching Proserpina with the potential suitors Ceres invited to the palace. Proserpina never reveled in their attention. Cora, on the other hand, radiates affection for Thomas. When he takes the mug from her and rewards her with a kiss on the cheek, Cora beams, sinking my mood deeper into shadow.

"Welcome be thou, Heaven King," he begins to sing, and a hush settles over the room. Though I despise him, even I must admit that he has a certain charisma. I scan the crowd, and everyone's eyes save for mine are locked on him. Their stares are carefree and jovial, unbothered by the fact that the hold he has over them is dangerous. It's slower than a song capable of driving them into the sea, but just as deadly. Would they be fawning so much if they knew he refused to send the scouting party to Scopuli even after that first snow melted away?

"Welcome born in one morning.

"Welcome for whom we shall sing.

"Welcome for whom we shall sing, welcome Yule!"

He raises his glass, and the room joins him in the next round to finish the song. Thomas pulls himself from the stump and invites another to take his seat. Will steps forward, and everyone hollers and claps for him, despite the darkness that flickers between the two. The black eye that Thomas gave him has finally healed, but a deeper rift remains. Thomas has been cold to Will. Not in an obvious way, but it's now Hugh Taylor whom he seeks to accompany him into the woods to hunt. It's Charles Florrie who joins him in the tavern to drink. It's Mauris Allen who's constantly sidled up beside him. I've tried to broach the topic with Will, but he dismisses my concerns.

"He didn't like losing in public," he says. "But he'll come around eventually."

When Will starts to sing, his notes melt my anxiety away, replacing it with a stubborn sense of pride. His voice is better than Thomas's, and relief that he won my hand washes over me.

No, he didn't, a nagging voice scolds. I press my index finger and thumb to the bridge of my nose to steady my thoughts. How have I done it again? Will isn't my betrothed, I'm not a princess, and my only reason for being here is to survive until spring so these men will follow me home. But the longer I'm in the City of Raleigh, the easier it is to forget. This life, so unencumbered by ancient curses, mythical beasts, and angry, vengeful gods, is starting to feel more and more real.

But it's not. Not for me.

I have a debt that must be paid, and its price is blood. When the weather breaks and we sail for Scopuli, my betrothed will die alongside Thomas. And though my heart breaks for Cora and Will both, I can't see a way out of this.

Perhaps I'm the one who's truly damned after all, and I'm too foolish to see it.

I take a large sip of warm wine, trying to push these thoughts from my mind and enjoy myself. Will makes that easy, his voice deep and rich. Like Thomas, he retires from his wooden throne after one tune, and the rest of the villagers take turns singing their favorite carols. Only once everyone is good and drunk do the men roll the log toward the large fireplace and set it ablaze. The meaning of today's spectacles is entirely lost on me.

Emme, halfway through her latest mug of spiced wine, finds me. She laughs sweetly as she pulls me into an embrace. "I'm glad you're here."

"Me too," I whisper into her frizzy hair and produce a tiny present from my skirts. After the challenge, Mistress Bailie reluctantly gave me the key to the locked room where they put my treasure for safekeeping. With Will as the official winner of my hand, she lost the pretense of protecting it, though she did insist I ask Will's permission before removing anything. When I broached the topic of giving gifts to some of the women over supper with the Bailies last night, Will simply laughed.

"We're not married yet, my lady. Those are your riches, not mine."

Rage ignited Agnes's features for the span of a breath, but though she regained her composure quickly, I still saw the crack. I could've kissed Will for that alone, if there weren't already a pair of petal-soft lips haunting me from across the table—a pair that was curled into a smile for someone else. Cora, distracted by Thomas, missed my victory over Agnes. My mood curdled for the remainder of the meal. Later that evening, I took great care sorting through the wealth, happy for the distraction of finding the perfect gift for each new friend, though the glimmering of gemstones and gold paled in comparison to Cora's radiance. What a fool Thomas is for not seeing that.

A sapphire for Emme, a ruby for Rose, an emerald each for Margaret and Wenefrid. Gold bracelets for the young mothers, Elyoner and Elizabeth. An opal for Liz, and a golden necklace with a large lapis lazuli stone for Margery. She nearly cried when she opened it earlier this afternoon, clasping the chain around her neck and hiding it beneath the collar of her dress. Although it went unsaid, we both understand it's best not to flaunt the gift in front of Agnes.

Emme's eyes sparkle with an intensity to rival the jewel's when she opens the small pouch, tears welling in them.

"Oh, Lady Thelia . . . It's beautiful."

"Come now," I tease, bumping my shoulder into hers. "It's just Thelia."

When Emme looks up to meet my stare, she's twinkling as bright as Venus.

Will slides behind me and smiles at her over my shoulder. Emme kisses the top of my head as if to say, *Go on, then,* and I laugh as Will extends a hand to invite me to dance. I still don't know the steps, but this doesn't faze him. He pulls me across the room in a series of spins and whirls, and we both erupt into laughter until the song ends and deposits us before the head table. Cora's there, alongside Thomas, a soft smile splashed across her lips as she watches us. Our eyes lock, and my fingers tingle with the desperate urge to reach for her, to invite her to join me here, but she winks and turns back to Thomas, lacing her fingers into his. A twinge of jealousy slithers up my back, but I'm not alone: Will's watching them as well.

It seems we both want what we cannot have.

"I need some air," I say, squeezing Will's hand before releasing it.

"Mind if I join you?" he asks with a sadness in his eyes, in the corners of his mouth, that he thinks he's hiding.

I retake his hand in mine. "Come on, then."

The night plants frigid kisses on my cheeks, but they sting less than watching Cora fawn over Thomas. Despite the cold these past weeks, she's still sought me out to walk along the beach with her, dangers be damned. At first, our conversations centered around the Bible stories she'd read to me, but those inevitably led to more spirited discussions. And in all those hours spent together sharing abbreviated histories and hopes with each other, she never spoke of Thomas.

But she also kept the conversation lighthearted. There was never an excuse to reach for her hand again.

"How long have you loved him?" I say after a time, bringing my mug of spiced wine to my lips.

Will nearly chokes on his. "I— Excuse me, my lady?"

Those eyes, so like his sister's that I could cry, are wide with shock. I give him a sad, knowing smile, and though he breaks his gaze away from mine, the tension in his jaw and shoulders melts away, leaving a softer Will before me.

"We've known each other since we were children. We're like brothers." His voice cracks on the last word, and I risk a hand on his shoulder. This moment is delicate, so much like the light snow that falls from above—beautiful and ephemeral, at the risk of melting into nothing if pushed too quickly. "He wasn't always . . . like this. But I don't know exactly when he changed."

"Is it hard to see them together?"

He shoots me a mournful look. "You tell me."

"There you both are!" Cora's sparkling voice splits Will and me apart. Her eyes linger on our reddened cheeks and our guilty faces. "Supper is about to start."

"Don't be silly," Will says with a grin, wrapping an arm around his sister's shoulder and pointing a finger at me. "Agnes won't begin without our guest of honor."

I laugh bitterly. "I'm not so sure."

Cora reads something on my face, and her brows crinkle with concern. "Are you having a good time?"

"Of course—are you?"

Her eyes wander past us to the snowy village, and she nods, a curious expression settling over her features.

"Will, would you check if Agnes started without us?" I ask. "I don't want to miss a slice of Margery's apple pie."

Will accepts with a nod, and then it's just Cora and me left in the falling snow.

"He's been really happy these past few weeks," she says, lifting her head to look at the sky. Tonight, Luna is nestled behind snow clouds, but Cora's skin reflects the meeting-house's light as if she's a moon herself.

"He's a good man," I concede. "I haven't met many of those."

"I think he's in love with you."

A surprised laugh escapes my throat. "In love with me? Cora, don't be silly—we barely know each other!"

"All right, fine, I think he's starting to fall in love with you. Is that better?"

"I don't know, Cora . . ."

"What about you? Are you falling in love with him, too?"

My eyes snap back to hers. "What? I— Why are you asking me this?"

"It's a rare thing for a husband and wife to love each other," she says slowly, and there's a glorious moment when hope blossoms in my heart before she crushes it in her hands. "I'm just hopeful you'll both be as lucky as I am."

Her words are like a slap in the face, and I turn away from her sharply, searching for a reply that might cut her as much as she's cut me. "I think I might be."

Her shoulders curl forward in my peripheral vision, a flower wilting. "Do you remember when you told me that he looks like someone you once loved?"

The question draws my focus back to her. A snowflake lands on her bottom lip, and another one catches on her eyelashes. My fingers twitch at my sides to brush them away, longing to feel her softness beneath them.

"Yes."

"Is that why you're holding back? Are you still in love with him?"

The emotion that washes over me has no name: sorrow at the loss of Proserpina and what will never be; joy at the thought of the moon reflected in her eyes, of the way her skin tasted on my lips. Guilt rises like bile into the back of my throat, and my arms snake around my stomach to steady myself.

"I'll always love her."

When I meet her gaze once more, those lovely emerald eyes are wide with shock, no doubt thinking of the laws pinned just behind us and their consequences—*upon pain of death*. Yet Cora doesn't appear disgusted or frightened, only surprised that I dare to admit it.

I smile weakly. "We were only girls. She was my closest friend."

"What happened to her?"

"What always happens. She married a man far too old for her, in a realm too far away to visit. Fate, some said. I don't know what became of her after that."

And I won't until I die, when the gods grant my ravaged heart an answer.

"Is she the only person you've ever loved?" The question is spoken so softly that I barely hear it before it's swallowed by the snow. Cora blinks the snowflake from her lashes. The other still graces her lip, and my entire world contracts until the City of Raleigh falls away. It's just me, Cora, and that glittering crystal. I can't help myself—I reach out to brush it away with my thumb, and when I touch her, every part of my body sings.

"No." The answer leaves my mouth without my mind's approval, and my heart twists at hearing it spoken out loud. But it's the truth, isn't it? Cora's eyes flick between my thumb and my stare. Her chest rises and falls with quickening breaths. Hope can be the sweetest ache when you believe you're on the cusp of attainment, but how quickly it darkens into misery once dashed.

"Thomas will be looking for me." Cora guides my hand away from her mouth before dropping it at my side. "Let's go back."

I have never hated Thomas more than I do in this moment. Raidne, our brilliant haruspex, will soon dig her fingers through his entrails, and oh, how I'll relish it.

※※※

At the head table, Mistress Bailie clinks a fork against her glass. Her daffodil hair is twisted into an elaborate bun on the top of her head, encircled in a crown of holly berries. Everyone's attention turns to her except for Thomas's, which finds its way to me. His stare makes my mouth run dry.

"Please, friends, find a seat," Agnes begins, motioning to the tables around the room. The most food I've seen since arriving here is distributed generously across each—apples spiced with cinnamon, cheeses, nuts, and even a few roasted birds and pies. People sit in the chairs closest to them, paying no mind to rank. During Yule, the traditional class separations don't apply. Will and I settle in beside Margery and Jeremie. I reach for her hand and squeeze it gently. The toddler giggles up at me from underneath a head of blond curls, the perfect cherub for the season. Despite my better judgment, the boy is growing on me.

"I know we're all preparing for a very rationed winter, but we've worked hard these past few days to prepare this beautiful feast. Tonight, let's enjoy the fruits of our labors as we celebrate the birth of our Lord!" Mistress Bailie concludes her speech with an exaggerated curtsy, and then everyone tears into their food.

"*We've* worked very hard?" I raise an eyebrow to Margery, and she laughs. Mistress Bailie hasn't so much as lifted a spoon, let alone helped prepare a meal.

The other women's work is a huge success, a stark departure from the last few weeks of hardtack and gruel. I let each bite sit in my mouth, savoring the decadence of the meats, the richness of the cheeses, and I wash the food down with large sips of mulled wine. I'm drunk halfway through supper.

Too late, it occurs to me that I should be embarrassed, but when I look around, everyone is equally intoxicated. It's almost pleasant until I catch sight of Thomas whispering something into Cora's ear. Whatever he says makes color rise along her throat, and she pushes at his chest gently, turning a flushed face demurely away from him.

Thomas grins.

Will sees it, too. Perhaps it's the drink, perhaps it's the

desperate need to feel something, anything, else, but he rests a warm palm on my leg beneath the table. My head snaps to face him, but he continues his meal with his free hand, engaged in a conversation with a man on his left. I can feel the heat of his fingers, even through my various layers of skirts. I know my cheeks must be turning scarlet.

Would it be so wrong to feel something other than guilt and loss for one night?

I could brush his hand away. Instinct tells me that if I did, he'd never touch me again. But there's something far more intoxicating than the wine in letting it remain. A power, however small, I haven't felt for centuries.

Memories of Cora's breath on the back of my neck, of her fingers lacing me into my gown, rush forward, and I choose this: I won't turn Will away. They have the same intense green eyes, the same night-black curls. Cora leads Thomas to the dance floor, and Will is here, extending an invitation. Is he not the safest way to be close to her? My punishment would be mild for lying with my betrothed—I'd hang if they discover it's his sister I ache for.

When he finally shifts his focus back to me, those sparkling jade eyes officially ask the question. Behind him, Cora throws back her head and laughs at Thomas as he lifts her by the hips off the floor in sync with the music's tempo.

I accept.

⊡⊡⊡

When we escape into the night again, I don't have time to process the chill before Will presses me against the meeting-house wall, his hands slipping beneath my cloak to find my hips. This is the second time I've found myself pinned in this shadowed corner, but I relish it now. Here, under the curtain of night, it's easy to pretend it's not Will's fingers that press into the silk, not his soft curls in my hands.

But his lips are soft as they brush against mine, more of a question than a kiss, so tentative that I fear he might break away. Where would that leave me? Without this distraction, there's nothing to keep my mind from wandering to Thomas's hands on Cora, to how she tossed back her head with delight and put the low cut of her gown on full display for him.

My fingers tighten their hold on his locks and my lips answer his, banishing the possibility of a night spent yearning for another promised woman. The kiss is slow, deep but gentle, exactly the kind that two people each thinking of someone else might share. It's not enough. I want, I need, to feel the pleasant warmth beneath my skin burst into flames.

"Like you mean it," I whisper into his ear, my teeth grazing along the lobe. "Like I'm him."

Will stills against me, and a painful moment passes where neither of us speaks.

"I'm sorry, I—" The words have barely left my mouth when he kisses me again, and this time, it's a wave crashing against the shore. The hesitation has vanished, replaced by hunger— what else to call the way his tongue parts my lips to taste me, the way his grip on my hips tightens? He presses the entirety of his weight into me, and the delicate silk of my gown snags against the meetinghouse's rough wooden walls, but I don't care. In this moment I'll let him consume every part of me, even my feelings for his sister, if it means she can't haunt me tonight.

When he parts my legs with his knee, I gasp against his mouth, reveling in how easy it is to trick the body into trading one ache for another. And unlike the longing I feel for Cora, this thirst can be quenched.

"Take me home." I barely recognize the sound of my voice, thick with longing.

Without a word, Will lifts me from the ground to spin me around. I can't help it—I laugh, tilting my head up to the sky to catch falling snowflakes on my tongue. The hood of my cloak falls back to my shoulders, but the shock of air on my neck feels incredible against the heat that radiates across my skin. When our eyes meet again, he pulls me in close once more and steals the snowflakes from my mouth.

There it is. The fire.

When we reach her—*his*—home, he pushes the door open so forcefully that the cottage shakes around us. My fingers find the clasp of my cloak before I cross inside, and as soon as the door clicks shut behind me, I drop the garment to the floor. It lies there unceremoniously, all the bed we need.

The room is dark but warm, the only light cast from the hearth's fire. It crackles gently, ready for another log, but that will have to wait until we're done. In its low glow, I linger on his similar features—the curve of his lashes, the gentle slope of his nose—as we close the space between us once more.

Our lips meet, and our fingers pull frantically at the strings of each other's clothes with little success. But then Will breaks the kiss to spin me away from him, making use of the firelight to unlace the back of my gown. I close my eyes, trying to pretend it's Cora who stands behind me now, but Will's touch isn't as delicate. The gown falls to the floor with a sigh, and then I'm before him in only my shift, hair still pinned beneath a simple white coif.

"Are you sure about this, my lady?"

His kindness catches me by surprise—I don't want it, not now, when every moment our bodies lose contact is a moment when thoughts of Cora and Thomas threaten to slip in.

One of my fingers finds his lips to quiet him, while the other hand moves to the band of his trousers.

"I'm sure. But enough talking."

There's a strangeness when we come together. The room's low light does its best, but it can't transform us into the people we truly seek. The more our bodies connect, the more a sense of desperation takes hold to try to defy this fact, to find pleasure in it anyway.

And pleasure there is—the lovely tingle of skin in the wake of a caress, the bittersweet ache between my legs. There's a pleasant sense of fullness when he's inside of me, but even after, when he teases that ache to release with his tongue, none of it's enough to banish Cora.

A long silence settles upon us once it's over, broken only when Will brings my hand to his mouth and places a warm kiss on my palm.

"You're so lovely," he says, but there's a distance in his voice. A mist that gathers in his eyes at the second half of his thought, which remains unsaid. *But . . .*

My hand slides to cup his face, as I try to blink away the tears that threaten to gather in mine. In this moment, with our limbs still draped across each other's, I must face the fact I've done my best to ignore these past few weeks—that Will is truly good. How can I possibly protect him from what's coming when he's the one who won my hand?

"I need to go."

His eyebrows furrow as he helps me from the floor. "My lady, I'm sorry, I . . ."

"There's nothing to be sorry for, Will." I reach for his hands and draw in close to rest my forehead against his. We stand like that for a moment, hands clasped and foreheads touching, a new sense of understanding enveloping us in its embrace. "It was worth a try, right?"

There's a faint crack in his smile, and something inside of me breaks at the sight of it. I wait for the safety of the darkened streets, still punctuated with the radiance of Yuletide candles in the windows, and then I let the tears fall freely.

ᛁᛋᛁᛋᛁᛋ

"Where did you sneak off to?"

The question accosts me as soon as I slip into the kitchen, sending my heart into my throat. There, at the table where Margery prepares our food, Thomas waits. He's leaning back in a chair, his dirtied boots propped up on the table's surface, where they leave little puddles of melting snow.

"Good evening, Master Thomas," I reply coolly. "I didn't sneak off anywhere. I just wanted a bit of fresh air and to watch the snow fall."

The confidence in my tone brings him to a standing position, and his lips curl.

"Oh, really? And your new prince wanted some fresh air as well?"

"I'm not exactly sure what you're implying. I bid Will good night outside the meetinghouse." I hang my cloak on its hook beside the door. "But do keep in mind that you don't have the rank to question me."

A low growl emanates from his throat. Thomas isn't used to being below someone in class, to being put in his place.

"How can anyone be certain you are who you say you are?" An ugly sneer cuts across his face. "Never forget that you're a guest in my home."

"How could I?" I snap back. "And I'll happily prove I am who I say once the weather clears. I would have already, if you didn't stall our return."

Gods, how I'll relish cutting his throat, spilling his blood into the sand and sending his body on the wings of flames to

Proserpina. His death will free my sisters from the chains of Ceres's curse.

His death will free Cora.

"Royalty or not, I won't tolerate you behaving like a harlot underneath our roof."

I push past him toward the stairs, digging my shoulder into his chest as I do. The force catches him by surprise, and he stumbles, the backs of his legs hitting the table with a loud *thump*.

When I reach the first step, I turn around to face him once more.

"Then good thing we weren't under your roof."

Thomas does not follow me; he does not say a word.

᠍᠍᠍

The turn of the year comes and goes, taking my third full moon with it, though her image is lost to me behind a curtain of snow that refuses to lift. For the next three weeks, each time it seems as if the clouds might part, another storm darkens the skies to re-cloak the city in a fresh layer of white. Long gone is the sense of calm brought by Yuletide, replaced by a quiet desolation that's fraying everyone's nerves, mine included.

Will and I continue to steal moments together, though it's not lust that draws us into each other's orbits—it's that we've somehow shared our silent truths. There's comfort in that for Will, and there would be for me, too, if it didn't complicate my plans for spring. I spend our time together praying for some sin to reveal itself, to justify what must happen to him, but one never comes. Will is as kind and as thoughtful as I feared him to be, and I have no way to keep him from voyaging to Scopuli.

When I'm not with Will, I'm with Cora. We spend most of

our days together now, after I finally convinced her and Margery to let me help with the housework. My wealth and status have slipped just far enough into the fog of memory for them to allow me to participate in the mundane. As soon as Margery and I finish cleaning the kitchen after breakfast, I head to the Waters house, where I spend the day helping Cora tend her hearth, mend and clean clothes, and care for her ailing father.

We spend long hours sitting before the same fire where Will and I sought comfort in each other. That night felt like a dream the moment it was over, but the first few times I find myself in the same room as the act, I'm terrified that Cora can read what transpired between her brother and me on my face. But she never broaches Yuletide at all—not my time spent with Will, and not the conversation we shared. At first, I worry that she's intentionally ignoring it, that my confession tainted whatever blossoms between us with rot. But she treats me no differently, and there are even times I'm certain that I catch her staring when she thinks I'm not looking; though as quickly as our eyes meet, she turns away, and the flush that creeps along her graceful neck always has causes more plausible than longing. Still, it's easy for my imagination to rewrite Christmastide's history—how I might have ended up here with her instead, had she not retreated. What would our hair look like tangled together, the red and the black?

I come close to finding out one evening after Margery retires. Thomas is off with the other Council members, and Agnes has locked herself in her chambers, leaving me free to revel in the warmth of the hearth fire unbothered. But a knock on the back door shatters the calm. I open it to find Cora before me, body trembling with cold.

"Cora." Her name is so sweet on my tongue, and I move to

let her inside. "Come, let me make you some tea. It's freezing out there."

I find the small cast-iron kettle and hang it on its hook over the fire. Cora closes the door behind her, then moves to rub her hands up and down her arms to generate heat.

"What are you doing here? It's late."

"Is Will here? He didn't come home for supper."

"The Council met earlier this evening," I reply, unable to hide the disdain in my voice.

"So they're at the tavern, then." Cora sighs. It's no secret that's where most of the meetings are held, making them more social gathering than civic duty.

"Will usually stops by to wish me good night. It's not too late yet. Want to wait here with me?"

"Thank you, Thelia. I hate being home alone with my father at night." Cora unclasps her cape, preparing to slide it off her slender shoulders, and I force my attention back to the kettle. I've learned the hard way that if I watch her peel one layer of clothing off, I'll be plagued the rest of the night by visions of removing the rest. Of her fingers teasing my gown's laces, of my thumb brushing against her lips. "His coughing fits grow worse once darkness falls—they rattle the whole house. It's hard to listen to."

I place a hand on her shoulder sympathetically, careful not to let it linger too long, then pull a mug from the shelf to mix herbs for her, red clover and lavender, the same concoction I prepared for Pisinoe more times than there are words for the numbers.

"Here, this will help soothe your nerves"—I hand her the cup, and she smiles gratefully—"and tomorrow I'll stop by to make your father a tisane to help with the coughing."

She steps deeper into the kitchen, putting more distance

between us. Despite all the time we spend together, it's not often that we find ourselves with idle hands. She raps her fingers along the edge of the mug, and her attention flits across the room. A charged energy radiates between us. It makes my stomach flutter.

"Let's wait in my room. It's more comfortable there," I say, not adding that it's also more private. She nods.

We wander out of the kitchen and up the stairs. Her shoes click against the wooden floor, while my steps are padded by my stockings. The closer we get to my quarters, the faster my heart beats. When I finally close us in together, my hands are trembling.

"Do you think they'll be much later?" she asks, her skirts sweeping toward the small fireplace as she moves to add another log. The flames accept it hungrily, and she watches with her back to me.

"You know how they are." My voice is breathy, and I cough to clear it. "It depends on how much ale they've already had."

"How should we pass the time?"

My pulse throbs in my ears, an unbearable *thump-thump thump-thump* that counts the length of my silence. There are no words to describe how I'd like to pass the time, only images that flash in rapid succession before me. Cora's delicate eyelashes fluttering against my skin, her salty taste on my lips, the ties of her dress unfurling beneath my fingertips. I'm frozen by these thoughts, made silent by my own desires.

I let myself laze over her features: the graceful arch of her neck, the curves of her hips. The wisps of raven curls that fall free from the knot she's pinned them in, begging me to release the rest. How badly my fingers itch to run through them, gently at first, and then harder. I want to use this moment to devour her, to sink my teeth into her skin. Would Cora, even with her strength, become a crushable flower between my hands? I don't remember the tenderness of love, its softness.

I only remember its bite.

She looks back at me when I don't answer. The flames crackle as they consume the fresh piece of oak, their reflection dancing in her eyes. The moon in Proserpina's and a conflagration in Cora's—I'm cursed to love women made of light. It's strange to remember believing that Cora was her exact mirror; our months together have given their differences time to make themselves known: Cora's calloused hands, her gaunter frame, realities of a mortal life. The kind of beauty that can be found only in a life so fleeting.

"I don't know," I lie, my voice catching in my throat, painfully aware that one wrong move could send her running to the tavern alone, propriety be damned. "Will you read me something?"

Her face pinches into a strange expression. "You want to hear a Bible story now?"

I exaggerate a groan, using the levity to draw in closer. "Oh, please, no! Surely there must be one other book in this house. Do you think the Bailies are fans of poetry?"

"Poetry?" Her voice is incredulous, but a smile appears on those pretty lips.

"Yes, or do the English not believe in such things?"

This makes her laugh. "Of course we do, but we don't exactly have the latest sonnets available here."

"All right, fine. You can't read me a poem, but surely you must know one."

A blush creeps along her cheeks, and her eyes fall back to the fire. I'm close enough now to see the reds and oranges of the flames reflected in them, layering atop the green, all sprinkled with the spark of embers—an entire universe inside her stare.

"Ah, so you do." I grin. "And it looks like it's a good one."

She nudges me gently with her shoulder, and it takes all my strength not to seize her by the forearms and press her in close. "I barely remember it. You tell me one instead."

"Oh, all right, coward," I say, keenly aware of the sweat on my palms. "Ready?"

Cora nods, so I begin:

*For just gazing at you for a second, it is impossible
for me even to talk . . .*

The verses spill from my mouth instinctively, as if one of the Muses has caught hold of my tongue. But I barely hear the words—my world is reduced to her eyes, and the fact that they're locked on my lips. I only realize I've finished speaking when she raises her stare to meet mine.

A look passes between us before she finally speaks. "That's beautiful."

"Yes," I whisper, trying to memorize her every angle—the way the firelight catches in her hair and dances across her eyelashes. She thinks I'm talking about the poem, and while I agree the verse is lovely, I want so badly to admit that I'm speaking of her. But I don't. Instead, I take a few steps back, clasping my hands behind my back so she can't see how they tremble. This metered, careful interaction needs to be enough, but that doesn't mean it's easy to watch as her expression melts into one of confusion.

"You need not retreat . . ." Her voice is so soft that I worry I've imagined the incredible coincidence of her speaking aloud exactly what I longed to hear.

"Is that the beginning of another poem?" The words sound crueler falling off my tongue than I anticipated, and there's only one way I can think to take them back. When I speak again, I offer my heart. "Don't I, Cora?"

It's she who closes the gap between us this time, reaching to take one of my hands in hers. I suck in a breath at the shock of her touch, and she turns my palm to trace its lines with her index finger. How is it that a caress so light nearly brings me to my knees?

But then her grip on me loosens, and her gaze drops to the floor.

"What's wrong?" I ask, desperate to fix the source of whatever hesitation now plagues her.

"What about Will?"

I feel my face twist in confusion. "What about him?"

"You've been spending so much time together. I . . . I don't want to hurt him."

I can't help but laugh. "Cora, it's not me he loves—it's you."

"What do you mean?"

"He didn't compete for my hand because he wanted it. He competed so that—" My voice catches in my throat. Thomas is the last specter that I want to invite into this liminal, fleeting space we've found—it's just for me, her, and the firelight. "So that your future would be secure."

Embers pop as she considers my answer, and when she lifts her chin once more, her eyes are clear and determined. "Do you remember that first day on the beach?"

I nod.

"I reached out to check you for a fever, and you pulled away from me."

"Cora, I . . ."

"I couldn't figure out why it bothered me so much. Well, that's not exactly true . . . But it seemed impossible that even then, I . . ."

My throat tightens as instinct draws my body closer to hers. This time, she's the one who inhales sharply as we press together, as she laces her fingers into mine to draw my arms around her.

"That you what?" I almost groan the words into her ear, savoring the scent of her hair—the warmth of a bonfire, and, of course, the pale kiss of roses.

"That I . . ."

"What?"

When she turns her head to me, our eyes meet one last time—there's a hunger inside hers that mirrors my own. The only question is who will be the one to close the distance between our lips.

"Thelia . . ." she begins, and my eyes flutter closed in anticipation. Every part of me quivers with need, unable to believe she's finally, blessedly, close enough to taste.

But the gods are cruel; our question goes unanswered. The loud thuds of Thomas's footsteps on the stairs shatter our fragile sanctuary, and the next thing I know, we're cleaved apart.

The haze of desire clears from Cora's eyes as quickly as a curtain lifting. "God have mercy," she whispers. "What was I thinking?"

I don't answer her—I can't. It's hard to breathe, my one small comfort that she's still in my arms, until she suddenly isn't. She quite literally slips through my fingertips. One moment, my palms rest on her hips, and the next, she's gone, bounding toward the door like a hound called to its master.

"Cora, wait!"

But she doesn't. The knot of desire in my stomach unfurls into nausea, and I watch, helplessly, as she throws open the door to him.

"There you are, Thomas!" she coos. The taste of bile in my throat brings a hand to my mouth.

I hear Thomas's voice before I see him. "Cora! What keeps you here to such an hour?"

"I was waiting for Will. I know he often visits Lady Thelia before returning home for the evening."

She stumbles, just barely, over the word *visits,* as if she doesn't want to think about what such rendezvous entail. I marvel at the incredible mess of it all: Thomas openly vying for my hand despite his betrothal to Cora, Will and I finding solace in our friendship as we long for others, and, somehow, Cora lusting for me.

"He isn't here, sweet one. He took John Chapman home from the tavern about an hour ago."

Cora sighs with relief and turns back to look at me. The stare that contained a universe moments ago has chilled. She's waiting to see if I'll somehow give us away. I don't know what hurts more: the fact she worries that I'm foolish enough to call her back to me now, or the way her trembling bottom lip begs me not to. From over her shoulder, a smirk crawls across Thomas's lips. Something about it is wrong, and now dread rises from my depths to keep my hurt company.

"Shall I walk you home?" he asks, and Cora pivots to him again. When she takes his hand, it requires all my self-control to swallow down a gasp. The sight of it makes my cheeks burn as if I've been slapped.

"That would be lovely, Thomas. Good night, Thelia."

My name at the end of her farewell catches me by surprise. The statement is a dismissal, one that I'd hoped she'd give to Thomas. I smile weakly, trying to conceal the bright bloom of pain the action stirs.

"Good night, Cora," I respond, and then add more coldly, "Thomas."

The hallway shadows swallow them both. I'm tempted to peer after them to see if Cora looks back for me, but I can't handle the very real possibility that she doesn't. Tears blur my vision as I pull the door shut behind them.

There was a time not long ago when I was certain that I'd never allow someone into my heart without Proserpina's explicit permission. Was this near-kiss a punishment for that transgression? Proserpina was never jealous as a girl, but so many other gods carefully track their worshippers' affections, and straying to another is a punishable offense. But I didn't intentionally open the door for Cora—somehow she found her way inside a locked chamber without a key.

"Scold me, then," I hiss into the flames. "Say something to me, anything at all. Please, Proserpina."

But if my beautiful queen hears me now, she doesn't make a sound.

༄༄༄

I wake to loud, frantic banging. In the fog between sleep and wakefulness, my mind goes to the city's palisades. To what they're meant to protect us from. Could the reckoning the colonists fear be upon us? I pull myself to my feet, fingers massaging my sore muscles. I fell asleep on the floor before the fire, and my body screams at me now for my carelessness. The knocks continue as I collect my hair beneath a coif. Dawn breaks over the horizon, but the house is still dark. There's barely enough light to guide me from the bedroom, down the twisted steps, through the kitchen, and on to the front room. Behind me, I hear Mistress Bailie stirring.

"One moment!" Margery shouts to the person outside, already at the door. Heavier footsteps falling upstairs indicate that Thomas is awake as well. Both he and his mother descend as Margery undoes the wooden latch.

A blast of cold air greets us. Cora and her father stand on the threshold, tears frozen against their reddened faces as if they're gilded with frost. Master Waters opens his mouth to speak, but he's interrupted as a violent coughing fit erupts from deep within his chest. It's so forceful that I fear each hack will bring up pieces of his lungs. Margery immediately ushers them inside, and when Master Waters stumbles, she rushes forward to catch him, supporting his weight as he works through the fit. The last time I saw him out of his bed was at the Yuletide celebration weeks ago. The realization makes my stomach twist. Something terrible has brought them here.

"Master Waters!" Margery exclaims, eyes wide with alarm. "You should be in bed, look at you—"

"Will," he gargles, and my heart sinks.

I turn to look back at Thomas, breath catching in my throat. He's standing in the kitchen, little more substance than a shadow. The light from Agnes's candle doesn't reach him, but its flame still flickers in his eyes. The effect sends dread skittering across my skin.

"What about him?" Mistress Bailie asks.

"H-he's missing!" The old man clings to Margery. She's too thin to support him for long, and he soon sinks to the floor. "Something must have happened!"

"Did you try the Chapmans'?" Thomas steps forward to lift Master Waters back to his feet. "John was a mess last night, and Will walked him home."

"We went this morning, Thomas," Cora says. Her eyes are frantic. "John doesn't remember how he got home, but Alis said she never saw Will. None of their children did, either. We've searched everywhere! He's not in the village!"

"Please, calm yourselves!" Mistress Bailie chides, albeit sincerely. "Especially you, Richard. You'll only make your condition worse if you don't relax. I'm sure Will is all right. Why wouldn't he be?"

Because of me.

My treasure put a target on his back. My stomach lurches at the realization, and my hands move atop it to try to settle it.

I watch Cora's face as she reaches the same conclusion. Mr. Waters still howls against Thomas, but Cora pays them no mind. Her eyes narrow to slits; her hands harden into fists.

"You," she growls, pointing an accusing finger toward me. "This happened because of you!"

"Cora, please—" I try to reach for her, but she sidesteps my advance.

"You think it's a coincidence that the man who won your hand is missing? Some jealous drunk wanted his chance to win the wealth of a thousand lifetimes, and who knows what he did to Will to get it! Because of you, my brother—" She wails, and what I hear in her voice makes me sick: She's furious. But how can I blame her? Her words are true. Though Will's disappearance is not by my hand, his death would be if my plan comes to fruition.

But wasn't he fated to die regardless?

No man shall commit the horrible and detestable sins of Sodomy, upon pain of death.

Does a part of her know that? Does she blame me for encouraging her to commit that very same sin?

"Enough," Thomas demands, but it only spurs Cora to lunge at me. Thomas steps between us and snaps her to his chest. She struggles against him as if rabid. "Take your father home. He needs to rest."

"I'm not finished, Thomas!"

"We'll find him, Cora." He answers in a tone gentler than I believed him capable of using. Still, something feels off about it, like a wolf trying to soothe a hare between its jaws.

But the words seem to comfort Cora's father, for his cries wane to whimpers.

"Where could he be, Thomas . . . ?"

"I don't know, Master Richard, but I promise you we'll find him."

The old man nods, and another coughing fit begins. The painful sound is the only thing that draws Cora's attention from me. She watches her father struggle to regain his composure as she struggles to regain her own. Only once her breathing has slowed to a manageable pace does Thomas loosen his hold on her, and she tears herself from him as soon as she can. Her green eyes are still wild, and she reaches for her father, linking her arm in his.

"Let's go." Her voice is soft when she speaks to him. "We must get you away from this witch."

The word is a knife in my side. She knows its weight as she levels it against me, the consequences it could have. It's a similar accusation to the one she could make about my nature, but she knows that *witch* will never circle back around to her.

"Cora . . ." I start, desperation rising in my chest, but she won't look at me.

"I'll alert the rest of the town. Margery, fetch my clothes, we must hurry," Thomas says, his eyes directly on Richard, who nods clumsily. The poor old fool actually believes Thomas has his family's best interest at heart. "You should be at home, resting in your bed. Will would never forgive himself if you got hurt."

Richard relents, but Cora hesitates. Her eyes dart between Thomas and me once more, but then she follows her father into the stark morning air. Thomas shuts the door behind them and leaves to prepare himself, Margery trailing behind him.

"Make sure Thomas's breakfast is ready before he finishes dressing," Mistress Bailie orders me calmly as she floats across the room to follow them. When I don't answer, she looks over her shoulder at me. "You'd better get used to your wifely duties."

The obviousness of what's happened hits me squarely in the chest, melting away the initial fear, leaving only a brilliant, fiery rage. My feet carry me to the kitchen, but instead of obeying orders, I fly to the table beneath the window where Margery keeps the knives. They did something to Will. The words repeat over and over, until they become an incantation guiding me to exact vengeance. My fingers wrap around the smooth handle of the largest blade. I find my reflection staring back at me in its polished metal, though my alarmed expression seems at odds with the sneer I feel myself wearing.

Stop, Thelia.

The knife topples from my hand onto the dirt floor. I whirl around, but my only company is the dying hearth fire that Margery's been pulled away from. Blood rushes through my ears, and for the briefest moment, I consider ignoring the message from the Underworld. How good would it feel to snatch the knife from the floor and storm up the stairs? To sink it into the soft spot of flesh between Thomas's ribs, and then tear its sharpened edge against Agnes's powdered throat?

But to do so would mean abandoning Raidne and Pisinoe, and though I want nothing more than to bring a bloody justice down upon the Bailies, now isn't the time. I must wait for spring.

The understanding does little to quell the fury that still thrashes in my chest. Now might not be the time to kill them, but that doesn't mean I have to sit idly by. After returning the knife to its proper place, I dash up the stairs.

I skip my bedroom and continue down the hall until I come to Thomas's. I pause for a moment, considering, but move on to the next. Whatever's happened, Agnes is the one who will know the entirety of it. My hand wavers before her door, but I need to know for sure, for Cora, and I grab ahold of the knob and push my way inside.

It's the first time that I've been in her bedroom. There's a large fireplace to my right and a four-poster bed directly across from it to the left. A rug made of an animal's skin covers most of the floor. Mistress Bailie stands in only her nightshirt in front of a large wardrobe at the back wall. She doesn't look at me as I walk to the center of the room, my bare feet caressed by the warm fur beneath them. The sensation should be pleasing, but it makes my skin crawl.

I'm walking on another being who was killed for sport. Even at our most violent, my sisters and I never kept trophies.

Agnes turns to me.

"Certainly breakfast isn't ready yet?" She's beautiful, almost handsome, with soft blond locks framing her face, her piercing eyes watching me smugly from underneath a thin brow. Her smirk is relentless. I see where Thomas learned his.

"What did you do to Will?"

She seems surprised by my boldness, but instead of admitting any wrongdoing, she closes the gap between us and reaches out to stroke the side of my face, her smirk morphing into a hideous grin. The gesture catches me by surprise, and I pull my head away in disgust. Her fingers twist around a lock of my hair.

"What an awful thing to suggest, Lady Thelia," she murmurs. "Will was like a son to me. He was Thomas's closest friend . . . Although, this does technically mean that Thomas is now the winner of your hand."

"You vile—" I begin, but she slaps me across the face, hard. The sting sends me stumbling back in shock.

"That sounds like disrespect," she says as she turns to continue dressing. "Which will no longer be tolerated."

"How dare you raise your hand to me!"

"Who will punish me?" She laughs. "By your own admission, Scopuli is dying. You need Thomas." Her words are true, but she'll never understand why. "Unless that's all a lie."

"I need a husband. It doesn't have to be Thomas."

"Choose another, then. Winter is dangerous here—hopefully he survives it."

The threat is clear; it makes my throat tighten. "What about Cora . . . ?"

"It's a pity, really. She would've made a more compliant wife, and certainly a prettier one. But her hand doesn't come with a fortune, and yours does."

"You'll pay for this," I hiss, far enough away from Agnes that I'm safe from another slap.

"We'll see." She pulls on her stockings, completely unbothered by my warning. "Now, if you'll excuse me, I have a search party to organize."

"How could you? He loved Thomas."

"Then perhaps this is God's punishment," she says, then ushers me back into the hall. "May the Lord have mercy, or else he'll burn for it."

The door slams shut in my face. My entire body trembles as I retreat to my quarters, where I push a chair against the door for good measure. Now that the Bailies believe I'm Thomas's property, who knows what they might do, even in the light of day.

I pace back and forth between my bed and the fireplace, mind racing. Cora will never forgive me for this, and the thought is so unbearable that it nearly brings me to my knees. My fingers find the mantel's edge to keep myself from toppling to the ground, and I spot her there—my little spider friend weaving a new web. Her presence doesn't bring the peace it usually does. I believed us so similar, but now, as my chest feels as hollow as one of the countless carcasses I've processed, I understand how different we truly are. This fierce little creature would never be foolish enough to get tangled in such a mess. She was born knowing the painful lesson I've refused to stomach these past few weeks: Sometimes, it's best to hunt alone.

I am, once again, entirely on my own, but gods, it hurts so much worse like this—with Will gone and Cora lost. Though it's painfully clear that, unlike this spider, I am no predator without my sisters.

The best I can hope for now is to not become prey.

13

〰〰〰〰

BEFORE

Thelia!
    Thelia . . . !
    "Thelia?"

I sit upright with a start. My hand rushes to my heart; it burns with terror, and it hurts to breathe. Pisinoe rests beside me, and she rubs my back, coaxing me into consciousness, into leaving the dream world behind.

"You were whimpering. It sounded like a nightmare," she coos, pulling my head to her chest. I nod and slide my arms around her waist.

"Was it about Proserpina again?"

Ah, yes. Jaquob's tale's distortion of Dis is only a new twist in a recurring nightmare, but the image of that emaciated face and those bloodied lips has me shaken. I nod again.

"You've been spending so much time alone. Have you been looking for more signs?"

I want to tell her that I've been taking care of the last sign I received. That he would have made a piss-poor sacrifice before, but even though I've nursed him back to health, I'll never give him to Ceres. I'll use him to force Proserpina to speak to me again, and if she doesn't, he'll sail away from here with my blessing. But I don't.

"I've been looking for her everywhere, Pisinoe."

"Have you found anything new?"

"I would tell you if I had." The lie slips from my lips with such ease that I startle myself. I expect Pisinoe to whisper into my ear that she knows I would, but she doesn't. Instead, she strokes my hair a few more times before releasing me from her embrace.

"I have the metal pieces that you asked for. The small ones are there," she says, motioning to a large bag that sits beside the door. Its seams are nearly bursting, mostly with nails. Pisinoe spends the most time poring over the treasure we keep in the sea caves. I'd never be able to locate the various parts that Jaquob described without her help. She was thankful for the task, a welcome excuse to dig through her hoard, but her next question doesn't come as a shock. "And the rest are on the beach. That anchor especially was heavy. What are you going to do with them, exactly?"

"I'm repairing a small boat."

She raises an eyebrow, no doubt recalling all our failed escape attempts.

I chew my bottom lip, waiting for the lie to materialize on my tongue. "Because of the women who washed ashore. What if more arrive, but alive? We're cursed to stay here, but that doesn't mean they would be. If it happens again, I want them to have a way out."

Pisinoe watches me, a mixture of sadness and relief in her stare. "You've been acting so strangely recently . . . so removed, so preoccupied . . . First the lily, then this. Try not to burden yourself with too much."

I smile softly, but it's too late to heed her advice. I'm trying to force a goddess's hand with a man she guided me to find, while hiding his existence so that he doesn't become another sacrifice to her mother—it's quite literally too much.

But after all this time, I'll do anything to hear that voice again, even if it's scolding me from the shore as he sails off into the horizon.

And so I help Jaquob build his escape.

Although he requested parts from his wrecked ship, he wanted only hardware and other metal baubles. When I offered to bring some of the ship's original wood, he bristled at the idea. Who'd want to try to escape in a coffin? Instead, we go to work with fresh materials, although obtaining new timber is no small task. Since there are no large trees on Rotunda, I spend several nights collecting wood from the southern end of Scopuli. An entire week elapses where Jaquob and I hardly speak because I'm too preoccupied with transporting the felled lumber from my island to his, from the moment the sun slips behind the horizon to the moments before it returns in the morning.

Jaquob wasn't wrong: Building a boat is a long process. Scopuli's trees lose their leaves, and one moon cycle slips into another before the craft looks sailable. Its progress makes me more anxious to complete it, especially since Proserpina's campaign of silence continues. Fear's roots entangle themselves inside me—what if Jaquob leaves, and she still doesn't speak?

"Does it need to be this large?" I ask him early one evening. He's doubled over the side of the boat, working to get the center thwart in place, one of the bench-like pieces of wood where he'll sit during his voyage. Cold air whips across the sand, a reminder that summer is a distant memory.

"I don't know how long I'll be at sea," he cautions. "I need plenty of room for supplies, especially since I don't know where I'll land. We've maintained good relations with the Algonquians, but I might be mistaken for British—or worse, Spanish—before I have a chance to explain myself."

I mull over his words. I'd have no idea how much food to bring, what supplies to pack, how to navigate the seas, but such questions are facts of life for Jaquob.

Soon we'll no longer be building, and we'll need to start packing. What comes next is still hidden from me. Is it truly possible for him to escape? He isn't cursed, but I'm haunted by the image of our beautiful boat shattering across the reef once he reaches the curse's boundary, drowning him in the process. What lesson would that be—to watch him die beneath the waves after all this?

What do you want from him, Proserpina? From me?

"Are you sure you don't want to come?" he asks as he wipes his hands on a small piece of cloth. His eyes are hopeful. "What's here for you?"

I turn away, looking out to the west. "I can't leave, Jaquob. You know that."

"I know you *say* that," he retorts, coming up behind me to place a hand atop my left wing. I shudder. His touch underscores the differences between us. "But I don't know why. You don't give me much to work with. How is it that after all these weeks, I still know so little about you?"

"Because you love to hear yourself talk," I tease, and then add, "My sisters are here. I can't abandon them."

"Ah, yes. The infamous sisters, the two soulless harpies who will surely kill me if they ever learn of my existence." His tone is light. He doesn't grasp the magnitude of his situation. "I managed to win you over, didn't I?"

He spins me around to face him, placing both hands on my shoulders. His eyes are so dark that they're almost black.

"You didn't win me over," I whisper, but the words aren't convincing.

"Then why didn't you immediately take me to your sisters as soon as you discovered me on the beach?"

"A feeling overcame me, and I acted without forethought. I'll admit that Pisinoe might be persuaded to let you live for sheer curiosity, but Raidne would never allow it."

"How would they kill me?"

The question catches me by surprise, momentarily seizing my tongue and, with it, my ability to speak, as images of his sacrifice swirl before me. I can so clearly picture his dazed expression in the flickering light of the ritual cave's fire, his wrists clamped in the irons, his artery throbbing in that muscular throat—but now that I know him, would I still be able to draw a blade across it? Would I still be able to step over his entrails to spill the last of his life onto the floor of the cave?

"Be glad you'll never find out."

"God knows how I'll explain what I've seen these past months should I survive this ordeal."

I smile weakly and retreat from his touch. "How much work is left?"

"I still need to add the mast, the boom, and the yard, but the construction should be done within the next few days."

"The next dark moon is in five days," I think out loud. "That's when you should go. It'll be the safest then. Is that enough time for you to gather supplies?"

"Yes, it should be plenty, especially if you bring more fruits." Jaquob winks. Scopuli hasn't withheld her bounty from him, and he insists on catching his own game, which is for the best. Raidne and Pisinoe would notice if a large quantity of the salted meat went missing.

My eyes wander up to check the time. A waning crescent punched out of the black fabric of the night hangs overhead. It casts little light, which brings me comfort. The billowing smoke from the bonfire would only be visible from the hovel with the light of a full moon, and we are mere days from its exact opposite.

I catch Jaquob watching me as he tosses another piece of driftwood onto the blaze before bringing a bottle of liquor to his lips. The fire crackles greedily to consume the new fuel, but he's too lost in the sight of me to notice. He stares at me often: sometimes with a mixture of wonder and fear, and other times with confusion, as if he can't decide if what stands before him is real. Right now his expression is leaning toward the latter, his brows furrowed so deeply it looks like the two black lines might connect across the bridge of his crooked nose.

"What is it?" I ask, arms drifting across my chest defensively.

"You barely speak, you know. Unless I speak to you first."

I sigh. "I've already told you—"

"I know, I know. We're not friends."

Hearing my own words tossed back at me makes me bristle. "Yes, but also . . . It's been a long time since I've met anyone new, and most of what my sisters and I communicate to each other can be said with little words."

"There, something I can work with!" Jaquob offers me the liquor, and I shake my head. "Tell me about the last new person that you met."

Those first sailors appear in my mind, their teeth stained black with wine, and behind them, Dis. His eyes are so dark that I can barely make out his pupils, smoldering with such intensity that I can't decide whether to look away in terror or let them set me ablaze. I can still feel the heat of his breath on the side of my face as he whispered in my ear, his fingernails digging into the supple flesh of my young arms, his coarse black beard tickling my cheek.

"I can't remember," I say after a time, though my shaking

voice betrays my lie. But Jaquob doesn't press me further. It's a little after midnight. I feel myself growing restless, eager for the comfort of my pallet. My sisters notice my mood swings. They don't question me yet, but how much longer can I expect them to leave me be?

He senses my nerves and chuckles softly. "I'm only here a few more days, and yet you're still desperate to return to them. You'll be thrilled once I'm officially gone."

I'll be thrilled once she speaks to me again, but that isn't what he wants to hear. "I'll miss the excitement you've brought. It'll be strange to not wonder what you're doing during the day, to not sneak out to see you at night."

"Does that mean you'll miss me?" He grins so wide, I can't help but laugh softly in return. "It looks like I did manage to win you over."

"I suppose you did, Jaquob."

The concession placates him, and he shakes his head toward the east. "Well, then. You'd best be off. I wouldn't want your sisters to come searching for you."

I embrace him in goodbye, taking note of the way he lets his hands linger on my body. It makes me ache with desire, but not for him.

Where are you, Proserpina? Why don't you answer me?

When I pull away, his smile falls; his eyes cloud with disappointment. I cup his face with my palm and then turn toward the trees with a gentle smile.

He doesn't ask me to stay.

⊐⊏⊐⊏

I've barely left the glow of his bonfire when rustling disturbs the path ahead. The noise is too loud to belong to some timid mouse or bewildered songbird navigating through the barren beach plum branches. Before I can retreat and warn Jaquob to hide, Pisinoe emerges from the darkness, wearing no jewels. When she finds me, she stops and rests her hands on her hips. Her pose is more than accusatory; it's hostile.

"Oh—!" I stammer, trying to buy time that I know I don't have. My strange behavior the past few months has finally come to a head. This fact is etched in the severe angles of Pisinoe's frown; it's been centuries since I've seen her this upset. "What are you doing here?"

She doesn't take the bait.

"What's going on, Thelxiope?" she asks, her tone saying for her what her words don't: *Do not lie to me.*

My face flushes, and I'm thankful that it's cloaked in shadow.

"What do you mean?" I try to feign innocence, but I hear the guilt that drips from every word. It paints shame across my features. These past weeks have given me practice at speaking tiny falsehoods and deceits, but I haven't been confronted so directly. I crumble beneath Pisinoe's growing anger. Thank gods she found me and not Raidne—her fury would already have me leading her to Jaquob like a dog with its tail between its legs.

"Stop. I know you're hiding something. That you have been since the wreck. We've been waiting for you to come to us, to admit it, but our patience has worn out."

"What are you talking about?" I squeak. "I'm around every day. I cleaned the wreck; I prepare meals. None of my responsibilities have fallen off. So what if I take a few longer walks in the mornings and afternoons?"

"Don't. Even when you're physically with us, your mind is somewhere else. Do you really think we can't tell?"

"I told you. I'm looking for more clues from Proserpina—"

"And you found something. Now I'm going to finally see what it is."

"I haven't!" I try, but it's too late. In my desperation to goad Proserpina, I let myself believe they couldn't sense my deception, but of course they could. We've spent eons together first learning and then memorizing one another's rhythms; they've known something was wrong since that very first morning. When, exactly, were they convinced? When I refused to go to the pool, or some earlier misstep? Were they able to see that my joy at my younger body was tempered by guilt? And still, out of care for me, they gave me space to lie, even as summer withered into autumn.

But now that well of tolerance has run dry.

Pisinoe pushes past me and begins toward Jaquob's camp. My heart rises in my throat, and instinct takes over. I grab hold of her arm, but this only fuels her suspicion. She hisses and pulls herself from my grasp, hurling her body farther down the path.

"Pisinoe, wait!" I beg, following behind her, reaching for her wings, clawing at her shoulders, trying to trip her, but she barrels forward like an arrow toward its target. Screaming will draw Jaquob to investigate, and that's the last thing I want.

She stops when she reaches the edge of the clearing. There, in plain sight, Jaquob sits with his back to us on a fallen log in front of his bonfire. Somehow, he hasn't heard us approach, and the bottle of liquor at his side reveals why. He's drunk.

All I can do now is watch in rapt silence as a tragedy unfolds across my sister's features: First, her mouth slackens, and she blinks rapidly, as if Jaquob is no more than a trick of the light, a bad dream she can banish by refocusing her vision. But he's no waking nightmare, and Pisinoe's astonishment quickly deteriorates into disgust as she tallies each lie I effortlessly told. The wide O of her lips curls back into a snarl, and her eyes narrow into slits. Her attention is locked

on him, but I know her bright blue stare has turned to ice—
the warmth that she usually radiates is gone. My throat tightens. Even at her angriest, I can usually dig to find a trove of
compassion, hot soil buried beneath a blanket of snow. But
now she assumes the posture saved for sailors: Her stance
widens, her fingers turn to claws. She bares her teeth and
draws back her shoulders, and the breath leaves my lungs.

Pisinoe is going to sing.

14

NOW

Thomas gathers men to search for Will. They clamber through the streets, banging on doors and shouting among themselves, before finally stomping through the village walls into the wilderness beyond. A somber hush falls over the settlement in their absence, enveloping its buildings in melancholy and whisper.

I stand vigil in the kitchen with Margery, stalking back and forth across the room as I offer silent prayers to gods I know aren't listening. Margery tries to busy herself with work, but her trembling fingers lose their grip on a large iron pot, and it crashes to the floor.

"God's blood!" she curses, and my stomach sinks. I've barely heard Margery raise her voice, let alone curse.

A series of horrible, heavy booms punctuate the air, joined by frantic cawing as blackbirds undoubtedly flee from their perches in the surrounding trees. The sound is otherworldly, and my mind races to find an explanation for it—Titans? The gods?

Margery sucks in a breath. "They're firing their muskets."

"Their muskets?" I parrot, perplexed by the word. I recall the metal weapon that Thomas slung over his shoulder as he left this morning. "What for?"

"Maybe they found an animal. Or"—her face darkens—"maybe the Secotans." After the first round of shots, the woods fall quiet once more. Somehow, this wretched silence is more agonizing than the volley of musket fire.

The men return under the banner of twilight. Like Margery suspected, Mauris Allen thought he saw a red wolf and tried to kill it. Apparently, the beast evaded not only his weapon, but Thomas's, Charles's, and Hugh's as well.

But they bring no news of Will. There was no evidence of him, and that fact alone is suspicious. His disappearance is too clean, too illogical. There was no reason for him to leave the confines of the palisades at night, though even if he had stumbled drunk through the forest alone, surely there'd be proof of that. Some scrap of clothing snagged on a branch, wafting like a flag in the frigid air. If he'd walked straight into the sea, the waves would have returned his body to shore by now.

I confide my belief of the Bailies' involvement to Emme, and she hushes me quickly, as if I've invited their Lucifer to break bread with us.

"Even if you're right, nothing will come of it," she cautions as she pulls me into an alley between two cottages, fearful that the others on the street might have read the accusation on my lips. "The Bailies are too powerful—such a statement will land you in the pillory if you're lucky. If you're not, you'll find your neck kissed by a rope."

I think of the pillory, the wooden contraption erected on a platform behind the meetinghouse. Intended for public humiliation, the device is little more than a wooden frame atop a post with holes for the punished to place their head and hands. No one has been forced into its clutches since I arrived.

Emme's warning leaves me restless, disturbed by the knowledge that even if anyone else suspects the Bailies in Will's disappearance, they won't breathe a word of it. I must carry this suspicion alone, deep inside me at the base of my stomach, where it agitates to no end. The only way I can keep calm is by imagining my future revenge. After Agnes's smug observation that Thomas is the next in line for my hand, I know she plans to join him on our trip to Scopuli. A scouting party is no place for a lady, but an exception can be made for the mother of Scopuli's future king. So be it. I won't stop her. Our vow not to harm women was never explicit, though we also never encountered one like Agnes, who so easily manipulates those around her into facilitating her own ascension.

A patrol of ten men, all Will's compatriots, spends the following mornings marching up and down the frozen streets under Thomas's orders, knocking on doors, asking questions. Watching them from my window brings the taste of vomit to the back of my throat. What a waste of time. By his own admission, Thomas was certainly the last to see Will alive, save for perhaps John Chapman, who was too drunk to remember. But this fact is never spoken aloud by anyone. Instead, his cronies perform the charade of grieving friends, forcing their way into people's homes, demanding answers that only the Bailies have.

Throughout all this, the Waters home remains as silent as a grave.

I try their door three times each day. Once, I'm certain that I catch sight of Cora sneaking a peek from a side window, but, painfully, the door remains closed. I press my palm to the wood, willing her to speak to me through the barrier. She doesn't come.

When I return home after today's final attempt, I find Margery in the kitchen preparing a watery soup. She's doing her best to flavor it with one of the few remaining bones from a long-dead sheep. Most of the town is eating much worse, if they're lucky enough to have food gracing their bowls at all. Will I even survive long enough for the weather to turn, or will I starve before then? I take a seat at the table with an audible groan, and Margery looks at me sympathetically.

"She still refuses me," I say, and Margery doesn't need to ask me who I am talking about. She's seen Cora and me grow closer; she's seen how her absence has me on edge.

"Give her some time, Lady Thelia." Her voice is kind, tinged with understanding. Every woman here is deeply intimate with catastrophe.

Tears well in my eyes. I know Cora is suffering, but I can't help but wallow in my own losses as well. I think of our last true conversation, of her breath against my lips.

It seemed impossible that even then, I . . .

A mere few days ago, the world held more promise than I ever dared wish for, and now those dreams have burned into ash. Margery steps beside me, placing a hand on my shoulder.

"She'll come around," she whispers, but there's an uncertainty in her voice that she can't quite hide. Margery knows more than anyone how dogged Cora can be when she has her mind set on something. "She just needs more time."

She's right, but the sentiment doesn't bring me any comfort.

"Do you think things would've been different if I had listened to you?" It's a thought that I haven't been able to shake.

"What do you mean?"

"Before the challenge. You told me to tell Thomas he couldn't participate—" My voice cracks beneath the weight of my guilt.

Margery's face crumples. "Oh, Thelia . . . Who can say? But whatever's happened to Will, it's not your fault . . ."

How many times have I heard those words before? How many times have I said them, more of a plea than a statement, desperate for them to be true?

Fault is a curious thing, too messy to trace. I can tell myself that I alone was not to blame for Proserpina's abduction—Dis, certainly, bears the bulk of that honor. But does Ceres hold any responsibility for placing the care of her daughter in the hands of three young girls? Or perhaps it's the fault of the oracle who visited us as girls for not warning Proserpina whose children she'd bear. Better yet, weren't the Fates the ones to weave her abduction into her destiny, just as they wove my traitorous act into mine?

But all of that feels hollow in the memory of Proserpina's screams. I was the one who was with her, and I was the one who gave her away. When determining true fault, all you can do is see who has the most blood on their hands, and I'm always covered in gore.

🙰

The Bailie home feels more like a prison than Scopuli ever did, with one notable distinction: No magic binds me inside its walls. Despite the cold, instinct draws me to the woods. Thomas will purposefully never find Will, or what's left of him, and given how confidently he struts around the house when he returns from his patrols, he believes no one else will, either. But this is Thomas's fatal error: He underestimates me.

And so, every day I leave the safety of the city walls to

search for clues. Margery accompanies me as often as she's able, waiting just outside the eastern gate. Cora has made it clear that she wants nothing to do with me, and our circle is too nervous to test her wrath. Margery's the only one brave enough to defy her, but even she won't walk beside me inside the palisades.

Which means I mostly explore the woods alone. Even the men don't stray as far away from the settlement as I do, but there's little reason for them to: Most have given up trying to catch anything in their traps, and the shadows that gather between the oaks and pines don't feel like home to them. But they do to me, even though the oaks here have the curious trait of retaining their leaves. Winter has gilded them with hoarfrost, and overhead, branches of all kinds shimmer with delicate, sparkling icicles. When the sun hits them, they glitter just as brightly as Pisinoe's jewels.

But there's no sun today, and it makes an already cold day feel even more frigid. My fingers stiffen in the deep winter air until the ache sharpens into pain. I welcome it. This hurt is physical. Manageable, and within my control—at any moment, I can return to the warmth of Margery's kitchen and end it.

The pain of Cora's silence has no release.

I'm far enough into the trees now that the settlement's sounds are lost to me. There's only the crunch of my boots against hardened snow, and the occasional soft thud when a branch drops its powder collection to the ground.

A large, unfamiliar oak looms ahead of me on the path, signaling that I've reached an unexplored area of woods. In the dull afternoon light, the tree's snarled branches look menacing, as if its arms are raised in warning. My gut tells me to heed it, but how can I? Frosted leaves shiver in the wind as I push forward into this unknown section of the forest.

Go back, they seem to whisper. Immediately, the trees feel wilder and the sky darker. This must be the section of woods that belongs to Sybil Browne. A shiver traces up my spine. Though I have no reason to fear her, when nature flashes its fangs, you should listen. I pull my cloak tighter to my frame to steel myself against the cold and defy every instinct that screams at me to turn back.

After a while, I ponder heeding the warnings, until I smell it. The scent is strange, a petrichor that has soured, a sweetness that masks something sinister. At first, it's faint enough that I can pretend I've imagined it, but it intensifies the deeper I go into the labyrinth of trees.

What could cause such a foul smell? An animal?

It's too cold for rot to touch an animal's corpse, and my stomach growls at the idea. A haze of hunger descends, and inside its fog I let myself believe it's a creature, perhaps even a buck, that the cold air has preserved enough to eat. Margery will be thrilled. For the first time in weeks, Jeremie will sleep with a full stomach.

Fallen branches claw at my wool cloak, as if the forest is begging me to stop. But the idea of fresh meat overpowers whatever internal warning mechanism the smell has activated. The scent is staggering now. It holds more decay inside its profile than before, and a warmth that's reserved for rotting things. A wave of nausea rolls through my belly, and my hands move to cover my mouth. Then I hear it.

It's the sound of beak tearing muscle, combined with a slow *plip . . . plip . . . plip*. The trees part to reveal a clearing. Directly before me, hanging from the limb of another ancient oak, is a body. A large, hideous turkey vulture sits on the corpse's shoulder, and although the bird is obscuring his face, I don't need to get any closer to know that it's Will.

The vulture lifts its head to appraise me with large golden

eyes. She's already consumed Will's, leaving behind two bloody voids that find me. But the worst part is his stomach. Someone has carved him open, leaving his intestines to spill out onto the snow. Pink ribbons, all tangled together in a heaping pile at the base of his feet, and although this scene should be familiar, it makes me want to retch. No one here practices haruspicy; only hate could drive someone to desecrate his body like this.

"Oh, Will," I whisper. "What happened to you?"

Having decided I'm no threat, the vulture burrows her hideous, bloodstained beak back into Will's neck. A primal growl rises in my throat as I rush forward. She raises her huge black wings, not unlike my own, and unleashes a hiss meant to ward me away, but she's calculated wrong—I *am* a threat, and I grab a large stick from the ground to prove it. One violent swing through the air is all it takes for her to decide that Will's body isn't worth dying over. She's a scavenger, after all. She takes to the sky, leaving Will and me alone.

A low wail rises from my gut and spills out from my lips. Will's body swings gently from the force of the vulture's ascent, his toes just barely caressing the red snow beneath him. The sight is so like the sailors I processed on Scopuli's shores; the only difference is that this exact shade of gore now paints snow instead of sand.

My stomach growls. My mouth waters.

Once again, my hand is at my lips, although this time I'm not sure if it's to prevent myself from retching or from drooling. Disgust and shame flood every part of me, and I turn away from Will. His shocked expression feels accusatory, as if he knows what my body, what my instinct, wants to do with him.

"This is Will!" The words come tumbling out in a desperate scream. But hearing them hang in the ice-chilled air isn't what makes the salivating stop—it's that violent open gash across his midsection, the source of the fetid smell. His bowels are torn; the meat is spoiled. Instinct sorts him into the pile for burning. Hot tears pool in my eyes, and I rub them away with the backs of my hands.

Gods, I really am a monster.

I move to the rope tied around the oak's trunk that keeps Will suspended. It feels like hours before I'm finally able to undo its knot, and when I do, he crashes into the snow. Another horrid, wretched sound tears from my throat. I wish it had its magic—the sorrow it carries would bring down the sky.

I nestle down beside him. His face, the face that holds so much of Cora, is mottled blue and purple, and I blink back tears as images of sailors twisting on the end of my rope flash before me. Will suffered the same fate, a realization that makes my hands shake. Ice crystals cling to his dark hair, and to his eyelashes, which still ring those hollow eyes. A bloated, blackened tongue hangs limp between his lips. Everything about his appearance is an affront to how he looked in life.

My fingers move to brush a tendril of hair behind his ear, and I place my head to his stiff chest, hoping against reason to find what I know I will not. No heartbeat drums, and my tears break free at this final injustice. The cold turns them to ice against my face.

The sun has fallen below the tops of the trees, and the temperature with it. I should go back, but the thought of leaving Will like this makes the tears come harder. Even in my dreams, I never turn around to help Proserpina. I can't abandon another person I care about to the darkness, and Cora needs to know—oh, gods. This will destroy her.

"Get out of here, girl." An unfamiliar voice cuts through the glen, as gnarled as the oak that held Will.

My head jerks from his chest to search the ring of trees

that encircles me, but I can't find the source. It's as if the woods themselves are speaking, ancient and all-seeing, though I know who the voice belongs to.

"Sybil?" I ask, pushing myself to my feet. "Sybil Browne?"

"If they find you with him, they'll blame you for this savagery."

"I could never—" The sentence dies in my throat, because of course I could.

I did.

Not Will specifically, no, but how many countless others? Did they have lovers they never returned to, who always wondered what fate they met, assuming the worst but never able to guess the true horror of it?

If Will had been on one of those boats, I would have killed him. Who knows how many Wills died at my hands. The thought is so disturbing that I let out another anguished wail as Sybil emerges from the trees. She's tiny, her face hidden beneath the shadow of her cloak.

"No need for that. I know it wasn't you."

"So you saw who did it, then?" My eyes are frantic now. "Was it Thomas Bailie?"

"It was a man, that's all I know. I heard him laughing." She tips her head to Will. "But by the time I got here, he was gone."

Grief sharpens into fury, an emotion I'm far more comfortable wearing. "He lured Will here on purpose. To do this."

"No one ventures here unless they have good reason."

"Because of you."

"Yes."

"I can't leave him."

"You must. How would it look, you dragging him back into town? Do you think they'll believe you had nothing to do with his death?"

Of course they wouldn't. It's painfully clever, and equally devastating. Thomas hid his treachery in plain sight, knowing that I, with my frequent forest venturing, was the only one likely enough to find it. When he led the search parties, all he had to do was avoid an area of the woods that everyone already avoided. Either his secret would remain safe or I would dig my own grave by trying to return Will's body to the City of Raleigh.

Such designs are far too thoughtful to be the work of Thomas alone. No, he's too brash, too excitable. This level of planning belongs to someone calmer, more collected. Agnes. She set a snare for me, and without Sybil's intervention, I would have walked straight into it. My fingers curl to fists, and if I had any reservations about her fate, they're gone in an instant, a drop of water lost to the waves.

The other men will be for my sisters, for Proserpina. Agnes and her son will be mine.

᎒᎒᎒

Abandoning Will in the woods is excruciating, but Sybil's right: I can't allow myself to fall into Agnes's trap. So I kiss his cheek gently and force myself to return home. The warmth of my bed provides no comfort, as two thoughts torment me: First, what Thomas must have said to bait Will that deep into the woods so late at night. Did Will mistake the moment as the time for his confession? Is that what made Thomas desecrate him so? And second, how can I possibly carry such a secret? Luckily, I don't have to for long.

The next morning, Mauris Allen discovers Will's mutilated corpse outside the southern gate. It's torn to shreds, left in such a state of carnage that the official conclusion is an animal attack. If Agnes and Thomas are shocked by the news, they manage to keep a straight face when they tell me about it. I have to keep one as well—how did Sybil manage to move Will there, and how was she able to disguise the exact nature of his death? Perhaps the stories women whisper about her aren't entirely fabricated.

What's left of his body is placed in the charnel house outside the eastern gate: The frozen ground won't easily accept the dead, but Master Waters can't wait that long. He demands a funeral, frigid earth be damned. Perhaps he fears he won't make it to warmer weather to see his son properly buried. Unable to refuse a dying man, the Council acquiesces. And so, three days later, on the morning of my fourth full moon, the town gathers to bury Will.

Sorrow and the strangeness of unknown customs work together to soften the edges of his funeral into no more than a series of discordant sights, sounds, and feelings: There's the loud, hollow tolling of the bell that guides his procession past the charnel house to the colony's cemetery. The forest that looms ahead, its trees twisted into a nearly impenetrable gate. The longing that fills me for the safety of their shadows, more home to me than the City of Raleigh could ever be.

The dark, exposed soil that will soon hold Will's grave, the ground around it scorched an unseemly, malicious black from where they lit a fire to thaw it. The sour taste of bile in my throat at the sight of it, and the smell that lingers in the chilled air—the same hideous scent of burnt earth as when the ground opened to swallow Proserpina. The strange sense of knowing that one day, the forest will reclaim this cemetery, and the wooden crosses that mark its graves will be lost to time. Will, and everyone else this island devours, will simply vanish from history. How this makes me feel so profoundly lonely.

There's Alis Chapman graciously offering me a handkerchief, and Cora standing before Will's grave, refusing to meet my eyes. The jealousy that needles between my ribs when it's Margery she leans into for support, and the shame that swirls in the pit of my stomach at the fact that even here, I yearn for her.

Me willing her to change her mind: *Look at me. Look at me. Look at me.* My fingers tapping against my sides as I think the words over and over, always three times in a row, counting on the magic that number holds to sway her: Three sisters banished. The Trinity. The Fates, who apparently didn't spin this concession into my destiny, for my incantation goes unanswered.

Cora never looks.

The dull thud of the coffin hitting the bottom of the grave, lighter than it should be, given how much of Will was missing. How Cora winces each time dirt hits it as men work to refill the hole that will cradle him until he's no more than dust.

The fog lifts only once the rest of the villagers have already gone ahead, making their way back inside the safety of the gates. A pang of guilt flicks at my heart, wind on a chime. This isn't what I wanted. Not at the end, not once I knew him.

"Goodbye, Will," I whisper down to the earth. I didn't see much death as a child. The emotions it brings are difficult to navigate. Sorrow at the loss of a friend, relief that his death wasn't by my hand, confusion as to why it had to happen at all. At least I know who's responsible for it—many people tonight will go to bed scared of an evil they can't place. Little do they know that one monster this city holds has already achieved his goal. For now, no more blood will be spilled in his pursuit of it.

Funeral feasts were common among the mortals of my time, and though the custom persists into this age, the meetinghouse holds no feast today. There are plenty of those offensive hard biscuits, and a few crocks of a watery broth, but there's simply not enough food left to do Will's life justice. Still, the eyes of the poorer residents of the village, like Margery and Jeremie, light up at the sight of it all. How dangerously close we all are to passing into oblivion.

We might all starve before the men follow me back.

What a terrible waste that would be.

People file into their seats, and a fresh wave of anxiety rolls over me. As Will's betrothed, I'm expected to sit at the head table, where I find Cora glaring at me: a warning not to get close. I heed it. The last time someone looked at me with such disgust, she banished me to Scopuli. Where would Cora send me if she had Ceres's powers? Master Sampson's Sunday warnings of scorching fires that burn eternal come to mind. Though her Hell doesn't exist, Cora might rest easier if she knew I was marked for the pit of Tartarus. From what I can tell, the two places aren't that dissimilar.

Emme motions for me to sit at the table with her, Wenefrid, Margaret, and Rose's friend Jane. The others bristle as I approach, but Emme shoots them a look that keeps their objections quiet. We're silent for most of the meal. I take a large sip of wine, hoping to either push the anxiety away or bury it with drink.

Cora excuses herself from the table, stumbling a bit from self-medicating when she stands. Without thinking, I hop to my feet to follow her. I catch Emme reaching for me from the corner of my eye, and though she means well, I've been waiting for this opportunity since Will disappeared. Nothing can keep me from Cora now.

I find her outside, leaning against the meetinghouse wall, close to where I kissed Will. How have five weeks already passed since then? Her face is buried in her hands as she heaves loud, grotesque sobs. I open my mouth, hoping to find something comforting to say, but what words exist for the weight of this moment? Instead, I take a cautious step forward. Snow crunches beneath my boots, and Cora whips her head up at the sound. When she sees me, she laughs. The noise is hateful, and I wither beneath it.

"What do you want?" she sneers, returning her weight to her feet.

"To make sure you're all right."

"I'm not," she growls, her words coated with venom. "Someone murdered my brother, most likely because of you."

"Cora—"

"It made me start to wonder . . . What do I actually know about you? Maybe Agnes was right to be suspicious—maybe you are an agent of Spain after all. Or perhaps something worse, sent here by Lucifer to lead us into sin. Whoever you are, you've done a great job turning us all against each other."

"You know who I am. I'm your friend."

"So you plan to rebuff Thomas when he proposes to you?"

"Cora, please—"

"Listen." Her voice drops to a register reserved for warnings: a snake's rattle or a lion's growl. "If you were my friend, you wouldn't have stolen my past and my future in the same night. Unless you mean to tell me that you'll decline Thomas's offer?"

"With Will gone, he's the winner . . ." The words are weak, for she's right: My actions are unthinkable. But even though I spend my idle moments imagining the sound of her voice whispered into my hair, the feeling of her sweet breath on my neck, I'm not here for her. She doesn't know, can't ever know, what's truly at stake.

My sisters, I want to scream. *They're depending on me.*

And I'm running out of time.

Cora spits at my feet, the glob of saliva barely missing my left boot to land in the snow.

"I don't want him, Cora! I never wanted him!" I reach for her hand, as if somehow our skin touching can convey the sincerity of this small truth. "You must know that all I've ever wanted is—"

"Don't." She flinches away from me before I can find her. "Don't you dare."

The hatred in her voice steals my confession from my throat. "Please, believe me. I never meant for this to happen . . . I care for you, Cora. And I cared for Will, too."

"Oh, I know you cared for him. You're a seductress. A whore."

I balk beneath the weight of her anger. Who exactly is she accusing me of seducing? Is it only Will and Thomas, or does she count herself among the ranks?

"I know what you two were up to, sneaking around when I was doing *anything* possible to keep Thomas's affection. But you must not have cared much for Will, given that you're already willing to sell your cunt to Thomas."

I've never heard Cora speak so profanely, and the word echoes in my mind, drawing shivers up my back. *Cunt. Cunt. Cunt.*

"You know it wasn't like that between us."

"So you never laid with him?"

I open my mouth to speak and then close it. It would be so simple to lie to her now, far easier than explaining the truth of what Will and I shared, but where would I even begin?

"This is your chance to speak honestly. And not just about Will. You've been hiding something from me, from us, since the moment you landed here. None of the men care to investigate because they don't want to jeopardize their chance at unimaginable wealth, but don't think that we can't sense something isn't right. Tell me everything now, or don't speak to me again."

If Sybil was exiled for healing an innocent man, I won't be given the chance to flee into the safety of the woods—my story will cost me my life, and swiftly. And yet, as I stand before those searching green eyes, there's a part of me that wants to tell her everything. If it were only my future at stake, I would drop to my knees and confess it all, from the very beginning. Every shameful secret I've ever kept, I'd give to Cora willingly.

But the gods aren't known for offering second chances, and my sisters need me to succeed. I owe them that, after all the years Scopuli stole from them. That *I* stole from them.

"I can't . . ." My chest tightens as the words leave my lips. Her stare hardens.

"Then keep your distance," she says. The words are cold, plated with a finality that chills my blood.

"Cora—"

"Goodbye, Thelia."

There's something in her voice, buried in the anger, a seed beneath snow. It's sorrow. The tone makes me reach for her again, but my hand finds nothing but empty air as she retreats around the corner, out of sight.

I catch glimpses of her through the windows, watch her figure vanish behind corners, and overhear her name on other lips. It feels as if Cora died, too, now no more than a ghost who haunts me with near misses.

I'm surprised to find that her absence hurts as much as Proserpina's did, although the pain is a different shade.

Proserpina was taken from me against her will, and the guilt of playing a role in that violent act warped my insides into something as monstrous as the exterior that Ceres gave me to find her. But Cora is still here, just out of reach, disgusted by me—and with good reason. I always assumed Proserpina must have despised me, too, but I never had to see it. The image of Cora's twisted face, of the twinge of longing in her goodbye, torments me just as much as those earlier memories of Proserpina, bathed in moonlight, smiling up at me from that secluded pool.

I've taken to following Margery around like a sick dog, eager for kindness, which is why I eat breakfast in the kitchen instead of in my room. Behind me, Margery stirs away at another crock of watery soup. I don't have the heart to ask her what she's flavoring this one with. The spoon clinks against the rim of the pot erratically, and I turn away from the woeful meal before me to watch her.

Her eyes are locked on me, and we both startle. I wasn't expecting her to be so intently focused on my form, but to be fair, she wasn't expecting me to notice. It's not common for people to pay her much attention.

"Are you all right?" I motion my head to her vigorous mixing.

"Forgive me, Lady Thelia, I didn't mean to stare . . ." Wisps of blond hair poke out from beneath her coif, further evidence of her nerves. Her eyes dart to the wall and then back to me, teeth chewing on her bottom lip while she searches for words. My heart begins to pound as I watch her. I imagine a stale smell filling the space between us, the anxiety I'm certain is dripping from her pores. "It's just something I heard from Elyoner this morning . . ."

"What did she say?"

"Well, she heard from Alis, who overheard it when her husband was talking with Master Lacie over an ale—" She wrings her hands in her apron.

"And?" I can't keep myself from interrupting her. The way she refuses to meet my gaze makes me uneasy.

"Last night Master Thomas went to speak with Master Richard—"

"Why?"

"I'm trying to tell you, Lady Thelia!"

I bite my tongue and motion for her to continue.

"He ended his engagement to Cora."

Despite being seated, I cling to the table for support; I can't breathe. I knew this moment was coming, but I hoped Thomas and Mistress Bailie would have the decency to wait. Will hasn't yet been buried a week.

"Master Waters was devastated . . . he tried to throw Master Thomas out on the streets but was too weak to do so. Even still, he made quite the commotion." She pauses for a moment, as if considering whether she should continue. "People are saying he did it so he could marry you, Lady Thelia."

I push myself up from the table so abruptly that my bowl clatters onto the ground with a loud bang, but thankfully doesn't shatter.

"Damnit!" I curse, before dropping to my knees to clean up the gruel that's splattered across the packed dirt floor.

"It's all right, let me . . ." Margery places a warm hand on my shoulder, and tears spring to my eyes at the kindness of the gesture. I look up at her, trying to will them away before they can spill over my cheeks. I don't succeed.

I've been here for only a few short months, and in that time, I've taken everything from Cora. How can I possibly begin to explain to her that none of it was personal? That I never meant to hurt her? That I know what it feels like to lose everything you've ever loved, and that excruciating pain is the last thing I wanted for her?

"I have to find her." My voice is frantic, the words tumbling out of my mouth one on top of the next.

"She won't want to see you. Not yet." Her tone is gentle as she moves to dry my wet cheeks, but her words cut like coral. No, sharper. Like talons.

I moan, nearly collapsing to the floor at the idea of being permanently exiled from Cora's Eden and into Thomas's Hell.

"Thomas is still the most powerful and respected man in the village. The men see this as an obvious next step for him, but I wouldn't count on any kindness from the women."

I look down to my hands. I can feel my cheeks flushing with shame.

"What do Emme and the others think?"

"Cora has been our friend for years . . ." Margery smiles sadly at me, answering my question without answering it at all. "Regardless of what they think, they know better than to incur her wrath."

"I didn't ask for this." The sentiment rings hollow, hanging in the air for Margery to examine. Yet it's all I can think to say.

"I know, my lady. We rarely do."

Her words twist my insides into knots as I mull over them. I spent eons imprisoned on a rocky shoreline as punishment for a savage act committed by a god. Proserpina was kidnapped by someone old enough to be her father thousands of times over. I know it was my cowardice that sent him to her, but I've been punished for it every single moment since. Where was Dis's punishment? The stability of Cora's future was tied to her betrothal to Thomas, and he tossed her aside without a second thought. How often were we warned as children to watch ourselves around men, to guard our purity with our lives until the moment our fathers deemed us old enough to be traded for status, wealth, prestige?

Margery's gentle gaze reveals a horrifying truth: Despite the slow, torturous passage of time, despite the changes in technology, and language, and dress, our lives are still ravaged by all the things we didn't ask for, and those who do the ravaging never have to pay for it. My jaw clenches so tightly that the taste of copper blooms in my mouth.

I spend the rest of the day moored in my room, awaiting the inevitable. This time, I don't lock myself in. It's the cosmic punishment that I'm owed, isn't it? And after losing Cora for good, I no longer feel compelled to hide from it. I watch the street from the window, praying for a glimpse of her slender frame through its wooden shutters, but she doesn't materialize. Those who do pass slow their gait as they cross beneath the house's shadow, entranced by the gossip born under its roof. Word travels quickly here, just as it did in Ceres's palace.

Thomas doesn't return to greet his new bride until after night falls, and when he does, he bursts through the front door with such force the entire house shakes. He laughs boisterously and bids good night to several other low, indistinguishable voices, perhaps accomplices in his treachery.

Then his footsteps begin up the stairs. He makes it to the landing, and, like always, he stops outside of my room. But tonight, he doesn't just linger; tonight, he throws the door open, enters my space uninvited, then closes himself inside it.

I'm sitting in front of the fireplace with Cora's Bible open on my lap. She left it here before Will disappeared, and even the word of God isn't enough to bring her back to reclaim it. I'd been trying to force meaning from its stories, as if by somehow understanding the core of Cora's faith, I could convince her to come back to me. I close the tome gently and set it on the floor.

Thomas grins as he strides toward the fireplace, holding his hands out to the flame's warmth.

"It's done, dear Thelia."

I don't answer him. He reeks of alcohol.

"Master Waters didn't take the news well, but Cora handled herself with grace." He pulls a golden ring from his pocket, turning to present it to me. "Your ring, my queen."

I allow him to slide it onto the same finger Cora wore it on when it was hers. How ugly this golden band is—a visible symbol that I no longer belong to myself.

He never officially asked me to marry him, never confirmed that his second place was enough to win my hand and the treasure that comes with it. He simply assumes he's entitled to me, and why shouldn't he? This is a man who has never been told no. He's both spoiled and wealthy, a dangerous combination.

He drops to his knees to crawl toward me, though not in supplication. When he's close enough, he grabs ahold of my legs and buries his head in my lap. My hands slide up the arms of the chair as my entire body recoils from his touch. He digs in deeper.

"I can't wait to taste you."

"Stay back," I hiss, pushing his face away. He looks up at me with a grin.

"You can only play coy for so long, sweet Thelia," he says.

"I'm not your wife yet," I growl, managing to kick my legs free. He falls onto his backside with a loud thud, and I jump to my feet. Thankfully, he's so slammed with drink that he can't follow me. He doesn't have the coordination right now to punish my petulance with a smack.

"Technically," he concedes. "But you weren't Will's, either."

"How dare you—"

"Don't bother pretending, my lady. Will could never keep secrets from me."

"You can have me as soon as we set sail for—"

"I know, I know. We'll go as soon as the weather permits. I have no reason to delay, not now." He crawls back to his knees, and then rises to his feet. "But I can keep a secret if you can . . ."

When his hand reaches for the top of my nightgown, I slap it away, staring daggers. For now, he heeds the warning and stalks to my bedroom door, miming disappointment.

"I won't wait much longer," he warns. My stomach flips.

Once he's gone, I rush forward to block the door, but the act brings me no comfort.

From now on, there will be only sleepless nights in the Bailie house.

15

〜〜〜〜〜

BEFORE

I dive for Pisinoe, knocking the song from her lips as we fall to the ground in a tangle of limbs and wings. Her surprise is my only advantage, and I make use of it, rolling my body on top of hers to pin her arms against her sides with my legs. Then my hands clamp down across her mouth. Pisinoe's blue eyes flare, hot as fire.

"I'll explain everything," I whisper, looking back over my shoulder. Jaquob's form has slumped into the sand, the now-empty liquor bottle at his side. He's too drunk to notice anything amiss in the thicket behind him. "Just don't sing."

She growls so fiercely behind my palms that my fingers flinch, fearing her bite. But two can play at this game, especially when it's Proserpina who's at stake. When I speak again, my voice is a hiss. "I'm serious."

Pisinoe grunts in assent, though she doesn't look happy about it. When I slide off her frame, she allows me to lead her out of Jaquob's earshot.

"How could you hide this?" she asks. "From the gods? From me?" I've never seen her warm face this shattered. Not when Ceres spoke those final words and sealed our fate, nor when we found ourselves deposited on this forsaken island. Not even after those first sailors bound us. Because all those times, it was never me betraying her.

I shake my head. "You don't understand. I didn't want to keep this from you, but—"

"But what? You hid him here by accident? It's been six weeks since the wreck! What have you been feeding him— gods, our food? *His companions?*"

"Pisinoe, please—"

She brings a hand to her lips, her teeth grazing at her thumb. An anxious habit from when we were children. "Raidne will know what to do."

"No." Even I'm surprised by the authority my voice carries. "You can't tell her."

Her eyes widen. The blue irises are still laced with fury, and she laughs at me bitterly. "You can't expect me to keep this secret for you."

"She'll make me kill him, Pisinoe!"

My cheek erupts with a bright bloom of pain at the same time a loud *crack* fills the air, and it takes me a few moments to understand that she's slapped me across the face, hard. My fingers reach gingerly for the site of the impact, and I wince when I find it. The initial contact was sharp, painful, but its prolonged stinging hurts more. The weight of Pisinoe's anger truly sinks in, and tears pool in the corners of my eyes. In my life, this is the second most unforgivable thing that I've done, but I never had to face Proserpina after I betrayed her.

"Kill him? *Kill him?*" She growls the words, leaning in close to me. "He doesn't belong to us, Thelxiope! He belongs to Ceres."

Anger flares inside my chest, and without thinking, I shove her away. Pisinoe stumbles back, her own ire waning in the sudden eruption of mine. There was no way for her to know that her words were the exact wrong thing to say, that while my guilt at hiding Jaquob grew, my resolve that he would never be Ceres's only strengthened. "Mark my words, Pisinoe. I'll never give that woman another sacrifice. She isn't listening, so why should we keep groveling at her feet?"

She throws her head back and laughs. The sound is cruel, and my feathers quiver beneath it. There was a part of me that thought Pisinoe would agree with me, and it feels like a fool now.

"Why? Are you serious? Do I need to remind you that it was our fault her daughter was kidnapped? That we'll never get off this island unless it's with her blessing?" And then her eyes are on me, filled with a malice I didn't know she was capable of feeling. "You should know that better than any of us."

The words are an intentional blow, and they extinguish the fury in my belly that roared mere moments ago. I recoil from them, from her, and suck in a breath with surprise. Only then does she recognize the boundary that she's broken.

"And you think I don't? I *betrayed* her, Pisinoe. How many times did I tell her I loved her, and yet, she was taken *because of me*. And instead of returning to us, she bound herself to that infernal place—"

Confusion softens the fury in Pisinoe's eyes. "What are you saying, exactly? You believe she chose to stay?"

"Maybe!" My voice cracks. "What if, as she held those cursed seeds in her palm, she decided she never wanted to see me again?"

"Then why send the lilies? The ships?"

I scoff. "You never believed that she did."

Pity crumbles Pisinoe's remaining anger away, which somehow feels worse. "Raidne should be here."

"Pisinoe . . ." Desperation weaves into my voice, and a

wave of self-loathing crashes over me. I'm still too weak, just like all those years ago. How can I explain to her what I haven't been able to fully articulate even to myself? That even after all these years, there's nothing I wouldn't do to hear her voice again.

That if she truly forsakes me for good, I'll never be able to ask her why she did it.

"I'm sorry, Thelxiope. It'll be better for you if we tell her together."

Pisinoe might as well have me pinned against a tree, the bite of its bark tearing into my back. And it's as true as it was then: There's no stopping the inevitable.

My body quakes as the elder sister leads the younger to face her fate.

⌘

The trek back to our cottage feels like it takes hours, though I admittedly do my best to slow it down. But Pisinoe doesn't let me dawdle for long, and soon enough she digs her nails into the soft flesh of my arm and pulls me to the sky, intent on delivering me. When we land on Scopuli's cliffs, Raidne stands waiting, a silhouette in our doorway.

At first, she doesn't see us. She's facing Scopuli's woods, her black hair spilling over her shoulders. She thinks I've been hiding in the meadow these past months. It's not until we're closer that her attention wanders toward the cliffs. She raises a hand in a wave, and then her face crumples as our expressions begin to register. Her eyes implore Pisinoe's as we approach, rapidly growing alarmed.

"What is it?" she asks. "Another lily? Another sign?"

Pisinoe pushes me forward to stand between them. "Tell her."

My breath catches in my throat, and I shake my head.

"Tell her, or I will."

Raidne turns to me, her muscles tense with worry. "Thelx-iope?"

I lift my chin to face her, this woman who raised and sheltered me as best she could. Determination lifts me to stand straighter, to show her that I'm a woman now, too. That I have been for centuries. That I get to decide what happens.

"I found a man."

Raidne's lips purse, as if I've spoken one of the countless unknown languages from the book pages she collects. She raises a questioning eyebrow at Pisinoe, who has suddenly become very preoccupied with her feet.

"A live man. The day after the wreck."

I watch as her mind clicks the pieces of the puzzle into place, clasping my hands behind my back so she can't see how badly they tremble. Raidne's dark brows crinkle together, her confusion deepening.

"That's not all!" Pisinoe interjects. Despite her insistence that I bear the news, it seems she can no longer stand to carry my secret. "He's still alive—she hid him from us. On Rotunda."

I brace myself for the rage that's certain to barrel toward me like a horse bitten by a fly, but it doesn't come. Raidne's eyes are locked on me, but where Pisinoe's held fury, hers hold only hurt.

"I don't understand," she says softly. "Why did you keep this from us?"

"Because Proserpina told me to."

A loud gasp tears from Pisinoe's throat, and I flinch beneath the doubt it holds. But the sound doesn't break Raidne's focus. She's appraising me once more, just like she did when I told them about the lily.

"So tell us now, then."

"I found him on the beach the first time we went salvaging. But when I started to call for you, I heard her. She told me not to. I've been hiding him ever since, waiting for her to explain why she wanted me to save him, waiting for her to reveal his purpose—"

"And has she?" Pisinoe interrupts, and my cheeks burn crimson.

"No."

Pity draws the corners of Raidne's lips up into a sad smile, and only now does she turn to Pisinoe. The two conduct the next part of the conversation in pointed looks, as if it's a language I don't understand.

Has she gone mad, Raidne? What are we going to do?

The only thing we can.

She'll never agree to it!

Raidne sighs softly, and she reaches her delicate fingers to cup my chin. "What about the women, Thelxiope? Why would Proserpina want to save someone capable of such brutality?"

Her voice is surprisingly gentle, and when I meet her stare again, so are her eyes. The care she takes brings mist to the corners of mine, and I blink back tears as I remember the wraiths from my dreams, as I remember their anger.

"He said he didn't know anything about them," I answer, but the words sound so foolish spoken out loud. My chest tightens at my naïvety, at my willingness to be deceived. Of course that's what he said, and I accepted his lie readily. But even if they're right, even if Jaquob is as much a monster as the other sailors who washed ashore here, I refuse to dedicate him to the Mother of the Fields.

"You should have told us," Raidne continues. "We could've been done with this weeks ago."

Anger brings the sour taste of bile to my tongue, and I

scoff. "If I'd told you weeks ago, he'd either be ash on the wind or salted meat in our stores. He wasn't fit to sacrifice until I healed him!"

Until I healed him. The ground tilts beneath my feet as understanding prickles across my skin, raising the hair on the back of my neck, nearly stopping my heart. I can't breathe, oh, gods, I can't— Of course! *Of course!*

Raidne's right: Proserpina wouldn't want to save a man capable of such brutality, not unless . . .

"Thelxiope? Are you—" Raidne reaches for my swaying frame, but I raise a hand to silence her.

"He wasn't a fitting sacrifice until I healed him," I repeat. A shaky laugh rises from my depths, and I can feel my gaping mouth curl into a slow smile. "But he is now."

Yes, Thelia, yes . . . !

That voice makes my head fall back and my eyes roll up to the heavens. Above me, the night sky twinkles with the brilliance of infinite stars, their light smearing together through the tears that now fall freely. I open my arms to them, ecstatic, as relief spins me in circles across the cliffs. She speaks, she speaks. My queen finally speaks.

"Did you hear that?" I call to my sisters as their blurred forms draw together. They must think me mad, but I don't care—let them. "I know what he's for!"

Yes, tell them . . .

"All those years, it was Proserpina sending us ships. And all those years, we gave their spoils to Ceres. Don't you understand?"

All I can do is clap my hands in giddy excitement as I watch Raidne solve the riddle, her gray eyes bright as the answer comes to her.

"So instead of Ceres . . ."

He's mine . . .

"Yes." My mouth is hers as my taloned feet carry me to my sisters, my arms extended to find their hands. Pisinoe grins as she accepts one, and though it's not as large, Raidne's smile is just as fiery, lit by the thrill of defiance. "The Queen of the Underworld is owed her due."

16

NOW

The City of Raleigh, filled with eyes loyal to the Bailies, doesn't offer many places to hide from Thomas. But the forest does. Now that I've discovered their bloody secret, the trees grant their protection, but the comfort I once felt here is gone. These oaks, with their green winter leaves, remind me that I'm an outsider here, haunting the paths created by others. As I explore them, I find myself wishing for a miracle—the gentle curve of a trail opening to my meadow, erupting with lilies.

Instead, in the hush of the late winter woods, I'm granted a different one.

I've been spared from Eve's curse for over two months now. When I first heard the turn of phrase a few days after my arrival, I didn't understand it, but Cora's Bible instruction offered the explanation:

I will greatly increase thy sorrows, and thy conceptions. In sorrow shalt thou bring forth children, and thy desire shall be subject to thine husband, and he shall rule over thee.

Incredible that despite the passage of millennia, Cora's god behaves in the same petulant ways that ours did. They all hate being bested by men, but they absolutely despise being bested by women. Like Jove, her god is laughably self-absorbed. Banishing his children from Eden was the only way to regain control, to ensure unending worship. It was a crafty decision, but it hardly inspires me to look to him for solace.

It seems all gods know that enlightened women are forces to be reckoned with, and that idea trickled down through the centuries. It's why Cora is the only woman here who can read.

And so they banish us to the domestic realm, but that isn't enough. Eve's cursed, after all. Her ability to create life is never regarded as a gift. It's a punishment, a way to make us ashamed of our achievements, heartbroken over the amazing feats our bodies can achieve.

Women can bear children.

And here, I'm a woman, too. In the safety of the trees, I cradle the swell in my belly, a child too small yet to be noticed by anyone else. The hours pass quickly with fantasies of returning to Scopuli, where there's no husband to rule my future. Instead, we three will shower her with love and protect her from all the evils in the world. And there are so many evils.

Three weeks after his last visit to my bedroom, Thomas grows tired of waiting. When I wake to the groan of the door creaking open, I know what comes for me.

The chair I've propped against it does little to keep him at bay. If anything, the added obstacle only emboldens him as he shoves the weight of his body against the door to push it away. Within the span of a few heartbeats, he's inside the room, taking in the space through hungry, narrow eyes. When he finds me in my bed, he pauses to see if I'm awake. I keep quiet. Perhaps he'll leave if he thinks I'm asleep, finding no sport in the act. My silent prayer goes unanswered.

"Ah, there you are." Though he's still across the room, the scent of ale hits my nostrils.

"What do you want, Thomas?" I try to keep my voice even, to project strength.

"You know what I want," he growls, and it's true. I do. I can feel it in the pit of my stomach. I don't have the strength to beat him back, and I fear for the child's life if he gets too rough with me. Instead, I lift the covers in hopes that my compliance will make it go faster.

He grins, a terrible thing to behold, then pulls off his shirt and undoes his trousers. Before I know it, he's on top of me, lifting the hem of my nightdress to my waist so he can force himself into my most sacred space.

My fingers dig into the flesh of his back. The indignity of it all. If I were truly human, my heart wouldn't be able to bear this. How he spreads my limbs apart like it's nothing to invade the root of me, like my body was always just his to use. How could the gods be so cruel, placing our souls inside vessels that so easily crack? But Proserpina was a lesson—the gods are the cruelest of us all.

When it's over, Thomas collapses on top of me. I feel his grin against my ear, and my fingernails dig deeper. He mistakes my grasp for pleasure, and in a way, he's not wrong. But what he, this man who didn't ask, assumes is from his body is actually from the image, a vision, that's appeared in my mind.

My fingers are no longer fingers; they're claws. The dark blue ocean unfurls beneath me, where Thomas's head bobs desperately up from beneath the water only for a wave to force him below once more. Letting him drown is tempting, but no, his sins are too grave to simply allow him to sink into the depths. That would be a mercy, one Thomas hasn't earned. Instinct takes hold, and I dive for him. Talons meet flesh, piercing the skin and digging deep into his muscle. He screams as his body splits apart, and saltwater rushes into his open mouth, as if even the sea is tired of hearing his voice. With a single thrust, I heave him from the waves, and we begin rising, rising, rising, until we're a silhouette against the sun. *See my strength,* I think. *It was here this whole time.*

He pulls out of me, and when he does, his eyes rush over the nakedness of my lower half, his conquest. He smiles. This final act of injustice seals his fate. In my vision, I let go. His body falls like a stone.

My body quakes with pleasure as I watch him shatter upon the cliffs.

᠋᠋᠋

The fifth full moon graces the sky, and I pray for spring. There's nothing else that can be done, no more preparations that can be made until the weather turns. But though each passing day loosens winter's jaws around our necks, its last weeks don't leave the city unscathed. The day-to-day tedium is punctuated with a staccato of deaths as Morta's shears sever thread after thread. Though most of the souls she calls to the Underworld belong to the city's poorer settlers, the wealthy aren't immune—Cora's father is among them.

I agonize over her dramatic reversal of fortune. Without a brother, a father, or a betrothed, she's all alone here. It's a dangerous position for a woman to find herself in, and I feel useless in the face of a world that continues to take from those I love. When will their sacrifices finally be enough? I think of our years banished. I think of Job from Cora's Bible.

I have my answer.

Losing Cora severs me from the rest of the women, save for Margery. Even Emme keeps her distance, unable to reconcile what I've stolen. Margery is kind when I encounter her preparing meals in the kitchen or hanging laundry on the line outside, but her days are filled with chores, and she doesn't need me following her around like a fawn on its mother's heels. She'd never admit as much, but I notice how her muscles tense in my presence. Despite the time we spend together, she still sees me as royalty, and she can't fully relax when I am around. It hurts, but I remember what it felt like to stand before Ceres. There was such incredible beauty in her power, but that same power also sparked fear: One misstep could lead to an eternal exile, to a monstrous metamorphosis. I was right to be afraid of her, and Margery is right to be afraid of me.

I hoped Thomas's appetite would be sated for a few weeks, but I'm barely granted one before he forces his way into my bedroom again. This time, I'm keenly aware of the blood coursing through the artery on his neck. Its pulsing is a clock counting the seconds of my violation. My eyes trace its trail to the place on his shoulder right above where his clavicle protrudes. The muscle there is flexed as he holds himself over me, and without thinking, I run a finger along the seam I'd cut if he were one of our sailors. What does he look like underneath his skin? What does he taste like?

I lift my head from the mattress and press my mouth to that quivering muscle. Thomas vibrates with pleasure. My lips part so that my teeth can find his skin, and I revel in the soft moan that escapes him, in the fact he has no idea what's coming.

I clamp my jaws down as hard as I can.

The moan cracks into a scream, and his keenly attuned self-preservation instinct tries to retreat from my grasp. But I bite harder, my hands snaking around his sides so my finger-nails can claw into the flesh on his back. Only once I taste hot, slick copper on my tongue do I release him, and my head hits the pillow with a contented sigh. Thomas stares down at me in shock, unsure of what to make of my bloodstained lips, my gory smile. He can't know that I'm imagining what he'll taste like cooked into one of Raidne's stews, but I am, and the thought makes me laugh. This time, he doesn't linger in my bed to gloat. For the first time in this body, I feel a surge of power as he scurries from my quarters to lock himself back in his own.

I relive the fantasy of dropping him onto Castle's spires over and over again, delighting in how his face contorts with horror as he falls through the air, how his body slams into the rocks with a singular sickening crack. But the best part of this daydream is watching the light fade from his eyes as his blood spills down over the stones, a sacrifice for me alone.

The physical toll of growing a child should be another rea-son to despair. Aurora's light no longer wakes me in the morn-ings. That task has fallen to my stomach, which spends the early hours before sunrise trying valiantly to keep down the previous night's meal. It's a battle that's often lost, forcing me into the predawn chill to empty my chamber pot before Mar-gery can discover how frequently it's filled with vomit. My breasts grow tender to the touch, but despite my body's in-creased sensitivity, I revel in this transformation. For millen-nia, I aged only until a fresh ship brought more sailors. I grew so familiar with the process: how my skin would sag, my hair gray, my feathers thin. But these changes are entirely new, and the fact I never believed they could be mine makes them all the sweeter.

If I'm honest with myself, Cora's distance is for the best.

I already struggle to avoid daydreaming of us crossing the channel to the mainland, heading northwest into the wilderness. The tiny part of an impenetrable forest where we would carve out a place for ourselves, where we'd build a tiny cottage beneath the protection of the pines, and where we'd raise this baby together.

These are fantasies I never dared entertain about Proserpina. Didn't I always know somewhere, deep down, that our love was ephemeral? Something to be enjoyed in our youth before Ceres found her a husband. Isn't that why my thoughts of her were always immediate? How we'd spend our mornings, our days, our nights. They never wandered to what our futures might hold.

The same barrier doesn't exist with Cora. She's all alone, just as I am, and if I could convince her to, what would keep us from escaping together?

That's the danger of dreaming—it's the same danger as our song. It tantalizes with a glimpse of the forbidden, assures you it's possible. And then it offers the details you ache for most: what the first snow looks like in that little cabin, flakes shimmering in the evergreens that envelop us, on Cora's long, dark lashes, on my sweet child's little nose. The picture it paints is so clear that I smell the logs burning in the hearth. I hear the combined music of their laughter as Cora bounces the baby on her knee. I feel the warmth of us curled together on a pallet, buried beneath a pile of furs and quilts. I see the first verdant kiss of spring pushing through the frozen forest floor, breaking through the white blanket that seemed so impenetrable only a few months before.

It's a destiny that doesn't—that *can't*—exist.

The promise of such a future would drive anyone into the sea.

ௐ

An ache in my lower back wakes me from an afternoon nap. I pull myself from the bed with a groan, arms stretching over my head. A gentle knock on the door signals Margery's outside, and I hobble across the room to push away the chair and open it for her. She smiles weakly at me as she enters, sidestepping my form to place a tray on my bedside table: a cup of weak tea and some salted meat. My stomach sours at the sight; I know I should be grateful, but the settlers have taken to eating rats.

"Thelia!" she gasps, raising a finger to my nightgown. "You're bleeding!"

My face crumples in confusion at her words. *I can't be,* I almost say aloud, catching myself at the very last moment before the words tumble over my lips. I whirl to face the bed. Sure enough, a dark crimson smear stains the white linens. A hand rushes to my belly instinctively, and the room begins to spin. I take a seat in the chair beside the fireplace to prevent myself from collapsing onto the floor.

I fall silent. Each breath is slow, measured, as if breathing too quickly will shake the babe free. *Am I losing her?* I have no one to ask. I bury my face in a palm, turning to the fire that still burns from this morning to hide my distress from Margery.

Her duties should distract her from analyzing my demeanor, but she makes no move to strip the soiled bedding.

"Stay here. I'll get help," she says, and then disappears from the room in a hurry. As soon as the door falls closed behind her, I drop onto the floor, swinging my legs up onto the seat of the chair to press my hips off the ground, womb to the sky, as if I can keep this child inside of me with the same downward force that makes fruit fall to the earth instead of floating away into the heavens.

Maybe such bleeding is normal, I repeat to myself over and over, trying to calm my racing heart. I think of the men on Scopuli, how the blood poured from their wounds more quickly when they panicked. Does losing a child work the same way? Will my anxiety quicken the process? Despite my best efforts, my breathing grows haggard. The more I try to relax, the more flustered I become.

"Please be all right," I whisper to my belly. "You're all I have."

I stay in that position for what feels like hours, waiting for Margery to return. Who can possibly come to my aid? If she brings Master Sutton, the closest person to a doctor on Roanoke, what will my punishment be? I reach between my legs tenderly only to find my fingertips stained crimson with fresh blood. Whatever bleeding occurred while I slept hasn't stopped.

"We are almost home, sweet babe. Hold on." The words are both a promise and a plea.

The sound of frantic footsteps up the stairs makes a cry catch in my throat. I try to push myself back up, but the door bursts open before I can hide that I'm curled up on the ground like a crumpled nightdress. I don't raise my chin to meet the new arrival just yet—shame and fear bring tears to my eyes. What a damning position to be found in: sprawled across the floor, clutching my belly as red seeps out from between my legs.

I barely have a chance to register it's her before she's upon me, green eyes wide with alarm as she rushes to my side to cup my face gently in her hands. When I open my mouth to speak, her beautiful black waves encircle our faces. For a moment, there's only us. The sight of Cora after all this time is so overwhelming that all I can do is stare up at her, mouth agape. I reach a hand up to touch her cheek, but my muscles seize, and I scream from the shock of it. Margery hovers on the threshold, looking over her shoulder anxiously.

"Shhh . . ." Cora murmurs, brushing my hair behind my ears and out of my face. The tendrils are slick with sweat. "We need to take you to Sybil. She'll know what to do."

"All right," I say, the words more sobbed than spoken.

"You must go quickly," Margery interrupts. "If Master Thomas finds out about any of this, he'll kill the child himself."

17

᠎᠎᠎

BEFORE

We hold rituals in the sea cave on Scopuli's south-western shore. It's accessible only when the tide is low, neither above the earth nor below it, neither a part of nor separate from the ocean, a sacred place between the worlds. The grotto's opening is oblong and curves up in the corners. Jagged rock formations stand guard along the ground, giving the aperture the appearance of a crooked sneer. Outside, the sun straddles the horizon, half in the sky, half below. Its last light spilling onto the waves, staining the sea red as blood. Soon Jaquob's will flow to meet it.

The sight makes me shiver, so I turn to Raidne. She's kneeling before a ring of stones we placed in the middle of the space centuries ago, striking two rocks together over the wood that sits within its sphere. A spark emerges and catches the kindling ablaze. Warm light bursts across the cave walls, giving life to all nature of shadows. Only once the bonfire roars does Raidne meet my gaze. Her eyes are sympathetic, though I don't need them to be. I know what must be done. This is why Jaquob is here; he was always meant to be a gift to her. They all were—it's their punishment. Otherwise,

Proserpina would never have sent them here. My skin crawls with anticipation, and each sense is heightened by the knowledge that for the first time since these offerings began, this will work.

Yes, she'd said. *He's mine.*

So I'll give him to her. A long overdue gift, more potent than those flowers I failed to gather for her.

The sound of footsteps draws my attention to the mouth of the cave. Pisinoe approaches on the exposed, rocky beach. Jaquob follows. One look at his slack-jawed grin and glassy eyes confirms that she sang to him, bewitched him into submission to follow her here willingly, like a dog follows a bone. He stumbles over the rocks beneath his feet, but Pisinoe waits patiently for him to catch himself each time he loses his balance.

A lump forms in my throat. The men I've killed before were all strangers, but Jaquob isn't. My fists tighten at my sides, forcing away the pleasant memories. If sacrifices were easy, they wouldn't be called sacrifices. Perhaps that's why all the others went unanswered—Ceres could sense the offerings were too easy to give. But Jaquob will hurt. Another reason why Proserpina chose him for me, out of all the others.

"Thelxiope." He beams when he sees me. He sounds like he's drunk, and in a way, he is, only this time it is on our voices and not on liquor. What future does he envision waits for him inside this cave? Pisinoe leads him into its maw toward the far left wall, where she slips shackles around his wrists and ankles, locking him in place, his body an X. He looks at the irons, eyebrows piqued. "What are these for?"

"Those women," I begin, knowing that the magic of our song will prevent him from lying. I already have the answer I seek—I feel it in my bones. But I need to hear it from his lips. It will make what I'm about to do easier.

"Who were they?"

He groans, eyes rolling up to the vault of the cave. Even in his current state, he recognizes what he's about to say won't be received well. "I knew you would be mad."

Every single muscle in my body constricts at the admission, so tight that I worry they might split my skin apart. "Who were they?" I ask again, my voice hard.

"Don't look so upset. They were Iroquoian women who were gifted to us. We're not barbaric like the Spanish. We were taking them back to France."

"Not barbaric? They were bound!"

"That was unfortunate, but we couldn't get them onto the ship willingly. They were too ignorant to recognize the gift they'd been given—the chance to be civilized!"

Revulsion skitters across my skin. His enchanted eyes are bright, pleading—Jaquob desperately wants to believe his own words, to ignore the hypocrisy they carry. He's trying to reassure himself that stealing the women from their homes, their families, and spiriting them across the sea wasn't an act of savagery simply because somewhere in the world, the Spanish are treating people worse.

"It was for their own good," he adds, but his voice wavers. Jaquob knows, deep down, that something inside of him is vile, rotten. And he knows the importance of keeping that part of himself hidden. Otherwise, he wouldn't have lied to me about their existence.

"You offered them a life in chains and wondered why they refused it. The only fool I see is you."

"Thelxiope, you don't understand."

Rage blazes inside my chest, and I rush forward and grab ahold of his precious relic, the piece of his saint that he wears around his neck. He opens his mouth to protest, but I've heard enough. I tear the necklace from his body in one rough tug and throw it to the floor. The golden pendant clinks when it hits the stone, but it doesn't break. Watching his most prized possession ripped from his chest makes his eyes widen. He calls out to me in alarm, but his words are incoherent.

"Bon Dieu, femme! Pourquoi fais-tu ça?"

I turn my back to him. He continues to babble, his tongue indecipherable. The words, devoid of meaning, wash over me with little effect.

"Let's begin," I say.

Raidne and Pisinoe say nothing as they follow me into the farthest recess of the cave to the small pool where salt water collects when the tide recedes. As much as I want to throw myself into its dark halo, to wash the filth of Jaquob's admission from my skin, there's an order that must be followed. Raidne doesn't make me wait. She submerges herself first, taking care to rinse any dirt from her body. Pisinoe follows. I'm the last to be consecrated in this holy water. As I sink below its inky surface, it takes all my strength not to scream into its depths.

Pisinoe waits with a towel when I emerge. We dry our frames; we don our ceremonial garb. We wrap our lower halves in white linen, twisting the fabric around our waists and tying the ends behind our necks. It's not the traditional style, but the open back leaves room for our wings, so it must do. I place a golden circlet on Raidne's head. She places one on Pisinoe's, who in turn places one on mine.

Once we're dressed, Raidne passes me a pitcher of blackberry wine. I take the clay vessel and step toward Jaquob. Our eyes meet once more. One final test. If he's meant to live, he will not flinch. He will not bow his head.

I dip my fingers into the sticky dark liquid. They're instantly stained black, and I pause to look at them. I have played this role countless times, but it feels different as I raise my hand and sprinkle the droplets onto Jaquob's fore-head. He doesn't know the significance of the act when he lowers his head to shield his eyes. He doesn't know our ways, doesn't understand that he's now consented to this.

It's settled. He must die.

Pisinoe begins to beat a makeshift drum, which is no more than a large bowl with a deer hide spread across its breadth. The beat is steady, syncopated, like our pulse, and for the first time in a decade, I feel the blood pumping through my veins. A throbbing begins deep within my stomach, and I'm hungrier than I have been in ages. My body starts to sway. Raidne fans her wings and then I'm fanning mine as well. Our wings fuel the fire, and the smoke billows up through a tiny aperture in the cave's ceiling before escaping into the moonless sky.

"Thelxiope?" Jaquob tries again, my name the only word I recognize in another garbled sentence. It's no use. Raidne and I circle the fire, lionesses stalking their prey, faces locked on Jaquob's. He frowns, his eyebrows furrowed with confu-sion. My pulse and Pisinoe's rhythm quicken in sync, and all three of us are swaying, frenzied. The bonfire roars. We three become one: a singular, insatiable beast.

Raidne unsheathes a long blade from its scabbard and ap-proaches Jaquob. This blade, like our butchering tools, has a sole purpose. It gleams in the firelight, its iron edges lusting for blood. The sight of it shatters his reverie, and for the first time since entering the cave, he lets out a long wail. I feel no sympathy. The women he captured float before me. I remem-ber their decaying mouths and rotting fingers. I remember their empty eyes.

He's no longer Jaquob. He's a gift to Proserpina. A good one, too.

With a swift and powerful movement, Raidne digs the

blade into the skin beneath his ribs and pulls it down to below his belly button, opening him like a present. His scream is shattering, projected by the cave onto the waves.

Entrails spill out of the wound, a dark and tangled gore. With surgical precision, Raidne, our haruspex, slides them through her fingers, checking for imperfections, for bad omens. When she looks up from the intestines with a rare smile upon her lips, I know she's found no damning messages. Jaquob shrieks, unable to believe this is happening. Raidne hands me the blade.

I approach him one more time, resting a hand on his cheek. He leans his face into my palm, wailing. With my other hand, I place the knife against his throat.

"S'il vous plaît . . ." he says between sobs. I don't need to speak his language to understand the meaning.

Please.

We usually recite an incantation before the final mercy is delivered. This time, only one name is necessary.

"Proserpina," I say. My voice booms through the grotto. It's a dedication. It's an offering. It's an apology. My hand on his cheek slides into his tangled mess of hair to draw his head down so he's facing the Underworld.

I slice.

His blood is dark, and it spurts from the wound like a fountain onto my frame. Jaquob sputters and gasps and sobs until he finally chokes on his own life force. I stand there, captivated, waiting for his last breath to pass between his lips before I remove my hand from his hair. Finally, he slumps over. I take his relic from the ground and place it around my neck before turning to the others triumphantly.

Raidne reaches for the blade and promptly removes his lungs, his liver, his heart, then tosses each organ into the fire. The smoke licks the ceiling of the cave, wrapping around the hanging rock formations like ribbons before escaping to the gods. When the organs have burned completely, we unchain Jaquob's corpse from the wall and drape it over the flames as well. If this were a gift to Ceres, we could butcher him and eat the meat, but Jaquob now belongs to the Realm of the Dead, and it's forbidden for the living to consume him. When only his bones remain, I toss a coin into the flames, the fee for his upcoming passage.

Take him to Tartarus.

Pisinoe slows her drumming. Our ecstatic frenzy reaches its low point, and we watch the fire swallow the last remnants of Jaquob's skeleton until nothing is left but ash.

With his body gone, the sacrificial fever begins to dwindle. Raidne moves to start cleaning the blood from her frame. I take a step forward to follow her, but a sharp pain erupts in my gut. I shriek, taken aback by its sudden appearance, but the agony doesn't relent. It intensifies.

I fall onto my knees, my arms wrapped around my stomach. The rough ground tears across my skin through the thin ceremonial dress, offering the linen two new blooms of blood to join Jaquob's. Raidne drops to my side. I feel the warmth of her hands on my shoulders, and I think she's speaking to me, but I can't make out the words. Concentrating on her speech requires too much effort, and all my focus is turned inward. Pressure builds in my abdomen, as if something is forcing my intestines up into my lungs. Before I can warn my sisters, I'm on my hands as well, vomiting darkness onto the floor of the cave.

18

ıƨıƨıƨ

NOW

Margery's statement chills the room. Cora slips an arm beneath my shoulder and lifts me slowly.

"Can you walk?" she asks gently. I have no choice; I nod.

It's twilight. I'm thankful for the coming darkness, but we don't have much time to make our escape. The men will be returning from their drinking shortly. Cora leads me, slowly but purposefully, through the hallway, down the stairs, and out the back door. We stop several times as dizziness threatens to overtake me.

I think back to the seer who wouldn't tell me how many children I'd bear. The memory makes me want to tear at my hair, to bang my fists against the wall. After we were banished, I understood why she refused my question. But being here, being human, it let me ignore a very important truth: This baby was doomed to death the moment it was conceived. And now Mercury draws close, here to collect both our souls for the Underworld. Will he recognize me as the same girl responsible for delivering the Realm of the Dead its mistress all those centuries ago?

Cora doesn't know any of this, doesn't understand this was predetermined by the Fates. To her, this child is the last piece of her brother that she has left. As much as I want to curl up in my bed and let my body purge her in peace, I must try to save her, or I'll lose Cora forever as well.

"If Thomas asks where she is, tell him she's with me. I'll have her back as soon as possible."

Margery nods, urging us on with a quick motion of her hands. "Go quickly!"

It's early enough that the night watch hasn't closed the settlement's doorways for the evening. As we approach the southern gate, Cora pulls the hoods of our capes over our heads, casting our faces in shadow. Thankfully, there's no need—it's manned by John Chapman, asleep at his post.

As soon as we're free from the village walls, Cora squeezes my hand to encourage me to move faster. I go as quickly as I can, but my stomach roils, and a cold sweat collects underneath my arms and behind my neck. Everything blurs, and I have the distinct feeling that if it were not for Cora's grasp, I would simply disappear.

The twisted branches of the wood all fade together, and with their distinctions gone, so is my sense of time. Have we been out here in the cold for minutes, or has it been hours? When I'm finally able to focus, we've arrived at the edge of a swamp. Trees I've never seen before shoot from the water like tall sentinels, their leaves more like hair than foliage. The sun has sunk completely beneath the horizon, and it would be pitch-black were it not for a soft orange glow coming from the windows of a small hut perched precariously close to the water's edge.

We've made it to the witch's cottage.

Cora takes a confident step toward the hovel when its door squeaks open. The silhouette of a woman twisted with time stands on its threshold. In the confines of the village, the swamp witch was a hypothetical, the only potential solution to my condition. Will seeing Sybil in the flesh give Cora pause? She carries me forward without faltering, and I moan softly with relief.

"Please," she says, her voice trembling. "We need help."

"Bring her inside."

I sway on weary feet, and the vertigo that's threatened me this entire time finally makes its move. Cora barely catches me before I hit the ground, and the display propels her to pull me into the cottage with renewed conviction. As we cross the doorway, I'm struck by the familiar scent of medicinal herbs and plants. I look up to find the entire ceiling is covered with muted greenery—Sybil hangs them to dry, like we do. In fact, the entire space is like my home on Scopuli. Despite Cora's tightening grip, I feel a sense of peace for the first time since the bleeding began. The yarrow, the purple coneflowers, the marigolds—these are plants for soothing and healing, not for malice.

"Lay her down here," the woman tells Cora, motioning to a makeshift pallet on the left side of the room. Cora helps me settle atop a pile of animal furs. I catch her running her hand over one, going against the grain of the red hair. A fox, perhaps. She chews her bottom lip, and I know exactly what she's thinking.

Foxes have avoided our snares for months. Is it possible that Sybil really did curse them? Sybil interrupts the question by settling between my legs. Although this is the second time we've met, she makes no indication that she knows me in front of Cora. Instead, she opens my knees and peers into the vastness between them. Long white hair is tied back in a braid that falls over her left shoulder. A frown forms on her lips.

"How far along are you?" She looks up at me for the first

time. Our eyes meet, and a surge of energy passes between us. The sensation makes her mouth drop, her wrinkled eyelids open wide with surprise.

"A little less than th-three months," I stammer, rattled by whatever's just happened between us. I feel that I've known her for centuries.

"I need to feel inside," she warns, and I nod. Her fingers land on my inner thigh and gingerly crawl inward. When she removes them, they're covered in blood. The slick, wet crimson confirms what I already know.

"I'm so sorry. The only thing I can do is quicken the process."

In my periphery, Cora's frame crumples.

"No," she says. "No! You must save it!" I can hear the tears welling in her eyes from the tone of her voice.

"The only thing left to save is your friend's life. The child is already lost. We need her body to expel it and to make sure the bleeding stops." The woman pushes herself back to her feet, her bones creaking as she hobbles to her large wooden table. She selects a bundle of plants from the ceiling that I don't recognize. The long green stalks are adorned with circular clumps of flowers that she cuts into small bunches and adds to a mug.

"How can that be? Isn't this what you do? You're a witch, after all!" The word comes out biting, an accusation.

"Enough, Cora." I groan.

She has to save the baby, her gaze says in return, but she snaps her mouth closed.

I shake my head slowly. *It's too late.*

Cora collapses beside me. The sudden drop is enough to shake her cries free, and she dissolves into weeping. I bury my face in her lap, and her hands tangle themselves in my hair. We cling to each other for comfort.

The woman adds warm water to the mug and returns to my side with it. I accept the drink from her and take a sip. "What is it?"

"Pennyroyal mint," she answers gently before turning to Cora. "This part won't be pretty. You should wait outside."

Surprise creases Cora's face. "I'm not leaving her."

"I don't want you to see this," I say softly. "I'll be all right."

"Of course you will be." She turns back to me, her eyes bright with resolve. "And I'll be right here beside you."

I don't have time to answer before the pennyroyal mint takes effect. Losing a child is a painful thing, soaked in scarlet. All I can do is marvel at the amount of blood that saturates Sybil's towels. How much can I spill before death claims me?

If I die, will I see Proserpina again?

Not yet, please. I'm not ready.

My vision is blurred by tears, by pain, but I find Cora's shape. Her hands take mine, and when I cling to them like they're the only thing that tethers me to this realm, she squeezes back just as tightly.

"You're all right," she says, her voice steady, but what I hear is *I won't let go.*

"It's done," Sybil finally says, and only now do tears rush to Cora's eyes. I reach trembling fingers to her cheek to brush them away, but Cora catches my hand and brings it to her lips.

"I told you," she whispers against my palm, and her goodness shatters something inside of me. What have I done to deserve it?

Sybil cups something in the palms of her hands. "Do you want to hold your child?"

I nod weakly, and she crawls on her knees to sit by my side. The tiny babe is no larger than a stone fruit, and I cradle it gently in my hands. The sight of its little pink body brings me to tears again, but it's not my daughter I'm holding.

It's my son.

A wave of revulsion overtakes me, and I move to hand the boy back to Sybil. Suddenly, the overwhelming sense of loss is gone, replaced by a mess of conflicting emotions that compete for dominance until I feel nothing at all. When she reaches out to reclaim him, though, I falter before bringing his little body to my chest instead.

He's so tiny. Even though I feel no outpouring of love, I'm still afraid I might break him. Only I can't, and even if I could, wouldn't the world be better if I did? The thought is like a punch in the gut. So is my next one.

What would Raidne and Pisinoe have thought of him?

I think of young Ambrose, of how sweet he is to Elizabeth, and how Margery fawns over Jeremie. Somehow over the past few weeks, I've grown tender toward them, but it was always an abstract affection, underscored with relief that I'd never have to make a decision about their future morality. When the scouting party leaves with me, the mothers and children will stay behind, absolving me of needing to answer any complicated questions. For have I not already? If I thought a boy could be different, wouldn't I be able to muster any emotion for the child I grip to my breast?

"Will you fetch me some more water, girl?" Sybil asks Cora, pointing to a wooden bucket beside the door. Though Cora looks reluctant, she slowly untangles herself from my side.

"You weren't destined to be a mother," the old woman whispers after the cottage door creaks shut, signaling we're alone. She interprets my silence as resignation, not as shocked detachment. "I suspect fate brought you here for another reason."

Her words offer a welcome distraction from my confusion and draw my attention back to her. "How do you . . . ?"

"There's a magic about you. I can't quite decipher what it is, but I do recognize it. You're so young, but somehow you seem to have lived a thousand lifetimes."

I bring his little body to my cheek. "I thought I could have a different life than the one already spun for me."

"An alluring thought, but this was a cruel reminder—you can't avoid your fate." The woman wipes the sweat from my brow, a loving gesture that I lean into. It reminds me of my sisters' touch. "Rest here as long as you need. The bleeding's slowed, and your body is healthy. You're going to be fine."

When Cora returns, she takes the little boy into her hands, weeping over his lifeless body, distraught by Will's death all over again. My heart breaks to see her like this, though it's easier to feel sorry for her than to try to parse my own feelings. I fell in love with a daughter that never existed; instead, my traitorous body was harboring a boy. I want to hate him, for even if he survived, how could I have stopped him from growing into a monster? I'm one myself.

But I can't. And I also can't love him. I don't know how to. I feel nothing except relief that it's too late for us to return home. The gates will already be locked for the night, and neither Cora nor myself wants to devise an excuse for why we were in the woods long past midnight. Exhaustion overtakes us both, and Cora hands my son's body to Sybil. The crone wraps him in a tiny piece of fabric, then looks to me for approval. I nod, and Sybil leaves, off to return the child to the earth.

I motion for Cora to join me on the mattress, and she does.

We entwine ourselves in each other's arms. She cries herself to sleep, but Somnus does not grant me peace.

After some time, I look to the crackling fire across the room and find I'm not alone. There, in the chair beside the hearth, sits a figure cloaked in shadow. For the span of a breath, I fear Mercury has come after all, here to guide my soul below. But then, in the half-light of the dying embers, I recognize him. How many times over the past few months did I stare at that face, desperately wishing for it to transform into his sister's? This time, he's thankfully intact. No exposed muscle hangs from his cheeks, no vulture tears at his eyes. His stomach hasn't been torn open to reveal a mess of bowels. The back of the chair fades in and out of sight as he rocks in it, watching the flames. His body isn't entirely solid; he's made of air. A spirit.

"Will?" I ask, not sure if he's simply a trick of my mind. Although I should be terrified, I find that I'm not. My pulse is steady, my breathing calm. When I speak, he turns to look at me, his soft lips turned down in a sorrowful frown. "What are you—"

"I'm sorry about our son, Thelia," he says, and the sound breaks something in me. I half expected he wouldn't speak, or when he did, that the sound would only fill my head like Proserpina's voice. But no, although it's soft, his voice still drifts across the room like a gentle spring breeze.

"I couldn't carry him. I'm not destined to be a mother."

"I know."

"What else do you know?" I whisper, afraid of the answer.

"Everything." His green eyes flare when the fire catches them, but there's no hatred or disgust in his expression. Only a sad understanding.

"Did Thomas—"

"It doesn't matter now."

"Of course it matters! He—"

"You'll punish him soon enough, I suspect."

My throat closes, trapping my voice inside it.

"I'm not here to talk about him. I'm here to talk about our son. About how you feel nothing for him."

"There's nothing to feel," I say, a little too quickly. "The child wasn't meant to live. Even if he had, wouldn't it be my responsibility to kill him? My purpose . . ." My voice cracks.

"Is to punish," he answers for me, before adding, "the guilty. A child is innocent. So are some men. Wasn't I?"

Tears well in my eyes. "I believe so, but how can I know for certain? I've been fooled before . . ."

"You don't need to steel yourself against him."

"I'm not trying to," I whisper. "I lost a child, and I don't feel anything. How is that possible?"

"You're too afraid to, scared of what it might mean. But it's all right to love him. Some of us are worth loving." He smiles mournfully.

"But how can I know who is and who isn't?"

"Monsters are made, Thelia. Not born."

The words make my throat tighten—shouldn't I know that better than anyone? I was innocent once, too, until the cruelty of men molded me into something else. This child, who never took a breath, is blameless.

It's all right to love him.

All at once, the walls I've built around my heart come crashing down, and the tears for Will now fall freely with tears for my son.

"Take care of my sister," he adds, nodding to Cora. The sound, combined with my crying, is enough to draw her from her slumber.

"Who are you talking to?" she asks gently, rubbing her

eyes. I don't know how to answer, so I look to the chair only to find that it's empty. Will is already gone.

"I didn't mean to wake you."

Cora pulls me back to the mattress and holds my head against her chest. "Shh . . ." she murmurs, not entirely awake. "It's all right."

I want to tell her it's not, but the warmth of her hands cradling me says otherwise. I allow myself to sink into her embrace, to be comforted by the scent of her, roses mixed with the sweetness of her sweat. Despite everything, it works.

This time, we fall asleep together.

In the early light of dawn, I confirm what I suspected last night: that this is a healer's home, not a witch's. Lions and wolves made docile by magic aren't guarding its perimeter, at least as far as I can tell, and I don't see any of the usual magical instruments—no looms, no wands, no altars to Hekate. No poisons grace the rafters. But there's no denying that some magic must reside within Sybil. She recognized that I'm beyond human. So the gift of sight, then. The corners of my lips curl at the injustice—this woman, now old and alone, lives on society's edge for her own safety, and yet she took me in without question. She saved my life. How many other villagers has she treated under the cloak of night only to be abandoned again come morning?

The people here fear those whom they do not know to the point of treachery. They despise women who seek knowledge. They subjugate, rape, and murder those who possess what they want. Just as with Jaquob, I cannot ignore their cruelty any longer. It's time for me to take Sybil's words to heart.

I can't avoid my fate.

It's a lesson I should have learned centuries ago.

All I can do now is shake Cora's shoulder gently to wake her. She rolls away from me, a long groan passing from her lips. I want nothing more than to watch her like this, in the dim light that filters through wooden slats that cover the windows. It's the first time in months I've seen her so peaceful—how easy it would be to let the gentle rise and fall of her back pull me to her side, to bury my face in that raven hair. Instead, with a lump rising in my throat, I try again.

"Cora, we need to go back . . ."

She grunts in response but pushes herself onto an arm, wiping the sleep from her eyes with her free hand. An awkward silence sits between us.

"Thank you for bringing me here," I whisper. "For trying to save him."

She turns to look at me. Her face is open, her forehead creased with guilt. "I'm sorry. For how I treated you after Will . . . It wasn't your fault, I know that, but I wanted someone to blame so badly . . ."

"Shhh," I coo, placing my hand on the side of her face. She nuzzles into my touch, and heat blooms in my cheeks. "You don't have to apologize . . . I hope this means we can be friends again. I miss you."

"I miss you, too," she breathes, and despite the sorrow that has settled within my bones, I smile softly. She returns mine, but then her teeth find her bottom lip.

"Was there something else?" I ask softly, but before she can respond, Sybil opens the cabin's creaking door and steps inside. The old woman holds three squirrels by the tail in one hand and a hare in the other, and Cora's eyebrows rise with surprise.

"Oh, good, you're awake," Sybil says as she places the animals on the wooden table. When she sees Cora's shocked expression, she winks at us both. "If you can stay a little longer, I'll send you on your way with full bellies. Lord knows you girls had a trying night."

We nod ravenously, which makes Sybil laugh. She makes quick work of processing her game, throwing the sinewy meat into a large pot. I flash back to my last carcass, a comrade of Jaquob's. What would Cora say if she knew? Sybil adds some herbs to the mix as well, then wanders to an end table where she starts to dice mushrooms.

A hearty, rich scent fills the room before long. I detect both thyme and rosemary, and my stomach gurgles loudly. Cora giggles softly into my shoulder, and Sybil smiles at us both. When the old woman deems the stew to be ready, she ladles our portions into wooden bowls. We slurp it up so fast that neither of us savors it, but Sybil offers servings until our stomachs are bursting.

We take our time eating these, lazing in the warmth of both the food and the company. I don't want to return. I feel at home here, with this woman who senses my destiny as if it were its own scent in the room, mingling with the thyme and rosemary. She and I have much in common, with our respective curses and banishments.

But Cora doesn't find the same comfort here. Although she's grateful for her help, it's clear by how the muscles in her neck have corded that she's not entirely relaxed in the old woman's presence. She finishes her meal first and turns to me.

"Are you all right to stand?"

I bob my head yes, and she extends a hand for me. I take it, gratefully, and then we turn to Sybil.

"Thank you for your kindness," I say. "I'll never forget it."

"Remember what we told you, girl," she cautions. Cora

glances at me, intrigued by the comment, but I fix my gaze on Sybil, bowing my head in acknowledgment. So she saw Will, too.

Cora curtsies slightly in deference and hands Sybil a pouch of coins. The old woman slips the gold into her skirts. Payment for my treatment, though what use Sybil has for it is beyond me. With the transaction complete, Cora exits the cottage. I linger in the door for a moment, considering my words carefully before speaking.

"I can't leave until spring comes," I say slowly. The faintest flicker of a smile threatens to crack across Sybil's face.

"I have a feeling the weather will turn around soon enough," the crone says, her gray eyes glimmering.

A grin overtakes my lips, and I nod as something catches my eye. There, a few paces away from the front door, is a little plot of freshly disturbed earth. Sybil has placed a flower on top as a marker. It's a lily, though it's far too early for them to bloom. And yet Sybil found one anyway. My chest tightens—*it's all right to love him,* Will said, and seeing Proserpina's flower here makes me believe him. Believe both of them.

Cora sidles up beside me, slipping her arm around my waist as I say goodbye. We stand together like that for quite some time until I finally pull back from her touch to meet her gaze. Her hand finds mine, and then she's leading me back through the woods.

It takes us nearly an hour to return to the colony's boundaries. The walk is mostly through forest, although every so often a break in the trees reveals a hidden marsh or a glimpse of the sea. The trip is calm and quiet, and over far too soon. The southern wall welcomes us back, and then there's nothing to do except part ways for our respective homes. She embraces me.

"I'm glad you're all right."

A loud sound rolls over the tops of the houses. Cora releases me, face crinkled with worry, and I hold a finger to my lips to quiet her. At first, it's hard to place what exactly the noise is. My mind races to name it, but it's not a singular sound at all. It's countless voices all roaring discordantly: a mob.

Color drains from Cora's face until it matches the shade of the snow that still covers the ground.

"Something's happening." Her voice quivers, and she grabs ahold of my hand. My palm grows clammy in her grasp, and nausea blooms in my stomach. Have I somehow been discovered? The sound of jeering leads us to the center of the village, where a large crowd gathers before the meetinghouse. Neither of us speaks as we push our way through the throng of people, trying to get a better look at what all the commotion is about.

There, locked in the pillory, is Margery. Her face is crimson with tears, and she sobs hysterically. Emme holds Jeremie a few feet away from her. He's just as inconsolable, screaming and tearing at Emme's arms, leaving red scratches in his wake. Emme tries to calm the child, but he can't be soothed—his hands remain outstretched for his mother, and she calls for him in return. My mouth falls open in shock, and Cora gasps. Thomas is holding up the lapis lazuli necklace that I gave Margery for Christmas. The gem spins in loose circles on its golden chain, as if to enchant the crowd. A hand on my shoulder startles me, and I nearly scream, but Wenefrid *shhhs* to calm me.

"What's going on?" My voice betrays my fear for Margery.

"Mistress Bailie discovered her with that necklace—" Wenefrid begins, but she's interrupted by Agnes, who stands before Margery with wild eyes.

"How dare you steal from our house after my husband showed you such incredible kindness?" Mistress Bailie shrieks, and moves to slap Margery across the face. Margery, with her head and hands locked in the wooden restraining device, turns as much as she can to dodge the blow, but there's nowhere for her to hide. The slap connects with her cheek with a sickening *crack,* and the crowd erupts. The villagers have grown restless over the long harsh winter, and the strike stirs them into a frenzy. One man shakes his fist at Margery. Lewes, the teen who was the first to try for my hand a few months ago, calls her a whore. Even Master Sampson, the man responsible for reminding us of God's mercy, doesn't speak in Margery's defense. Alarm takes root in my stomach as the crowd grows more restless. Is theft also punishable by death?

"I didn't steal it, mistress!"

"You dare to lie to me? My son holds the evidence in his hand!" Agnes spits down at the girl. Wenefrid grimaces as Mistress Bailie raises her hand again, and the crowd goes wild. Margery's face falls toward the ground, a large red splotch already forming on her cheek from the first slap. A thin line of blood traces its way from beside her right eye to the corner of her lip, and I realize with startling ferocity that one of Agnes's rings cut her.

"Enough!" I scream. Cora and Wenefrid watch me wide-eyed as I push forward through the warm bodies to emerge before the pillory. Mistress Bailie looks shocked at my interruption; she's not a woman used to being told no.

Agnes's surprise lasts only a moment before a look of steely conviction settles back across her face. "Enough?" Mistress Bailie laughs coldly. "Who do you think you are, telling us 'enough'?"

"I'm the princess of the land your son seeks to inherit, and that necklace was a gift from me, as you know. Release her at once!"

"I will do no such thing," Agnes replies, her voice alarmingly calm. "You are my son's betrothed, so the dowry belongs to him. Therefore, the necklace wasn't yours to give."

"How dare you?" I growl, my eyes turning into slits. "You can't do this—"

"If the story you told us is true, my son is to be king of Scopuli. Do you deny this?"

"No—"

"Then you have no power here."

"That's not—"

"Put your betrothed in her place, Thomas."

Before I can comment on how pathetic it is that he requires such instruction from his mother, Thomas inserts himself between Margery and me. He puffs his chest outward in a grotesque display that makes my hands curl into fists. "Silence, woman, or you'll find yourself in the pillory in her stead."

"You wouldn't dare."

"Hugh, Charles." Thomas snaps his fingers at two men in the crowd behind me, who jump at the sound. Dogs. They're no better than dogs. "Release Mistress Harvie. We have a new bitch that needs to be punished."

It all happens so quickly: Hugh and Charles grab ahold of my arms so forcefully that bruises will flower beneath their fingers, and they pull me onto the platform. The crowd becomes a blur of screaming faces. Suddenly, I'm a child again, being dragged from Ceres's throne room. Agnes unlocks the top of the pillory and lifts it off Margery's neck and hands. She stumbles backward out of the device, stunned, and Emme rushes forward with Jeremie to catch her.

"N-no, wait . . . !" Margery stammers. I shake my head to

silence her. Hugh and Charles deposit me in her place as if I weigh nothing, and Thomas slams the pillory closed with a sickening *thunk*, trapping me inside.

"This," he hisses coldly in my ear, his voice no louder than a whisper, "is for biting me."

A whole slew of thoughts rush forward, and it takes all my strength not to shriek the worst of them at the crowd. Instead, I seethe silently, vowing not to give them the satisfaction of seeing me fight back.

"Let this show us that no one, not even a princess, is above our laws," Mistress Bailie says soberly, as if she's imparting a great lesson to the villagers. In actuality, it's a warning. I find Elyoner's and Margaret's shocked faces in the crowd. Wenefrid pushes her way forward to stand beside them, but Cora remains where she is in the back.

"It's not a woman's place to talk back to her betrothed. A few hours in the pillory will help Lady Thelia learn this lesson."

A pounding echoes in my ears as Agnes's voice draws my focus back to her. *Monsters are made, not born,* Will said. Trapped in the blaze of Agnes's vicious grin, I see that he's right: If my son's sex doesn't inherently condemn him, then Agnes's doesn't absolve her. The suffering wrought by men is easier to spot—it's razed villages, stolen land, and violated bodies. But such obvious violence wouldn't be possible without a quieter brutality, the kind Agnes excels at, to clear the way for it.

How many nymphs survived a god's assault only to fall prey once more to the misplaced wrath of his wife? And the punishments rendered by goddesses were just as cruel. Wasn't mine?

The crowd lingers in the square for a while, delighting in the entertainment my imprisonment provides. My cheeks burn beneath their taunts, but I won't give them any more of a spectacle. The quickest way to end this is for them to grow bored, and so I do my best to make it clear that the exciting part has passed. Inside, though, I rage. I commit the most gleeful faces to memory, imagining how they'll look when our song takes hold, when I slide our sacrificial blade across their throats.

Slowly but surely, people lose interest in my stoic frame gracing the pillory. Their days beckon them away, though the Bible study group remains. Young Rose runs home to fetch a bucket so she can ladle water to my lips, while Jane, Alis, Elyoner, Wenefrid, Margaret, and Liz form a circle around me, as if to shield my pathetic form from any lingering gawkers. Through the gap between Jane and Elyoner, I see Thomas find Cora, but then the women draw closer together, and the space that contains Cora and my captor disappears. Why is Cora with him, after what we've just been through? Only now do the corners of my eyes grow damp. With my hands bound, I can't wipe the tears away, and so they fall to the wooden platform floor. My only choice is to trust her, but her absence still makes my chest ache. It's a different pain from the soft cramping that makes my legs tremble beneath my skirts, but it hurts just as badly.

"Where's Margery?" I croak, straining my head as far as I can to my right to try to catch sight of her. I barely move it before my cheek brushes against the rough wooden board that locks it in place, my limp right hand blocking my peripheral vision. "Is she all right?"

"Emme took her and Jeremie back home," Wenefrid explains, gingerly brushing a lock of my hair behind my ear.

"What the Bailies did to her is appalling." Margaret's words whistle over the gap where one of her teeth is missing.

Elizabeth nods. "How could they, after Margery has worked so hard to keep their house in order?"

"What will she do now?" Rose asks, delicately lifting a cup of water to my mouth. I drink it gratefully, and she brings me another.

Without the extra money she earns working for the Bailies, Margery will likely need to find herself a new husband, although the public shaming she just endured will effectively scare away the more decent men, if they exist here at all. No one wants to say this out loud, so we all fall silent.

"You don't have to wait here with me," I say eventually. "Who knows how long the Bailies will keep me here."

Alis, usually so soft-spoken, surprises me with an astonished laugh. "Of course we do, Lady Thelia! You gave us all gifts. It could have been any one of us in her place. The fact you were willing to stand up for her . . ." She trails off, searching for the right words.

"Well, it just means you'd be willing to defend any one of us," Wenefrid adds slowly, and Alis nods.

"Especially since none of us were particularly kind to you after Will disappeared . . ." Rose says, and the other women shuffle back and forth on their feet uncomfortably.

"I hold no grudges," I whisper softly. "Cora is your friend—"

"So you forgive us?" Rose interjects. She's so young, she can't contain her excitement. It makes it hard not to smile, even though my body still aches from last night, from being locked in this position.

"I do," I say, and the other women grin to one another. With the matter settled, all there is left to do is wait for my release.

Thomas doesn't return to free me until the sun is nearly three-quarters of its way across the sky. When he does, Rose helps me stand, and Wenefrid puts her hands on my shoulders to steady me. No one acknowledges the Bailie man, and he senses the anger roiling beneath our collective surfaces.

While the women are distracted with me, fussing and making sure that I'm all right, Thomas slinks off to the tavern.

"Good riddance." Margaret spits at the ground in his direction once he is out of sight.

The women all murmur in agreement. Elyoner slides up beside me, looking concerned.

"You can't go back there tonight. It would give Mistress Bailie too much pleasure."

Emme, who returned with Jeremie to the square about an hour after helping Margery rest, suggests that we all retire to her house. "I'll fetch Margery. She'll be awake by now, and we can spend the evening together."

I can't help but smile a bit. An evening away from the Bailie home sounds like exactly the blessing I need.

While Emme collects Margery, Margaret and Wenefrid set to stoking the hearth to prepare supper. They barely finish adding scraps of meat, vermin of some sort, to a large iron pot before a series of rapid knocks distracts us from our conversation. I peer up at the door. Has Thomas come for me? Emme pushes herself to her feet to open it, but before she can, Cora bursts inside and slams the door closed behind her. She gasps for air; her eyes are wild.

"I'm sorry I couldn't stay with you . . ." she says between breaths. "Thomas—"

"Did he hurt you?" I interrupt, jumping to my feet. My hands find her shoulders, and I guide her into the chair I previously occupied.

"No, no . . . He believes I hate you still, and that's ground I didn't want to lose. When he asked where we were, I told him that I saw you leaving the village and followed you into the woods."

"You were gone all night," Margery wails. "How did you explain that without damning her?"

Cora's eyes blaze. "Don't you understand? She's already damned. Thomas met with Master Lacie and Master Florrie this afternoon—"

"Sailors," Emme says. Her eyes grow dark.

"Yes. They're preparing for the journey to Scopuli. They have been for months."

"What do you mean?" My face pinches with confusion. "Thomas said we couldn't go anywhere until the weather lifted."

Cora looks apologetic. "The weather was only part of it."

The room holds its breath, waiting for her to continue. She fingers the edges of her sleeves nervously; her eyes wander to the ground.

"Tell me," I say softly, kneeling before her. Her green eyes grow glassy with tears.

"This entire time . . . Thelia, they've been building another boat across the island. One large enough to carry us all."

"Why would they do that?" Margery asks.

"By Thelia's own admission, there are no eligible men left on Scopuli for her hand. They assume that since she arrived alone, there must be very few men left at all." She turns to me. "Why else would your family risk sending a woman without protection to an unknown land?"

"And?" My voice is barely a whisper.

"They plan to steal it from you."

Several of the women gasp. Rose's hand flies to cover her gaping mouth, and Emme's hands curl into fists.

"The men don't trust you. Some openly call you a witch behind your back. All of them call you a heathen. Thomas has been circulating rumors that you're responsible for Will's death, but everyone is willing to play nice until you lead us to your gold . . ." Her voice cracks, as if she can't bear to continue. "Once you do, they'll kill you. Your family as well, and anyone else who might stand in their way. After that, Thomas plans to marry me." Her face crumples into despair. "He told me all this, and I had to pretend to be thrilled! Thelia, I didn't know what else to do—"

"You did well," I whisper, my hands holding her legs in encouragement.

"I think he murdered Will," Cora whispers, the words catching in her throat. "And now he plans to murder you, too . . . Oh, Thelia! What are we going to do?"

The treachery should be shocking, but it's painfully consistent with what I've already witnessed these men to be capable of. My teeth dig into the side of my mouth as I look for the words to say next, but a growl from Emme breaks the silence. "Who knows of this?"

"Mistress Bailie, John Sampson, James Lacie, Hugh Taylor . . . a handful of others."

"How can they be so cruel?" Rose barks with surprising ferocity. "We're planters, not soldiers!"

"Maybe," Cora says, her eyes finding mine. "But aren't we only here because our soldiers came first?"

"But to agree to this . . ." Rose says, the color leaching from her cheeks.

"It's not just them. It's everyone in this town!" Emme adds. "No one said a damn word when they dragged Margery into the pillory today."

"Nor did we," Elyoner whispers, not quite ready to condemn the entire village to Hell. She has the decency to look ashamed, and she reaches for Margery's hand to squeeze it apologetically.

"Who would have listened to you if you had?" Margery snaps to defend her. "Look what happened to Lady Thelia. The Bailies would have jailed us all for interfering with their plans, and everyone else would have let it happen."

"I hate them," Cora says. "They did nothing when Will went missing, nor when he was found. God's blood, some of them probably knew what Thomas planned, and no one warned him!"

"None besides you have helped me when John loses control," Alis adds softly, agreeing with the growing resentment.

"And no one punished Charles after what he did to Emme . . ." Rose trails off, not wanting to finish the sentence. Emme's expression hardens. Although she speaks no words, her pain is etched into hard lines across her face.

"And Sybil . . ." Margaret says, looking to Wenefrid with large, sad eyes. "What other choice did she have but to flee into the woods? If she'd stayed, they would've certainly killed her."

I hate them, they take turns saying. *I hate them, I hate them, I hate them.* I feel the truth to their words, the weight of the years they have spent straining beneath this society's cruelty, and beneath the other women's indifference to it. A seed of rage forms in the pit of my stomach, and it grows with each story that's shared. Suddenly, everything that seemed so morally nebulous is now simple. I can't speak to all men, but I don't have to. I need only to judge the ones before me, and the verdict is painfully clear.

These men are thieves.

These men are rapists.

These men are murderers.

These men will receive the punishment they deserve.

However, Cora's confession adds a new wrinkle to the original plan. If they intend to resettle on Scopuli, women and children will be aboard the return ship, too. How do I keep them safe?

An idea crystallizes on the edge of my mind. Before I can overthink it, I let my thoughts come tumbling out.

"So you hate them," I say slowly. They turn to look at me, their eyes inflamed with the same rage that I've seen reflected at me in Raidne's and Pisinoe's stares, that I have felt burning in my own. "All of them?"

They nod, and I take a deep breath before speaking the words that will change everything.

"Then will you help me?"

19

BEFORE

My wings are heavy, too heavy, and their weight drags me down into my sticky, dark vomit. But even pressed against the cool floor of the cave, every part of me burns as if it were my body placed upon the pyre. Pisinoe strokes my back, but her hand recoils in terror. Black feathers stick to her fingers—my feathers. I wail. Each twist of my body tears more away.

Darkness gathers in the corners of my vision. I try to blink it back, but it descends with the same intensity as the pain, narrowing my world to only agony and shadow. "Raidne? Pisinoe?"

"We're here, Thelxiope!" Pisinoe's voice is strained. I hear the horror of this scene inside it, and it brings more vomit up my throat. We were never beautiful creatures, some terrible combination of woman and raptor, but there was a dignity in our ferocious appearance. That's gone now.

The muscles in my legs and my wings constrict so tightly that they're sure to snap, but the sensation doesn't relent. It's as if they're retracting inside of me, called back to my core by some unseen force.

It's too much. Were Raidne and Pisinoe right to question

my connection with Proserpina? Was her voice no more than the manifestation of a guilty conscience, and now I'm suffering Ceres's wrath for keeping Jaquob as long as I did? For dedicating him to someone else?

Or worse—is this punishment from Proserpina herself, overdue vengeance for the part I played in her abduction?

All I know for certain is that I'm dying.

Raidne's hand cups my face. I picture her assuring me that I'm fine, but I see nothing in the blackness and hear nothing over the sound of my screams.

"What's happening to me?" I reach to touch my featherless wings. The limbs, once the span of two men, are now as small as a hawk's. They're shrinking, swallowed away between my scapulae.

The shadows abate long enough for me to see scales fall from my talons. Beneath them, there's skin. Human skin. As my claws recede, understanding emerges from the blinding pain.

The monster I was is gone.

"Raidne . . ." Pisinoe gasps. "She's . . ."

Raidne's palms shift to slide me into her lap. I tremble as her hands trace down my spine, unencumbered by the large appendages that once rested there. Sweat plasters the fallen feathers to my skin, and I struggle to breathe. But the cutting pain begins to lessen, and the tears that now grace my cheeks are from relief. Raidne gently wipes the sweat from my brow.

"She's human," Raidne finishes, but I can't tell if the words are real or if I've imagined them, because the world once again dissolves into darkness.

ᗄᗄ

My sisters carry me from the cave, an arm slung over each of their shoulders, my body hanging limp between them. It doesn't take long to reach the cabin. They're used to carrying the weight of men; my frail frame poses no challenge.

Once we're inside, Raidne lays me down gently on my pallet and Pisinoe warms a pot of water over the fire. When it's ready, she cleans the mixture of tears, sweat, vomit, and feathers from my skin.

The room is foggy, as if I'm looking through a lens of milky glass. Every part of me aches, and I toss and turn, unable to find a position on the straw-stuffed mattress that doesn't irritate my raw skin. It's still flushed, hot to the touch, and fresh beads of sweat stream from my pores faster than Pisinoe can wipe them away.

Fragments of my sisters' hushed whispers float down over me.

"What does this mean . . . ?"

"How did this happen . . . ?"

"Will she survive . . . ?"

Finally, thankfully, I slip into unconsciousness.

But it's not a quiet darkness that I find myself in. Scattered visions appear: a small town, the shadow of a man. I see Jaquob at the edge of a vast and dark subterranean river waiting for the ferryman; I see Proserpina.

She was still a child the last time I laid eyes on her, merely sixteen years old. Now she's a woman, a beautiful one, with long, dark tendrils of hair that billow around her face like a lion's mane. Her lips are painted a deep red, almost magenta. The color of pomegranates. How often I've pictured her popping those tiny berries, so dark that they're nearly purple, between her teeth, savoring the sweet juice that trickled over her lips. How did their nectar taste? Did Dis kiss it from her mouth?

She stands at the edge of our secluded pool wearing a shimmering black gown. What I first believe to be silver thread is actually the soft twinkling of stars. Constellations ripple across the fabric. The most beautiful woman I've ever seen stands before me cloaked in the heavens.

I want so desperately to speak to her, but when I try to talk, all I can muster is empty hot air.

"Thelia." She breaks the silence with the name I haven't heard in millennia, her voice as sweet as honey. When she opens her arms to me, it's all the invitation I need. I collapse into her embrace. She nuzzles her head against mine, and though I'm sure this is a dream, I can still smell her. It's no longer the scent of morning dew and lilies like I remember, but something darker—it's ceremonial incense, ash, and flame. It's sweet, dead earth. The smell doesn't match the memory of the girl I once knew, and when she releases me, I don't see a child.

I see a goddess.

"We don't have much time. My mother grew bored with torturing you and placed Scopuli outside of any ship's path. I don't think she expected you to live this long, but before she did that, I was always able to help."

"So it really was you." My heart flutters with the confirmation that I was right. "You sent the ships."

A sad smile settles over her lips. "Of course I did. Without men to hear your song . . ."

". . . we'd fade into dust."

"I thought I was going to be powerless to stop that from happening, but when that last ship wandered astray, I convinced Tempestas to knock it farther off course."

"The goddess of storms?" I remember how quickly that squall appeared, its wall of stygian black clouds gathering on the horizon. How had Jaquob described it?

It was like Hell opened above us and let loose its fury.

"I need you to listen carefully, Thelia. I'm a powerful ally, but my mother is an equally powerful enemy. Tempestas was leery to help this time—she won't do it again."

"What do I need to do?"

"You're not trapped here in your current form. No more ships will pass, so you must leave Scopuli and convince more men to return with you. I can save you all, but I need more blood. Their sacrifices will return you all to your divine forms; they will free you from this place. But without them this new body will only last six turns of the moon. You must hurry."

Six full, round moons—one for each pomegranate seed.

"Why send me?" I choke; it's all I can muster.

"Because you listened for me," she whispers, cupping my face in her hands. "And you shouldn't have been punished for a destiny that was already decided."

"That's not why I'm being punished."

The Fates might have tied Proserpina to Dis, but they didn't deliver her to him. I did that alone.

"Then because I know you can succeed."

The words make my body tremble; they are seismic. I don't deserve her compassion, and if she truly knew what transpired that day at the pool, she wouldn't give it so freely. I retreat from her, ashamed.

"You shouldn't," I say, weeping. "I've failed you before. What if I fail you again?"

"Thelia . . ." she begins, but I'm distracted by a hole that appears in my chest. Inside the gaping aperture, there's only darkness—and it grows, swallowing my body into that inky black. Instead of feeling frightened, I'm flooded with relief. This shadow will devour me whole, and I won't have to face the woman whom I betrayed, won't have to watch her features crumble with disappointment when she realizes the mistake she's made trusting me with this task.

"You won't."

Her words are claws to my heart, and she repeats them over and over until even her voice fades into shadow.

The rest of my sleep is as cold and dreamless as a tomb.

I wake to my sisters' relieved faces. Pisinoe tells me with a trembling voice that I slept for three days, twisting with fever the entire time. My temperature broke only shortly before I rose, and even Raidne looks shaken as she brings water to my lips.

I tell them about my dream, about Proserpina's plan to save us from Scopuli. Pisinoe is elated at the news, and Raidne is as well, though her jubilation is more subdued. At one point, I think I catch her wiping tears from her eyes, but I can't be certain that it's not my recently fevered mind playing tricks on me.

"It's settled, then," Raidne says, always the one to make the final decision. "You must go."

On the day I'm set to depart, I make my way to the meadow where wildflowers enchanted me all summer. The first frost has already come and gone, so I don't expect to find any blooms waiting for me. But Proserpina has sent one last message.

The pasture is overflowing with lilies. Their orange crowns stretch proudly toward the sun despite the ice that coats their stems. I kneel before one of the regal blossoms, its delicate petals gilded in hoarfrost. The sunlight bounces off each gracile stalk, each thin leaf, each vibrant petal, radiating thousands of beams of light across the field, thousands of diamonds shimmering for me, wishing me luck, saying goodbye.

The crunch of ice beneath talons signals I'm not alone.

Raidne appears from the woods, wringing her hands with nerves. But when she sees the lilies, awe overtakes her. We stand in silence for a few moments and bask in the sight.

"Everything's ready," she offers slowly. She doesn't know how to tell me it's time to leave, doesn't know how to send me away.

I look down at my hands, suddenly petrified. This rocky island is our prison, but it's also our home. A part of me is afraid to leave it behind. Raidne slides in close and places a thin golden circlet on my head. She beams at the result and nestles her face into my shoulder.

"Whatever happens, this is for the best, Thelxiope. I know you have no choice but to go, but this gives Pisinoe and me something to hope for. I never thought we'd have that again."

I reach for her hand and squeeze it gently. "Walk me to the beach?"

She nods.

I feel like I'm watching from above as we stroll side by side, arms linked, down the path that leads to the skiff that will carry me away: two women—one human, one myth—moving toward something greater than themselves.

Pisinoe waits for us on the same stretch of sand that brought me Jaquob. She's filled the tiny boat with necklaces, jewels, gold and silver coins, weaponry, anything that can conceivably count as wealth. It's an impressive hoard. Perhaps I'll find my way into legend again, this time as someone who redeems herself, not only as a monster who tears men apart. Then Raidne hands me the letter we spent hours crafting together, my new history inked across its surface. I press it to my chest, reveling in the fact that these past centuries won't be my only story. This single piece of paper is proof of that.

Their eyes well with tears as they help me climb into Jaquob's vessel and push me into the surf. I'll head south out of the archipelago, and then it's up to the Fates where I land.

The water today is calm, and I raise the sail. Wind rushes to fill it, and then I'm off, coasting on the surface of the waves. I turn back to look at the shore.

Raidne and Pisinoe have ascended into the sky to follow me until the curse forbids them from going any farther. Like this, they're magnificent—with their wings spread wide, with the wind blowing through their hair. But it's what happens next that steals my breath.

A song floats down from the heavens. Their voices are so beautiful that tears blur their forms, and only now do I understand the overwhelming desire to follow its notes wherever they may lead me. It contains everything that Raidne and Pisinoe feel right now: There's the sadness at losing me and the jealousy of being left behind. But more important are the notes that overpower those: the hope for a new beginning, joy at the end of the monotony, and, more than anything else, love.

Our song spins promises of the future, and for the first time that I can remember, I have no idea what mine holds. But with the sea unfurling before me, their voices sing the answer, as clear as Scopuli's waters.

In them, I hear salvation.

20

NOW

"Of course we'll help you, Thelia," Cora answers. There's a sharpness to her voice that takes me a moment to place. Hurt. She thinks I question her willingness to protect me. "We'll take you back to Sybil's. If she's still in contact with the Croatoans, perhaps they can be convinced to take you to the mainland—"

"No. I'm going back to Scopuli."

"My lady, you can't!" Margery clasps her hands together so tightly that her knuckles shine white. "The Council voted to seize Scopuli by force! If it's mostly women on the island . . ."

"There are almost a hundred single men here eager for their company," Emme answers when Margery's voice trails off, a dark expression settling over her usually soft features. "And nearly all of them would like the opportunity to change that, though the spoils of raiding aren't often made into wives."

I think of the Iroquoian women on Jaquob's ship. Gifts, he called them. "I know what they'd do if given the chance. But the only other women on Scopuli are my sisters, and they expect me to return with men—men with treacherous hearts."

Confusion pinches Cora's features, and that soft red mouth I've dreamt of kissing for weeks falls open with surprise.

"What do you mean?" Rose asks. The other women wear similar confused expressions.

I take a deep breath, steeling myself for my confession. The colony's articles pinned proudly on the meetinghouse's door flash before me. They beg me to keep my mouth shut.

1. *No man may speak impiously or maliciously against the holy and blessed Trinity or against the known Articles of Christian faith, upon pain of death.*
2. *No man shall use any traitorous words against her Majesty's Person or royal authority, upon pain of death.*
3. *No man shall commit the horrible and detestable sins of Sodomy, upon pain of death.*

My throat tightens. Oh, gods, I'm guilty of all three counts, and though these women have been kind to me, will they truly forsake their countrymen, their queen, their god for me? A stranger? But what other choice do I have? If I don't trust them now, I risk having to bury their corpses on Scopuli's bluffs. I risk having to bury their children's. Raidne and Pisinoe wouldn't want freedom, not if it came at that price. And I don't, either.

"You're not an agent of Spain, are you?" Emme asks.

"No. But I'm also not a princess."

A collective gasp ripples across the room.

"I'm going to trust you, but you must trust me, too. Can you do that?"

Each woman nods.

"My sisters and I . . . we're cursed. When we were girls, I angered someone very powerful. She was a goddess to us—I don't know what you'd call her. A witch, perhaps, though she'd punish you severely for diminishing her like that. A fallen angel, then. A fairy queen. I was given a chance to break this curse, but it can only be done by spilling the blood of treacherous men. *These* treacherous men. I wouldn't have landed here if it wasn't supposed to be them. But without your help, I can't stop our magic from endangering the innocent."

I hear my heart beat once, then twice, but no one speaks. Cora's chin drops to her chest, and dread swirls in my belly, its claws looking for purchase to tear through the rest of me. The other women watch her just as intently; we all hold our breath waiting for her verdict. But when she lifts her face again, her eyes are glistening. She nods to them, determination settling into her features.

She believes me.

"God works in mysterious ways, but what can we do?" It's Elyoner who speaks. A few short months ago, she would've delighted in watching my neck grace the pillory, but tonight, she joins my side.

"We need a plan, and quickly," Cora says. "Thomas will ask you about Scopuli tonight, and as soon as he knows its location, they're going to imprison you."

I take a few moments to appraise them. My friends. Their faces are creased with worry, yes, but Cora's conviction is infectious. One by one, courage makes them each stand a little taller, and I know my faith has been well placed.

When I speak, there's a smile on my lips. "So we'll let them."

᛫ᛋᛋ᛫

After we settle on a rough course of action, Wenefrid finds me to tell me she intends to remain behind.

"I'm too old for another voyage," she says with a smile. "I'll be happier here."

"With Sybil?" I ask.

"With Sybil," she confirms, and her eyes sparkle like stars as they wander from me to Cora. When she speaks again, her voice is as soft as a sigh. "If you love someone, make sure they know it. Don't make the same mistake I did. You can lose so much time that way."

Her words haunt me as Cora and I walk through the darkling streets to the Bailies', Cora's hand swinging dangerously close to mine. My fingers itch to take hold of hers, but I force my arm to stay at my side. We need the colonists to believe that Cora's one of them, that they've all caught me unawares. Which means that for now, the ghost of her touch must be enough.

"What's going to happen to us all?" she whispers, eyes scanning the shadows between the cottages for potential spies. But the village is quiet.

"I can't say. But I'm serious about the bayberry wax, Cora. Wenefrid will show you how to make it, but you need enough to seal everyone's ears."

"Don't worry, Thelia. We'll make enough."

I nod, her assurance a balm on my anxiety.

"I don't know if we'll get another chance to be truly alone," she continues. "They'll lock you in your room while we prepare to embark, then they'll transfer you to the new ship with the rest of us before we sail."

"It will be all right, Cora."

"How will we stop them? Truly?"

"You'll see." I allow my fingers to graze against hers, a warm smile on my lips. Even in her most wondrous dreams, Cora would never be able to imagine it.

᠄᠄᠄

Cora's warning proved true several nights ago. When I arrived back home, both Bailies were gathered in the dining room with the rest of the Council. Thomas feigned an apology for my time in the pillory. His penance, he said, was an invitation to help them plan the scouting party's voyage to Scopuli. Just as Cora predicted, Thomas presented me with parchment and a quill. My fingers trembled as I lifted the quill above the parchment's clean surface. Most of my time at sea was a blur—how could I possibly commit my path to it? But the moment that the tip connected with the paper and ink soaked into its fibers, my hand moved of its own accord. Proserpina, I believe, showing us all the way. As soon as the roughly sketched map of Scopuli's location was in Thomas's hands, Hugh Taylor and Charles Florrie were on me, dragging me to my bedroom to bar me inside.

And so I watch from my window as the colony prepares to steal my home. Now that I'm safely locked away, there's no need for them to hide their treachery. Under James Lacie's command, they dismantle the cottages and other fortifications, should they need to return for the lumber after sacking Scopuli. They make a show of parading their possessions past me on their way to the northern gate, but their actions don't have the desired effect of making me wither with fear. Instead, I commit the wealthier families' chests to memory so I can guide Pisinoe to them when the waves return them to our beach.

Of the two ships now in the colony's possession, only the pinnace is small enough to navigate the narrow inlet that

separates Roanoke from the open ocean. I imagine it traveling back and forth between the island and the new ship, *Endurance*, ferrying the colony's possessions to the larger vessel.
Planks will be erected to connect their decks so the men can
cross between them freely, hauling barrels and chests over
the thin stretch of sea. Then the heavier items will be ma-
neuvered aboard with a series of ropes and levers, including,
to my surprise, the cannon they rolled past my window. They
plan to blow Scopuli to pieces.

All the while, they watch me as they work, and their gazes
hold a smug satisfaction now that my riches are no longer
meant for a single man alone. They, too, will be able to plun-
der from me after all. But I no longer hide my treachery, either. When they're unlucky enough to meet my eyes, I
unleash a blazing grin that desiccates their pompous smiles.
They recognize the threat it contains, and they slink away,
defeated. It makes my skin vibrate with giddy anticipation.
The City of Raleigh had already become a prison, even before
now—the unusual clothes, the forced politeness, the constant stares, each a bar on a cage smaller than Scopuli. I miss
my rocky shore, its familiar folds. I crave the comfort of my
sisters' presence. I imagine what they'll say about Cora, reveling in the fact that, soon, I won't have to imagine it at all.

Inside the *Endurance*, the clean scent of fresh timber mixes
with the brine of the sea. My new cell is a locked closet
where the gunpowder is stored. I run my palms along the
wooden walls. Their edges are still raw, a reminder that the
Endurance was built in a hurry, and a rogue splinter pierces
my index finger. A bubble of blood erupts from the wound,
but instead of bringing the digit to my mouth to suck it clean,
I rub it into the wood.

Consider that an offering.

Signs of life filter through the locked door. Lantern light leaks in through the seam where the door meets the floor, and that sliver becomes my sun. In its glow, soft songs seep into the closet. The colonists sing to distract the children from the monotony of sea travel, but their music is also a comfort to me.

Every few hours, the *clink* of a key in a lock announces it's time for John Chapman to check my chamber pot. I suppose I should be grateful for this small mercy, but it's for their benefit as much as mine. It doesn't take long for the main deck, where the colonists are housed, to grow fetid with the haze of excrement, urine, and sweat. It's enough to almost make me grateful to be locked away—inside the closet, the worst of the noxious cloud can't reach me. Still, the sharpness of stale urine settles into my clothes, the sweetness of vomit nestles into my hair.

For the few moments the door is open, I search the space to the outside world for signs of the women. Occasionally I'll catch glimpses of Elizabeth and Elyoner. Rose smiled at me once. But Cora never graces the slender aperture. As Thomas's betrothed once more, she likely occupies quarters separate from the rest of the colony's.

When the sliver of light disappears, the singing and soft chatter stop. I mark the days by counting its loss, carving lines into the soft wood floor with my fingernails. In that near total darkness, one week turns to two, then two spills into three. Luna will be close to full again if she's not already, and all I can do is pray that the *Endurance*'s larger sails carry us to Scopuli's shores faster than my skiff carried me to Roanoke's. Tonight, I've barely finished chipping my daily notch into the floorboards when the deck suddenly tilts beneath me, sending me toppling into the wall, and a collective scream tears across the main deck. When the ship rights itself, a chattering panic rises. A loud crack of thunder shakes the sky, followed by the sudden sound of rain beating against the ship.

Emme's voice floats through the door, sharp and biting. "Aren't you going to check her chamber pot again?"

"John emptied it half an hour ago," Master Florrie snaps. "That's enough royal shit for one day."

My throat constricts—Emme's avoided Charles since the night he was too rough with her, before my arrival. And now she's purposefully seeking him out on my behalf.

"If the weather looks as bad as Mauris says, we'll all suffer if it spills on the floor! Lady Thelia, can you hear me?"

"Stop! Master Bailie forbade anyone to speak—"

"There's a storm coming—" Her speech is interrupted by another wave swell. In the darkness, I hear the empty chamber pot slide across the floor. "Does your chamber pot need to be emptied?"

There's a frenzied pitch to her voice. Someone else might attribute it to her fear of the storm. Or of Charles. But to me . . .

"Yes!" I call back. "It's full, Mistress Merrimoth."

Loud footsteps stomp across the deck overhead, combined with the sound of yelling. Each muscle in my body tenses, readying me to run.

"Go wake up John," Charles orders. "It's my duty to guard her, not to empty her piss."

"God's blood! Just unlock the door and let me deal with it before another wave knocks it over."

Charles grumbles, no doubt plotting a punishment for her harsh tongue, but the familiar *clink* of the key in the lock indicates Emme's won. The door swings open, and she crosses into the gun room, hand outstretched to receive the empty stoneware pot. Behind her, someone strikes a match to light the lantern that swings overhead, silhouetting her against the door. I hold my breath as I hand it to her.

Emme steps to the side, out of the doorway. When she speaks again, her voice hits the perfect key of alarm. "Master Florrie! Come quickly!"

Charles hears her fear, and, without thinking, he charges into the darkness to face the treachery Emme's discovered. But all he finds is me, wide-eyed, as Emme slides behind him and, without a word, swiftly brings the heavy crock down onto his head.

The man crumples to the floor. The lantern behind Emme lowers to reveal Margery with a black cloak hanging off her left arm. She closes us into the gun room together, safe from any potential prying eyes.

"God's blood, that felt amazing." Emme laughs as she retrieves the conical gray hat from Charles's head and hands it to me.

I grin.

"Everyone's distracted by the storm," Margery explains, as Emme retrieves the cloak to place it over my shoulders. "Cora's room is in the cabin directly above us. Take the ladder just outside to the floor above, then knock on the door behind you. She's waiting."

"But—"

"They won't be looking for you because they won't know you're missing," Emme says. "We'll drag him back out and lock the door. The sea was so rough, he simply slipped and hit his head—thank goodness Margery found him when she did!"

I nod. "Thank you."

"Good luck," Margery whispers, then reopens the door for me. The tension in my muscles springs me forward through the shadows to the ladder, and I scan the darkened room for stray eyes that might catch my ascent. But Margery's right—most of the able-bodied men are above deck helping to rig the sails, and those who remain are terrified by the ship's increased rocking. No one wants another problem to appear, so they aren't actively searching for one. I almost laugh when my hands find the first rung.

Within moments, I'm at Cora's door. I rap my knuckles against the wood once, then twice. With each second that passes, my heart races faster, but then there's the blessed sound of a latch being lifted, of a door squeaking open.

Cora's eyes widen, unable to discern who stands before her. The brim of Charles's hat casts my face in darkness that the low lantern light can't penetrate; I lift it slowly, my heart soaring as recognition melts her confusion into a slow smile.

"Thank God," she says, pulling me into her arms and slamming the door closed behind her.

A particularly violent wave smashes into the ship and sends us tumbling to the floor. Cora crawls to her feet as quickly as she can, bolting the door behind her. When she finds me again, her face is twisted with fear.

I've seen ships tossed in waves like this from the sky, but the feeling of being inside one is a horror new to me. Only now, as water rains down on us from a leak in the wooden floors above, do I truly appreciate how fragile this vessel really is.

"W-what do we do?" Cora stammers, her eyes their own large, verdant planets. I reach for her hand, and she takes mine without hesitation.

"We have to wait it out."

"There was a storm during our voyage from England. It nearly destroyed the ship—"

"Shhh, Cora, don't think of such things. It's not our fate to die here."

I hope my voice projects the confidence that my heart doesn't feel. In truth, I'm just as terrified as Cora, if not more so. Did Ceres discover our plan and, on the cusp of my victory, convince Tempestas to drown me instead?

"Come." I wander to her bed and motion for her to lie beside me. To my surprise, she listens, and I slide my hands beneath her head to guide it into my lap. My fingers brush her hair gently, although I'm careful to keep their touch light—the last thing I want is to scare her away. Only now, locked safely away in her chambers with my hands in her curls, do I realize she's just wearing a shift.

Slowly, she softens, and my racing heart follows suit. The waves still sway the boat, but, at least for now, they aren't intensifying.

"I'm so sorry," she whispers up to me. I use the opportunity to lie down beside her; she slips her hand into mine again. "There was no way for me to go belowdecks without Thomas noticing. Are you all right?"

"I'm fine," I whisper back. "Much better now."

"I'm scared, Thelia."

"Don't be, Cora. Everything is going to be all right."

"You can't know that. Once Scopuli's in sight, they're going to . . ." She buries her head in my shoulder, unable to make herself finish the sentence.

I hold her there, stroking her hair. "I won't let him hurt you."

"Can we really stop them? There are so few of us."

"I won't let him hurt you," I say again, this time more firmly. Cora cranes her head to look at me, and I feel tears welling in my eyes. "I'll kill him, Cora. I won't be responsible for another forced marriage. Not again."

There's a long moment where Cora says nothing. She simply stares at me, green eyes unblinking and expression unreadable. But then she speaks, and her voice is as soft as I've ever heard it, as gentle as a spring breeze. "Again?"

Breaths catch in my throat, one right after the other, a trapped chain of words I've never repeated to anyone in a single sitting. My back stiffens as my right hand finds my heart, as if the placement could possibly soothe the organ's quickening beats. It pounds against the back of my ribs, *lub-dub, lub-dub, lub-dub,* as I choke for air. Now it's Cora's turn to soothe me. She envelops me in her arms and guides my head to the crook of her neck. I bury my gasps in the warmth of her bare skin; it sends my own ablaze.

Her hand rubs circles into my back to melt away the panic. But I linger after it passes, still frightened of the silence. Her muscles tense beneath me, her body repeating the word for her: *Again?*

She's as curious as Proserpina was, unable to help herself, unable to remain on the outside of a secret.

"You asked me once to tell you the truth," I murmur into her curls. "I couldn't then."

"And now?" she whispers.

"Now I'll tell you everything."

טטט

Tears stream down my face as the story spills out, and I lift my head to meet Cora's gaze. She's crying as well, but where I expect disgust written across her features, I find heartbreak— not *by* me, but *for* me. "Oh, Thelia . . ."

"I won't let another love of mine fall prey to the cruelty of men."

Cora presses her forehead to mine as her fingertips make sensuous promises on the back of my hand. A stone forms in my throat as every part of me comes alive beneath her touch. Overhead, the lantern swings back and forth with the waves, its reflection captured in two warm sparks that set her emerald eyes alight. "A love?"

Her voice is so soft that I'm not entirely sure that I heard her question. I think of how she withdrew from me those weeks ago, of the sharp ache left in her wake. I say nothing.

"You need not retreat," she whispers. An invitation, and this time, I don't question her.

The ship moans on the crest of each swell, as if it's unsure it can scale the next one. The commotion outside should be a distraction—men yelling indistinctly, boots stomping across the deck, the *clangs* and *scrapes* as they try desperately to steer through the squall without falling victim to its fury—but it isn't. There's only Cora, her soft pink lips turning upward into a tentative smile, her mess of black curls spilling over her shoulders. Warmth radiates from our bodies. There's a charge in the air, the same energy that precedes a summer storm, so potent you can taste it—an entire atmosphere born from our desire.

My heart races against my ribs. She lets her hand wander from mine up to the side of my face, brushing a lock of hair behind my ear. Each caress is gentle, exploratory, working up the courage to ask the greater question. The time for thinking is over; I press my body against hers, erasing the space between us, encircling her in my arms.

Our lips meet, an answer. Her kiss is fiery, almost desperate, with an intensity that I match. Her hands leave my face to dig into my hair, fingers entangling themselves so tightly into the locks that it almost hurts. After a time, I break away—I need to catch my breath.

"It wasn't your fault, Thelia," Cora whispers into my ear, her words an absolution. It's what I've been desperate to hear for centuries. I find her mouth again, and finally, after all this time, we melt into each other.

With Will, our intimacy was hurried, a poor attempt to fill the void left by others. It's different with Cora. I want to savor every second, every detail: how she trembles as I plant delicate kisses along her jaw, how her breath hitches each time my lips make contact with her skin.

"Can I touch you?" I whisper into her shoulder, and she nods.

"Please."

A few months ago, I was certain I'd forgotten love's softness. That if given the chance, my desire would crush us both. But now, as a hand slides from her waist to slip beneath her nightgown, the idea seems foolish. I won't devour her.

I'll worship her.

Cora twists beneath my touch, and I think of all the times she grazed against me and set my skin alight. She must be burning beneath the weight of my palm, but I take my time dragging it along her skin, trying to memorize the rise of her hips, the swell of her breasts. Suddenly, our clothes are an excruciating barrier.

"I want to see you," she says on a sigh, so we peel off each other's gowns, and then nothing separates us but skin.

Her hips grind into mine, and she laces our legs together, guiding me with her embrace to rest on top of her. My hair encircles our faces in our own private grotto, and when I look down at her, she's smiling, lips slightly parted. I can't resist brushing a finger against them, and before I realize what she's doing, she takes it into her mouth and swirls her tongue around it.

The sensation shoots through my entire body and settles between my legs, and I must look shocked by the thrill, because she laughs sweetly before releasing me. The act emboldens me, and I let my lips travel to her jaw, down her neck. She sighs, pressing her body up into mine, asking me to continue. So I do.

I bury my head in her chest, letting my tongue work its magic there, while my wet finger slides down her side. Her back arches in response, and then my hand is climbing over the curve of her thigh to rest between her legs. I lift my head to meet her eyes once more.

"Is this all right? Can I keep going?"

Cora's entire body flutters against mine, and she nods. It's all I need. My finger traces its way into her slickness. She groans softly, biting her lower lip to try to keep quiet, but I can tell it's hard for her. Seeing her like this, pliable to my touch, needing more, makes me desperate for her, and I slide my body down hers until I'm nestled between her legs. I catch her watching me between them, her mouth open in a surprised little O, so I add a second finger.

It has the desired effect, and she crumples back into the pillows, rocking her hips against me. This time my tongue finds her most sensitive spot, and within moments, her entire body quakes. Her legs close around me, overwhelmed by the sensations I've led her to.

I move back up to bury my face in her nape, and her arms encircle me while she catches her breath. When I look up, I find that she's crying softly.

"Cora—" I whisper, alarmed.

"Shh, it's all right, Thelia. They're happy tears," she says before bringing my lips to hers again. She kisses me slowly, and when she finally pulls away, that beautiful mouth is twisted into a playful grin.

"It's your turn."

With three short words, she sets my entire form aflame.

21

NOW

Outside her door, the deck is quiet. The storm has settled. I turn to Cora, my fingers tracing the side of her face, not wanting to disturb her but knowing that I must.

We're close. Scopuli's pull pulses inside of me, the same way birds know where to migrate for the winter, following that instinctive, ancestral path to safer havens.

I place a gentle kiss on her cheek and whisper her name into her ear. She stirs, slow to rise. When her eyes find mine, it's clear that she's processing what's happened between us. She wonders what it means for her soul.

There's nothing I want more than to reassure her, but we don't have time.

I slide from the bed to kneel before the wooden chest at its base. Its heavy lid creaks with resistance, but I find what I seek: a large crock filled with bayberry wax.

"Do you remember what to do with this?" My tone conveys my seriousness, and Cora's hesitation is replaced with resolve.

"I do."

"Their song will drive the men mad. If we have any hope of ever leaving Scopuli, we need to keep them away from the whipstaff, otherwise they'll purposefully steer the ship into the rocks."

"I know—Emme and I will keep them away from it."

"And Margery and Elizabeth will load the others into the longboat just in case, right?"

"Yes, Thelia." She reaches for my hand and squeezes it. "We know what to do. You can trust us."

"If . . . if something happens to me—"

"Thelia—"

"Please, Cora, let me say this. You can trust us, too. My sisters look frightening, but they won't harm you."

She reaches into the chest and withdraws a small cloth bundle from its depths. Nestled inside are the dragonfly fibulae Pisinoe gave me before I left. Tears blur my vision at the sight of them—the last place I saw them was on my fireplace mantel before I lost my son.

"How did you . . ."

"I know what they mean to you," she whispers, sliding them into my hair. "Please be careful, Thelia. I can't lose you."

"You won't."

"Do you remember the night before the challenge, when I followed you to the beach?" she asks.

I nod.

"This is going to sound absurd, but as I listened to you singing, I could so clearly see my life with you. It seemed impossible then, but now . . ."

Emboldened, I lean forward to kiss her again. She doesn't turn away. Our lips tell each other all the things we're too frightened to say aloud.

"I'll find you when it's over," I whisper against her open mouth.

She nods, quivering against me.

Her tears taste like fear on my tongue.

🙰🙰🙰

Scopuli's call carries me to the main deck, dressed in only my thin linen smock. The predawn air draws goosebumps on my skin, but though I know it's cold, I don't feel it. The blood is rushing too quickly through my veins. Sailors gawk as I brush past them, but they're of little concern to me now. The bow is my destination, and I stare ahead, willing Scopuli to appear in the endless blue gradient of sea and sky. The sun sits low to the east, spilling its warm glow onto the waves.

Three tiny needles appear just left of center on the horizon, and every hair on my body rises. It's a familiar, unmistakable sight, and it leaves me breathless: the rocky formations of Castle.

I've dreamed of this moment for months, thought through every minute detail, but now that the time is here, I'm frozen in place.

"Thelia?" Cora whispers, and her voice shatters my suspension. I whirl around to meet her.

"Cora." The desperation in my voice catches us both by surprise. She throws a shawl around my shoulders, always concerned for my decency. I take it readily. With my reverie broken, the chill finds my skin, and I pull the shawl tight around my frame. "Go, now."

My tone sends her back a few steps, but I don't have time to calibrate my reactions properly. If we can see Castle's spires, it won't be long before Raidne and Pisinoe discover us approaching from the south.

Cora takes off toward the gun deck, and I look north once more. The trio of rocks grows larger; there's no denying it. I tear myself from the view and head for the Bailies' cabin. No one answers when I knock the first time, so I knock again, louder. A few moments pass before Mistress Bailie answers, wiping the sleep from her eyes. Mother and son have both just woken.

"Lady Thelia." Her eyes widen in surprise. Just as Emme and Margery suspected, in the fury of the storm, no one bothered to confirm if their story about Charles was true.

"We're approaching Scopuli," I say cheerfully. Excitement radiates off my words. The elder Bailie stiffens at the news.

"What do you mean?" Thomas's voice is pitched, no doubt alarmed by my appearance in his doorway. "Your map says we're still a few days out."

Saliva pools beneath my tongue, and I laugh at this little gift from Proserpina. "Did you think I'd tell you Scopuli's true location?"

"Go warn the men," Agnes orders, twisting to face her son. Her tone pushes him to pull on his leather boots. "And ready the cannon."

His expression darkens at the order, but he obeys it, stumbling shirtless from their cabin. I let him pass and then close myself in with her. The corner of her lip twitches at the sound of the door clicking into place, but even now, she's too proud to let me see her fear for long. Instead, she moves to stand before a mirror that hangs on the wall to our right, eyeing herself in the looking glass. Gracile fingers collect her yellow hair to twist it into a bun, then she reaches for her hairpins to secure it in place. I want, no, I *need* to see her jaw drop, her carefully constructed exterior crumble into ash.

"You taught me an important lesson, Agnes."

That piques her attention, and our eyes connect in the mirror's reflection. "And what was that?"

"Before I met you, it wasn't in my nature to wish harm upon women. So many of us have suffered at the hands of men. It seemed wrong, no, *perverse,* to inflict that same cruelty on each other."

I deposit Cora's shawl on her bed, then slide beside her and pluck the pins from her grasp. She still holds her unsecured bun with her other hand, and I slip the delicate metal pieces into those daffodil locks for her.

"But then you showed me it wasn't simply the sex between your legs that can corrupt a person. That although we bear unimaginable burdens, women can curdle just as easily when lusting for power. Tell me, why did you kill Will?"

She turns to face me, intrigued by my candor. The smirk on her lips reveals that she doesn't believe herself to be in any real danger. "I didn't."

"You know what I mean. All of this"—my hands motion to the room around us—"was your idea."

"Will meddled where he shouldn't have, and after, it was clear that he was never going to do what needed to be done."

Her voice is steady, calm, as if she's discussing her favorite Bible verse or her preferred flavor of tea. But then her eyes narrow. "You had something to do with his body ending up outside the walls—how did you move him there without being caught?"

I ignore her question. "Why would you do such a terrible thing?"

"For Thomas, of course. He needs to be guided to greatness."

"You've hurt a lot of people."

"The world is a dark place, Lady Thelia. The weak don't survive it."

The back of my throat begins to tingle, although the exact sensation is difficult to describe. It's not painful, but there's a pressure that builds, and it begs to be released. It's my song, trying to break free. Now that Scopuli is close, its magic has returned.

"If I wanted to, I could enchant you. I'd lead you off the ship's edge and let you drown in the waves below. If the gods deemed you fit, you'd wash ashore alive, and I'd slit your throat as a sacrifice to them."

Her eyes widen in disgust. "I knew something was wrong with you from the very first time I saw—"

"Most men don't survive the gauntlet of the waves and reefs. But you're stronger than most men. I'm so tempted to see if you'd live. I'm almost certain you would. And what an incredible offering you'd make! Proserpina would love that pretty porcelain neck of yours and the treacherous blood in your veins. But I'm tired of waiting for the gods' approval." I pull one of the fibulae from my hair and press its pin into my finger to test its sharpness. A tiny bubble of blood erupts from my flesh, and I smile. "When I kill your son, his death will be for me. Just like yours."

She lunges for me, and we fall to the floor. Despite her age, she's strong, and it doesn't take long for her slender hands to find their way around my throat. She should call for Thomas, now that she has me in her grasp, and I think a part of her knows that. But she can't resist the urge to choke the life out of me herself.

I anticipated such a reaction, and with a single, swift movement, I jab the fibula's pin, Cora's gift, into the side of her neck. Her eyes widen with surprise, and, without thinking, she pulls the brooch from her flesh. A thin line of blood sprays onto the floor, painting the wood crimson.

Agnes slides off me and fumbles around on her hands and knees for something to press against the wound. While she's distracted, I wander to her bedside table. There, resting atop the gleaming wood, is a slender knife.

"That was for Will," I say, straddling my legs across her frame to peer down at her. "But this is for me. For those nights you stood by and did nothing to stop your vile son from taking what wasn't his."

She looks for me over her shoulder, but I sink the blade into the other side of her throat before she finds me. This time, she knows the blow is fatal. She slumps to the ground, her fingers caressing the handle, too afraid to pull it out.

My hand pushes hers out of the way.

"Don't," she pleads. But it's too late for that—I tug. Her blood paints me, and Agnes chokes on her own sins just like Jaquob did, but this time, I don't feel compelled to watch. Let her die scared and alone. It's what she deserves. I wrap myself in Cora's shawl to hide the worst of Agnes's mess and exit back onto the deck, into chaos.

Thomas is nowhere to be seen, but he's clearly given orders. The men who rush past are distracted, too lost in their assignments to notice as their captive sneaks to the helmsman's cabin. As instructed, Emme and Cora are posted outside, waiting for the signal to begin. Once they have it, they'll knock out the helmsman and drop Endurance's anchor.

"Thelia," Cora says with a gasp, taking in the crimson on my gown. "Are you hurt?"

"It's not mine," I say gently, watching as their expressions shift from fear to surprise. To agree to a revolution in a quiet room is one thing, but to stand before its bloody reality is quite another. What if they change their minds?

But then Emme spits and says, "Good riddance," and all I can do is smile.

"Are the others in place?"

"Yes," Cora says. "Elizabeth gathered everyone, and Elyoner and Liz are sealing their ears. When it . . . when it starts,

Rose will give us the signal before joining the others to head for the longboat."

I nod, an anxious energy thrumming in my gut. All that's left is to wait for my sisters to make our first move. "Do you have yours in?"

"Not yet, we—"

Emme catches sight of my expression and presses a glob of the light green substance into each of her ears before she turns away to peer through a small window onto the main deck. It's all the privacy I need.

"Now, please, Cora."

She looks reluctant, but she concedes.

"Can you hear what I am saying?"

Cora shakes her head no.

I lean forward and kiss her, too painfully aware of all the ways this moment could be our last. Cora's lips tremble beneath my own.

"Thelia, I—"

"There's no time, Cora—" I start, but my objection falls on unhearing ears.

"I love you," she says. "I don't care what it means for my soul."

I press my forehead to hers and close my eyes, reveling in her roses one last time. "I love you, too."

𐌔𐌔𐌔𐌔

Anticipation carries me across the upper deck toward the long-boat. Already, Castle's spires loom larger on the horizon, and to their right, the elevated cliffs of Scopuli finally rise to join them. There was a part of me that didn't believe I'd make it home again, and yet here I am, just as Proserpina decreed. My eyes scan the sky for signs of movement. A dark figure dips between the clouds, but it's only a gull, and my heart sinks.

Hugh Taylor appears around the opposite side of the long-boat. He stops in his tracks when he sees me, his eyes flooding with confusion.

"How did you—" He cranes his head to the half deck above, no doubt scanning for Thomas. A dog without his master, unable to create his own orders. I won't let him ask for them. My hands dive for his arm, fingernails finding purchase in his flesh.

"You bitch!" he growls, yanking out of my grasp. My nails leave bloody trails in their wake, and though he raises a hand to hit me, I can't help myself—I laugh. "You have no idea what's coming for you—"

I hear them before I see them. The wind carries their melody, soft at first, over the miles that still lie between us. It's a haunting sound, wind blowing over a glass, a loon calling across the gloaming. It stops Hugh's hand midair, and he follows my gaze to the heavens.

Two shadowy figures approach from the north. Hugh's eyes grow into large circles; his mouth falls agape.

He smiles like a man who's seeing angels. I didn't understand Jaquob's confusion before, but now I do—witnessing their winged forms soar through the clouds is like watching a star fall. There's an unmistakable magic in it. Before, I could see only our ugliness, but now I finally understand.

We are angels of destruction, and this ship is Gomorrah.

"No." I laugh again, pulling Hugh's attention back to me. "It's you who has no idea."

ᛅᛅᛅ

Their song grows louder, and Hugh wanders to the edge of the boat for a better look. Elizabeth appears on the upper deck, the other innocents in tow. They too stand in reverent awe at the sight of winged women in the sky.

Now's the time.

I cross the deck to shake Elizabeth's shoulder, and when our eyes meet, it takes her a moment to find me from behind her wonder. But then her mouth tightens in firm resolve, and with a nod, she turns to the other women and children and begins ushering them inside the longboat. Rose rushes past us, off to alert Emme and Cora.

Which leaves me free to find Thomas. How desperate I've been for this, and now, after all this time, it's finally here.

Pain erupts between my shoulders, eclipsing my fantasies of revenge. I reach a trembling hand back to run my fingers between them. The skin there is too taut, stretched thin by something hard pushing up from beneath. I recoil with horror at the same time that a sickening rip interrupts the enchanting melody that filters down from above.

The sixth full moon hangs heavy in the western sky, and as dawn banishes it beneath the waves, it takes the magic of Jaquob's sacrifice with it. Talons erupt from my bare toes, slashing the wooden planks beneath them, and agony brings me to my knees. This great unfurling, of feathers that push through skin, of wings that split open my back, hurts far worse than when my body absorbed them only a few months ago. But this time, I bear it without succumbing to the darkness that beckons, even when those magnificent black wings unfold and spray the deck with viscera—a mixture of my blood, my muscle. In the longboat, now safely lowered into the ocean, people scream.

But not because of me. They can't see me over the edge of the ship, on all fours, desperate to keep myself from collapsing entirely. It's because of Hugh, who has climbed over the low wall that separates him from the sea. Despite my cries, Hugh never looks at me. He's transfixed by my sisters, and when they're close enough that I can finally make out their faces, even blurred by tears, Hugh jumps out to them, then falls into the churning waves below.

What image was it that called him into the raging sea? Was it a kingdom of gold and a wife to own, or a different, secret wish he'll carry to his watery grave?

Raidne and Pisinoe should lead the ship to the north to dodge the worst part of the reef. They don't know we plan to anchor it, only that this part of the cove is vicious, and we need as many sailors alive as possible. But they spot me. Pisinoe takes Raidne's hand, and before I know what's happening, they crash onto the deck and sweep me into a tight embrace.

It's Raidne who speaks first, pulling herself away just enough to take stock of me. "Are you all right? Look at you . . ."

I nod weakly, too overcome for words to form.

"Can you stand?" Pisinoe asks gently, and the two help me onto my feet. It doesn't take long for the enchanted sailors to find us, driven mad by my sisters' voices. Their eyes are glassy, their expressions hungry, as they pour onto the upper deck to find us huddled together. Terror sends me deeper into my sisters' arms. The men are so frenzied by their proximity, so desperate for their futures, that they'll tear us apart to look for them in our entrails. Though I've forgotten what I am, Raidne and Pisinoe haven't. They open their mouths and let their song envelop them.

Immediately, the sailors stop in their tracks, swaying in sync with the melody, wearing slack-jawed grins. The notes bring tears to my eyes, and I'm overwhelmed with gratitude for the protection our song brings. But my heart still beats wildly in my chest. My body doesn't trust that I'm truly safe; I can't forget the weakness of my human form.

Raidne stretches her wings, and then Pisinoe follows, and

both look to me expectantly. I take a deep breath, filling my lungs with sea and salt, and close my eyes. One powerful beat is all it takes before we're in the sky, out of danger's grasp, and I scream once more.

This time, it's with joy. We climb higher and higher into the heavens, twirling through the clouds and basking in the golden glow of dawn. Raidne and Pisinoe are laughing, and then I am, too. When we find one another again, we join hands to form an unbreakable ring in the sky.

"You're here," Raidne says, eyes shimmering with tears, voice painted with awe. "I can't believe you're here."

"Did you think I wouldn't return?"

"We knew you wouldn't purposefully abandon us," Pisinoe says softly. "But as the months passed . . ."

". . . We were afraid something might have happened," Raidne adds.

Something did happen, I want to cry. I made friends and buried a lover. I carried and lost a child.

I fell in love.

Cora.

I look for her below, but if she's on the deck to drop *Endurance*'s anchor, she's hidden beneath the clouds.

"You must have thousands of stories for us . . ." Raidne says, seeing how my eyes are searching.

Before I can answer her, a loud *boom* cracks across the sky and a flash of light dazzles from below.

"What was that?" Pisinoe asks, alarmed. I pull them both higher into the heavens.

"A musket," I say, unable to hide the surprise in my voice. "A weapon."

"But how?" Raidne's brows crumple in confusion.

Her question makes my palms sweat. But how indeed. Was it one of the women, unable to bear the sight of us bewitching their men? No, Cora would never allow that . . . unless she, too, was revolted by what she saw and felt compelled to try to fix it.

"Stay here."

"Thelxiope—"

"Someone's stuffed their ears with wax—they aren't enchanted. Just wait here until you hear me sing."

"But—"

"Please. I need you both to trust me one last time."

I cling to clouds as I descend back toward the ship. The sailors still stand stupefied on the main deck, looking for any sign of us. As soon as they see me, they'll start calling out, alerting whoever has the musket to my presence. I hang suspended, unsure how to proceed, when Raidne and Pisinoe's song begins again, this time from the opposite side of the *Endurance.*

All the men turn to the south to face their sound. The distraction is enough. I drop to the side of the ship and skirt along its edges until I spot the longboat in the water. It's nestled against the *Endurance,* a baby animal hiding beside its mother for protection. From here, I can read the faces of the women, and they're terrified, including those who knew something was going to happen.

The children wail, and the din swells so loudly I fear it might mask my sisters' song, but the damage to the men above is already done. A loud crash into the waves reveals another sailor who grew tired of waiting and took to the sea to try to reach Raidne and Pisinoe.

Little Ambrose sees me first, and when he does, he lets out a bloodcurdling scream. The wax isn't strong enough to block it out entirely, and it doesn't take long for the others to spot me, too. Some shriek and point, trying to warn the sailors above, but thankfully, the men don't listen. I search for familiar faces—Rose watches me with confused, wide eyes. Elyoner makes the sign of the cross.

Elizabeth blinks back tears and holds a hand over her mouth.

But no one has the musket.

Thomas.

I hold a finger to my lips, desperately miming *shh*. I don't know if he'll be able to hear the commotion that they're making from wherever he is above, but if he spots them all flailing, finding me won't be difficult.

"Please," I mouth, and to my surprise, it's Ambrose who stops crying first. Elizabeth turns to the others, her hands finding their shoulders, their backs, though what she says to try to calm them is lost to the waves. When she finally looks over her shoulder at me, she nods ever so slightly—I nod back, and then I climb onto the ship.

I make my way down to the half deck. There below, in the middle of the swaying sailors, is Thomas. His left arm is wrapped around Cora's neck, and she struggles to break free of the choke hold he has her in. Emme lies in a crumpled mess at their feet. Her frizzy red hair is matted with crimson.

His bright expression reveals my worst fear. Thomas isn't enchanted. Behind him, several of his closest allies are bound to the main mast. They writhe and demand to be released, to be allowed to seek out the otherworldly creatures who sing their fates, but Thomas disregards their pleas.

He's too busy searching the skies. His right hand holds the loaded musket, though there's no way he'll be able to aim it accurately with Cora in tow. The key is to make him fire it. After the round is released, he'll need to drop Cora to reload it. That's time I can use to strike it from his hands, and then, finally, he'll be mine.

Cora spots me before Thomas does; she gasps at the sight of me, unintentionally drawing Thomas's attention to the half deck. A large grin slices across his face when he finds me, and he raises the musket.

"Think you're so clever?" he shouts. For a moment, I wonder why he bothers addressing me at all, but then I realize— it's because I'm not quite within the weapon's range. He needs to draw me closer. "I'll admit, you almost had me. But imagine my surprise when I stumbled upon Margery on the main deck trying to seal her son's ears with bayberry wax, of all things!" His grin is predatory, vile, and my stomach churns with the realization that I never saw Margery or Jeremie inside the longboat.

"What have you done to them?" I growl back, forgetting that he can't hear me.

"And now a young boy will pay the price for his mother's treachery. Remember that, Margery. This is your fault."

Only then do I find her face among the men tied to the mast. She thrashes against the ropes that bind her in place, and though her mouth is stuffed with something, her frantic screams still escape around the fabric. Thomas cocks his head to the left, and I discover the source of Margery's panic: There, standing on the ship's edge with a few of the other sailors, is Jeremie. Thomas must have stolen his wax, and without it, he's not protected. The wind blows through his mousy hair, so much like his mother's. It makes his linen shirt billow like a cloud.

There's no time to wonder if a future version of Jeremie deserves to drown. There's only this moment, where he's just a child, not yet two. Instinct takes hold, and I call out to him, spreading open my wings. My voice must cut through some of the song's magic, because he turns to look at me over his shoulder. But after the briefest flicker of a smile, he jumps.

He's gone.

Margery's screams shatter something inside of me, and I rush forward after him. I don't understand the situation I've put myself in until I hear the musket boom.

The sound is so startling that I instinctively throw my body to the left, though I have no way of knowing where the musket ball is as it tears out of the gun's barrel to find me. It grazes my right arm, spraying a trail of blood and feathers across the deck.

The gun kicks back against Thomas's shoulder, and Cora uses the force of the blow to tear herself from his grasp.

"Go, Thelia! Run!"

The pain that radiates from my wound, Cora's plea, even poor Jeremie—they can't distract from the singular truth that this, right now, is my moment. I've never hated anyone as much as I hate this man, not even Dis, who at least had the excuse of being a god. That hatred fuels me as I stretch out my wings and prepare to dive.

The horror of my full form erases the grin from Thomas's lips. His fingers shake as he tries to reload the musket, but there was never going to be enough time for that. I soar down to him, my talons outstretched. Thomas abandons the gun, and Cora pulls herself along the deck to curl her fingers around its barrel. Once it's safely in her hands, I begin my song.

This time, the notes are desperate and hurried, full of rage. They call back my sisters, who appear above. Now that they're in sight, there's nothing to stop the men who linger freely on the deck from jumping into the waves to try to reach them.

"You're a monster!" Thomas shouts. "A demon!"

I beat my wings a few times to lift myself higher, surprised by how good this body feels, how natural. I missed it. My talons find him easily, an owl snatching a mouse from beneath the snow. They dig into his shoulders and flex between his muscles. Thomas shrieks with pain, and my grip tightens.

The sound is so pleasing that I toss back my head and laugh as my fingers move to claw the wax from his ears. When I speak, I want—no, I *need* him to hear the triumph in my voice. "You're the true monster," I hiss down at him. "Or your god wouldn't deem it fit to punish you so. Tell me, Thomas— do you think he's going to save you?"

"Damn you, damn you!" he cries. I take to the air, carrying Thomas with me. Raidne and Pisinoe circle above. I don't hear their song; they've been holding their breath.

"What's going on? Are you bringing him to shore?" Pisinoe asks, tilting her head to Thomas.

"No," I growl. "This one's mine."

Thomas struggles to break free, but he can't flail too much without causing my talons to constrict tighter. I wiggle them inside him, slicing through tendons as easily as a knife slices through butter.

My sisters nod knowingly. There's something ugly in Thomas's core, a rotting pit they recognize from their memory of how gods would let their gaze linger too long on our young bodies, of how Jaquob defended his actions. They didn't see Dis or his power, but I did. Thomas shares something with him, just as Jaquob did, and as all those men did years ago. Dis might be the ruler of darkness, but there's a darkness, a little piece of sin that can fester if it goes too long untreated, in some mortal men as well.

Some, but not all.

"A little boy jumped. I need you to save him."

There, in the raging water below, Jeremie struggles to keep himself afloat. Raidne, my violent, vicious Raidne, doesn't ask for an explanation: She simply dives to rescue him.

Finally, there's nothing left to hold me back. I drop Thomas.

He falls into the sea like a stone, the force of the fall sending him deep beneath the waves. They hold him below for the span of several breaths, but I don't panic. How many times have I seen this happen before? Sure enough, Thomas resurfaces, his arms flailing for something, anything, to keep him afloat. He unleashes a scream for help, but I'm the only one who can answer, and I let the ocean pound him. His pain, his fear, they send a victorious shiver up my spine.

The blood loss from his wounded shoulders will speed along his demise, and when he's at risk of passing out, I lunge for him again—I need him awake for what's coming. He screams up at me as I descend, but there's nothing he can do to stop me.

See my strength, I think. *It was here the whole time.*

My talons find his back again, and a thrust of my wings pulls us both from the water. We begin rising, rising, rising, until we are a silhouette against the sun, then I turn toward Castle's dangerous rock formations. The three spires glow red in Aurora's dawn, covered in countless jagged protrusions, thousands of tiny blades. They'll easily tear his body open. His blood will be the sparkling rubies in its crown.

Thomas moans, realizing what I have planned for him.

"No, Thelia . . . !"

I've fantasized about this moment since the night he took me without asking. Now I'll take from him. My grip loosens, and I can feel his skin sliding off my claws when I look down to the *Endurance*'s deck one last time. There, balancing a soaking wet Jeremie on her hip, is Cora. Her free hand points desperately at me in warning, and though I find the sound of her frantic cries amid the chaos, I can't make out their contents.

By the time I understand, it's too late.

A sudden pain in my side snaps my attention to Thomas. I release him in shock, but the agony tears down with him as he falls. There's a knife in my flank, right beneath my left rib. He's stuck it in deep, and Thomas is keeping himself from falling by holding on to the handle for dear life.

My fingers move to claw at his hands, and he releases the knife but grabs on to my waist. I growl, and he looks up at me, a mixture of disbelief and pleasure washing over his face. There's no sight of Raidne and Pisinoe. They must be on the beach with our captives.

I throw my entire body to the left, sending us spiraling down, and then to the right, and then up on an air vent, trying to loosen his grip on me with sudden and unexpected movements, but he doesn't relinquish his hold. I tear at his face, but he uses my fury against me and takes the opportunity to pull the knife from my side.

This time, he sinks it into my stomach.

I scream. The sound pierces the air, and Thomas howls triumphantly as he twists the blade in deeper. I feel every excruciating second as it tears through my muscle, as it punctures my organs. My fingers find his eye sockets, desperate to stop him. Thomas releases his hold on the knife as his eyes burst from their orifices with a sickening *pop*. Now the shrieks that fill the air are his, but this brings me no comfort.

I've gutted enough men and animals alike to know that the blow Thomas dealt is fatal. With willing ears and blood, we can turn back time. But we're not immortal. He's sentenced me to death.

I hover there, my wings beating at a steady pace to keep us aloft, my thumbs still weaving around inside his skull as my breathing slows. I think about the night I washed onto Roanoke's shores, about my desperate plea to the gods. I asked them only to free my sisters. I didn't ask to be saved as well—one final cruel twist of fate for the gods to revel in.

Tears pool in my eyes, blurring my vision. I don't have much time. Already, Thomas feels heavier, harder to bear. Soon I won't be able to hold him at all. I've reached the end of my thread. Somewhere below, the Fates open their shears, but where I expected to find terror, there's only a strange sense of resignation. I fulfilled my duty to my sisters. I freed Cora from the grip of a vile man. They'll go on to live long lives, far away from here. And gods, though I wish more than anything that I could join them, there's only one thing left to do.

I'm sorry, Cora. I wish you didn't have to see this.

I fold my wings behind my back. Cora screams my name from below, but there's no way to stop this now. Thomas and I plummet through the air, gaining speed as we go, quickening us to our fates.

In the blur of sea and sky that rush past, I see Raidne and Pisinoe returned to their divine forms, finally allowed to rejoin the gods.

I see Wenefrid and Sybil laughing over ale in the abandoned ruins of the City of Raleigh.

I see the other women and children returning to England's shores.

And finally, there's Cora standing before the sea, on the cusp of an unimaginable adventure of her own making.

Dying for this is worth it. After all, a sacrifice has to hurt, or else it isn't a sacrifice.

Castle's spires grow closer and closer. My eyes flutter closed; my lips part in one last prayer.

Our bodies break upon the cliffs.

22

NOW, BELOW

The sweet scent of damp stone brings me back to the waking world. I'm in the antechamber of a large cave. Outside, the light is blinding. Even straining my eyes, I can't make out what lies beyond its threshold, so I turn my attention back to the dark interior. A single torch mounted on the wall beckons.

I begin to understand. The only direction to go is deeper. To descend. The flame flickers as I tread forward into the shadows, casting an orange halo around me. But the small perimeter of afforded light offers few clues as to what lies ahead. With each step, the light outside begins to dim, like an eye slowly closing, until I'm left in total darkness.

The stone beneath my bare feet is surprisingly warm. It's strange to be comforted by this, but it reminds me of my sisters. Of the times we spent in Scopuli's many sea caves.

If I'm here, I didn't survive. But my sisters will. I fulfilled my pact, brought back a ship filled with men so greedy and corrupt that their blood will give Proserpina all the power she needs to free Raidne and Pisinoe from Scopuli forever. I smile, thinking of them, of Cora. The small glimpse I saw of the world outside our cliffs was cruel, merciless. But it was also vaster than it ever was in our youth and filled with unending chances for a real life.

The antechamber opens to a hallway so large that I can't find its walls. I walk for a few moments with my hands outstretched until my fingers finally graze against stone. Beneath my feet, the floor slopes gently downward. I'm not only venturing deeper into this cave; I'm venturing deeper into the earth.

The only way forward is down, so down I go. My steps reverberate against the vaulted ceiling, falling in with the sound of my breath. It's surprisingly steady, given the circumstances. A *drip, drip, drip* punctuates my own rhythms from somewhere beyond my torch's reach; I never learn its source, but despite its secrecy, the sound brings me peace.

In life, I thought of caves as dank and musty places, but this tunnel into darkness doesn't meet that characterization. The air is cool, yes, but it's also crisp and clean, like a fresh winter snow.

And so I progress, farther and farther underground. I have no idea how long I walk—it could be for mere moments; it could be for days. The torch still rages brightly, as if it were just lit, a seemingly inextinguishable source of fire. Time doesn't mean much here, but why would it?

The gurgle of water is the first thing to break the monotony of the journey. It starts out quiet, no louder than a gentle stream, but as I continue, the babble grows into a roar.

My eyes slowly adjust to the darkness. Up ahead, the hallway terminates in a doorway to an even larger space. I cross its threshold and find myself on the ledge of an impossibly huge cavern, so vast that it holds an entire raging river that curves off into a deeper void. The ceiling is so far overhead that it's cloaked in shadow; it's impossible to know how high up it goes.

The cavern is illuminated by a mysterious light, the source of which is billions of tiny fluorescent strands of silk, spun by indistinguishable creatures that glow a ghostly blue. They hang from the ceiling like glass beads on fishing lines, too far away for me to see exactly what they are, but that's all right—this way, I'm able to pretend that they're the spectral sisters of my little spider friend. Their effect is beautiful.

Green mushrooms sprout at my feet, also radiating a subtle bioluminescence. Their light reveals a staircase carved into the cliffside that descends into the cavern. I follow the path with my eyes: The mushrooms lead to the bank of the river.

Standing at the water's edge is a cloaked figure beside a small boat. The apparition carries its own torch. It appears to watch me on the precipice.

My heart suddenly pounds so heavily, I fear I might collapse. I know who this psychopomp is; I also know I have no coin to pay for passage. Will I be doomed to roam the shores of this place for a hundred years? Have I already found a new prison to replace the one I just escaped? I look back at the hallway behind me, but, as if to underscore that there's no returning, my unassailable torch extinguishes in a sudden burst, as quickly as the snapping of fingers.

An empty sconce sits expectantly on the wall to my right, so I deposit the used torch into it and continue down the steps. They're ancient, rocky things, and if it weren't for the soft light of the fungi to guide me, I know with complete certainty that I would fall to—what? My death? I suppose I've already arrived.

I reach the bottom of the steps. The figure is indeed watching my procession, its obscured head following my movements. I start to feel faint, but I continue forward because there's nothing else to do, and nowhere else to go.

When I'm no more than an arm's length away from the guide, it reaches up with its free hand to take down its hood. I stare for a few moments, eyes blinking, trying to make sense of who stands before me.

It's not the ferryman of the dead. A gasp escapes from the back of my throat as the pieces fall together: the warm red lips, the cascading black curls of hair, the unmistakable vibrant emerald eyes.

"Hello, Thelia."

Proserpina's voice is so gentle that tears spring to my eyes, and, without thinking, I throw my arms around her, sobbing heavily into my queen's shoulder. Proserpina wraps her arms around me, too, pulling me into a tight embrace.

"My dear, dear friend. At first I feared I'd never see you again, and then I feared I'd see you too soon."

"I'm so sorry." I choke on the words I couldn't say when we last talked, right before I left Scopuli. "I'm so sorry, that day at the pool—"

"We were children, Thelia," Proserpina whispers. "Nothing you could have done would have changed my fate."

"But I told him," I whimper, lifting my head to look her in the eyes. "I told him where you were because I was afraid."

Proserpina's hands cup my face, and she nods, knowingly. "He was coming for me no matter what. I'm glad he didn't hurt you in the process."

"I can't forgive myself . . ."

"But I forgive you, Thelia." She brushes the tears from my cheeks. "I forgave you that very day." The words hit me like rocks to my chest, and the blow is so hard that I fall to my knees. Proserpina descends alongside me, holding me as I cry, as the centuries of guilt and shame and loss pour out of my soul. She runs her fingers through my hair; she coos gently into my ear.

"I forgive you," she repeats, again and again, until my sobs slow and there are no tears left.

"Why did you eat those seeds, Proserpina?"

A coy smile dances across her lips, a beautiful and dreadful thing to behold. "You never did believe that I was tricked."

"Not at first, no. I feared that you hated me enough to make sure you'd never have to see me again. But as the years passed, I started to wonder if the reason I didn't believe it was because that meant what happened to you wasn't entirely my fault."

"It wasn't, Thelia. You understand the thrill of finding power in an unexpected place more than most. I was always going to be someone's wife, but to be the Queen of Shadow is to be my mother's equal. As I held those pomegranate seeds in my hand, I felt the thrum of fate. I saw all the things I could do with that power, and I knew I belonged here. You've felt something similar recently, haven't you?"

I think of who I left behind, of how close our fates came to truly threading together. "What will happen to my sisters? To Cora? Will they be all right?"

Her eyes sparkle knowingly at Cora's name. She recognizes the longing in my face; does she remember when that same expression was directed at her? But when Proserpina speaks, her voice holds no jealousy, only glittering possibility. "Don't you want to see for yourself?"

The tears come again, because I do, more than anything. But I saw the twist of the blade in my gut, I felt what it meant to hit those rocks. "Thomas . . . my body . . ."

"My darling Thelia, don't you understand?"

The Queen of the Underworld, my first love, breathes the words that follow into my hair like they're an incantation.

You've already sacrificed enough.

23

NOW

For a few painful, blinding moments, there's only white. My eyelids rush to blink it away, and then, slowly, shapes emerge from the vastness.

There are two young women, one with black hair and one with blond, crying with relief. No monstrous wings grace their backs; they kneel beside me on human legs. Pisinoe slowly lifts me to a seated position, and Raidne brushes the blood-soaked hair from my eyes.

Oh, gods, the blood—the gash. The fall. My hands rush to my gut, but there's no gaping wound to find. Only the soft flesh of my stomach, perfectly intact. I run my palms over my arms, my legs, expecting to discover bones protruding through the skin. But I'm no longer broken. Proserpina has remade me, remade us, just as she promised she would.

My sisters speak excitedly, but I can't hear their words over the ringing in my ears. When something behind Pisinoe catches her attention, Raidne follows her gaze.

My eyes instinctively trail my sisters'. They push their bodies away from me, parting to reveal someone new.

A sea of raven curls. Cheeks stained pink by salt—both

from the sea and from tears. Trembling slender fingers that reach out to just barely brush my face, as if they fear contact will cause me to vanish.

Large green eyes, wide as if beholding a miracle. And finally, soft red lips parted in awe.

There's no reason to hold back—I pull her close, tangling my hands into her midnight hair. The gentle scent of roses floods me with warmth.

"Come, stop your ship so you may hear us." I whisper the words into the curve of her shoulder. She trembles beneath my lips, and fresh tears roll down her cheeks.

"I don't know all that happens on this bountiful earth." I kiss each tear away, following their salty trail up her neck, over her cheeks, until my mouth hovers above hers. "But I do know this—the future is finally ours."

Cora closes the gap between us, and her lips are sweeter than honey, than ambrosia. When we finally part, her fear is gone. Now she beams.

It's this last image that takes my breath away: Of all the transformations I've seen during my impossibly long life, Cora's smile is the most beautiful.

EPILOGUE

History remembers only our shades. Our names are lost, our millennia truncated into fleeting stanzas inside the stories of men. Epics depict our bone-littered beaches, but never the reason for them. Our wings and claws become fins and scales. Now we are temptresses, the danger of our mouths lost to images of honeyed lips. It's our beauty, not our knowledge, that drives men into the sea.

But I don't care. The centuries will rewrite our story countless times before the dark doors of Dis open for me again. In some retellings, we'll be heroes, in others, villains, but I no longer crave verses singing our absolution. I don't need them—I am forgiven.

I am free.

With the curse broken, the island's wildlife returns from the shadows, and her trees bear fruit once more. But most important, Scopuli's gates open to the outside world. Divine forms restored, Raidne and Pisinoe escape into its arms, and now I'm the one who watches from the beach as they're swallowed by the horizon. But my sisters are never gone for long, drawn home by Scopuli's call. Cora and I throw welcome feasts in their honor, and they regale us with tales of the changing world—how wooden ships become metal, how buildings kiss the sky. But soon after the stories fall from their lips, freedom's song lures them away again to a new corner of the earth, with new myths and new monsters to behold.

Maybe Scopuli's magic was unrelated to Ceres's curse, or maybe it's a gift from the Fates, a consolation for all the years they made me wait for Cora. Whatever the cause, time here moves slowly. Weeks take decades to write themselves into our bodies, and Cora and I make use of them. One day, we'll venture from the safety of these shores with Raidne and Pisinoe, but until then, it's each other we explore.

And now when ships appear on the horizon, there is no call to arms. Instead, we stand together on the cliffs and watch in rapt silence as the world passes us by. Cora takes my hand in hers and leans the entire weight of her body into mine. That beautiful human body, growing only more magical as the centuries pass, each gray hair and new wrinkle that graces her skin a miracle as incredible as my resurrection, because somehow, impossibly, I'm the one fated to behold them. She's a constantly shifting landscape that I'll study for as long as I'm able.

With Cora at my side, my former prison blossoms into paradise.

ACKNOWLEDGMENTS

Before I set out to write *Those Fatal Flowers*, I rarely read a book's acknowledgments, foolishly assuming that creating a novel is a solitary act. But as any novelist knows, that couldn't be further from the truth. As I began on the road toward publication, I finally started paying attention to the love letters authors write to their community at a novel's end. I can't believe I'm here, penning my own.

The fact that this book, and quite possibly my entire writing career, exists at all is only because of the guidance and support of so many beautiful people I've been fortunate enough to cross paths with.

My wonderful family—I am so lucky to have such incredible cheerleaders in my corner. Mom, Dad, you believed I could do this long before I ever did. Thank you for letting me take that private driver's education course all those years ago so I'd have enough room in my high school schedule for those early creative writing classes. Dad, when I decided to put writing on the back burner, you never let me forget that you believed I was capable of this. I hope you know how much that means to me. You've both gone out of your way to seek my work in places I never expected you to follow me—when you told me you'd read my cosmic horror short story, it meant the entire world. Thank you for always making me feel like I've made you proud.

My brother, Daniel—when I told you I was going to try to write a book, you acted like I was embarking on my life's inevitable next step instead of pursuing an unlikely dream. Thank you for that.

Sheryl—when you asked to read an earlier version of this story, I was so nervous to share it. But then you sent me the bouquet of flowers, of lilies, after you finished it and made me feel so loved. Your support means the world.

Donna, Tim—you always make sure to ask about my writing and make it known how excited you are for me. I am truly so lucky to have you both in my corner, and I hope you know how much it means to me.

My daughters, Ruby and Sylvia—I can only call myself a writer because you've pushed me to be a mother worthy of you.

Mrs. Peters and Mr. Thill of Geneva High School—you both fostered a sense of creativity and inquisitiveness in storytelling in me that, quite simply, I never managed to shake. For that, I am so, so grateful. This book began with you.

Professors Josh Langseth, Marcia Lindgren, and the other amazing folks in the University of Iowa's classics and anthropology departments—thank you for instilling me with a love of the ancient world.

Kathryn Ormsbee, Caitlin Alexander, and Zo Nicole—you were the first friends with whom I sheepishly shared the fact that I was attempting to write a book. Thank you all for being so, so delicate with that fragile dream, and for believing I could do this.

Zach Zehr and Angela Rodriguez—I am the luckiest person to have such incredible friends in my court. Thank you for actively seeking out my work and hyping me up. I don't know what I did to deserve you both, but I am so grateful.

John Curtis—you're one of my closest and dearest friends. I am so grateful for you, and for everything we've built in the twelve years we've worked together. It's not lost on me that I was only able to learn to write a novel after I learned how to build *something* from *nothing* while working with you.

Alyssa Lennander, Alyssa DeGilio, and Leta Patton— where to even begin? You three have been my constant companions through some of the most monumental moments of my life. Your friendship kept me company during Covid, during newborn days (and so many newborn nights), and through all of publishing's incredible highs and lows. Thank you for always pushing me to be better and for always having my back. I'm so glad we all found ourselves in that querying group chat all those years ago. I would be lost in this wild world without you. Of all the gifts writing has brought me, your friendship is easily my most cherished.

Cath—you were one of the first people I shared *Those Fatal Flowers* with, and wow, was I petrified. I admire you so much, and your kindness in those early days of querying is what kept me going. I am so very proud to call myself your friend.

SJ—I'm so grateful you slid into my DMs in those early days. Like Cath, you were so tender with that early draft you read. Without that support, this book wouldn't exist. You've become one of my closest friends, which completely boggles my mind given how incredible you are. I'm so glad we're on this wild writing journey together, and I can't wait to see what the years bring you. The day I finally get to give you the biggest hug will be one of my happiest.

The other incredible people I met on X's writing community who supported me along the way: Rosa, Melo, Sarah, Amalie, Hailey, Chloe, Brooke, Charlotte, Julie, Isa, Rose, Syd, Miriam, Katie, Kayla, Ally, Gabriela, and so many more. Your kindness keeps me going.

My agent siblings, who inspire me daily: Sam, Matt, Lore, Sarah M., Erin, Mo, Stew, Allison, Ashley, Bitter, Bori, CJ, Danielle, Dorothy, Jamie, Kes, Lily, Mahmud, Mikayla, Nadia, Poppy, Salma, A.M., Kenechi, Kathryn, and Sarah D. I can't believe I can count myself among your ranks. You are all truly incredible.

My agent, John Baker, for being Thelia's biggest champion. You always believed her story would take flight, long after I'd already said goodbye to that dream. Without you, she would still be trapped on Scopuli. I can't wait to see what other dark and beautiful stories we usher into the world together.

The entire team at Dell, starting with my amazing editor, Mae Martinez—thank you for your incredible insights. Under your care, both this story and my writing ability grew in ways I never could have imagined. Thelia owes her happy ending to you, and so do I.

Aarushi Menon and Rachel Ake, you gave me the cover of my dreams. I am forever grateful.

Laura Dragonette and Cara DuBois, thank you for your incredible eye for detail.

And finally, to you, John, the love of my life:
In some way, everything I create is an ode to you.

THOSE
FATAL
FLOWERS

SHANNON IVES

Random
House
Book Club

Because ™
Stories Are
Better Shared

A BOOK CLUB GUIDE

AUTHOR'S NOTE

Some stories flash into existence in the span of a few minutes, while others take years for the necessary components to reveal themselves. The seeds of *Those Fatal Flowers* began, as is so often the case, as an assignment for a high school creative writing class. For all intents and purposes, it was the very first draft of Thelia's transformation scene in the ritual cave. But it wouldn't be until nearly a decade later that this story really gained legs—or, in this case, wings.

Aside from a handful of short stories, I didn't write for the entirety of my early to mid-twenties; self-doubt convinced me that I'd never be "good enough," whatever that means, and I listened to it without trying. But a love for words is a hard thing to banish entirely, so in 2017, I challenged myself to complete NaNoWriMo, just for fun and just for myself. It was during those feverish writing sessions that I had the idea to place the sirens in an American setting. Why not, given their agelessness? So I wrote a Scopuli inspired by Acadia, Maine, and began toying with the idea of Thelia landing in a Puritan colony. And then inspiration struck when I remembered that America already had a "lost" colony. And thus, Thelia set her sights on Roanoke.

I minored in Latin in college, but I'm by no means a classicist, though they remain some of the most brilliant and dedicated people I've been lucky enough to meet. While many popular myth retellings use Ancient Greek sources as their inspiration, I can thank the class titled "The Golden Age of Roman Poetry" for introducing me to mine: Ovid's *Metamorphoses*. I'd like to think this book is a nod to those incredible teacher's assistants and professors I was so fortunate to learn from, so hopefully my research isn't too off the mark.

Despite the sirens having such a lasting impact on our culture's psyche, there is very little said about them in the major Greco-Roman sources. Their appearance in the *Odyssey*, while iconic, is only a few passages long. I adored that Ovid gave them a history as Proserpina's handmaidens who were with her on that fateful day she was picking "those fatal flowers." But after they're given wings to find her, they fall out of the spotlight once more.

In addition to Ovid, I also referenced mythological elements from *Fabulae* by the Roman author Hyginus and the *Aeneid* by Virgil. At one point, Thelia remembers her sister Pisinoe reciting a poem by the Roman poet Horace (Ode 1.5). In it, Horace laments the loss of his love, Pyrrha. The ending of the poem references an ancient practice where sailors who survived shipwrecks dedicated votive tablets to the gods in thanks and sometimes included the garments they were wearing when saved. It seemed oddly fitting for Thelia to unknowingly hear a poem about a man surviving a woman's storm.

As far as names are concerned, anywhere an Ancient Greek name is used (Thelxiope, Scylla, Charybdis, etc.), the name also appears in the Latin version of these texts. Cora's name was inspired by Proserpina/Persephone's epithet Kore, the maiden. While many of the characters in this novel bear the names of real people from the Lost Colony, their depictions are one hundred percent fictionalized.

The decision for the sirens' song to be enthralling because of its promise, and not because of its beauty, was an explicit nod to Dr. Emily Wilson's translation of the *Odyssey*. She has an incredible thread on X where she outlines that there's nothing in the original Greek text to suggest the sirens are seductive in the way we think of them today: Where previous translations refer to the danger of their honeyed *lips*, the Ancient Greek word is for *mouths*.

I loved the idea of mouths as a metaphor for what's truly dangerous to a patriarchal world order. Obviously, Thelia exemplifies this in her siren form, but she also does on Roanoke. There, too, mouths are a very different kind of threat, but a threat nonetheless—the women can rebel by talking to one another.

Agnes Bailie's fear of the Spanish is a real detail from history. The Lost Colony never intended to remain on Roanoke. Its waters were too shallow to support the major port city Sir Walter Raleigh envisioned, and their original destination was the Chesapeake Bay. So why did they stay? One theory posits that during a resupply in Dominica, they learned that Spain was aware of England's plans. One of the main goals of "the City of Raleigh" was for it to be a hub for English privateering (state-sponsored piracy) against the Spanish, so Spain naturally had a heightened interest in preventing its establishment. Given that the Spanish had murdered a Huguenot colony in Florida a few years before, the (also Protestant) colonists would have rightfully been terrified of them. And Roanoke, safely tucked away from the open ocean behind other islands in the Outer Banks, was the perfect spot to hide until they could be sure of their safety.

The articles pinned to the meetinghouse's doors come

from Jamestown's "Lawes Divine, Morall and Martiall," regulations that the colony was intended to follow beginning in 1610. Jamestown was the next English colony established in the Americas, in 1607, and would go on to be the first permanent English settlement on the continent.

History lovers may notice that Manteo, the Croatoan liaison to the English and a very prominent figure in the Lost Colony's story, is missing from this book. Specific tribes are named in *Those Fatal Flowers* to make it clear that there were complex social histories and relationships occurring in the Americas thousands of years before Europeans stepped foot on this soil. But I purposefully chose not to center an Indigenous character because the effect of European colonization on Indigenous communities is not my story to tell. My goal with including the violence I did was to shine a spotlight on the western world's cruelty during the Age of Discovery.

Though Manteo and the Croatoans allied themselves with the English when they first arrived in 1584, other Indigenous groups in the region were wary. Those suspicions proved to be justified a year later when Richard Grenville, the leader of the first Roanoke expedition, ordered the destruction of the Secotan village Aquascogoc over the perceived theft of a silver cup.

As we see throughout western history, European colonists happily capitalized on existing rifts between Indigenous groups for their own benefit. Manteo was open about his hope that the English would aid the Croatoans in their war against the neighboring Neusiok tribe. They never did, though they happily accepted the Croatoans' help to survive in the New World.

Many European sources from the Age of Discovery describe Indigenous people "visiting" Europe, but historians are now rightfully noting that many of these people were in fact abducted. "New France," present-day Quebec, was founded on such a kidnapping: After claiming the land for France in 1534, Jacques Cartier returned to Brittany two years later with ten abducted Iroquoians, which is why Iroquoian women were on Jaquob's ship. Illness killed all but one within a few years of their arrival: A little girl, about ten years old, survived. For more information about this time in history, I recommend reading *On Savage Shores: How Indigenous Americans Discovered Europe* by Caroline Dodds Pennock and *The Other Slavery: The Uncovered Story of Indian Enslavement in America* by Andrés Reséndez.

And finally, as intriguing as the idea of a lost colony is, the most recent archaeological data suggests that while the City of Raleigh's location has been lost to time, its people likely integrated into the Croatoan villages on the neighboring Hatteras Island . . . but history is always open to interpretation.

QUESTIONS AND TOPICS FOR DISCUSSION

1. How does the author's use of mythological creatures and Greco-Roman mythology enhance the themes and messages of the book?
2. What did you know of sirens before reading *Those Fatal Flowers*? And now, having learned about them, discuss depictions of sirens in popular culture and media.
3. In what ways does Thelia's journey reflect universal human experiences and struggles?
4. What do you remember learning about the Roanoke colony? Did you speculate about why it disappeared?
5. How does the author challenge societal norms and expectations through the characters and their actions?
6. Discuss Thelia's moral ambiguity and the ethical dilemmas presented both on Scopuli and Roanoke.
7. How does the author explore the concept of identity and self-discovery throughout the story?
8. Analyze the role of secondary characters in shaping Thelia's development and the overall narrative.
9. Discuss the dual timeline and its impact on your experience and understanding of the plot.
10. How does the author's writing style and narrative structure contribute to the overall impact of the story?

SHANNON IVES writes from the deep, dark woods of Vermont. She graduated with honors from the University of Iowa with a BA in anthropology and a minor in Latin. Her studies focused on myth, religion, and magic—themes that she continues to explore in her writing. Her work strives to capture the beauty in the grotesque and explore how traditional power structures perpetuate violence. More often than not, you'll find her characters behaving badly; they are monsters, after all. *Those Fatal Flowers* is her debut novel.

shannonives.com
Instagram: @thestickwitch
X: @thestickwitch

ABOUT THE TYPE

This book was set in Fairfield, the first typeface from the hand of the distinguished American artist and engraver Rudolph Ruzicka (1883–1978). Ruzicka was born in Bohemia (in the present-day Czech Republic) and came to America in 1894. He set up his own shop, devoted to wood engraving and printing, in New York in 1913 after a varied career working as a wood engraver, in photoengraving and banknote printing plants, and as an art director and freelance artist. He designed and illustrated many books, and was the creator of a considerable list of individual prints—wood engravings, line engravings on copper, and aquatints.

RANDOM HOUSE BOOK CLUB

Because Stories Are Better Shared

Discover

Exciting new books that spark conversation every week.

Connect

With authors on tour—or in your living room. (Request an Author Chat for your book club!)

Discuss

Stories that move you with fellow book lovers on Facebook, on Goodreads, or at in-person meet-ups.

Enhance

Your reading experience with discussion prompts, digital book club kits, and more, available on our website.

Join our online book club community!

 randomhousebookclub.com

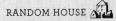